TEN

D0696101

TENEBREA'S HOPE

BOOK TWO OF THE TENEBREA TRILOGY

ROXANN DAWSON
AND
DANIEL GRAHAM

POCKET BOOKS

New York   London   Toronto   Sydney   Singapore

An *Original* Publication of POCKET BOOKS

POCKET BOOKS, a division of Simon & Schuster, Inc.
1230 Avenue of the Americas, New York, NY 10020

ISBN: 0-671-03609-2

First Pocket Books printing October 2001

10 9 8 7 6 5 4 3 2 1

POCKET and colophon are registered trademarks of Simon & Schuster, Inc.

For information regarding special discounts for bulk purchases, please contact Simon & Schuster Special Sales at 1-800-456-6798 or business@simonandschuster.com

Front cover illustration by Gregory Bridges

Printed in the U.S.A.

TENEBREA'S HOPE

chapter 1

The artificial time, synthetic food, enforced idleness, and incessant hum of space travel plagued her sleep. Andrea slept fitfully in her berth aboard the armed merchant *Benwoi*. Her mind grappled with a collage of memories.

The teak decks are damp. Morning dew collects as cool droplets on the railings. *The Deeper Well* rocks slightly—more from movement on board than from the glassy water. Steve comes up from the cabin with a steaming cup of aromatic coffee. He kisses me. The stubble of his beard rubs my cheek, a touch more stimulating than caffeine. He seems distant—preoccupied—as he walks to the forepeak to raise the jib. Little Glendon, my little pixie, scampers up the ladder wearing an orange life vest and nuzzles her cheek into my breast, jostling a bit of hot coffee that splashes on my bare leg, but I ignore the insignificant pain. Glendon's hair smells of lilac shampoo. She says "I love you, Mother," with perfect diction, too old for a child of three. Glendon's voice has lost its innocence. Glendon looks into my eyes. I watch as those pixie eyes dim. I'm confused. Glendon stops breathing! Then she slumps into my arms, cold and lifeless. I shake my child who suddenly is covered with blood. I can do nothing but scream, "Steve! Help me!" The man at the forepeak raising the jib turns. He is irritated by the commotion. He says coldly, "I'm not Steve."

Andrea woke to a shrill pulsating alarm. She dismissed her dream and sat up sprightly, slapping the comm-panel on the bulkhead above her berth. With the alarm silenced, the quiet hum of the ship returned like a long somnolent note played on an oboe. But Andrea was instantly and completely awake, perspiring.

Even in her sleep, she'd anticipated this important wake-up call. She glanced at the status panel: systems nominal. Tara, her partner and the only other soul aboard ship, was already on station. Not surprised—Tara was a clone. Andrea held the common bias that clones worked not from need or virtue, but from habit.

At the top of her panel, the chronometer counted backward: four hours, twenty-eight minutes until they slid out of faster-than-light speed into kinetic speed. Enough time to dress, eat, and rehearse their critical first minutes in the Jod system. Andrea touched the intercom button, "Tara, I'm awake. What are you doing up so early?"

After a pause, a sleepy voice replied, "I prepared a hot . . ." The message collapsed into a long yawn. "Excuse me. A hot meal, and I brewed some black gaval."

"You'd better have another cup." Andrea waited for a reply but caught the last audible part of another yawn over the intercom, which she clipped short, saying, "I'm switching off before you put me to sleep." She touched the pad closing the channel.

Andrea slipped her long legs out from under the thin cotton sheets till her feet touched the cold floor. Her plain undershirt had hiked up over her stomach during the night while she'd slept. Standing in her small quarters, she bent over, stretching her hamstrings, placing the palms of her hands flat on the floor, then grabbing her ankles, she stretched her strong leg muscles. She gracefully unbent herself and stretched her arms above her head as she rolled her head in slow, grand circles to limber her neck. Her shoulder twinged slightly from a wound not completely healed.

Her purloined clothes lay draped over a chair where she'd carefully laid them. She'd plundered the clothes lockers of the all-male crew—one of whom was quite small. She'd consigned her own set of foul, tattered clothes to waste disintegration; all but the wilderness cloak that Brigon gave her. Brigon, how is he? The cloak hung from a hook on her cabin door. Stained with smoke, blood, and sweat, the cloak smelled dank, but she dared not launder the garment and risk damage, because she did not know the secret of the cloak's technology—how it perfectly camouflages the wearer.

With a sense of practicality and irreverent mirth, she mixed and matched the crew's wardrobes to fit herself with a tunic, shirt, and trousers. The white pullover shirt fit well although roomy at the waist. The tunic hung loose on her shoulders and the sleeves were a bit short. Trousers were a much harder fit and she settled for the diminutive crewman's trousers that hung low on her narrow hips. Fortunately, the cloth had some give, as the trousers were tight about her seat and thighs. Serviceable, clean clothes, yet on her the outfit lost its military aura; instead, it broadcast a mixed signal of authority and tease. She fastened the belt with an audible click, then pulled on a pair of small boots—the smallest boots aboard the ship.

She looked into the long mirror to adjust her gig line, a habit held over from her days as a cadet. Her short black hair stood in a cowlick where her head burrowed into a firm pillow. She'd gained a couple pounds during this trip, pounds that brought her back to her correct weight. Her long ordeal on Cor had left her looking gaunt, her face showing the greatest deprivation of food and sleep. Her eyes still showed fatigue. She longed for the sleep of complete resignation, an outpouring of consciousness that refreshed mind and body.

Nevertheless, sixteen days of forced rest and full rations had done her good. She smiled slightly with self-satisfaction. She and Tara had stolen a comfortable Cor ship, the *Benwoi*, an armed merchant cruiser provisioned for a crew of eight, plus forty passengers. Yet, looking in the mirror, Andrea could see the latent anxiety about her own eyes, tension written in small telltale lines on her otherwise smooth olive skin. Now, she wished they'd managed to hijack a more formidable fighting ship, not this armed merchant. This comfortable ship—this pig, using loose nautical lingo—lacked long-range weapons, speed, and maneuverability. As best as she could tell, Andrea believed the Cor had dispatched two warships in pursuit.

On previous mornings, Andrea knew that she'd awake in the relative safety of traveling at FTL speed, a demilitarized state of physics where weapons are useless. Ships chasing them could not fire forward lest they fly instantly into their own ordnance. Likewise, the *Benwoi* could not see aft to target the pursuers, but not for long.

In four hours, they'd come out of light speed into the Jod system, where according to plan, her comrade H'Roo Parh waited with a heavy cruiser. *He'd damn well better be there waiting with his finger on the trigger.* This kind of fight was new to Andrea—not the tactile struggle of close combat where peripheral vision, reflex, and strength mattered. She knew physical anatomy better than warship structures. She knew how to use a variety of handheld weapons, not shipborne lasers and torpedoes. For her the proper distance between combatants was measured in one or two arm's lengths, not hundreds of thousands of kilometers. However, one principle applied to both situations: the party who inflicts the first blow usually wins. The Cor had the advantage of being at her back, at present invisible, possessing superior firepower. Andrea paused by the galley long enough to pick up a warm cake made of coarse cornmeal on which she spread a rich butter and a sweet chutney. She poured herself a large mug of steaming black brew, gaval—a synthetic that she recognized as insipid coffee buttressed with chicory. She loaded it with four heaping teaspoons of sugar to mask an unfamiliar aftertaste. She drank for the effect of the stimulant.

Andrea walked down the short spine of the ship and stepped onto the bridge, the arena of today's battle. The hiss of the door announced her.

"Morning."

Tara turned around in her seat and she offered a wan smile. She looked pale. Her gold-specked, hazel eyes sparked with anxiety. But her spirits picked up just having a companion. She wore her auburn hair loose, pulled behind her ears.

Sipping her gaval, Andrea put her free hand on

Tara's soft shoulder, trying to transfer some of her calm to her nervous comrade: words of encouragement were superfluous. Andrea looked at the screens. The forward screens showed them approaching Jod space. The ship's computers filtered the ambient light from the screens to present a picture of approaching stars, drifting from the center toward the edges as the perspective changed, each star eventually absorbed into a milk white glow at the edge of the screen—a blur of white light reminded the viewer that the screen was a representation, not physical reality.

Meanwhile the rearview screens displayed only charts and a virtual image. The aft sensors were useless because they outran all matter and energy. She glanced at the small weapons console and shook her head ruefully. The ship had no torpedoes in inventory. The laser cannon was small, suitable for intimidating other merchant ships or pirates, but Andrea thought to herself, *If we get close enough to use it, we're already dead.*

Andrea asked, "Have you figured out where we'll come out of light speed and become fully kinetic?"

"Yes—sort of." Tara brushed a wisp of auburn hair from her face. "The probable error is significant. The ship's computers have detailed charts leading up to the Jod system, and the Jod system itself—even the location of artificial satellites and space stations. But we can't confirm our position because we can't get a decent star fix until we come out of light speed. In short, we've been flying dead reckoning, just bearing and time, and I'm not an experienced navigator. This trip will last sixteen days, seven hours, forty-four minutes, and thirteen point six two seconds."

Tara pointed at the ship's red chronometer counting down the seconds, minutes, and hours in the flight.

She shook her head. "So the trip takes close to one and a half million seconds. If we're off by just two of those seconds, we'll find ourselves about three hundred sixty thousand miles off course. A ten-second error is not out of the realm of possibility."

"Not very encouraging." Andrea looked at the sensor readouts—all flat, and she muttered in frustration. "We're deaf, dumb, and half-blind."

Right now, Andrea wanted more than anything to send H'Roo Parh some kind of warning. First, she might not appear in the Jod system where they had planned. Second, she was bringing company, at least two armed Ordinate ships ready for a fight. She knew that a Jod battle cruiser could outmaneuver and outgun the Ordinate ships, providing H'Roo was not taken by surprise. But any message she transmitted to H'Roo would arrive in the Jod system about five hundred years after she arrived to deliver it in person. Andrea leaned stiff-armed against the console. The amber lights reflected from her high cheekbones and forehead. Her deep-set eyes were lost in shadow.

"Maybe the Cor didn't follow us?" Tara's eyes betrayed her own doubts.

Andrea stepped away from the flat screens and stifled a bubble of sardonic laughter. "Oh, they're behind us. Count on it." After all, she reflected, we saw two Ordinate ships accelerating in hot pursuit when we engaged the FTL drive and just barely escaped with our skins. They're motivated. We burned down their Clone Welfare Institute, ruined their crop of NewGen clones, killed scores of their security forces, started an insurrection between the old-order clones and the Ordinate, stole their ship, and set a course straight toward the Jod system.

Andrea smiled grimly, "I'll be pleasantly surprised if we discover that we've got only two Ordinate vessels on our tail. The Ordinate want our heads on a pike. Our best chance is to come out of light speed then pour on the speed in kinetics."

"Maybe we lost them. After all, we traveled in a broad arc—not even a straight line. They are bound to have the same navigational problems." Tara offered up some hope.

Andrea looked down at Tara and wondered how best to explain to a simple clone who'd never experienced space flight, let alone faster-than-light travel, the phenomenon of quantrails. But Tara seemed to have a gift for thinking in the abstract world of computers, so why not physics? "We're leaving a trail. Even in the vacuum of space, there are hydrogen atoms. We are traveling at such speed that we collide with billions of atoms a second. When the hydrogen atoms smash against our inertial dampeners, the atoms break into their elemental particles—muons, positrons. The particles spin off in a momentary life, but they leave a brief trail to follow. Have you seen aircraft on a clear day leave long thin clouds behind them?"

"Yes." Tara leaned back in her chair and nodded.

"Those thin clouds are the contrails that come from the tips of the wings—water droplets or ice crystals left in the wake of an aircraft. Something like that happens with a spacecraft traveling faster than light."

Tara thought for a moment, then observed. "If that's the case, they know our direction, but how will they know the instant we come out of light speed?"

Andrea smiled, seeing where Tara's thought was leading. "Very good. Suddenly they'll run out of quantrail, but by that time they will have passed us.

They'll be ahead of us. What kind of time lag are we talking about?"

Tara swung her chair around and tapped her console to bring up some ship's data. Andrea watched her scroll through charts of data, amazed at the speed with which this clone from Cor assimilated information. *Can this be? This once timid clone is acquiring self-confidence.*

Tara brushed her short auburn hair from her face and said, "Assuming their sensors are roughly equivalent to ours and their onboard computers operate at the same speed, and they can switch down their FTL drive at the same speed . . . we're looking at a half second—max." Her face fell: she'd expected a greater buffer.

But Andrea brightened. "Yeah, but that puts ninety thousand miles between us. At kinetic speed, it'll take them a half hour to come about, then catch us."

"That still isn't much time."

"It's thirty minutes I didn't think we had. We need to take advantage of every second. When we come out of FTL, we must have a programmed maneuver. We'll come about and reverse our course for two minutes at maximum kinetic speed. How fast can the ship's sensors pinpoint our position?" Andrea set her cup of gaval down on the console and crowded next to Tara.

Tara answered from memory. "Assuming we show up without a clue as to our position, the computer can identify stars from the charts and triangulate our position within a hundred meters in less than eight seconds."

"Okay. As soon as we have coordinates, we send a distress call to H'Roo. We'll pick a direction, and run like hell."

"The Cor will hear the signal as well. What if H'Roo can't get to us before the Cor do?"

Andrea looked Tara in the face and replied with certainty, "Then we're dead." Andrea picked up her cup and took a sip.

Andrea and Tara prepared to decelerate to kinetic speeds. They rehearsed their actions and anticipated decisions. Then, for the last twenty minutes, Tara sat at her console and silently watched the chronometer count down, waiting for the ship's computer to execute a series of maneuvers.

Andrea paced the bridge with an eye on the screens. She wiped a film of nervous perspiration from her forehead as she riveted her attention to the sensors, trying to grab even a half-second's advantage of knowing the disposition of her adversaries before they spotted her.

The final seconds dragged themselves off the clock. The hum in the ship changed markedly to a lower pitch. The screens blinked off, then back with live images fore and aft. The sensors came alive, and the computer strained with the flood of data, attempting to reorient the ship. The engines groaned as the ship jerked to a stop, then scrambled backward. The abrupt shift in speed and direction overwhelmed the inertial dampeners, jarring the ship and knocking Andrea to the floor. Down on her haunches, she looked up at the screens. "Look!" She pointed to the forward main view. "Quantrails!"

Two eddies of sparkles sped past and converged instantly in the distance, then disappeared.

Tara reported, "Two ships: ninety-two thousand miles forward. We are increasing our distance from them—accelerating." She looked back at Andrea.

Andrea raised her voice to the computer, "Forward screen; full magnification."

The screen zoomed in, delivering a grainy picture of the two Cor ships stopped dead in space. Then in graceful unison, the Cor ships came about, their bows pointing directly at the screen and they loomed larger. Andrea announced what Tara already knew, "They've found us."

Tara attended a message on her console. "We have coordinates and full navigation back on-line. Your message to H'Roo is gone."

"Where are we?"

"Well, we are in the Jod system—barely. We passed Jod. We're about two hundred million miles from the Jod sun."

Andrea looked at the charts. She jabbed at the screen with her finger. "H'Roo was supposed to wait in the vicinity of the planet Lobar, here." She asked, "What's the distance to Lobar in miles?"

Tara deftly stroked her console keys and the ship's computer flashed a star chart onto the forward screen. A thin red arc on the screen plotted the course and marked an endpoint: 257 million miles farther. Andrea's quick mind needed another piece of data. "How soon will the Cor battle cruisers have us in their weapons' range?"

Tara looked at the tactical display above her and answered. "They can close to torpedo range in twenty-one minutes. Maybe we can make another short jump at FTL."

Andrea looked at Tara and shook her head. "I thought of that. We don't have enough fuel. We could accelerate to FTL, but we would never be able to decelerate: we'd be a permanent streak in the cosmos until we hit something. But H'Roo can make the jump."

"He won't get our message for twenty-three minutes. He might be able to make the jump from kinetic speed in less than two minutes. Nevertheless his travel time to us is at least another five minutes. Best case, we won't see your H'Roo person for at least thirty minutes."

Damn! Andrea rebuked herself for missing the obvious. She lacked experience in this arena: deep space tactics. But she dared not let her nerves show. The bridge seemed to swim around her now, a flood of data, and only experience tells one which data are important, and which aren't. "We need to buy some time. This is just happening too fast." She pressed her fingers to her temples as she thought.

"We need more speed!" Tara exclaimed. Her wide eyes pleaded with the inanimate console.

"No! Not enough fuel. We can't go faster. Not possible." Andrea shot back with a note of exasperation, but her face transformed as her mind seized an idea. "We can't go faster, but perhaps we can make them go slower." Andrea looked at the charts, dragging her finger over the plastic screen along their projected bearing.

"What are you looking for?" Tara asked.

"A tree to climb. A rock to hide behind. There!" Andrea pointed to a planetoid, a mere piece of astronomical flotsam spinning lifelessly in space. "Now, we're going to play this game by my rules. Tara, change our bearing to intercept this rock, Qota Two. Quick, send a message telling H'Roo to meet us there."

"Done." Tara obeyed without question. She played the console like a musical instrument, then wiped her perspiring hands on her smock. Then she opened a channel and broadcast.

Andrea immediately followed with another request.

"Give me whatever specs the sensors can provide on Qota."

Tara consulted her console and the screen flashed a detailed set of data with enhanced photography of the planetoid. Tara looked up, surprised to see the rich detail in the virtual image of Qota. "The ship's library has complete survey data on Qota. Do you still want sensors directed there?"

How can that be? Andrea thought. *How can Cor have details on a cold dead rock in the Jod system?* Andrea postponed that question as the more pressing business of survival seized her attention. She skipped the detailed mineralogical studies of the planet and focused on the data affecting orbital mechanics. Qota: 4,765 miles in diameter, mass is one point one seven, with a veil of methane—a thin atmosphere. Density three point seven times water. Escape velocity three point one seven miles per second. . . .

Tara interrupted. "The two Cor ships got your message; they've set an intercept course for Qota. We just lost twenty seconds. We'll arrive in Qota's gravity well just ninety seconds before the Cor do."

"We'll make the time back—don't worry." She fixed her eyes on the forward screen.

"How?"

Andrea pointed to the virtual image on the screen. "We put ourselves into a low equatorial orbit around Qota. There, we hide behind the horizon and keep rock between them and us." Andrea calculated: If they keep their same speed up to overtake us quickly, they fall out to a higher orbit. Qota's gravity removes their advantage of raw speed. Each low orbit takes about fifty-eight minutes. If they continue to chase us, they must slow down, then maneuver. If they choose to wait for us, so much the better. In either case, by the time they devise a set of elliptical orbits to put us into weapons' range, H'Roo arrives. She said aloud, "Each orbit we make buys us about forty minutes. All we need is one orbit." She held up one finger.

Andrea and Tara set a course to put themselves in a close orbit only ninety-seven miles above Qota's surface. If the Cor ships tried to close the gap at their present rate, they'd find themselves in an orbit almost twenty thousand miles farther out—out of weapons' range. Andrea's small ship disappeared behind the horizon, where, out of sight, she fired thrusters to set her ship in a seven-degree west-walking orbit.

Tara asked, "What's that for?"

"Just in case they parked in a higher orbit to take pot shots at us, I don't want to come over the horizon where they expect us." Andrea put the planetoid's surface on full screen magnification. The thin methane veil reflected the little bit of light that traversed so far from the Jod sun. The shimmering veil hid the surface. Sensors painted a picture of a smooth surface. They could land, but Andrea had hoped for some terrain feature to hide behind. Nothing. The chronometer sloughed the seconds slowly. The relief of being out of the Cor ships' line of sight was palpable. But the relief was corrupted by fresh fear of not seeing her adversary. Andrea strained her eyes at the screen. She noticed how dry her mouth had become in the last twenty minutes of the chase. She felt overwarm. She unbuttoned her tunic and threw it aside on the floor.

"H'Roo should be here by now." Again, Tara wiped her hands on her smock. "What if he doesn't come?"

Andrea snapped back, "He'll come: he's my friend."

Tara grit her teeth, "I didn't mean it like that. Maybe

he jumped before he got our second transmission. He'd be sitting at the point of our first transmission. We're out of his sensor range by now."

Andrea balled her hand into a fist. "Start broadcasting our position."

"We're on the wrong side of the planet to send a transmission or receive an answer from H'Roo."

Damn physics! Andrea shook her head in frustration. She turned to Tara and said, "Then we must give up our position." Andrea bit her lower lip then, muttering, "We may need to make a second orbit just to get a good transmission out."

Andrea looked at the forward screens and the over-the-horizon sensors for any sign of a Cor ship. If the Cor were smart, and there was nothing to suggest otherwise, they'd park one ship in a high orbit and send the second to flush them out into the open. From a high orbit the one ship could see a third of the planet. The other, if it followed with a lower orbit, might be constrained to viewing a tenth of the planetoid or less. "Change course. Shift our orbit toward the pole. We've got to go under the planet and come up behind them. While we cross the pole, we can get a good transmission out and we can stay out of sight for maybe another twelve minutes."

"When we transmit, they'll know where we are."

"Yeah, but I don't think they're willing to make the same kind of U-turn we're about to make."

Tara entered the navigational data into the computer. She interpreted the results. "I'm not sure we can make that kind of turn either. We'll lose relative speed to the point where we put ourselves in a rapidly decaying orbit."

"How decayed?" Andrea asked.

"A free fall. We drop from an altitude of ninety-seven miles to less than thirty miles in just forty seconds. At the nadir of our turn we lose altitude at five miles per second."

"The engines can pull us out of the fall," Andrea said with false confidence.

"Barely." Tara looked back, fear showing in her hazel eyes.

"Are you sure?"

"You can check my math, if you wish." Tara answered with equal exasperation. Tara took a deep breath to steady herself and continued, "We'll hit that methane atmosphere and really heat up the skin of this ship. Not much room for error. If the engines so much as hiccup, we're cooked. You don't know what this ship can handle. We might spin out of control."

Andrea decided, "We've got to take the risk. We'll come 'round the far horizon in less than four minutes. I'd rather take our chances with the atmosphere than with those Cor battle cruisers. All we need is another couple minutes. H'Roo can make a short jump beyond kinetic speed, slip in here, and cover us."

Tara glanced sideways. "I suppose I should be dead already." With the stoic resignation typical of her model of clone, she typed in the instructions. "I armed the manual override in case you change your mind."

Andrea pursed her lips at this seeming lack of confidence, but the truth was she had no more confidence than Tara did. "Do it."

The ship banked hard as the engines delivered power to turn it almost ninety degrees. The artificial gravity stuttered as it compensated for the sudden rise in centripetal force. The forward screen showed the horizons expanding as they plummeted toward Qota's surface, and the black of space turned into a dimmed, diffused turbid green. The bridge lights dimmed as the ship automatically sounded an alert.

The hull temperature rose rapidly. The ship's computers, having never anticipated that a sentient being would purposefully put the ship into a crash dive, surmised that the ship was out of control. The computer barked a warning: *Helm control! Helm control!*

"Kill that noise!" Andrea chided.

Tara complied, overriding the computer's alert. The aft screen showed ionized gases trailing behind. The altimeter showed them dropping like a meteor, accelerating in Qota's gravitational pull. "We're less than fifty miles up." Tara's voice betrayed her anxiety.

The engines strained to accelerate the ship back to escape velocity in their new bearing toward the pole. Tara's voice rose a halftone higher, "Thirty miles."

"Oh, shut up!" Andrea snapped back. She slapped the console, exhorting the ship, "Come on, you pig! Come on!"

Tara's face flushed. She turned back to her console. She muttered under her breath, "Twenty-six miles . . ." as if she looked forward to auguring the ship into the frozen planet and in the last split second saying, I told you so.

The engines fought back. The ship shuddered as the thin methane buffeted the hull. The ship's retractable wings automatically extended, slightly increasing the surface area, slowing and stabilizing their descent. Then the altimeter reversed itself and showed a steady climb as the ship accelerated on a new heading. The forward screen faded to the crystal black covered with stars.

Andrea exhaled. "Hold this heading."

Both women dismissed the past thirty seconds of tension without comment and focused on their immediate tasks. They passed under the pole where they transmitted their message to H'Roo.

"We should get a reply in a moment," Tara said.

Andrea nodded. "He's bound to hear us now. Put audio on."

Tara complied and immediately they heard a loud, crackling oscillating screech against a background of groaning bagpipes. Tara quickly turned the volume low and looked up at Andrea. "What does that noise mean?"

"It means we're being jammed. It means the Cor did park a ship on the other side. It means they know where we are."

"Can they keep our signal from getting to your friend?"

"They can jam our receiver, but not our transmitter. I doubt they have the power to jam H'Roo. If they did, he'd come to the source—if he's out there." Andrea stared at the screen. "He's got to be out there."

"That's a comfort," Tara said sarcastically.

Andrea started to chide her until she recognized her own tendency to sarcasm now adapted by this clone. Instead she merely said, "Stay alert. As soon as sensors see anything coming over the horizon . . ."

"Well, sensors indicate that you've got one ship coming from sixty-seven degrees port, just over the horizon. Altitude: twelve thousand miles. Descending to intercept us."

"Estimated time to weapons' range?"

"As soon as she has line of sight—one minute fourteen seconds."

"Accelerate to maximum speed. Get us out of here."

Tara obeyed with relish. The ship rose in a sweeping arc in a run for deep space. As they rose, they caught sight of the pursuing Cor ship. Then their plan turned to ashes as the second ship appeared on the forward screen. They were caught in the open.

Andrea looked at her companion, whose face had turned pale. "Got any ideas?"

Tara looked up from her console. Her face glistened. "The forward ship has got a weapons' lock on us. We're in torpedo range. Shall I open fire with our lasers?"

"It's pointless. We can't breach their shields at this range." Andrea shook her head. "I'm sorry, Tara. You did well. Bad odds. God keep you."

Then she turned her back to the screen. She knew death would be instantaneous: she need not watch further. Death was not something she was curious about; simply accepted. Of all the deaths she'd endured, hers would be the easiest. A torpedo would pulverize the ship in one cataclysmic concussion. The overpressure would crush her completely, then toss her pieces into the vacuum of space. In that moment, she'd be with Steve and Glennie again. . . .

"Andrea!" Tara yelled.

Andrea braced herself for the impact.

"Look!" Tara reached over and grabbed Andrea's shoulder.

Andrea turned and saw a large bulbous Jod battle cruiser with its beak-shaped bow appear on the screen. Easily one hundred times the displaced volume of the Cor ship, the Jod battle cruiser looked like the head of a serpent protecting her brood. The Cor ship began an abrupt turn to face the greater threat, but with no chance of success.

The Jod battle cruiser fired a broadside of three

crimson lasers. The Cor ship returned fire, more a defiant gesture as the Jod shields rebuffed both lasers and torpedoes. Then the Cor shields failed under the massive beating; the lasers sliced amidships, breaching the hull, sending a shower of sparks at the point of laser impact. The Cor ship's hull blew apart with a burst of yellow light and chunks of metal flew in every direction, followed instantly by a blinding scorch of blue—a ring of light—as the Cor ship's engines exploded.

All systems on Andrea's ship dimmed to black as the electromagnetic shock passed through them.

"Oh, no. What's happening? Our shields are failing!" Tara said with a slight tremor in her voice as she watched her consoles die, leaving them in total blackness. "The artificial gravity is off!"

Andrea spoke in Tara's direction. "Don't move. Hold on to something. The ship's electronics must have shut down automatically for the shock wave—mechanical self-preservation. Look, the shields are coming back online." She felt herself weighted again. The forward screen flickered back to life with a splotchy resolution from the after-effects of the explosion, just in time for them to see chunks of debris flying at them. In the distance, Andrea could see the second Cor ship turn and disappear into FTL speed.

A small window opened on the lower left portion of the black screen, and Andrea saw a grainy, blinking image of H'Roo's face. His face showed a mix of hope and deep concern, his eyes searching his console. Through crackle and hiss, H'Roo's voice asked, " 'at i- -our stat-s?"

Andrea laughed in an outburst of nervous energy. She moved in front of the communications screen so

H'Roo could see her. "I was beginning to think you'd forgotten about me, H'Roo."

"I ca- -arely ma- -ur transmiss---." H'Roo asked again, uncharacteristically stiff, "Wha- is your status?"

Andrea answered, "Our systems went off-line from the blast's pulse. Our shields and some of our outer electronics are cooked." The screen resolution continued to improve as processors recovered.

H'Roo allowed a tight smile, but his voice was cold. "I see you now. Mat Flores. Welcome home. Can you navigate?"

Andrea noted the small crew working behind H'Roo on the bridge of the Jod ship. They wore the tan uniforms of the Jod regular fleet, while H'Roo wore the gray and black uniform of the Tenebrea.

H'Roo's face was outwardly aloof, but his hazel eyes sparked. Andrea noticed that the amber and indigo rings beneath his eyes seemed to smile, clashing with H'Roo's refined nose and straight lips. She noticed an older Jod with captain's rank giving orders to younger officers. She discerned that H'Roo's formal demeanor was to frustrate prying eyes and ears. Perhaps wishful thinking on her part. Therefore, she answered with similar professional coolness. "I think so. Our computers are back on-line. We need fuel."

"We'll refuel you from our stores. Then, follow us to Vintell. Travel under dead sensor emission control. We'll keep this local channel open at five watts to feed your computers navigational data." He abruptly changed the subject. He spoke softly, "Mat Flores, we'd almost given up on you. Thought you were . . ." H'Roo grappled with one word then substituted another, "unsuccessful."

"Just delayed." Andrea added coyly, "Maybe too successful."

H'Roo quickly cut her off. "Tell me later." He glanced sideways to his crowded bridge.

Andrea beckoned Tara to step in front of the screen. "H'Roo, we have a lot to talk about. Where is Hal K'Rin?"

"The admiral plans to meet us at the Vintell safehouse. I informed him immediately when you entered Jod space, and the *Tyker* is en route."

"Good. I have some information he wants. Also—" Andrea's face clouded with dark emotion, but she prudently checked herself. She forced a smile on her lips. "I have a couple questions of my own."

chapter 2

Andrea leaned against the bulkhead and looked out a porthole at the chocolate brown surface of Vintell. A weak message flashed on the screen, providing navigational data to the *Benwoi*'s computers and a reminder to maintain emissions control. Andrea looked across the bridge to Tara who sat passively, arms folded, in front of her console, noting course changes.

Andrea turned back to her porthole and a glimpse of a horizon illuminated dimly by a distant white dwarf star. Several thousand kilometers to port she saw a moving point of light, the dim reflection of the Jod cruiser. The Jod ship blinked out as it disappeared into the shadows. Down on the planet's surface, the day and night were demarcated by a stark line—not dawn or dusk, no gradations of light and dark, just the brutal distinction of light and dark. Andrea turned to Tara and announced, "Vintell has no atmosphere."

Tara replied perfunctorily, "We've begun our descent."

Andrea nodded and pressed her face against the small window. For some reason she wanted to see this

new place with her eyes, not with the augmentation of
the forward screen. Far below she saw massive chasms,
black crescents carved through the chocolate soil disappearing over the horizon. They looked like deep cracks
radiating from some shattering impact, perhaps a colli-
sion of two worlds.

They settled into an orbit to make a more graceful
entry into the gravity well, their course slipping them
into Vintell's shadow, then back into light for the final
leg of their journey. Andrea saw just how large the
chasms were. The ship began a vertical descent directly
into one. Easily twelve miles deep and two miles wide,
these yawning jaws of rock swallowed all light. Andrea
felt like a speck as they disappeared inside the fissure.
Blackness, not even starlight.

A message scrolled across the forward screen, inviting them to switch on all systems. Ahead, Andrea saw
H'Roo's ship switch on landing lights, a pinprick of
light in an otherwise black hole. She left the porthole
for the forward screen.

Tara reported, "Almost a vacuum: torr to the minus
two. Hull temperature minus two hundred seventy-six
degrees. Sensors detect thermal radiation at the bottom of
this pit: plus six degrees." With some manipulation, Tara
brought the forward screen to life and used enhanced
radar images to create a picture of this forbidding world.
Port and starboard, sheer walls of rock rose miles above
them. All proportion was lost to them. Seemingly small
shelves latticed the walls, small shelves on which one
might build a city. H'Roo's ship turned. With lights blazing, it maneuvered toward a shelf near the bottom of the
chasm. The shelf was the lip of a cavern.

Tara looked up from her console. "Almost pure

nickel and iron ore. The planet has a strong magnetic field."

Andrea muttered, "Good place to build a hideaway." Twelve miles deep within a crevice, the Tenebrea maintained a small facility shielded from prying eyes by miles of heavy metal. "Even the best sensors would mistake a ship for a flaw in the rock way down here."

The *Benwoi* turned automatically and followed the Jod ship. They passed over the shelf into the cave. Bright yellow lights switched on to illuminate the landing bay, a natural cave of ample proportions blasted from the igneous rock.

From her porthole, Andrea watched the Jod ship set down on five thick legs among a set of scuff marks on the landing bay floor. The Jod ship occupied one of six landing stations. Three small star-skiffs without military markings sat parked in a row near a maintenance bay. Andrea figured them for Tenebrea light transport.

Tara looked up and announced, "We have docking instructions." Tara eased the *Benwoi* down, near the skiffs, unconsciously grouping the smallish vessels together: the small *Benwoi* didn't need the room of a whole landing quad.

A command, the first voice they'd heard since going to emission control, bid them, "Do not disembark until we establish the artificial atmosphere. Remember, Vintell is a secure area. All nonstation personnel must be escorted. Thank you."

Andrea thought, *I'm back in K'Rin's world with his set of rules—and his secrets.*

She looked out her porthole. Two halves of a geodesic structure, like a giant crystal clam, rose from the landing pad arching overhead. The two sections rode shiny rails and they came together with tongue-and-groove precision.

Very gradually, the whine of turbine pumps increased, and Tara reported the results of the sensor readings. "The outside temperature is rising to nominal levels—seventy-four degrees—and the atmosphere gauge shows eighteen PSI with an O2-Nitrogen-CO2 mix. Humidity forty-two percent."

Andrea took a peek at the console. "Same as the air on Jod."

"Then we must be in the right place," added Tara sarcastically, looking somewhat pleased with herself. Toggling a row of red and black switches, she shut down the main engines, engaged the auxiliary generators, and put systems in maintenance mode. Then she spun out of her seat and started for the main hatch, brushing past Andrea in her haste.

Andrea raised an eyebrow. "Where are you going?"

"To see if Eric's here." Tara didn't stop.

"Slow down, Tara—Eric might not be here waiting for you."

Tara stopped and slowly turned. Her anticipation withered. She lowered her voice. "I haven't seen Eric for more than three years, but I thought about him every one of those days. You don't want him to be here, do you?"

Andrea defended herself although Tara's accusation was awkwardly accurate. "I didn't say that."

"Well, you'd act the same way if your mate—" Tara caught herself.

Steve. Andrea's face flushed, and she recoiled slightly as if slapped. Tara saw immediately that she'd touched an old wound, and whispered, "I'm sorry."

Andrea broke eye contact. Startled by her own swelling emotion, she held her hand over her eyes like a small curtain to hide her pain. Her imagination splashed the image of a face before her mind's eye: Steve's face. But Steve's arched eyebrows furled into a knit brow. His face grew pale. Lines of care marred the smooth skin and the porpoise smile turned flat with cold anger. His cheekbones seemed to protrude slightly as his image changed into Tara's hand-drawn picture of the clone Eric. *I can't tell them apart!* Neither could the Hunters. When they murdered Steve, they thought they had killed Eric. *If only I could correct their mistake . . .* Andrea struggled with her memory to recall the differences that must exist between the two faces, but the fresh imprint of Tara's picture overwhelmed her memory. She felt guilt for having neglected Steve's memory, for there was no other explanation for her confusion. This interloper, Eric, had robbed her of her last shred of comfort. *What am I going to do when I see his face?*

Andrea closed her eyes tight and cleared her scattered mind and caught her breath. She admitted, "It's not your problem, Tara." Andrea put her hand on Tara's shoulder. "It's just that I doubt Eric is on that Jod cruiser. Eric is K'Rin's prized secret. He'll most likely bring him on the *Tyker.* He'd never give Jod regulars access to Eric. You can ask H'Roo Parh."

Tara led the way down the ramp onto the cold floor of the landing bay. Moisture condensed on the floor, reflecting the glaring lights. Tara held her small bag of personal effects in the crook of her bare arm. They watched the Jod disembark.

Trying to hide her relief, Andrea pointed to the assembly of Jod in their tan uniforms. "You see, he's not here." She noticed the disappointment on Tara's face and added, "But you won't have to wait long." *I must wait forever. . . .*

Distinctive in his black and gray uniform, H'Roo trotted down the ramp of the *Benwoi*. His hairless head was more perfectly round than most Jod—his neck longer, even graceful. He reached out and grabbed Andrea's hand. His grip conveyed much more than a greeting. Restraint. He didn't smile. Rather, he shifted his eyes ever so slightly in the direction of the Jod maintenance crew working outside the Jod cruiser, directing Andrea's attention to the eyes and ears that did not belong to the Tenebrea. Then he led Andrea away and whispered, "I brought an injection of the enzyme: you are almost into your grace period."

Andrea acknowledged with a nod, then pointed to Tara. "H'Roo, this is Tara Gullwing."

"Oh, the clone?" H'Roo punctuated the introduction with the unflattering epithet. He did not extend his hand to Tara. Andrea noted this lapse in H'Roo's otherwise impeccable manners. Like most Jod, H'Roo deplored clone technology as a perversion of nature. Like most Jod, he associated the clones themselves with the Cor Ordinate threat: fear, distrust, and a sense of distasteful unnaturalness, even uncleanness—not the polite subject for reunions or dinner conversation. Although H'Roo had none of the innate Jod bias against humans, he did resent the clones, or at least the uneasy predicament they presented. Like most Jod, H'Roo wished the whole clone issue would simply disappear.

Tara withdrew to Andrea's side. Andrea felt herself stuck between sympathy and annoyance. She looked at H'Roo sideways, "When does K'Rin arrive?"

"Five days, ten hours."

Andrea noted H'Roo's curt behavior. She wondered if H'Roo still harbored ill will from their contretemps

on Clemnos. He had objected vociferously at first and
then with stony silence when she killed and mutilated
the Ordinate Hunter, Lt. Tapp. H'Roo had to haul
Tapp's mutilated body outside the Clemnos walls—
dirty business—while Andrea took Tapp's place on the
transport to Cor. Andrea remembered his disapproving
glance as they parted company without saying good-
bye. At first she dismissed H'Roo's pique as unprofes-
sional; now that he acted with dry professionalism, she
wondered if she had severed their friendship. I can't
change the facts now, she thought.

H'Roo pursed his thin lips. "Let's go inside where
we can talk." He hustled Andrea and Tara to the door.

Andrea ignored his admonition to silence and tried
an innocuous question. "Did you bring my uniforms?"

Finally, H'Roo let loose his affable grin. He pointed
at her makeshift clothes. "Lucky for you that I did. You
wouldn't want K'Rin to see you arrayed in this outfit
with all these flaps." He ran his finger down a lapel.
"What are these for? Wind rudders?"

Andrea welcomed the lighthearted abuse. "I wore
this outfit just for you, H'Roo."

Side by side, Andrea and H'Roo walked the short
distance to the small airlocks. Tara trailed. A guard in a
black Tenebrea uniform stopped the trio at the entrance
to the Vintell station. H'Roo produced orders with
K'Rin's seal that vouched for the two women. The airlock hissed shut, sealing them from the prying eyes of
the Jod regulars who worked in the landing bay
offloading supplies and preparing for their voyage
home.

H'Roo's neck warmed and he immediately said, "I
missed you these past months. I hope Hal K'Rin
assigns us to work together again." Without waiting for

a reply he walked quickly down a brightly lit corridor. Andrea and Tara followed. H'Roo led them up a steep ladder to an empty observation deck overlooking the landing bay. When they stopped, Andrea said, "Tara wants to know if K'Rin is bringing Eric on the *Tyker.*"

H'Roo turned to look sideways and down at Tara. Tara stood in his shadow, her eyes wide with anticipation of his answer. He then turned and spoke to Andrea, "Yes, I think so."

Andrea noticed that Tara's face flushed slightly. Was Tara reacting to the good news, or this second snub from H'Roo? Andrea wanted to tell H'Roo to mind his Jod manners. Tara could no more help the fact that she was a clone than Andrea could help the fact that she was a hairy Terran. However, Andrea simply changed the subject. "Any other news?"

H'Roo brightened. "I've got news about the rest of our class's assignments. Gem-Bar is assigned to special ops security, plumbers. Soon, he's scheduled to rotate to duty aboard the *Tyker.*"

"Good." Andrea nodded. "I like Gem-Bar. I'd like to see him again."

"You remember Tamor-Kyl?"

Andrea wrinkled her nose as if offended by a smell. "That blowhard."

"You'll be pleased. K'Rin denied him a billet in special ops. Instead, he put Tamor in a desk job as a Fleet Liaison Officer at Heptar. At first Tamor was furious— blamed you in part, blamed me, blamed everybody but himself. But I hear that he's calmed down."

Andrea nodded approvingly. "Good, then we'll not likely run into him." She leaned against the white plastic wall, and noticed how intently Tara listened to this idle conversation.

"Correct, but we are more than likely going to rely on him. In effect, he's our supply officer." H'Roo enjoyed sharing his gossip and commentary. "For example, Tamor-Kyl arranged the assignment of this Jod cruiser to our operational control. He can send up plump gramfles or powdered eggs, real smoked holstys, or the synthetics. My stomach has already made peace with Tamor. I suggest you do the same."

"I'd rather starve." Andrea looked through the thick glass porthole at the heavy cruiser that had a few hours before saved her life. She did not like being beholden to Tamor-Kyl in even the slightest detail, because she did not trust him. "Did he know the cruiser was for my benefit?"

"I doubt K'Rin felt obliged to tell Tamor why we needed a cruiser. Ironically in liaison work, the less one knows the better. The Fleet Liaison Officer is usually the last to know what the Tenebrea missions are. The Fleet likes it that way. If we make a mess, they prefer to know nothing, and it helps their case if the liaison officer knows even less."

Andrea approved. "Last to know? Wonderful. K'Rin will keep Tamor in the dark like a mushroom. Now, that will drive Tamor crazy. I'll bet he's ready to cut his own throat."

"I hear that Tamor is coping rather well."

"Pity. If I were K'Rin, I would toss Tamor out the airlock."

H'Roo grinned. "Not a chance. Tamor's decided to be the best mushroom that K'Rin ever had. He figures he can get promoted into a field assignment. You never know, Andrea, we may have misjudged him."

Andrea shook her head. "People don't change."

"Well, you haven't, except for your sense of fashion."

H'Roo laughed, reached over, and tugged at the loose sleeve of Andrea's tunic. He beckoned her to follow him deeper into the Vintell facility, walking past Tara as if the pale clone with the auburn hair were invisible. "When K'Rin arrives, you will have your triumphant homecoming."

Andrea walked down the sterile corridor beside H'Roo with Tara behind. Homecoming? I don't have a home. Triumphant? Then why do I feel as if I'm about to be caught and punished?

Admiral Adan Brulk arrived from a tense private meeting with the Cor Prefect, a tough woman with a mediocre cabinet that lacked vision. She relayed a barrage of criticism that emanated from the cabinet members. They can't see past the five-year budget! No sense of Cor's destiny . . . Nevertheless, Brulk was serene. Despite the recent catastrophe, the Prefect trusted him. The Prefect had vision. The private meeting was a politic means of warning Brulk about his detractors.

Brulk looked at the sparse model of levitated orbs circling an amber star: the Cor system not precisely to scale—the model was more a work of art than science, an orrery. The enameled blue and tan ball that represented Cor floated along the long leg of an elliptical orbit, heading away from the amber star. White patches at the polar regions grew, anticipating the change in climate: a hard winter. He reached out with his large hand and gave the blue and tan ball a gentle poke.

Admiral Brulk was a man of average height but uncommonly strong. He looked every inch a military man with short hair peppered with gray. His square, clean-shaven face featured a broad nose and an impassive mouth. Deep set beneath thick eyebrows, his crisp blue eyes sparked with intelligence honed on the two-edge steel of sentiment and malice. Brulk wore his uniform tailored to his broad shoulders, thick waist, and heavy legs. On each shoulder board, his admiral's rank was a shiny onyx insignia depicting two serpents tied in a Gordian knot, devouring each other.

He was a practical man, a modern man, and he sought the opportunity in change. Recently, his predictable world exploded with opportunities, the inexorable shift in climate, the technical advance in NewGen clone technology, and now open conflict. Destiny is a thousand practical considerations: the NewGens make the troublesome old-order models obsolete; the open conflict makes eradicating the old-order clones morally palatable, and the imminent permafrost will kill the vast majority of the old-order clones, keeping the Ordinate neatly in line with Nature.

He glanced out the large plate-glass window and saw the burned wreckage of the Clone Welfare Institute, and a tinge of anger colored his face. The political power in the Ordinate blamed him for a breach of security that allowed a rabble of old-order clones to perform this stupendous act of sabotage: the single largest edifice on Cor reduced to charred ruins; almost a complete loss—more than ninety-eight percent of the first NewGen crop; years of careful planning set awry. No rabble did this. Brulk bit the inside of his lower lip. No undisciplined rabble could decimate his elite security forces; rather, this unseen foe comprised of old-order clones fought with cunning and determination. He closed his eyes to contemplate the question: How many? Who leads them? Brulk looked at a thin file sitting on his desk. In the file, he compiled evidence of the wilderness clones. He drummed his fingers on the file and thought about the critical information missing from the file, information that he and possibly one other person knew, if that person were still alive.

Brulk closed his eyes tight as his mind visited his own past. He was only seventeen and spoiled. Now, Brulk could admit that peccadillo to himself, but not to others. His father was busy with government affairs; his mother was busy promoting her husband's career. So he spent too much time alone, rattling around a large empty house, intermittently studying, watching the shadows crawl across the parquet floors. He dreamed of one day doing something great, something that his father and mother must admit eclipsed their efforts. He had no one to tell his dreams, no confidant, except the pleasant but dull house servant.

She was a strong woman, ten years older by appearance, yet she'd been in service only six years and seemed charmingly naive. She listened with almost childlike attention to Brulk. She enjoyed the young master's attention and to show her appreciation, she began to do little things for Brulk: bring him food and drink, lay out his clothes. Around her Brulk felt very adult.

She was a PLV model, number 8218, one of the more popular domestic versions. She took the name Plova. She had strong features, an almost exaggerated jaw, and deep chocolate eyes. Brulk recalled that she was slightly taller than he was. Although her arms and legs were sinewy and she appeared, as most clones, underfed, Plova had solid hips and an inviting breast.

Brulk shook his head as he remembered. Thirty-two

years ago, his adolescent loins obliterated his common sense. He took Plova to his bed. Confession was impossible because of the certain punishment, but if he could ever tell anybody about the experience, he'd say he had become addicted to her touch. At first he swore he'd never touch her again. He tried being cold. Plova never complained. She imitated Brulk's aloofness, not knowing any other behavior for her circumstance. She complied with his requests to work in other rooms to give him solitude. But there she was in the otherwise empty house. He'd hear her rustle down the hall in her long silky house smock. He'd catch a glimpse of her looking at him, she turning abruptly to avoid his eyes. At first, he might restrain himself for a couple weeks, then a couple days. Finally he abandoned what he considered pretense. The pleasure was exquisite. Either his parents had withheld this marvelous truth, or they had failed to discover it. He'd certainly not seen any evidence that they had. As for the consequences, what harm could he do? Clones are engineered to be sterile.

Even now, Brulk could not recall her without knotting up inside, partly in longing for her and partly in fear of exposure. Their affair was a capital crime—capital in the sense that Plova would be immediately canceled. For his part, Brulk would be ruined as far as his career was concerned. His father and mother would reject him completely. The scandal of clone-whoring was crushing, especially for those in the ruling class.

Nevertheless, he lived for the afternoons when he returned from his formal studies. In what became an almost daily ritual, he'd bed Plova and they'd bathe. For an entire year, Plova was his passion and no one, not classmates, not even his parents, suspected any impropriety.

The female clone, Plova, fell in love in with Brulk, something Brulk had considered a remote possibility, but dismissed as inconsequential. But the limits of his incredulity were about to expand tenfold, and the consequences would haunt him. The impossible happened. Plova got pregnant.

Brulk did not panic. He considered killing Plova. In retrospect that was the better plan, but he feared—naively—discovery. He had never killed anything, and he did not yet appreciate how dispensable clones were or how easily one can make a body disappear in the wilderness. He was woefully inexperienced. Also, he had a morbid curiosity about the child he had sired. Foolish perhaps, but even now, he felt that the clone child transcended the normal. Brulk felt he somehow had acquired insights that the other Ordinate could never know. As a practical matter, the reminder of this peccadillo—as carefully hidden as it was—helped Brulk maintain a fastidious distance in other relationships. He remained a bachelor.

He didn't kill Plova. He settled for a second plan. As inexperienced as she was, Plova knew that failed sterility was an automatic cause for cancellation for quality assurance. She was, in contrast to Brulk, terror struck. Brulk helped her flee into the wilderness, where rumors said a small band of runaway clones subsisted until the elements killed them.

He remembered Plova's curious gratitude for what she thought was Brulk's selfless aid. It was proof of his reciprocal love. Brulk might have laughed out loud had he not been so terrified by the prospect of being caught. A hunt ensued for the fugitive domestic, but she was never found.

Another year passed. Brulk entered the elite academy for Ordinate government service. Brulk assumed Plova had died conveniently of natural causes in the wilderness.

The wilderness was a hard place. Even security patrols took great precautions when they operated east of the mountains for fear of the venomous creatures there. Brulk relaxed in the self-satisfied knowledge that he'd solved his problem without the trauma of killing his own progeny with his own hands. Brulk settled into a carefree existence inhabited only by his ambitions. He was determined to live without regrets.

Then he received a small sealed and somewhat weather-beaten note. He found the scrap of paper wedged in a stack of data cubes on his desk. Brulk remembered opening it, assuming the note came from a female cadet, also from a prominent family, a woman who might be useful as a wife. He opened it. *"My love. We have a son."* The note was unsigned. He recognized Plova's left-leaning staccato handwriting. The note was infuriating with its lack of detail. Where is he? What does he look like? What's his name? Even now, Brulk hadn't those answers.

Brulk burned the note immediately, and from that day, fear of discovery plagued him like lower back pain. He learned to live with it. Moreover, he learned from the episode.

Brulk rubbed his eyes as he replayed the painful memories for the thousandth time. At least he learned, and ironically—and Brulk appreciated irony—his transgression against the Ordinate and his illicit spawn taught him a lesson essential to avoid the inevitable demise of the Ordinate.

Most graphically, Brulk learned that the old-order clone engineering was flawed. Plova was fertile. With two billion clones in production, now outnumbering the Ordinate almost forty to one, incidents of clone fertility must increase. Moreover, this simple clone, Plova, had obviously survived the deprivations of the wilderness to carry a child to term. She must have learned far beyond her neural programming—another flaw. The clones were more resourceful than previously thought. If they ever organized themselves. . . .

Brulk rose in rank by his own merits. As one of the first voices to propound the dangers of the old-order clones, he was considered prescient. He predicted the failure of the technicians' attempt to breed a clone constabulary—a mess he later cleaned up with ruthless efficiency. His strategy for maintaining internal order while eradicating two billion clones earned him epithets such as genius. Only forty-seven years old, he was the youngest man to ever serve as an admiral and the only military man to get a portfolio in the government. Now this horrific breach of security and the destruction of the Clone Welfare Institute and the threat of clone insurrection instantly undermined his position in the government.

Brulk muttered aloud, "The truce is broken." He opened the folder with the scant information about the wilderness clones.

The file was a few flimsy pages. For the past twenty years, since he had had the power to intervene, Brulk had limited efforts to find and execute wilderness clones.

He did not want the government to launch military operations against the wilderness clones for three reasons. Foremost, he did not want to take the chance of someone hearing his son's story—easy enough to prove with a simple DNA scanner. Like all men of ambition, Brulk had his share of enemies. Armed with knowledge of his illicit union with a clone, they could reduce his life's work and his ambitions to ashes.

Second, the wilderness clones demonstrated in a very real manner the flaw in the old-order technology. Their sporadic raids on the precincts were ironically a useful reminder to the government that Brulk's strategy of replacing the old-order clones with NewGens was essential to Cor's long-term survival. Occasionally, Brulk sent a patrol, usually a handful of ill-trained and expendable men, into the wasteland. Brulk could point to the casualties as visceral proof that the old-order technology was dangerous. Finally, the wilderness clones provided a mechanism whereby the old-order clones who possessed initiative could separate themselves from the main body. The last thing Brulk needed was the emergence of leaders within the precincts.

So he let the wilderness clones know through a few hypothetical statements that the Ordinate had no reason to squander troops in the wilderness chasing a minimal threat. The message was clear enough: Remain minimal and we won't bother. Until now, the wilderness clones had kept their end of the tacit bargain. The government, in turn, convinced the nervous population that the wilderness clones were more myth than reality, a disorganized handful of aging clones dying in a wasteland, a nuisance—not an immediate threat.

So much for myths. Now, the wilderness clones were real—no longer minimal. Two hundred seventy-three Ordinate dead, the smoldering pit that was once the Clone Welfare Institute—the signs pointed to the wilderness clones. The government screamed for action and intimated that this devastating raid was in part

Brulk's dereliction of duty. They argued—no, accused—that had Brulk done his job, there would have been no wilderness clones to carry out the raid.

Yet something about the raid puzzled Brulk: the lack of numbers. He looked out his window at the ruins of the Clone Welfare Institute. He had long predicted that the clones would pour into the city in great numbers, or not at all. Nevertheless, in large numbers they would eventually come to wreak cataclysmic mayhem. Brulk gambled that he could quietly raise battalions of NewGens before the deluge. What he had not considered was a tactical strike with a limited objective, especially a tactically brilliant strike directed at the one limited objective that might upset his plans. Moreover, he was amazed that such a small number, fewer than a hundred, could wreak havoc in Sarhn against his best troops.

He looked at the brass clock on his desk. His calendar showed a series of follow-on briefings from the officers involved in or investigating the events of the past two weeks. The initial reports provided mounds of data and precious little information. Today he'd hear their findings. Soon he'd have some answers. He needed answers. Tomorrow the Prefect and her government would demand answers.

From his window perch, he saw small crews building a temporary cement barrier around the acres of destruction. Men in orange thermal suits climbed about the ruins extinguishing hot spots left after a two-week effort to contain the blaze. Sensors showed that deep within the subterranean levels near the center of the Institute, a pool of molten glass and metal had begun to congeal; nevertheless, searing heat forced its way up fissures to set new fires.

Brulk shook his head. What a mess. Reconstruction must wait till the spring. Further, albeit limited, NewGen production would continue at the Qurush facility in the south. He'd have the first of his NewGen armies within the year.

A clipped rap on his door pulled his attention from the smoldering ruins. Brulk looked at his appointment list on his desk and gruffly commanded, "Come in."

Two officers marched into the admiral's office. The taller man, wearing captain's stripes and pilot's chevrons, masked his anxiety with a face of disciplined resignation. The smaller man, an intelligence officer, was a bundle of apprehension, stoically fighting the urge to cringe like a small lab mammal half expecting an electric shock, caught between relief and mounting anticipation. The intelligence officer wore lieutenant's rank, but no nametag, in keeping with the tradition of his dark profession. He had bright, quick eyes. Brulk had never seen the young man before, but he knew ship's captain Tuley. Brulk spoke first. "Sit down." He turned to the younger officer and said, "You must be Botchi."

"Yes, sir." The intelligence officer found his seat first. Brulk eased himself into his highback chair. Leaning forward with his hands folded on his empty desk, he asked, "Captain Tuley, what happened out there?"

"We pursued the armed freighter *Benwoi* as ordered." The captain tactfully attributed the beginning of his misadventure to higher authorities.

"Yes, yes." Brulk impatiently waved his left arm. "I have a transcript of everything to the point where you jumped past light speed. Just tell me what happened at the Jod system."

Tuley sat ramrod straight in the plush chair. "We decelerated deep into Jod space and continued our pursuit of the *Benwoi* at kinetic speed. The pilot of the *Benwoi* proved clever. She sent a distress signal requesting help, then sought the cover of a small uninhabited planet, Qota. I set my ship in a high orbit, and sent the cruiser *Raye* to flush out our prey . . ."

Brulk interrupted, "You did know that we wanted you to take the two women aboard the *Benwoi* alive, didn't you?"

Captain Tuley crossed his arms over his chest, annoyed at the admiral's suggestion. He answered with bitter sarcasm, "The two women on the *Benwoi* are still alive, sir. The captain and crew of the cruiser *Raye* are not."

Brulk ignored Tuley's ill humor. "Continue."

"A Jod battle cruiser appeared twenty thousand miles to our port side on an intercept course with the *Raye*. The Jod ship closed at great speed and fired from well outside our maximum effective range. Their gunnery was precise, even at great range, and the discharge of energy collapsed the *Raye's* shields in two seconds. The *Raye* exploded. I ordered immediate withdrawal from Jod space before the Jod ship could turn her weapons against my ship."

Admiral Brulk stood and ambled to a tall glass and chrome bookcase filled with athletic trophies, awards, and porcelain figurines of birds. With his back to Tuley, he said, "You did the right thing, of course. Do you think the Jod ship was waiting for the *Benwoi?*"

The intelligence officer answered this question. "Yes sir. They came ready to fight. Also, the power of their weapons is beyond our technology."

Admiral Brulk shook his head. "We were warned that Jod long-range gunnery was better than ours."

"Better!" Captain Tuley started to rise. "That's a fatal understatement."

Brulk turned to the intelligence officer. "Botchi, why do you think the Jod sent only one ship?"

Tuley cut Botchi off. "They needed only one ship." Tuley's words were bitter. Botchi sat silent waiting to see if the admiral rebuked the captain.

Admiral Brulk walked to his window. The glass reflected his opaque image. He didn't address Tuley directly but continued the conversation with his reflection. "The Jod couldn't know how we could respond. They still don't know our capabilities." Turning his attention back into the room, he continued, "If I were a Jod admiral planning this mission, I'd have a half-dozen battle cruisers stationed to intercept any pursuit ships. Sending one Jod cruiser doesn't make sense." Brulk directed a question to the intelligence officer. "The two-woman crew of the *Benwoi* were clones, not Jod. Right?"

Botchi glanced at Captain Tuley for assurance that he might speak without interruption. He answered, "Definitely not Jod, Admiral. But I believe only one of the women was a clone. I think the other was a Terran."

"What?" Brulk became rigid, taking notice. "Explain yourself." The intelligence officer pulled out a tablet screen and consulted his notes. "Sir, a couple months ago, one of our Hunters, Lt. Tapp, was found buried in a shallow grave in the desert outside the Clemnos city walls. She had been due to rotate back to Cor for a new assignment. Witnesses state that Tapp was last seen in pursuit of a clone female. The Chelle found Lt. Tapp's body: her throat was cut, her ears missing."

"Mutilated? I've never heard of clone laborers mutilating a victim."

"Neither have I, sir. I don't think a clone killed her.

There's more. According to records, Lt. Tapp boarded the *Vasartrans* for her flight home. Sarhn spaceport control has records of Lt. Tapp disembarking. Tapp's husband reported seeing a female that he mistook for his wife in a Hunter's uniform. His description of the woman matches the description given by the cadet who survived the hijacking of the *Benwoi*."

"How do you conclude that the infiltrator is Terran?" Brulk began to pace the floor, contemplating the significance of the scenario presented to him.

The intelligence officer answered, "I've heard of clones killing to get out of the Cor system. I've never heard of them killing to get in."

"How did this impostor get past our DNA screens?"

"I presume she had some of Lt. Tapp's DNA, the lieutenant's ears to be precise. The scanning record from the *Vasartrans* shows that Lt. Tapp had a second set of DNA: they presumed Tapp was pregnant."

Brulk winced. "A Terran female. She knew our technology and how to exploit it." He rested his fist on his chin. He rubbed his hand through his short peppery hair as he muttered to himself, "Significant. Most significant."

He turned to gaze out his floor-to-ceiling window again, surveying the smoldering ruins of the Clone Welfare Institute. "She's a professional, no doubt. But who trained her?"

Botchi answered, "Well, sir. It's obvious that her mission concluded in the Jod system. Sir, I think the Jod have been part of this attack from the beginning."

"Why wasn't I told of this earlier?" Brulk's voice had the edge of accusation. The implication of the Jod was momentous.

Lt. Botchi straightened in his chair. "Sir, the investigating officer was killed during the assault on the Clone Welfare Institute. I found his records just four days ago and just now finished his work."

Brulk's face suddenly softened. "I've been right all along about the Jod. I always knew we'd eventually have to confront the Jod, although, not so soon. We've got to find out if the Jod are working in consort with the Terrans."

Botchi shook his head. "The two systems are allied, although they have never participated in any joint operations."

"We'd better find out." Brulk walked behind his desk but remained standing. He picked up a large polished lump of amber used as a paperweight and looked at the occlusions. "You captured two wounded clones during the assault on the Institute. Can they shed any light on the Jod-Earth connection?"

"The two prisoners are still on life support. Both have multiple wounds in major organs, but the doctors think they can keep them alive on machines. One is unconscious; the other just rambles on in delirium. We've got a recorder on him. Neither prisoner is strong enough to endure the interrogation chemicals or pain."

"Don't be too patient with them. We need the information now," Brulk admonished. He set the amber gently down on the desk.

"Yes, sir. I'll crack them as soon as the doctors think they can stand three hours. I figure what they know, we can squeeze out of them in three hours."

"Good. Can you tell me anything about the clone combatants?" Brulk sat down.

"We inspected their dead and ours. All of the dead clones except three were past the age of retirement. The

Institute archives—what's left of the archives—recorded them as renegades."

"So we're dealing with wilderness clones."

"Yes and no."

Brulk chafed at Botchi's cryptic response. "Just tell me what you know."

"The dead clones we found were pale, malnourished. They had not been exposed to the elements as one would expect in the wilderness. I think those clones came from one of the precincts—probably Precinct 15. But sir, I'm afraid it's more complicated. We examined their weapons: all stolen, most of them quite old. The bullets were a mix of captured rounds and reloads. Some of the reloads were mediocre, crudely cast lead balls with a standard powder load. Our body armor stopped most of their rounds. As the fighting moved closer to the city wall, then into the barrier forest, we encountered another kind of bullet, also a reload. But those bullets had a machined bronze ball and at least a two-hundred-grain load. The bronze bullets not only went through the body armor; they went through building walls, through trees. Sir, I think we fought two separate units. I think the wilderness clones are cooperating with some group of precinct clones. I think we have the beginning of an insurrection."

Brulk's eyes narrowed. He had always expected that an insurrection was inevitable. That threat was precisely why he wanted to phase in the NewGen clone model and cancel the entire old-order line. However, he had expected large numbers when the dam broke. A billion clones ought to be able to muster a hundred thousand combatants, who if armed with sharp sticks could defeat the Ordinate. He never expected a handful of renegades mounting an assault. Nor did he expect the wilderness clones to intervene.

Brulk turned sideways in his chair and looked through the window at the distant snowcapped mountains. On the other side of those granite walls lay a vast expanse of badlands. The beginnings of an insurrection. Was the assault just a demonstration for the masses? Or a demonstration for the Jod? That's it! The satisfaction of knowing overcame the grim reality of the truth. "Gentlemen, I believe the Jod instigated this attack to demonstrate the clones' ability to mount ground operations against the Ordinate. Unfortunately, the clones succeeded and proof has gotten back to the Jod. Nevertheless, we are still missing one piece to the puzzle: Why did the Jod muster only one cruiser? Can we assume that the Jod government is not yet committed? If so, we can exploit their disunity to buy time."

Captain Tuley reiterated his personal and painful experience. "Sir, the Jod Fleet is immense. I saw what one Jod cruiser can do. The Jod have seven dreadnoughts."

"Soon we will have millions of NewGen warriors. We can use them to pilot thousands of J-Class ships. If we take the initiative, we can still win this war." Brulk smiled for the first time in two weeks. "We can replace the Jod Empire with our own. Now that would look good on your résumé."

Lt. Botchi left the staid headquarters building for a short walk back to the barracks. As he stepped outside, a guard reminded him, "Sir, your mask."

Botchi acknowledged with a grunt and fished a nose-and-mouth covering from his pocket to protect himself from the occasional whiff of smoke that bore traces of heavy metals. Clones drafted as firefighters—bedraggled from three weeks of nonstop work—continued to pour water and chemicals onto the smoldering rubble, formerly the Clone Welfare Institute. The clones did not wear masks.

Finally upwind from the mess, Botchi ripped his mask off and proceeded toward the security barracks, past pockmarked buildings. He stepped aside a bouquet of flowers left by some family of a fallen Ordinate soldier.

Inside the barrack courtyard, he saw a company of NewGens, one hundred and twenty of the new breed of clones standing in close ranks. An Ordinate officer inspected these new replacements, the first of millions.

Botchi stopped to ponder these new walking, thinking weapons. Many were disfigured from burns and their faces glistened from ointments. Few wore bandages. The doctors did not bother to reduce the scarring, and many of the NewGens' faces looked like soft wax. Hair grew in odd patches from raw red scalp. These were the lucky ones. Botchi had seen the burn ward. Many more of the salvaged crop remained in rehabilitation, undergoing painful treatments to restore muscle mass gouged and melted away by flame, some fitted with prosthetic limbs. The government believed that the eight hundred or so surviving NewGens clones were the main force that stood between the Ordinate and two billion old-order clones.

Fourteen months. All we need is a lousy fourteen months. Then the other clone factories begin hatching NewGens at the rate of thousands per day.

chapter 3

Andrea gave up trying to will herself to sleep. She glanced at the pale illuminated numbers on the wall. Middle of the sleep cycle . . . She dressed in the comfortable baggy clothes and slippers she brought from the *Benwoi*. Then she left her small billet, stepping into the dim corridor and the oppressive quiet of the sleep cycle. She wandered past the communications suite where the lone watch officer kept himself awake with busywork. Her faint shadow passed over the watch officer's desk giving him a start, which he acknowledged with a sheepish smile. She set him at ease: "I'm just going to make myself some flora tea." The galley was likewise empty, the equipment shining, and the sink dry. With the press of a pad key, Andrea ordered her tea and the small machine hissed, seeming to chafe at her request, nevertheless relinquishing a large cobalt blue tumbler of aromatic brew.

She reached into her pocket and pulled out a small stiff paper. Carefully she unfolded it to see the copy she'd made of Tara's hand-drawn picture of Eric. She looked for flaws to distinguish Eric from her Steve, and it pained her to admit that she had to exert her memory to recall details about Steve that had been part of her everyday life, part of her personal landscape, details that she assumed she'd never forget. This isn't healthy.

Andrea looked at the galley clock. More than two full marks until the end of sleep cycle. The tea did not have the somniferous effect she wanted. She left the galley and walked backed to the billets, pausing at H'Roo's door. Oh, what the hell? She announced herself with the chime, then listened to the rustling inside the room.

H'Roo appeared as disheveled as a hairless Jod can be, stuffing lose ends of a pale green cotton shirt into his gray duty pants. His sleepy eyes were two slits, blinking at the light. He complained when he saw Andrea dressed in mufti. "What do you want?"

"I want answers, H'Roo." She was angry but her voice sounded tired, even forlorn.

The rings under H'Roo's eyes appeared darker than usual. He sighed. H'Roo needed his sleep. But he gathered his wits quickly and said sympathetically, "You look worse than I do. Don't stand in the hall; come in." Turning into his room he said, "Lights one hundred—belay that—eighty percent." He sat on his unmade bunk and grabbed a pair of socks. Andrea refused the chair.

"So what answers do you want to know at this late hour?" H'Roo asked.

Andrea handed H'Roo the picture of Eric. "Do you know the man in this picture?"

H'Roo blinked and shook his head. "No idea." He yawned, showing his straight teeth.

Andrea pointed to the paper. Her eyes flashed and

she spoke through clenched teeth. "I got this picture from Tara Gullwing. It's a likeness of Eric, K'Rin's clone."

H'Roo's genteel face became tight. "I've never seen Eric."

"Are you sure?"

H'Roo bristled. "Of course, I'm sure!"

Andrea's eyes narrowed as she took the measure of H'Roo. "If you're lying to me—"

Stung by the accusation, H'Roo dropped the socks and stood up. His neck flushed. "You wake me up to insult me? I'm about ready to wash my hands of you, Mat Flores. You know me better than that!"

Andrea didn't flinch. "I know that you played me false at Dlagor Island."

"I was under orders. You know that."

"Are you under orders now?"

"I don't know what you're talking about. Why are we arguing over a bad picture of a lousy clone?" H'Roo's bruised feelings were beginning to change into righteous indignation.

Andrea took the picture back from H'Roo's hand and held it to his face. "Because," she answered, "this picture strongly resembles my husband, Steve."

H'Roo's eyes widened with surprise and confusion. Andrea continued. "The Ordinate Hunters who murdered my husband and daughter thought they had killed Eric—convenient for Eric and K'Rin, don't you think? Plus, K'Rin just happens to be in Baltimore at the time of the massacre. I don't believe in coincidence. Now, what do you know about Eric?"

H'Roo lowered his eyes. "Only what we both heard in our mission briefings. I—" H'Roo stammered, "I don't know."

Andrea spoke through clenched teeth. "H'Roo, if you're lying to me . . ." She didn't finish the threat. Rather she said, "K'Rin arrives tomorrow. I'm going to ask him the same questions. It would be better for all of us if I went into the interview knowing more rather than less."

H'Roo withdrew. He stood under a small ceiling light, where he looked pale and sad. Andrea sensed the distance compounded by new suspicion. H'Roo said, "If I learn anything about Eric or Steve, I'll tell you first. Please don't do anything rash. I'm sure there's an explanation."

Andrea knew that H'Roo didn't believe his own words. She returned a wintry smile, said nothing, and left the room.

Disjointed suspicion competed with fatigue. Back in her billet, Andrea could not sleep. She sat at her empty desk in silence. The artificial climate of Vintell was like the artificial climate aboard any Jod ship. The light rose slightly to simulate dawn and the temperature rose a few degrees—all designed to coax the body's natural rhythms to shake off narcosis. She let her imagination loose as she watched the light rise from a dim orange to a bright yellow.

She remembered the first time she witnessed this artificial dawn. Four years ago in the sick bay aboard the *Tyker,* she woke from the stupor of sedatives, disoriented. Even then, she had the presence of mind to know that her immediate environment was artificial. The only reality she had was the pain in her shoulder, a bullet wound, and from that painful marker, her mind gathered the horrible pictures of her husband and daughter slain in her arms. Four years ago, she watched the artificial dawn and contemplated burying her consciousness in autism. Her father's voice seemed to mock her then: Better to light one candle than to curse the darkness. Curse the darkness? Never! She coveted the darkness. She wanted to pull the darkness over her like a black blanket and hide.

Andrea pondered this kind of mental or emotional suicide. In due course she decided that although such complete withdrawal was possible, it was impossible for her. Her only escape in this life was blocked.

Physical suicide was not an option for Andrea. She had the vague notion that the reality of suicide was the endless repetition of artificial dawns and a feast of bad memories—a punishment for fleeing the struggle. The prospect of an eternity holding her murdered husband and child was a crushing weight. Death is the irony of life: resist both; accept both.

What were her options now? She wanted to know the truth about Steve, but did she? She wanted to see the clone, Eric, but did she? She had prepared herself to confront Hal K'Rin and now she wavered. What is K'Rin hiding? K'Rin had to know that Steve and Eric look alike. Why didn't he tell me? Does he mistrust me? Then why did he adopt me into his family, train me, and make me part of his Tenebrea? She felt hollow inside, an unfamiliar gnawing indecision. Andrea clenched her teeth.

Yet, in a strange sense she was relieved. Although she was plagued with doubts, she had few if any options, making her doubts moot. A Tenebrea could not resign. She was bound by oath and Quazel Protein. Without regular injections of the correspon- ding Quazel enzyme, a Tenebrea would die. Resignation, treachery, or banishment: all spelled certain and awful death. Andrea looked at the dark plain walls in her billet.

The only question left in her mind was whether or not to confront Hal K'Rin and risk banishment. For Andrea, it was not really a question or doubt, only hesitation. Andrea could not run from the truth she had so tenaciously pursued. She recognized two imperatives: I must confront K'Rin, and I am trapped in his Tenebrea.

Unable to sleep, Andrea dressed in her uniform. She sat in the brooding darkness of her room. She tuned her intercom to listen to any ship-to-surface chatter. At last the silence broke. "Vintell, this is the Jod cruiser *Tyker*, entering a synchronous orbit 52,410 kilometers. Request landing instructions for the admiral's shuttle."

Ground control announced estimated time of arrival in forty-seven minutes. Andrea left her room. She took a leisurely breakfast alone, drinking black coffee and watching the clock tally another thirty minutes.

She went to the observation deck and watched the heavy shuttle slowly land, extending five metal legs, and gently settling down between rows of blue lights. Andrea strained her eyes to look at the portholes, but she saw nothing but mere shadows eclipse the lighted portholes. Her heart skipped a beat when she thought she saw a human profile. She berated herself.

She took a deep breath and left the observation deck. She found most of the Vintell staff standing in the landing bay, each nervously checking his gig line. Andrea ignored the nervous excitement of the men. The small ground crew wearing padded gloves fastened the discharge cables to the hull of the shuttle. Tara and H'Roo arrived separately. Andrea found herself standing impassively between the two. Tara's eyes sparked. Her auburn hair was combed severely back

and held with perfumed oil, a cosmetic Andrea had
never seen her use before. Tara wore her smock off the
shoulder exposing the blue gullwing tattoo that
stretched below her collarbone above her round
breasts. Tara had bleached a collage of stains from her
smock and leggings and the white offset Tara's ruddy
complexion and hair.

Andrea thought with some bitterness, *Showing a little skin, are we?* Immediately, she admonished herself,
Not Tara's fault. Instead, Andrea braced herself and
looked at H'Roo for support, but H'Roo stood rigidly
at attention, eyes forward. Andrea wiped her moist
palms on her pants legs.

The side of the shuttle opened and a short ramp
lowered to the ground. Andrea saw human feet step
down. The black leather boots had round toes unlike
the bulky square-toed boots of the Jod. The first figure
down the steps was a man of average height wearing
long black pants and a skintight charcoal gray shirt
with long sleeves and a high neckline. He walked with
confidence. At the bottom of the steps he turned and
faced the welcoming party. Andrea's knees buckled, but
she caught herself. Steve! The man looked so much
more like Steve than Tara's picture! She felt dizzy
watching Steve's ghost—not a ghost but flesh and
blood—walk toward her. She wasn't dreaming. The
hairline tapering to a point in front, the straight nose,
and eyes! Where's Glennie? She was momentarily
bewildered. The landing bay began to blur. Steve
wouldn't come all this way and leave Glennie. Look at
me! Steve looked at Tara, smiled at Tara, ignored his
own wife! The scene began to swim out of focus. Settle
down. She told herself: Steve is dead. This cannot be
Steve. Unless—Andrea grabbed her head and pressed

her palms to her temples trying to stem the sudden
pain she felt between her eyes. Unless Steve isn't really
dead. In four years she had forgotten so many of the
little details about her husband, all the little details so
perfectly displayed in the man walking toward her,
walking toward her but ignoring her. Have I changed
so much? Don't you recognize me? She couldn't
breathe. It can't be. I held his dead body in my arms.
Aloud, she groaned, "Steve?"

Tara cried out, "Eric!" Then she broke from the ranks
and ran across the hangar. She threw her arms around
Eric's neck. Eric embraced Tara tightly. Arching his
back slightly, he lifted her inches from the ground, and
they kissed, oblivious to the curious Jod.

Andrea groaned, turned, and ran away before the
tears began streaming down her face. H'Roo broke
protocol. "Andrea!" His voice echoed. The small assembly of Tenebrea turned to see the commotion.

Hal K'Rin stepped down from the shuttle stairway
in time to see Andrea flee the landing bay. He closed
his eyes and shook his large head.

The thin smoke haze rising from the smoldering
ruins of the Clone Welfare Institute mingled with cirrus
clouds and turned the Cor sunset red. The evening sky
looked like a bloody hand with distended fingers
stretching over Sarhn. The superstitious in the city
spoke of red sunsets as an ill omen. They saw the
bloody hand of retribution overhead until blacked out
by night. Throughout the city the populace spoke
about the unspeakable: death.

Admiral Brulk shook his head with disgust. He had
enough problems without a bunch of moribund civilians hauling out the old animist religion.

Brulk walked into the biting cold without his over-coat. He saw his breath. The evenings came earlier as Cor approached the winter solstice. The temperature fell suddenly as daylight failed. Already frosts burned the pink and purple flowers that filled formal gardens and hung raggedly from stone window boxes. Snow would come soon. The deciduous trees, poplars and linden, had given up their leaves early this year. Now, the naked branches looked like black lace against the red sky. Approaching winter added to the specter of death.

The destruction of the Clone Welfare Institute abruptly ended clone production as well as the mecha-nism to gracefully retire old-order clones. In a knee-jerk reaction, the government declared a state of emergency. Brulk objected. At best, declarations are impractical. He believed such declarations have a way of becoming self-fulfilling prophecies. But the Madame Prefect insisted that the government react immediately to the breach of Sarhn's security with word and deed. React how? The government didn't have a consensus how to react. Ironically, the cabinet left much of those elusive details to Brulk.

During this state of emergency, the Cabinet met each evening. The Cabinet became increasingly impa-tient for Brulk to provide a course of action. Brulk stalled as he waited for a clearer picture of the situa-tion. Now, he believed he knew. The Jod had commit-ted an act of war.

Brulk walked across a courtyard to the Executive Mansion. A flock of grackles blocked the cobblestone walkway. They scattered to roost in the bare linden trees and carp at Brulk as he bullied his way through.

He saw a pair of Chelle leave the Executive

Mansion. Brulk thought their grayish skin looked diseased; their beige smocks looked like hospital gowns. This diminutive species had long ago abducted and transported Terrans to populate the planet Cor, more than forty-five generations ago.

The Chelle outwardly professed to forget the old days, but Brulk knew better. The Chelle had never fully accepted Cor independence. Brulk believed that the Chelle would someday try to reassert itself on Cor. However, in the meantime, the Chelle would use the Cor to unsettle the Jod. Convenient, because Brulk also considered Jod as the main threat to Cor, and his erstwhile allies, the Chelle, provided him with intelligence and technology. "Firbin!" Brulk blocked the Chelle's path. "What are you doing at the Executive Mansion?"

Firbin looked up with large dewy eyes. He pointed behind with a long delicate gray hand. "The Madame Prefect asked to see me."

"What about?"

"Oh, she suggested that the Ordinate and the Chelle might conduct more trade if the Chelle quit the Alliance."

"And?" Brulk prodded.

Firbin pursed his thin lips. "I told her that for the foreseeable future, Cor is best served by having the Chelle in the Alliance."

"Good answer. I'll have some information requirements for you shortly. Please stop by my office tomorrow morning." Brulk walked around the pair of Chelle.

A guard opened the lead crystal door for Brulk, and he stepped across the carpeted hall into the unpretentious cabinet room. His abrupt arrival killed a conversation among the cabinet members. They had been arguing about Brulk's schedule for exterminating the old-order clones. Brulk ignored the obvious chill he brought into the room. He knew that the cabinet blamed him for their present quandary. He knew full well that the long-term shift from old-order clone technology to NewGen technology was his brainchild.

In the bluntest terms, they blamed Brulk for upsetting the status quo, which brought about the assault against the Clone Welfare Institute. Heretofore, Admiral Brulk replied that their charges were a non sequitur: insurrection was inevitable and not caused by the introduction of NewGen technology. Before today, Brulk had refused to elaborate, especially about his theory of the possible involvement of the Jod. Instead, he stalled the cabinet members with the challenge to come up with a better solution to the inevitable failure of the old-order clone technology. Today, he came prepared to elaborate.

Brulk sat down at the long table of polished granite. He put his data chip in the slot activating his screen built into the tabletop. Judging by the cold silence in the room, he guessed that the cabinet had finally answered his challenge: he fully expected to hear their better solution momentarily.

The Madame Prefect entered the small wood-paneled room and took her seat at the head of the oblong table. She was a stout woman with graying hair, pulled starkly back into a twist. She had a high forehead. Her face was unnaturally taut, except for telltale lines about the eyes. The Prefect folded her hands on the table with her long fingers interlocked. Her hands looked older than the rest of her well-maintained body. She spoke softly with an economy of words, her voice strained and gravelly. "News?"

The Minister of Support Services spoke first. He was

a fat man with a ruddy complexion made redder by his agitated state. "Madame Prefect, citizens continue to dismiss their domestic help. We have hundreds of clones malingering at the East and West Gates waiting for the end of the workday. Now the citizens are afraid of a riot."

A small woman who held the portfolio for capital improvements interjected, "I think that if the owners turn their clones away, they lose their property rights, and we simply apprehend the clones and cancel them without restitution."

"That is the law," the Prefect stated perfunctorily.

"True, but with the institute destroyed, how do we cancel the clones after we apprehend them? We can't just stack their bodies outside the walls. Can we?"

An uncomfortable minute of silence lapsed, then the Prefect looked down at her agenda and directed her attention back to Support Services. "Other news?"

"Yes, ma'am. We have an unprecedented number of requests for transfer to other cities on Cor. We cannot possibly accommodate even a fraction of the requests to leave. Also, citizens are beginning to hoard food and fuel. We are experiencing short-term shortages. We are beginning to see signs of a growing black market. In short, we are watching the collapse of order. The citizens are afraid."

The Prefect directed her next comments toward Brulk. Frustration edged her voice. "They are afraid, Admiral Brulk, because they don't believe your security forces can protect them. May I remind you that the entire strategy of transitioning from the old-order technology to NewGen technology is yours."

"Yes, Madame Prefect." The light from the screen illuminated his face. He set his jaw, pleased with himself.

True, the grand strategy was his. He was responsible. Now, circumstance placed the weight of Cor's future on his shoulders. He enjoyed the responsibility as much as the others chafed at the burden.

The Prefect's voice was artificially calm, underscoring the anxiety in the room. "Let me tell you what I'm hearing from the people who petition my office. They want the military to exterminate all the old-order clones immediately . . . they say that any delay on your part is tantamount to treason."

"Yes! Yes!" Half the cabinet erupted to support the sentiment. "Get rid of them all!"

Brulk's cheeks showed a tinge of red. "Exterminating the old-order clones has always been my plan. But I don't think the people quite know what they're asking for when they ask us to exterminate a billion clones just like that!" He snapped his fingers.

The Minister of the Economy interjected. "Admiral Brulk is correct. The people say they want the clones canceled immediately, but if we cancel all the clones, those same frightened citizens will starve to death in six months."

"Is that true, Master Grundig?" the Prefect asked the Minister of Support Services.

Grundig picked a piece of lint from his pleated shirt and said with professional exactness, "We keep a sixty-day reserve of food for the Ordinate and a two-week reserve for the precinct clones, which would be available to us if we canceled all the old-order clones. We could ration food to a thousand calories per person per day and import grain from the Chelle. Theoretically, we could survive the deprivation of food, but I'm afraid the bigger problems include the collapse of energy production and our systems for hygiene."

Gloom settled around the table.

Grundig looked at his soft, clean hands. "You are not only talking about going hungry, but you are talking about going without light and heat. You are talking about the end of running water. You'll see mountains of garbage piling up in the streets. Disease will kill us long before hunger."

Brulk added, "Tell us, where do you dispose of a billion clones all at once? You don't wave a magic wand and make a billion clones disappear. No, for the time being we must continue our policy of gradual attrition."

"You must consider how the citizens think," the nervous Minister of Capital Improvements interjected.

"We must consider what the clones think," Brulk snapped back.

"What clones think?" The entire table recoiled at the seeming heresy.

"Yes." Brulk answered confidently. "How will the old-order clones react when they finally realize that they are marked for extermination? The old-order clones are not as docile as our engineers advertised. Witness the destruction of the institute. What happens if the old-order clones, motivated by self-preservation, rise in mass against us? I assure you, our small security force would be overwhelmed. Are you prepared to arm yourselves to defend your homes from a deluge of clones?"

Nobody answered. The Prefect nodded in the affirmative. Brulk looked around the table wondering if any of the other pampered cabinet members could defend themselves. Soft people make expedient choices. He said, "No, the extermination of the old-order clones must be gradual. We cannot risk a full-scale insurrection before we have the NewGen clones on line."

The Minister of the Economy nodded morosely. He was slight, almost birdlike, but intelligence exuded from his pores. Not given to hyperbole, he sat with his hands folded on the table. He said plainly, "We're already feeling the pressure caused by Brulk's policy of attrition, gradual or not. Now, you are talking about a total breakdown in our system from food production to hygiene. When our citizens begin to starve, they'll forget all about their fear of renegade clones. They'll want their way of life back. If we cancel the entire crop of old-order clones before the NewGen models arrive, we ruin our economy for at least twenty years—maybe, fifty. What one can tear down swiftly, another must rebuild slowly. Madame, we must not acquiesce to the people's fears of the moment. If we do, we'll have no options when the economy collapses."

"What do you propose?"

"With the admiral's permission"—the Minister of the Economy waited for a nod from Brulk—"actually, instead of canceling the clones, we need to extend their operational lives to offset the losses at the institute."

The pro-extermination faction of the cabinet gasped. The Minister for Capital Improvements seethed. She slapped her hand on the stone table to get attention. "Everybody out there has a family to think of—"

Admiral Brulk interjected, "—and they count on us to be practical. You know damned well that no self-respecting Ordinate would stoop to perform work heretofore done by clone labor." Brulk turned to the Minister of Support Services. "Can you even imagine Cor Ordinate men and women shoveling manure from the cattle pens and hauling it to the agro fields?"

"That is disgusting." The fat minister pulled on his double chin and scowled.

Brulk turned to the Prefect and continued, "If I thought our citizens would perform menial labor, I'd argue with those in favor of immediate extermination. I'd ask you to conscript our citizens. I'd organize them into an army and teach them how to fight, but I know—as all of you know—that the vast majority of our citizens will not do menial work, nor will they fight."

The cabinet members grumbled at Brulk's insult obliquely directed at them. The Prefect held up her hands to stifle the dissension. With a nod of her gray head, she let Brulk continue.

Brulk glowered, allowing some of his contempt for the cabinet to show. "Fighting is dirty work, and Master Grundig," Brulk turned to his left and directed his next comment to the obese Minister of Support Services, "very few of us in the Ordinate are willing to do the dirty work, while everybody seems willing to supervise."

"That's enough!" Madame Prefect rebuked Brulk with her gravelly voice. The cabinet members sat silently.

Brulk felt confined in this small room of chestnut brown walls and no windows. He always thought better when he could see the horizon. He turned to the Prefect and announced, "I have news that may interest the cabinet. We are convinced, albeit by circumstantial evidence, that the Jod are involved in the attack on the Clone Welfare Institute."

A pallor fell over the cabinet members. The Prefect held her breath. "Are you sure?" she finally asked.

"Fairly sure. The Jod sent an agent provocateur, a human, who worked with the precinct and wilderness clones. We extracted information from a clone prisoner and learned that the Jod agent was a Terran female working with the Clone Underground in Precinct 15. The Terran was part of the attack. She escaped to Jod space with a TRA model clone, number 2862, a former clerk in the Clone Welfare Institute. The prisoner said nothing of cooperation with wilderness clones although I suspect some level of cooperation. We know that a Jod cruiser was stationed to receive their agent and repel our pursuit."

The Prefect blanched, "A Terran female? Is the entire Alliance mobilized against us?"

Brulk saw the Minister of Support Services break into a cold sweat, patting his broad forehead with a folded handkerchief. Brulk resisted a smile, but he enjoyed the fat man's discomfort. He said, "I think not. I contacted my source in the Chelle government. He assures me that the Chelle have no knowledge of any Alliance plans directed against us. Alliance policy remains containment with the long-term goal of incorporating us into the Alliance. Apparently the Jod are acting on their own."

The Prefect ordered, "I want you to send your best Hunter team to Earth to find out everything you can about that that Terran. We cannot defend ourselves from the entire Alliance. Can you discover the origins of that Terran?"

"Yes ma'am. I have already done so. We have the record of her DNA scan when she boarded the troop ship *Vasartrans.*" Brulk shook his head, deciding not to explain the details of how the Terran bamboozled their vaunted security. "If she has any connection with the Terran military or police, we ought to be able to get her history."

The color returned to the Prefect's cheeks. "Is it possible that the institute attack is not an act of war?"

Brulk answered succinctly, "Anything is possible, but I think this attack was just the opening salvo in a war. Call it reconnaissance in force. Frankly, I think fortune smiled on us. The Jod blundered."

"How so?" The Prefect was caught between genuine incredulity and sarcasm.

"The Jod should have come at us with everything at their disposal, but they didn't. This operation reeks of hesitation and compromise."

"Why?" Madame Prefect asked.

"I don't know, and I'm not sure that their reason matters. Perhaps the Jod wanted to see how the Chelle react. Perhaps they wanted to start an insurrection and trust the clones to eliminate us as a threat. In any case, they erred when they let us recover the initiative." Brulk allowed a thin smile.

"What do you suggest we initiate?" She addressed the question to her entire cabinet, and everyone except Brulk shrank from the question.

He said, "Madame, first we stall for time. Then we boldly eradicate the threat to our future—and I mean the Jod. Let's not blind ourselves to reality: coexistence is eventually impossible. The Jod are acting logically. They know that if we continue to prosper, their hegemony is doomed. Their only mistake is that they acted in half measures. I suggest we duplicate their logic, but not duplicate their mistake."

"That's insane!" The birdlike Minister of Capital Improvements mewed.

Brulk silenced her with a look. He activated the screens around the table with a push of a button. "Madame Prefect, if I may, I'd like to brief you on my concept of operations."

The Prefect nodded gravely.

Brulk stood to begin his presentation. "Madame Prefect, we need fourteen months to complete our transition to NewGen technology. These are critical months. The Qurush facility will start producing small numbers of NewGens within six months. The other large hatcheries don't come on-line until the third quarter of the year 482, eight months later."

Brulk pressed a button at his console and called up a scheduling diagram. "First, we need to stall the Jod by means of diplomacy." He explained how they should use the offices of the Chelle to mislead the Jod into believing that Cor wants to join the Alliance. The Jod, after all, would be just as happy to have Cor submit to their hegemony peacefully.

"If they see us as potential members in their Alliance," Brulk explained, "the Jod will refrain from further attempts to destabilize our old-order clone population while we negotiate. I further recommend that we blame the institute sabotage on the Jod to let them know that we are not blind and helpless. Give them pause, so to speak. We ought to demand reparations, immediate return of our ship, the surrender of the renegade clones for cancellation, and the extradition of the Terran provocateur to stand trial—" Brulk raised his eyes to assure the cabinet that such sentiments were for Jod consumption.

"In addition, we employ the Chelle to inform other Alliance members, Earth and Artrix, that Jod aggression in lieu of negotiation may embroil everyone in a galactic conflagration. The allies will pressure the Jod Council to be reasonable and negotiate. We insist that the Jod stand down their fleet as a show of their peaceful intentions. Any questions so far?"

Everyone sat still, some looking at their screens, others gazing back at Brulk. He became more animated as he explained the military portion of his grand scheme. He explained how his work progressed on Lynx. The four hundred and eighty J-Class attack ships were in final tests and they had begun arming them with quark torpedoes. The NewGen pilots met all expectations. At the appropriate time, they would overwhelm the seven Jod dreadnoughts with a swarm of J-Class ships, wiping out the capital ships in the Jod Fleet. Brulk said with conviction, "The Jod will not wage war without their dreadnoughts, and it will take them two to five years to rebuild their fleet. By then, we'll have our NewGen hatcheries operating at max capacity. We'll have the ability to expend five hundred J-Class attack craft per month if need be."

Brulk stood up and walked to the Prefect's end of the conference table. "We can do this." He held up a confident fist. "I have about eight hundred NewGens that we salvaged from the institute fire. I am already programming them to pilot our J-Class attack craft. If I can catch the Jod Fleet in one place, we can do enough damage to stun them into inaction. Then we can beat them in the race for mobilization. We need only fourteen months and the galaxy belongs to us."

Grundig's squinty eyes widened. "What if your attack fails?" Standing behind the Prefect, Brulk answered, "Then we are no worse off than we are now. The Jod have declared their intentions by attacking Sarhn."

Grundig raised his voice. "Madame Prefect, I object! This plan is too hasty!"

The Prefect took Brulk's side. "A half hour ago, you wanted to exterminate the entire old-order clone population and plunge us into chaos. Now you are afraid of the mere preparation for a preemptive strike. Grundig, I think you are just afraid of everything but the status quo."

The Prefect looked around the table and prudently said, "One step at a time, Admiral Brulk. Summon the Chelle emissary. We shall begin with the diplomatic ruse and see where that leads. In the meantime, you may prepare your fleet."

chapter 4

"**B**ypass the lock," K'Rin whispered to the Vintell technician. His voice resonated in the narrow, brightly lit corridor. Then, he straightened himself to his full, albeit stocky, height and adjusted his uniform sleeves. He clenched his large square jaw and furrowed his brow. He wore the Rin Family sash and Triskelion medallion.

The technician opened a panel and inserted a data chip. "Done. I replaced her code with yours." He backed away.

"Now leave me." K'Rin spoke in sharp, clipped words. Cowed by K'Rin's brusqueness, the technician gathered his hand tools and left without closing the panel.

Kip, K'Rin's aide, stood by grimly. He wore his simple black duty uniform with handlance strapped to his utility belt. He said, "Sir, you knew this day was coming."

"Yes. I did. I want you to leave, too."

"But sir!" Kip protested. "In her state of mind, she's capable of anything."

"Silence." K'Rin cut off the argument. He sighed. He looked and felt tired. "Kip, don't make more trouble for me. I'm in a bad mood. Go back to the comm suite and tell the council courier that I acknowledge their summons and I shall report to Heptar in due haste. Now leave me." K'Rin stood and watched as Kip reluctantly obeyed.

Alone, K'Rin used his code to unlock Andrea's door. He paused, took a breath, then entered. The room was dark in contrast to the glaring bright lights in the corridor. He stepped into the shadows. He left the door open, muttering, "Light one hundred percent."

The ceiling lights came on. The room was untidy: bed unmade, a baggy beige tunic and pants draped over the foot of the narrow bed. He saw Andrea slumped over her desk, facing the wall. She wore the Tenebrea uniform, but the tunic was unfastened at the neck. At first, he thought she was asleep, but he saw her back arch as she took a deep breath. With her forearm, she shielded her eyes from the light and said, "My father once had to take my bedroom door off the hinges."

K'Rin said sternly, "I cannot believe that you of all people are hiding in your room, refusing to answer your door. I came to congratulate you on your mission."

"No you didn't," Andrea replied petulantly. She sat up. Her face was pale, her eyes dark and menacing. She held a crumpled paper that bore the image of Eric.

K'Rin controlled his temper although he felt a tinge of red about the neck. He relaxed his tight jaw muscles to control his rising ire. He clasped his hands behind his back and said, "I can well understand that you are upset. I wanted you to see Eric before I got your briefing on the mission—give you time to collect and sort your feelings."

"I'm trying to numb my feelings. I'm trying to collect and sort my thoughts."

"Well, you seem to be having some trouble. Perhaps I can help."

Then she stood from her chair and shoved it backward violently, knocking it on its side. She balled the picture in her fist and shook it at K'Rin's face. "When were you planning to tell me the truth?"

K'Rin didn't move despite her threatening gesture. "Today. Now." He patiently stepped past Andrea, set the chair aright. "Sit down, please."

Andrea took a couple quick breaths. She measured her words. "You knew all along. You knew that the Hunters killed Steve, believing they had killed Eric."

"Yes, I did." K'Rin exuded authority although he knew his rank would not mitigate the wrath blowing his way.

"Then, you are a coward, K'Rin, for hiding the truth from me." The tendons in her neck tightened as she growled at K'Rin.

K'Rin accepted these rebukes from his subordinate with grace. "I thought I was doing the right thing. If you will compose yourself, I'll tell you the particulars."

Andrea glared at him. Keeping her eyes on K'Rin, she slowly sat in the chair.

K'Rin folded his arms across his chest and lowered his eyes. "The story goes back before I set eyes on you at the Baltimore Harbor. The *Tyker* was on a routine mission tracking a Hunter team in the Terran system. By chance, a Jod merchant ship reported a stowaway— a male clone. I took the two-parsec detour to acquire the clone, whom we now know as Eric. In making the detour, I lost contact with the Hunter team and valuable time. As soon as I had Eric, I pressed the *Tyker* at maximum speed to Baltimore to make up lost time."

"How did you know to go to Baltimore?" Andrea asked.

"I had corroborating intelligence and a hunch. Baltimore is the Jod's primary port of call for Earth, a fact that the Cor know as well."

Andrea steeled herself to hear the next part of K'Rin's story, for she knew it too well. K'Rin's words were deliberate but his tone was paternal. "We confirmed that the Hunters were in the Baltimore area, but we arrived too late to save your Steve, your child, and the other civilians."

K'Rin braced himself for his next admission. "Had I been a better ship's captain and not let myself be sidetracked from my primary mission, I would have maintained contact with the Hunter team. Your Steve and your child would be alive today. I blame myself for your husband's death. When I saw you cradling your husband in your lap . . ." K'Rin's voice failed him.

The disembodied words that he had rehearsed congealed into that awful moment. In his mind, K'Rin saw Andrea wailing over her husband riddled with bullets. The man's arms lay limp. The pale child lay at the base of this heap of anguish. K'Rin blinked away the memory, collected his breath, and continued the apology. "I knew immediately that the Hunters believed they had killed the clone Eric, who was at that time safely aboard the *Tyker*. I admit that for these past years, I used their mistake to my advantage."

Andrea turned her face away toward a blank wall. "You should have told me sooner."

"I didn't know how. I wanted to repair my mistake

by helping you, so I brought you aboard the *Tyker*. I took great pains to keep you and Eric apart, partly for your benefit. Shortly after the massacre, we tracked the Hunters to Kent Island, and we dispatched them— sending their disrupted bodies back to Cor in a waste bladder."

"Why didn't you just tell me the truth?"

K'Rin brushed the rumpled tunic to the floor and sat on the end of the bed. He was now eye level with Andrea. "I had my reasons. I didn't know you, and I had no reason to trust you with sensitive information, certainly not to risk an asset like Eric. Frankly, when I first met you, you were very unstable, even irrational. When I found that you had no family left, I brought you into my clan. I might point out, cousin, that you were not completely forthcoming with me either. In fact, you've been a bit of liability. But I don't blame you for mistrusting me. You shouldn't blame me for mistrusting you at first. I didn't know you then." K'Rin reached out and touched Andrea's chin. "I trust you now."

Andrea glared back, unappeased.

K'Rin again tried to press reason into Andrea's whirlwind of emotions. "You must admit, cousin, after Steve's murder, you spent two years not trusting anybody or anything—not even yourself. Why should I have trusted you when you did not trust yourself?"

"So you kept the truth from me because you mistrusted me—that's it? What were you afraid of? I couldn't hurt you then. What was I to you?"

"You're right. I could have flown away and put you out of my mind. Why did I take you aboard?" K'Rin exhaled deeply. "Fate, perhaps. Atonement?"

He paused to assess the conversation so far. He grudgingly admired the distraught Terran who sat before him, despite her disheveled appearance. Her unwashed black hair seemed grotesque to him. He would normally associate her red eyes with disease. When he first recruited her into the Tenebrea, he thought she possessed animal simplicity, an instinctive cunning so necessary for survival in covert operations. But now he perceived in her a wonderful complexity. Her intellect and emotions seemed to operate almost independently with disturbing disunity. A Jod would lose his or her mind trying to juggle the morass that was in Andrea's head, yet Andrea's questions and comments remained lucid, even penetrating. She amazed K'Rin, who asked, "Do I need a reason?"

Her eyes softened but she didn't answer.

K'Rin explained, "At the time, I was afraid that in your state of mind, you'd do something self-destructive. You were wounded by the loss of your kin. I thought that I could strengthen you. I hoped that in time you might understand how a soldier like me tries to do his duty. I hoped that you would see how we soldiers face decisions and the consequences of our decisions." K'Rin's voice softened. "I could not explain myself to a civilian widow and bereft mother—I still do not have the words, nor does the civilian have the understanding. So I made you into a soldier. But I guess I err again. You still do not understand."

Andrea turned in her chair. She replied coldly, "I understand distrust better than guilt or compassion."

K'Rin realized that he was as yet not forgiven, and that forgiveness was not a possibility in this meeting. He retreated to practical matters. "So." He slapped his knees. "What do we do now? Obviously, this Eric business is most upsetting to you, so I have decided to assign you to duties where you'll never see Eric again."

"I don't care where you send Eric. I have unfinished business on Cor."

K'Rin rubbed his large hand over his hairless scalp. "Send you back to Cor?" He shook his head. "I must send Eric and Tara back to Cor. I was thinking of assigning you to operations in the Artrix system."

"I made a promise to someone on Cor—that I'd return with help."

"That's not a problem." K'Rin raised an eyebrow and shrugged.

"After we talk some sense into the council, I can make good on your promise to get them some help."

"You don't understand. I promised that I'd return."

K'Rin's countenance hardened. "I'll repeat myself for your sake. I am going to send Tara and Eric back to Cor to organize a clone resistance. If you return to Cor as you say, you will find yourself in the constant company of Eric and Tara. I don't think you can cope." K'Rin saw that this interview was failing on this second point, and the frustration began to show in his eyes. He stood so he might look down on his subordinate.

Andrea remained seated and replied, "I don't have a choice."

"You always have a choice. Your promise on Cor means nothing to me. The mission matters. For purely operational reasons I prefer that you no longer be involved with Eric and Tara. I discussed the matter with Kip. He agrees with me. We think we should reassign you to Artrix operations."

"Kip can hang himself." Andrea stood nose to nose with her mentor. She spoke with cold deliberation. "You forget, I have a score to settle with the Cor Ordinate. You may have been negligent, but let's not forget: the Cor murdered Steve." Andrea poked a finger into K'Rin's broad chest. "Don't reassign me to some do-nothing outpost. I might get the notion that you are just trying to get rid of me."

K'Rin felt he was no longer speaking to a subordinate but to a peer, perhaps even to the mirror image of himself. His eyes narrowed as he said, "If I were that cynical, I would simply kill you."

"Perhaps you are only half-cynical."

He appreciated her combative wit. He chuckled. "Never half-cynical: that's a fatal condition, as you well know." He paused to reflect, then added, "Very well. Against my better judgment, I'll keep you assigned to Cor operations. I figure I owe you that much."

Andrea did not thank him.

Then K'Rin taunted her, "You seem to have recovered quickly from the shock of seeing Eric." He picked a loose undergarment from the end of the bed and dropped it to the floor. "You've become your old marginally insubordinate self." K'Rin again fixed his eyes on Andrea. "Nevertheless, you are the best Tenebrea I have. Tell me, how do you plan to work with Eric and Tara?"

Andrea fastened her uniform tunic, improving her bearing. "Eric isn't Steve. Eric's just a clone and not worth my consideration."

"I see. Prejudice against clones, I presume, is not just a Jod sentiment. How you cope with Eric is your business as long as it doesn't interfere with the mission."

K'Rin stood and Andrea followed. He said, "I'm glad we had this conversation. For my part, I'll forget the insults you heaped on me—this time."

Andrea bowed her head. K'Rin reached over and with his forefinger raised Andrea's chin. Her face was still ashen. Her brown eyes were dry and exhausted.

K'Rin started for the door saying, "Tomorrow at the beginning of the first cycle, I want a complete briefing on your mission. I'm deeply concerned by the fact that you did not remain covert."

Andrea started to defend her actions, "But, sir—"

K'Rin cut her short. "Not now. Tomorrow, I want a tour of the Ordinate ship. I want you rested and ready for duty." K'Rin stepped into the corridor, closing the door behind him.

Andrea woke with a firm resolution to keep her thoughts regarding Steve and Eric to herself. She believed Steve's murder was not K'Rin's fault, not directly. She thought part of his confession was almost gratuitous. But K'Rin's explanation was consistent with the tradition that the captain is responsible for everything that happens on his or her watch.

But he should have told me . . . She tried to tell herself that her remaining doubts were, as K'Rin suggested, irrational. Andrea admitted to herself that she had been blinded by her fury. In fact, K'Rin had once told her that she would be far more dangerous to the Cor when she shed the cataracts of anger. More than anything, she wanted to be more dangerous to the Cor—Steve and Glendon's murderers.

Andrea took extra time with her uniform, planning to arrive at the briefing room at the stroke of the second hour. She did not want to arrive early and fill the time with awkward silence or more awkward chatter. She had nothing to discuss except business today; the less said the better. She used a piece of chamois to polish her dagger. She carefully wiped the ornamental handle, but when she ran the cloth down the blade the razor edge sliced the chamois and the ball of her thumb.

The pain didn't startle her. Rather she was almost surprised at her indifference. She held the bleeding cut to the light and grabbed a dirty undergarment to staunch the bleeding. With one wipe, the bleeding stopped. She marveled, *How quickly Quazel-enhanced blood coagulates!*

When Andrea arrived at the briefing room, she found H'Roo standing by the door with his arms crossed over his chest. Tara sat at the table, fidgeting with her hands. Her hair was pulled tight with a clip. Eric was noticeably absent, Andrea presumed for her benefit. She took a seat next to Tara who spoke softly: "I can guess how you feel."

"Feel what?" Andrea quipped.

"I am used to seeing people who look like each other. When I first met Eric, for example, I was seeing several ERC models every day. I knew Eric, not by the way he looked, but by the way he looked back at me."

"That's exceedingly poetic, Tara," Andrea jabbed. "Over the top—a . . ."

Tara blushed. Determined to finish her thought, Tara said, "The point is . . ."

Andrea shook her head disdainfully and thought, *By all means, get to the point.* However, Andrea bit her tongue.

Tara shrank but blurted out her prepared script. "The point is you can't go by outward appearances. Everything of value is hidden, and—"

Andrea interrupted. "I know Steve and Eric look alike, and it's a problem for me, but I'll be okay. Even on Earth, they say everyone has a double. The less we talk about Eric, the better."

"As you wish." Tara turned away.

*   *   *

K'Rin breezed into the room with Kip in his wake. H'Roo and Andrea stood smartly and Tara awkwardly followed their example. Kip announced, "Take seats."

K'Rin launched into his piece of the briefing. "First, I've already seen Tara Gullwing's video of the NewGen clones. My staff is at present analyzing the data cubes she brought back and I think we have enough information to convince even the most recalcitrant doubters on the council that the Cor Ordinate presents a threat to the Alliance. Also, while Mat Flores was feeling ill, I took time to question the clone, Tara Gullwing, and I learned about the assault on the Clone Welfare Institute."

K'Rin lowered his voice, "Although I can't find fault with your tactical decision, Mat Flores, the simple truth is that we now have an incident, when we were supposed to have a covert operation. However, what's done is done."

He sat down. "I want you to know the political situation so you can put everything in context. Let's begin with what the council knows. A flash report from the deep space sensors shows three nonregistered ships entering Jod space and one departing. In particular, they know that an Ordinate merchant ship is here on Vintell. They know that two Ordinate light cruisers pursued the merchant into Jod space and that our Jod cruiser just happened to be in the sector to intercept. They know that we destroyed one Ordinate ship, allowing the second to get away. The council will correctly surmise that because I requisitioned the Jod cruiser and put it under the operational control of H'Roo Parh, the Tenebrea is at the root of this incident. Moreover, the council is correct on the particulars. They sent a rather terse order that I return to Heptar. I leave in seventy-two hours."

Kip grumbled, "They will certainly use this incident against you."

"I'll get the obligatory tongue lashing." K'Rin closed his hand into a big fist. "However, this time the weight of evidence is with me." K'Rin's voice exuded confidence but his eyes betrayed the usual wariness. "Here are my orders to you. I want H'Roo and Andrea to take the *Benwoi* to Yuseat Sigma just inside the Artrix quadrant."

He handed H'Roo a data chip. "Everything you need to know about Yuseat is on this chip. Update the *Benwoi*'s data banks. If you need more star charts or navigational data, ask Kip. H'Roo, I want you to continue the technical exploitation of the *Benwoi*. I want to know everything about Ordinate hardware. I want you to take Tara and Eric with you." K'Rin looked at Andrea. "Are you sure you want to go with them?"

Andrea noted that K'Rin turned his gaze on Kip, a silent reminder that Kip must mute his misgivings. Andrea, devoid of emotion, said, "I insist that I go with them." Looking sardonically at Tara, she added, "We're a team."

"As you say." K'Rin made a note on his data pad. "So ordered. Andrea, I want you to help Eric and Tara devise a plan to organize and train the old-order clones into an effective ground force. At a future date, we'll infiltrate your party back to Cor. Meanwhile, you must work on Yuseat in total communications blackout. In effect, I want you to hide there until I figure out what the council wants. Understood?"

H'Roo answered for all. "Yes, sir."

K'Rin reiterated, "You'll stay on Yuseat until you receive word from me—and that may take a couple months, depending on our success with the council. No one outside the Tenebrea knows about our secrets at Yuseat. Even within the Tenebrea only a dozen of us have ever been to the Yuseat lab."

Then K'Rin rose and all the others stood in military fashion. He said, "Now Andrea, the *Benwoi* is your trophy. Why don't you give us a tour." He beckoned Andrea to lead the way.

The small party left the secure briefing room and went to the open landing bay. Andrea introduced the ship. "Gentlemen, the *Benwoi*: she's an armed merchant. Tara Gullwing can answer your questions about the onboard systems." Turning to K'Rin she said, "Sir, I thank you for the compliment, and I'll contribute what I can, but I am not rated to pilot anything bigger than twenty tons. I cannot give you much of a tour."

"You brought her this far."

"In that case, sir, I can give you a better briefing on luck than astrodynamics."

K'Rin laughed. "Save that briefing, Mat Flores. I'm going to need it before I go back to Heptar."

Andrea walked behind Kip and K'Rin as they walked around the Cor ship. K'Rin pressed his hand against the ship's skin, inspecting the weldless seams in the hull, speculating to Kip about the composites used. He compared the width of his finger to the caliber of the weapons: laser cannon and pulse grenades. He looked at the scorching around the engines, then at the array of sensors protruding from the belly of the craft. He examined most closely the quarter-inch copper-colored band around the ship.

"Kip. Look at this. Ever seen this design?"

"No sir. What is it?"

"The band around the gunwales: it's their inertial dampener and field generator, Chelle design." K'Rin commented briefly on the technologies. "She's built for

speed. Multipurpose. Aerodynamic in atmosphere."
K'Rin ran his fingers over the stout wings, probing for
hinges or hydraulics. He found none.

Andrea anticipated his question. "The wings expand
on their own. They are made of a shape-memory alloy."

K'Rin brightened. "Ingenious." K'Rin led the small
group to the boarding ramp and into the belly of the
ship, saying, "Too bad you couldn't bring back one of
their military craft."

Andrea answered, "Sir, all their military assets were
busy at the time. We had to take what we could get."

"Of course." K'Rin raised an eyebrow. Inside, he
walked directly to the small bridge and looked over the
instrumentation. He sat forward in the captain's chair,
noting that the chair was small for Jod hips. "Rather
uncomfortable." He flipped to the communications
panel and briskly brought up the call signs of the merchant ships.

"How did you do that?" Andrea asked.

"Chelle design." K'Rin leaned back and gave her a self-
satisfied smirk. "I've exploited a couple Chelle ships in
my day." Then he counted the number of call signs and
announced, "I figure the Cor have about eighty-four
armed merchants. Let's see if they have the call signs for
their military craft." K'Rin stroked the keypad. The screen
returned with a list of call signs. K'Rin didn't understand
the symbols but looking at the patterns of letters, he spec-
ulated, "I'd guess that they have zero dreadnoughts, two
heavy cruisers, about a dozen light cruisers, and about
twenty small destroyers. In addition, they have a set of
five hundred registered but unassigned call signs." He
turned and smiled. "If the council gives me permission, I
can eliminate the Cor fleet in a week."

"That might not be accurate," Andrea demurred. "I

think those Ordinate call signs will soon be assigned. When I was on Cor, I heard talk about Cor's production of a fleet of small assault craft—upwards of five hundred craft. Maybe a coincidence, but the five hundred craft were due for completion at the same time the first NewGen crop was due to hatch."

Kip echoed, "Eric made references to a ship building program, too."

K'Rin sat straight in the chair and said nothing for a long time.

"Five hundred small attack craft? They could overwhelm our ships' defenses."

Kip echoed, "Yes, sir. If they can get within our perimeters at high-end kinetic speed—even with atomic torpedoes—they might drag down a dreadnought."

K'Rin directed his next question to Tara. "How fast can the Cor make a new crop of NewGen clones?"

Tara cleared her throat and replied, "The gestation cycle is five years."

"Good, then we have five years to prepare."

Tara interjected, "Maybe not."

H'Roo frowned at the female clone offering an opinion not asked for. Andrea elbowed H'Roo gently to keep him from intervening. Tara said, "The Cor have other clone factories, not nearly as advanced or large as Sarhn's Clone Welfare Institute. However, we must consider the possibility that the Cor have already converted other factories to manufacture NewGens. To change a factory to NewGen technology is just programming, processing, and DNA material."

"I think we need to assume the worst." K'Rin looked sideways at Kip, whose face turned grim.

Kip said, "Sir, I think we need to tell the council everything about Andrea's mission."

"Let's not compound our problems with haste." K'Rin interlocked his fingers and put both hands behind his head. He obviously enjoyed sitting in a captain's chair again, even if it pinched. "I agree that time is of the essence, but we get just one chance. Perhaps we ought to quietly contact some of our kinsmen in the fleet."

"And tell them what?" Kip shook his head. "If Pl'Don ever gets a shred of evidence that you are trying to subvert the fleet against the council's authority, you, the Tenebrea, and the House of Rin are finished. Your only defense against Pl'Don thus far is that everyone rejects out of hand even the notion that you might be disloyal."

K'Rin grunted. "I am stretched thin on that point now."

"That's why you must lay out your case as best you can, then accept the council's ruling."

K'Rin smiled wryly. "Your solution seems too direct and I'm almost embarrassed to say that it, therefore, makes me uncomfortable." Turning to Andrea he added, "It is ironic that you of all people may have forced my hand."

Andrea replied almost as a reflex, "I don't see the irony."

"I hope you never do." K'Rin struggled out of the small chair. He looked around the tactical displays, then said, "Show me the rest of the *Benwoi*."

As they walked through the hold, K'Rin stopped to inspect the smallest details: a minor pump or vacuum valve, noting with a sense of admiration the simple, rugged, and relatively inexpensive design. "We must not underestimate the Cor."

As they toured the crew quarters, Andrea paused to

show K'Rin the wilderness cloak she kept bundled in her locker. She explained the oddity of Brigon, the wilderness clone who saved them during the assault on Sarhn.

Then she demonstrated the cloak, wrapping herself in it. As her body warmth powered the cloak, she disappeared before K'Rin's eyes—that is, the cloak projected the image of the bulkhead behind her. K'Rin reached forward until his hand felt the resistance of the cloth and where he jostled the fabric the image failed, revealing for a moment the nappy cloth. As he removed his hand, the cloth again disappeared into the image of the bulkhead. He whispered, "Great Mani's ax!"

Andrea shed the cloak. "Tara and I were able to sneak aboard the *Benwoi* wearing these cloaks."

"At Yuseat, ask Dr. Carai to reverse engineer this cloak's technology, if he can. Be sure to tell the staff at Yuseat that the *Benwoi* is basically Chelle design. They'll know how to get at all the ship's libraries. Perhaps you can break their encryption. I want to know the Cor's technical capabilities. I want to know their standing orders, policies, and procedures. In short, I want to know what they know and what they don't know."

Andrea scowled. "One thing you'll learn soon enough: somebody's selling the Cor information. The Ordinate have precise charts of Jod space—way beyond the capabilities of long-range sensing. They know the location of asteroids, even comets. They know the coordinates of major Jod cities. I think the Chelle are working both sides of the Alliance."

K'Rin looked down his nose at her. "Andrea, my dear cousin, Chelle duplicity is the oldest and most

poorly kept secret in the galaxy. Yet the council culti-
vates them as allies, so your point is timely."

Turning to Kip, he added, "She's right. If I tell the
council everything, they will in turn divulge the particulars to the Chelle, and the Chelle will sell the information to the Ordinate. Instead of telling the council, I
might as well sell the information directly to the
Ordinate and at least show some profit for our pains."

chapter 5

H'Roo lay on the floor of the *Benwoi*'s bridge with his head deep in a compartment. "Typical . . . tight . . . Ow!" He banged his elbow on the side panel. He continued to fuss. "Miserable Chelle design, modified by dysfunctional Ordinate."

Andrea sat cross-legged on the floor and watched. "I didn't know you could fix these machines." She held a data chip in one hand, and a tool belt in the other.

With his head buried and his voice muffled, H'Roo replied coolly, "I paid attention during sparks class. You didn't."

She smirked, "My inattention has paid off again." She leaned back, bracing herself against her outstretched arms.

"Cute." H'Roo's breathy voice echoed from the stuffy compartment. "I got the binary adapter in place, assuming I got the optical fibers reconnected in the right order." H'Roo breathed heavily. "Now hand me the data chip." He waved a hand blindly behind his back.

Andrea placed the data chip into the palm of

H'Roo's outstretched hand. A moment later, H'Roo grunted, "Done." He shimmied backward. He was unaware of the smudge of brown that crossed his forehead. She enjoyed the incongruity: H'Roo was by birth one of the wealthiest Jod alive, destined for rank and privilege, and here he labored as a mechanic, looking and acting like a mechanic.

H'Roo replaced the panel cover, popped in the four corner rivets, and said, "Now, we can download the data and read all about Yuseat." H'Roo pushed his bulk back onto his haunches, then stiffly rose, taking a seat at the console. By contrast, Andrea rose in one fluid motion.

A flickering yellow light counted off the terabytes of data transferred from the cube, whereupon the *Benwoi*'s computer flashed a message: *Indexing files: eight seconds*. H'Roo muttered contempt. "Slow system. Nonstandard keyboard." He hunted and pecked instructions. "We ought to get that Tara clone in here."

"She's still getting reacquainted with her"—Andrea hesitated—"husband."

Andrea settled into the navigator's chair. H'Roo stood at the console. The forward screen flickered to life. H'Roo pointed to the forward screen and three orbs lined up. Consulting the text on his console, H'Roo said, "The closest is Yuseat Sigma, a moon. She is locked in orbit with the planet Cloe, roughly one hundred thousand times larger than Jod, and uninhabitable. In the distance you see the star Thule at the edge of the Artrix system."

"Magnify Yuseat, if you can."

"You want imagery or cartography?"

"Imagery," Andrea replied.

"No problem. I'll simulate an equatorial orbit about

two hundred miles up, all daylight." H'Roo zoomed in on the dark blue ball that turned slowly.

Andrea observed, "The oceans seem a normal blue. What are those long stripes of green and red?"

H'Roo consulted the text. "Some kind of surface algae."

They sat still for a moment and watched the image of Yuseat turn slowly. The landmasses were almost totally shrouded in a thick gray fog, not like cloud cover, but like a heavy smoke. A few spikes of snow-capped rock poked out of the thick shroud.

Andrea asked, "Besides the algae, is there life on the moon?"

Hunched over his console, H'Roo paged through material several times faster than Andrea could read. He answered, "Oh, most certainly. The Artrix call Yuseat Sigma the fungi moon. The dominant life forms are filamentous, spore-bearing organisms devoid of chlorophyll. Most are benign."

"Benign? You mean they've got poisonous mush-rooms that we mustn't eat, or something?"

H'Roo paged through the text, paraphrasing. "On Yuseat the mushrooms do the eating. The fungi are can-nibalistic; that is, they feed on each other. Any weak-ened organism immediately falls prey to the stronger. Nothing passive about Yuseat."

"Good old Mother Nature taking care of business," Andrea mused.

H'Roo paused as he read more. "Listen to this: at the top of the food chain, Yuseat has a rare but aggres-sive form of slime mold, known as slime cats." He looked up. "They eat anything that doesn't eat them first."

"Right." Andrea chuckled.

"Really. Slime cats secrete a mild neurotoxin that kills, then digests flesh. The slime cat grows on the skin, spreading."

H'Roo looked up, somewhat alarmed. "Sort of like getting skinned alive. There's a whole chapter on slime cats and how to avoid them."

"Then we'd better watch where we step. What other life forms does Yuseat have?"

H'Roo paged down the file. "On land, bacteria and yeast participate in a feeding frenzy of microorganisms."

Andrea wrinkled her nose. "The whole place must smell like the inside of an old wet boot."

H'Roo raised an eyebrow as he perused the next screen full of text. "Doesn't say anything about smell, but does talk about irritation of mucous membranes. Yuseat has a thick atmosphere with a high level of carbon dioxide. Yuseat rotates in forty-four-hour days. During daylight, the land lies under total cloud cover. However, half of the mass of those dark clouds is spores, not water vapor. One can see the sky only at elevations eighteen hundred feet above sea level where a few mountain ranges comprise about two percent of the moon's surface. At those altitudes, cold temperatures and high levels of ultraviolet light inhibit fungi."

Andrea shook her head. "What a hellhole."

H'Roo continued to read. "There's more. With almost no wind, the planet seems to breathe in and out with each rotation, a diurnal raising and lowering of clouds. At noon, the clouds rise to about five hundred feet above mean sea level. Each night the clouds descend as dense ground fog, misting everything, prompting the trophic fungi to produce spores. During the day, swarms of fruit flies come out to feed on rotting vegetation." H'Roo forced a smile. "It's going to be hard to pick a shift: so much to choose from—spores and fruit flies."

Trying to understand the phenomena, Andrea said, "A global weather inversion with stale air trapped over land—like Denver or Los Angeles."

"I suppose." H'Roo turned back to his screen. "The cloud convection causes electric storms in the upper atmosphere—more a bother at night when the clouds are at ground level. They don't get many ground strikes, just a lot of noise and some flashes from above."

Andrea shrugged. "You haven't seen lightning until you've been in a kkona storm on Cor."

H'Roo brightened, "Ah, but here's some good news. The oceans by contrast stay cloud free." He tapped the console, accelerating the rotation of the image until he saw the oceans with their lazy green and red stripes.

Andrea pointed to the algae. "Then Yuseat's oxygen must come primarily from the oceans."

"Correct. The algae pump most of the oxygen into the atmosphere. But on land the oxygen-rich air stays trapped above the cloud cover. On the surface below the cloud cover, we need level-three breathing masks for sustained outdoor activity."

"Right." Andrea guffawed. "Nothing like the great outdoors on Yuseat."

"At high altitudes or over the ocean, masks are not necessary. Also, Yuseat's poles are barren ice."

"Ice sounds good. Mountains, ice, oceans. So, just where is the lab?"

H'Roo queried the system with a few key strokes. The image of Yuseat spun quickly, then stopped. A red speck of light marked a spot on the cloud-covered continent. He zoomed in closer, showing the dense shroud of vapor and spores.

Andrea groaned.

"I'm changing to cartography." H'Roo typed in a command and instantly the black clouds vanished. The red dot signifying the location of the lab was in a bowl-shaped valley near the edge of a lake. Hundreds of spidery streambeds raked the surrounding hills, feeding into the large lake. Deltas of sludge upset the otherwise round shoreline. The east edge of the bowl rose to four thousand feet, just grazing the upper limits of the ubiquitous clouds.

"A good hiding place." Andrea wagged her head, disgusted with her future home.

"Without a doubt." H'Roo consulted his text. "Yuseat doesn't have many other kinds of plant life that you'd recognize—just a particularly hardy type of cypress, the Papuyoosa tree that survives in wetlands among the fungus. Yuseat isn't all vegetation." H'Roo scanned the text. "They've got insects: fruit flies, of course, that feed on decaying fungi. Also, the oceans are filled with krill and" —H'Roo squinted—"the landmasses have various terrestrial crustaceans of the genus armadillidium." He looked at Andrea and shrugged.

"Roly-polies . . . pill bugs. Haven't you ever looked under a rock?" She held up a thumb and forefinger to give the approximate dimensions.

H'Roo furled his brow. "Crustaceans or insects?"

"Tiny land crabs. We call them bugs; don't ask me why."

H'Roo looked up from his screen to smile wanly. "I hate crabs—filthy scavengers."

"They're harmless enough." Andrea turned back to the screen. "Did anybody ever try to colonize Yuseat?"

H'Roo turned back to the text. "No, the Artrix never attempted colonization. Apparently, they thought about it, surveyed the moon, conducted a lot of on-site research, but determined that they'd have to sterilize the entire surface to make it fit for habitation."

"How did K'Rin find this hiding place?" She added sarcastically, "Have they've got indoor plumbing? I hope so, because I wouldn't want to sit on a slime cat or a bunch of pill bugs or . . ."

H'Roo shushed her. "Yuseat is a lot more than just a hiding place. The Yuseat Lab houses Dr. Carai and a staff of five Tenebrea technicians. They produce the Quazel enzyme."

Andrea interjected, "I wondered where they got the stuff."

"Says here, the lab has only eighteen thousand square feet of living space, and a small landing platform." H'Roo turned and grimaced. "Only eighteen thousand."

Andrea looked around the bridge. "Damn. The *Benwoi* has more living space than that. I pity the poor bastard who pulls a long tour on Yuseat. How long did K'Rin say we might spend there?"

H'Roo ignored her question. "Only fifteen Tenebrea know of the existence of Yuseat. I guess we make it nineteen, counting the clones." H'Roo turned from the screen. "The file gives coordinates and directions."

"Skip that."

H'Roo returned to the screen. "Travel protocols. Navigational data and such. We must run silent with complete emissions control. As soon as we jump to FTL speed, we shut down the engines and make the trip on inertia."

Andrea observed, "Slow trip. K'Rin's not taking any chances, is he?"

"None. We must shut down all systems, including the environmental suite, and survive on ambient air for at least one hundred hours. Therefore, if any sensing post detects our relatively small mass, they presume we're a piece of ice or rock, not a ship, or if a ship, then a derelict." H'Roo scratched his chin thoughtfully. "Do you think the *Benwoi* can go a hundred hours on batteries alone?"

Andrea shrugged. "Tara can figure that out."

The sallow light of mercury lamps filled the Vintell landing bay. The ground crew manhandled heavy equipment, preparing the *Tyker* shuttle and the *Benwoi* for space travel. Kip and K'Rin stood by the worm gears that held the landing bay doors closed against the vacuum. Kip was meticulously dressed, even over-dressed for the occasion.

Kip planned to use these final minutes of flight preparation as a last chance to caution K'Rin to coop-erate with the Council of Elders. He broached the sub-ject tentatively. "Sir, in less than a week you'll be standing in front of the council."

K'Rin mused, "I haven't been to Heptar since the council expelled my father."

Kip tried to sidestep the bitter memory. "We need to keep our minds focused on the near future."

K'Rin looked down his nose at Kip. "You can bet that the council will focus on my recent past. I expect the council will reprimand me for meddling in Cor's affairs. They'll say I disobeyed their orders."

"You did, didn't you?" Kip tried to discern whether K'Rin was being ironic on purpose.

"True," K'Rin admitted through tight lips. "The major difference is that I am trying to save their skins, while they are looking for a way to skin me."

Kip allowed a judicious pause. He watched the ground crew as they gingerly loaded fuel pallets into the shuttle. He reiterated an old point. "All the more reason why you should have every fact at your disposal. Sir, you should take the *Benwoi* and the two clones with you to Heptar and make your case as completely as possible. When the council learns the truth of the situation, they will be grateful that you took the initiative."

K'Rin spoke as if lecturing a son bound for boarding school. "Kip, the first lesson in politics is ingratitude. Never, never presume gratitude. First, the council will seek their own political advantage, then they might consider the security interests of Jod. Right now, they are trying to determine the greater threat to their power: me or the Ordinate."

Kip relished these rare moments where he served as K'Rin's confidant. That K'Rin shared his thoughts with him was a great compliment. Occasionally, K'Rin took Kip's advice. Those heady moments more than paid for the times K'Rin curtly dismissed Kip's suggestions. Although K'Rin had never said that Kip was his protégé, Kip assumed he was, and Kip would do anything to further their shared fortunes.

Kip advised, "We must not poison this opportunity by prejudging the council's motives. I think you can sway them with the weight of your new information. An open dialogue is long overdue."

K'Rin raised an eyebrow. "Exchange of information is irrelevant. No matter what I say, the council will question—perhaps prejudge—my motives, despite my oath of allegiance. If I show them everything, I must admit everything. Right now, they have no hard proof—only circumstantial evidence—that I'm connected with the incident on Cor. I'm not going to hand Pl'Don enough proof to convict me."

"Then what are you going to tell them?" Kip asked rhetorically. He knew K'Rin's mind on the matter. He simply disagreed.

"Just what they need to know—that the Cor Ordinate are developing the capability to destroy Jod, that Jod must mobilize, and that we must conduct a preemptive strike to eliminate the Cor threat. I have already dropped hints to the assembly by way of Hal B'Yuon that I would serve on the council throughout this military crisis, then resign my seat. My best hope is to convince the council that they need me at present and that I'll go away quietly when I'm finished with Cor."

The part about K'Rin resigning his seat was news to Kip. Clever ruse. Kip said under his breath, "You will of course change your mind after you are securely on the council with command of the Fleet."

K'Rin shook his head. "You think like they do."

"That's part of my job." Kip smiled wryly.

"You assume Pl'Don will invite me back to the council."

"I do."

Throughout the conversation Kip and K'Rin watched the hustle and bustle in the landing bay, never facing each other. Each spoke impassively. Kip continued, "I believe the old saying: Keep your friends close, your enemies closer. Besides, the Cor Ordinate will determine if you are right or wrong. Pl'Don has everything to gain and nothing to lose. If Cor attacks, then Pl'Don will need you desperately. If they don't attack, Pl'Don can pin another fiasco on you."

K'Rin scowled. "Another fiasco?"

Kip felt himself blush. "I didn't mean . . . I was just trying to put myself in Hal Pl'Don's frame of mind. I still think you are best served by disclosing everything. Pl'Don is no fool. Reinstating you is in his best interests."

K'Rin put a hand on Kip's shoulder. "His best interests? Perhaps. Nevertheless, Pl'Don is what he is. I doubt Pl'Don can resist the opportunity I've given him. A serpent, caught in a flood, cannot help but bite you even when you reach down to save it from drowning: such is its nature. The other council members have the desire but lack the gumption to bite. No, Kip, I won't disclose everything. Instead, I'll hide my assets at Yuseat for the time being until I know whether the council is disposed to listen."

"In any case"—Kip folded his arms across his chest—"I think your meeting at Heptar is a positive sign. They could have reprimanded you just as effectively through Fleet channels. I think your fears will prove baseless. Try to be optimistic."

"Cautiously optimistic, perhaps."

"I'll stake a wager that you come out of the meeting stronger than when you go in." He watched the ground crew remove equipment from the launch area.

"Care to wager a case of Vorlach brandy?"

Kip paused to calculate the cost of the rare liquor. "Done." He looked sideways at K'Rin's dour countenance.

Without looking back at Kip, K'Rin mused, "I hope to lose this bet."

The shuttle commander stepped down the short gangway and waved to Kip, signaling time to depart. At the far end of the bay, Andrea carried her personal gear in a gray bag thrown over her shoulder. As she got ready to board the *Benwoi*, she paused. From a distance, she saluted K'Rin. K'Rin held out his hand as if to touch her across the yawning bay—a gesture recognized by all Jod as a blessing.

Kip did not mimic his boss, thinking the gesture profane, directed as it was toward a Terran. He cleared his throat. "At the risk of yet another rebuke, I'll remind you that I think it is a big mistake to let Mat Flores and the clone Eric work together."

"Duly noted." K'Rin kept his gaze on Andrea as he added, "Has it ever occurred to you that I might tire of your repetitive misgivings? Eric has specific instructions to avoid contact with Andrea." K'Rin started walking toward the shuttle.

Kip shrugged off K'Rin's criticism. "Care to wager another case of brandy?"

K'Rin stopped and turned. His neck flushed and nostrils flared, a sight that froze Kip to a rigid attention. K'Rin growled, "You cocky two-ringer, don't press your luck."

The ancient fortress of Heptar stood on a stout butte, a nine-hundred-foot pillar of black obsidian, the core of an extinct volcano stripped away by millions of years of sandstorms. The black pillar was twice as wide as it was tall, providing a seventy-acre perch. A wall of massive chocolate-brown stone skirted the ragged obsidian cylinder. Round towers—some squat, some tall—lined the walls. Weatherworn arrow loops and crenellation seemed fanciful.

Within the protective barrier stood a complex of interconnected pavilions. On the flat roofs, lush gardens added a fringe of green to the bellicose countenance of Heptar's walls. Three onion-shaped domes, enameled in blue, green, and gold filigree, dignified the council chambers.

Although now the center of Jod power, most Jod considered Heptar's history as a footnote. Heptar's preeminence was a convenient accident.

Heptar survived the Clan Wars, in part due to its formidable walls, in part due to its geographic isolation. Heptar held no strategic advantage, and therefore posed no threat to other clans. They remained unaligned and friendless, and thereby spared themselves centuries of bitter war. But Heptar's isolation and inconspicuousness had a price. At the end of the Clan Wars, famine and pestilence ravaged the land. A ten-year drought sucked the artesian wells dry. Meanwhile, the other clans sat on their hands and watched the heretofore unallied and uninvolved citizens of Heptar perish in large numbers.

The desperate remnant at Heptar gave up everything to the fledgling council. In exchange they got food, water, and medicine. Although humiliated, Heptar survived. The timely demise of Heptar solved a thorny issue for the council—where to put the new central government. All their cities had been ravaged, and no clan would allow general funds to rebuild the city of a rival. The fall of Heptar into the status of community property helped bring about a swift end to the wars. All Jod believed Heptar's loss was providential. Heptar had been the seat of Clan Don.

In modern times, the government of Jod expanded. Civil authorities occupied the Heptar Fortress and built the Lower Barracks at the foot of the butte where two thousand elite Jod regulars atrophied in endless drill and ceremony.

Over the years, a modern city grew, sprawling around the base of the obsidian butte. The population expanded to one million Jod. By law, no building could stand more than half the distance to the top of the butte.

Most of the land surrounding Heptar was arid. Yet to the south, a great quilt of many shades of green and yellow stretched to the horizon. Artesian wells provided water to the otherwise parched land. The commerce of Heptar was agriculture and bureaucracy.

Above the frenzy of daily life, the council lived in resplendent seclusion. Council members represented the major Jodic clans. At the beginning of the Federation, their seclusion made all the clans' headmen mutual hostages. In the simple logic of survival, they learned to cooperate in their seclusion without ready access to their kin. Otherwise, life on Heptar would become a living hell.

The experiment succeeded. For a thousand years Jod enjoyed internal tranquility, and clan allegiances became social and cultural instead of military. Skirmishes of opinion were fought in decorous debate. Intrigue was still the currency of government, but the highest compliment paid to a council member was that he was flexible, compromising, and above all practical. Hal Pl'Don understood the council politics as well as any. He exuded compromise, but inside he was as a hard as the obsidian base upon which his ancestors built Heptar. He took special pride in his ancestral home. He took pride in his political skills. After all, he was the first of the Clan Don to wend his way through the political maze, from the General Assembly of Clans to the powerful council. He basked in the justice of ascending to the First Among Equals, titular head of Jod government, which meant he occupied the Great House, the former home of his direct ancestors.

Pl'Don sat on a simple stool, working at his desk. Tired and slump-shouldered, he read reports from outlying colonies: requests for labor, requests for water, requests for transport, requests. . . . Some documents he approved without comment. On others, Pl'Don scrawled marginalia that aides would later transcribe into lawful orders for council approval and his signature.

The weight of the Jod Empire lay squarely upon his shoulders. More than ten billion Jod relied on his good governance. Ten billion mouths to feed. The strain of leadership showed on his face. His saffron robes hung loose about his shoulders. He wore a simple necklace advertising his rank: delicately filigreed links of gold with a solitary emerald as a pendant.

From his desk, Pl'Don peered through the beveled glass panel, his window into the Audience Chamber. He was upset by the news: the Chelle ambassador requested an audience to issue protest regarding Jod violations of the Alliance Treaty, specifically an alleged aggression against Cor. He was sure that this unpleasant news was somehow tied to the report of the Qota incident—three Cor ships trespass; one stays, one flees, and one is destroyed by Jod gunnery. Pl'Don's eyes narrowed to slits. K'Rin's doing.

The Audience Chamber was empty. A curved table made of milky onyx sat upon a platform of dark red stone. Eleven chairs—ornately enameled with disproportionately large backs—lined the table. Each chair displayed the crest of a great clan represented there. Behind each chair stood a wooden staff and a banner.

Pl'Don's chair was in the middle, and from that seat

he ruled the council. In turn, the council ruled the General Assembly that met after each full moon to ratify council policy. Talk of the Cor ships violating Jod space buzzed through the halls and Pl'Don fully expected to answer tough questions at the next assembly. Now this—a protest from Chelle.

Pl'Don left his desk and entered the imposing chamber. Immediately two uniformed guards, tall and muscular, bearing heavy ceremonial weapons, came from opposite sides of the room to escort Pl'Don to his seat at the center of the table. The remaining ten seats sat empty. The guards crisply retraced their steps to their posts, whereupon one announced in a loud baritone, "Executive session of the council: Hal Pl'Don is seated."

Moments later, the door at the far end of the chamber opened. Pl'Don watched three sylphlike Chelle enter the Audience Chamber. The larger two dressed in Chelle beige, the third in the metallic gray cassock that indicated ambassador rank. Their thin arms hung at their sides. The long fingers slowly flexed and relaxed as if timed with their breathing. The three Chelle looked about the room and whispered together in apparent agitation. Then from a distance, the ambassador spoke, his shrill voice echoing from the polished stone walls, "I am directed to deliver this message to the entire council."

Pl'Don did not stand. He disliked the Chelle. He thought the Chelle an officious species, constantly reminding anyone with ears that the Chelle were innately superior, although woefully underappreciated—destiny's favorite, yet perennial victims. He wished they would make up their superior minds. But most of all, Pl'Don despised their tortured efforts to

justify themselves at every level. For cultural reasons
that Pl'Don did not comprehend, the Chelle cared less
if they won or lost. No, they cared more if other species
agreed with them, completely, without the slightest
odor of reservation. The ultimate irony was that when
one agreed with the Chelle, the Chelle immediately
became suspicious. But the Chelle were a fact of life
and a major force in the galaxy.

Pl'Don allowed an uncomfortable pause, then
replied, "The other members are busy at present. I act
as the council in executive session." Pl'Don purposefully wanted to take this interview alone. He made a
point of always granting the Chelle less than they
asked. Pl'Don knew the Chelle practice of overreaching
with their demands. He bowed politely and said,
"Therefore, I represent the entire council for this interview."

The three Chelle put their heads together. Their
faces did not betray any emotion other than some confusion. Then they approached Pl'Don's seat and without the normal courtesies, the ambassador pulled a
small palm screen from a pocket to consult notes. He
spoke in a high register that grated on Pl'Don's ears. "I
have come on behalf of the Ordinate."

Pl'Don displayed his irritation by cutting the ambassador short. "The Ordinate can speak for themselves.
We have offered to open a dialogue with them."
Pl'Don's fuller voice echoed through the empty chamber.

The Chelle ambassador opened his mouth to continue his prepared text, but Pl'Don again cut him off—
a practiced tactic of intimidation. "In fact, we Jod prefer
that the Cor Ordinate speak directly with us, without
intermediaries, so we can avoid any misunderstandings

that might occur from the lost nuances inevitable in the exchange of messages through a third party." The Chelle ambassador put his palm screen in his pocket and spoke extemporaneously. "Jod-Ordinate dialogue may no longer be a possibility—especially after Jod's unprovoked attack against Cor."

Pl'Don leaned forward to blister the Chelle with the facts. "Two Cor combat vessels came into Jod space in pursuit of one of their merchant ships. They violated our space." Pl'Don raised his voice to impart his government's displeasure with the Ordinate incursion. "A Jod cruiser intercepted the two combat vessels that were prepared to destroy the merchant ship—an egregious violation of our prerogatives. Our Jod cruiser fired upon one of the Cor vessels, destroying it. The second Cor vessel retreated. Neither the Cor Ordinate nor the Chelle have any cause for complaint."

The ambassador smiled and nodded. "I think we do. Understandably, you left out the more interesting aspects of the incident, the Jod attack on Cor's capital city, Sarhn, which was the provocation that justified Cor's pursuit of the perpetrators into your space. I am here officially representing the Chelle and the Ordinate to ascertain whether or not Jod and Cor are in a state of war."

Pl'Don sank back into his chair, speechless.

The Chelle ambassador approached the dais, trying to subdue a note of triumph. His clothing appeared liquefied in the strong lights. He blinked once, momentarily blanking his large black eyes. "Shall I deliver my message uninterrupted?"

"Yes. Do."

Recovering his notes, the ambassador intoned, "On Cor Julian date one-eighty-six, two-eighty-three, a pair of Cor light cruisers pursued a Cor armed merchant into Jod space. A Jod vessel attacked the Cor ships as they tried to retrieve the Cor merchant."

"Yes, yes. We know that. The attack was hardly unprovoked. Two Ordinate war ships show up unannounced with their weapons hot. While I regret any loss of life—"

The ambassador raised his hand. "Please, let me finish. The Ordinate have proof that Jod sent an agent provocateur into their capital city, Sarhn. Your agent is apparently an Earth woman in your employment."

"An Earth woman? That's preposterous!" Pl'Don clenched his teeth. *K'Rin! You crazy bastard!*

"Your agent organized a clone insurrection. The clones assaulted the city, destroying the Clone Welfare Institute, a magnificent building. They destroyed other valuable property as well, including ninety-five percent of the clone crop therein." The ambassador lowered his palm screen and added his own dig. "The loss of the fifty thousand NewGen clones requires special reparation."

"How so?" Pl'Don fumed.

The Chelle ambassador recited his calculations. "Each clone has a service life of approximately twenty years. Therefore, your liability calculates to one and a half million labor years."

Pl'Don raised his eyes to the ceiling and shook his head.

The ambassador continued his litany. "Your agent hijacked the merchant ship *Benwoi* and escaped with the leader of the clone insurrection. Cor logically surmises that the Jod are planning further operations to destabilize their clone population, possibly in anticipation of a Jod invasion."

Pl'Don glowered. "Our days of empire are long past. Everyone knows that we seek coexistence with the Cor Ordinate. I personally have been the chief proponent of bringing Cor into the Alliance."

"The facts suggest that you speak one way and act another." The ambassador continued, his face growing stern. "The Ordinate demands return of the merchant ship, the *Benwoi*, and restitution for the destruction of their property and the pursuing cruiser." Again, the ambassador offered an aside. "The Cor Ordinate authorizes Chelle to act as their agents in these transactions." Returning to his notes, the ambassador added, "The Ordinate also demands return of any clones in Jod custody, specifically the TRA model clone that escaped on the *Benwoi*. They also demand that you surrender the agent, the Earth female, for interrogation and trial. She is wanted for espionage and murder, among other charges."

Pl'Don kept his composure. "What evidence do you have?"

"We—I mean, the Ordinate have enough evidence to prevail in the Alliance's Intergalactic Court. Our appraisers are at present surveying the damage. Jod is culpable. The evidence points directly to you."

"We'll see." Pl'Don loomed large from his chair on the dais. He looked down at the ambassador, but his mind was on K'Rin. He would have K'Rin's head if half of what the ambassador said was true.

The ambassador raised his pointed chin. His large dark eyes sparkled as he said, "Now, the Chelle also have a demand."

"A demand?" Pl'Don bristled. He folded his hands on the onyx table.

"Yes. The Alliance Treaty of Mutual Interdependence,

article three, section two, paragraph two, states that any party may unilaterally—"

"I know what the Treaty says."

"The Chelle demand that the Jod withdraw their ships from Chelle space. We want to reassess the reliability of your command structure. Frankly, our sources do not show any signs of Jod mobilization, which makes us doubt that the assault is council policy."

Pl'Don stood. He looked past the ambassador at the flags that lined the Audience Chamber—spoil from another era when war was the natural order. Even in the past millennium, small wars marred long periods of peace. Even in recent times, when Pl'Don was a young man, his elders waged a short war of retribution against the Chelle—a war of egos and overwrought principles. Pl'Don eschewed military service and thereby kept himself pure. The Rin household ruled then. Pl'Don shifted his gaze down to the Chelle ambassador. Perhaps the Chelle ambassador fought in that ridiculous war: Pl'Don had no way of knowing.

Pl'Don said, "I just assured you that such an assault, if factual, is not my policy." Pl'Don fought to keep his neck color pale. Inside he roiled with anger. This is K'Rin's doing! "You may assure your Cor clients that the Jod government has no designs whatsoever against the Ordinate. I have long hoped that the Ordinate would eventually join us in the Alliance. You know that I have tried to persuade other members to drop their objection to Ordinate cloning. I firmly believe in self-determination of species."

"I am inclined to agree with you, Hal Pl'Don, but our concerns remain. The assault did take place—an act of war, no less. We quite naturally wonder if your Fleet is sufficiently under civilian control."

Pl'Don studied the pair of large black eyes, wondering how much the ambassador knew about the fractious nature of clan politics and the importance of controlling the Jod Fleet. He wondered if the ambassador knew that Rin, although deprived of their council seat, remained a potent family because of their strong presence in the military. He replied in his most conciliatory tone, "I have complete confidence in our command and control. However, I will investigate the matter fully."

"I recommend it. Also, the Ordinate permit me to say that they would consider as a sign of good faith the stand-down of the entire Jod Fleet." The ambassador raised his sylphlike arm to point accusingly at Pl'Don. "After all, we quite naturally suspect duplicity on your part, since recent events contradict your words."

Pl'Don swallowed this gratuitous attack on his integrity. When he was finished with this crisis, he would deal with the ambassador at his leisure. Pl'Don said, "Take this message back to Cor. The Jod government desires peace. We will investigate the incident from our end. If we find that any Jod, inside or outside our government, is responsible for this breach of the peace, we will inflict punishment according to our laws, and if—and I stress if—we discover that Jod is in the least bit culpable, we shall make full restitution."

The Chelle recovered the palm screen from his pocket and waved it. "I have the full record of our conversation and I shall deliver it promptly."

Pl'Don straightened his robe and said, "Now turn that cursed recorder off for a moment."

"As you wish." The Chelle ambassador pressed a button, then showed the blank screen to Pl'Don.

Knowing that his next remarks would be broadcast

more than the official record, Pl'Don chose his words carefully. "I need a month to sort some things out. Deliver your message and return as soon as you can. Suppose we can devise a solution, a remedy that satisfies the Ordinate. The Jod would be willing to compensate the Chelle and you in particular for your good offices. War impoverishes all parties concerned. Peace, my dear ambassador, enriches us all. We need to arrange diplomatic relations with the Cor. Can you make arrangements with the Cor whereby we can send an emissary to Cor? I would make it very much worth your while."

The Chelle ambassador bowed. "We are always and everywhere at the service of peace."

chapter 6

The *Benwoi* left Vintell with her four-person crew. Andrea hunkered down for a long stretch of inactivity. She sat on the floor with her back against the wall of the ship's bridge, brooding.

On a heading toward the Artrix system, Tara engaged the FTL drive, confirmed their heading, then cut power except for the inertial dampener that held the ship intact. Tara keyed off the communications suite and powered down the environmental suite. Screens dimmed to black. The navigational console ran calculations based on dead reckoning and some sketchy triangulation taken from ambient points of light.

H'Roo locked the hatches to the aft crew compartments. He likewise blocked the storage compartments—all to squeeze hours from their batteries, maintain on-board temperature, and preserve the precious oxygen.

Eric sat in the back with the logistician's console, studying maps of Cor, occasionally glancing up to watch the sparse activity. Eric appeared sinister in his bastardized version of the Tenebrea uniform, a black

pullover shirt with long sleeves tapered at the wrist,
long pants with a single crisp crease running down
each leg allowing the pants legs to flare slightly at the
shoe. He has no right to wear the uniform. Everything
annoyed Andrea. Even the silence.

With engines off-line, silence was the only rhythm of
the day. Awkward silence. For one hundred hours, their
universe was going to be the bridge and the captain's
ready room, which offered the only amenities: a couch
long enough to sleep on, a small galley, and a head.
Andrea sat facing the blank forward screen. She
drummed her fingers on the console. She wore her gray
and black uniform, her hair pulled severely back to a
black whisk of a ponytail.

Preparing for the voyage, she had successfully avoided
direct contact with Eric. She saw him occasionally. She
noted that Eric's mouth and eyes—the same clear blue
eyes as Steve's—turned slightly down in a perpetual
frown. Steve's face was in contrast optimistic.

She had heard Eric speak. The timbre of his voice
was like Steve's, although he lacked Steve's brackish
accent: the Chesapeake's peculiar backwash of old
tobacco farmers and watermen combined with his parents' more refined dialect. Welsh, she always thought.
Steve had a unique patois that always left folk guessing
where he was from.

Andrea concentrated on the differences; she had to.
At Vintell, Tara and H'Roo conspired to keep Eric and
Andrea separated, but for the voyage to Yuseat and in
the confined Yuseat lab, she would be face to face with
Eric more often than not. She thought about Eric
although she fixed her eyes to her busywork. She knew
that the other three watched her to see how she would
act. Andrea felt their curiosity and resented it.

This situation is not improving with time. Andrea stood up and walked to Eric's chair. Tara and H'Roo both watched with interest. Andrea stood over Eric, her arms folded across her chest. Looking down she said, "We haven't been formally introduced."

"So?" Eric slowly raised his eyes. His thin lips tightened. His eyes showed disdain.

Andrea spoke with cold authority. "I am Mat Andrea Flores, and—"

Eric interrupted, "I know who you are. Tara told me all about you and how your husband took a bullet for me. Listen, Mat Flores, I don't owe you a damned thing. Got that? I'll do my job. You do your job."

Andrea stared down at Eric and slowly a thin smile crept over her face. She thought: *You are just a boorish clone, nothing like Steve, thank God.* She said aloud, "Works for me."

Falhal R'Oueu carried a small worn book of verse that she cradled in her arms. She was a beauty, despite her age. Her five rings shone bright beneath her eyes. She used a touch of gold liner to accentuate each ring. Her richly embroidered green and gold gown hung from her broad shoulders to the ground, cinched at the waist and pleated to accentuate her lack of girth. She did not wear the high collar typical of Jod gentlewomen, because she had mastered her species' tendency to broadcast emotions by the blush on their necks. Her naturally purplish lips added to her cool, aloof aspect. Hers were thin resolute lips that only occasionally offered a grave smile or her appreciation of some irony. She had every reason to be vain, but she was not.

R'Oueu crossed the rooftop garden into the cooler

shade. She sat on a sun-bleached wooden chair behind a screen of jasmine flowers, and opened her book. She liked to memorize verse.

Voices disturbed her solitude: her husband's voice. She tried to force her concentration back to the verse, but the temptation to eavesdrop overpowered her and she set the book aside. Her husband, Hal Pl'Don, asked questions. A stranger's voice answered. She peered through the jasmine and saw Pl'Don and heard his questions plainly, but she could not hear the stranger's answers. All she saw was the stranger's back.

R'Oueu was intrigued. The stranger with her husband was a younger Jod, too young to be in private conversation with the chief executive of the Jod government. He did not wear any marks of rank or family affiliation. Instead, he wore the plain indigo robe of a clerk, cut too short for his frame—a disguise, most likely. She could see that this stranger was no slump-shouldered functionary. He lacked the necessary obeisance of a clerk; he was tall and muscular.

She cocked her head sideways and listened. They talked about growing old—an odd conversation for two strangers, her aging husband and a young courtier. Pl'Don became animated as the stranger talked of a drug that can double a lifetime. Then they talked about Hal K'Rin. R'Oueu did not want to hear about K'Rin, not in *her* garden, *her* sanctuary. R'Oueu stood up with the intention of interrupting her husband and meeting the stranger, but when she rounded the privet hedge of jasmine, she found Pl'Don alone. "Who was with you just now?" she asked.

Pl'Don recovered quickly from his surprise at seeing his wife standing behind him. "A useful person, no concern of yours as yet."

"Keeping secrets from me again?" Her purplish lips darkened.

"I tell you everything in time." Pl'Don smiled charmingly. "I learned a lot of interesting things today."

"For instance?" R'Oueu walked past him and gazed over the wall toward the expanse of Heptar's plains. The sunshine shimmered from her dress.

"I learned of matters concerning Hal K'Rin."

The name settled on R'Oueu like a cloud. She fixed her gaze on the horizon and checked her emotions. The distant mountains progressed into faded shades of gray. Often she stood at this parapet, staring at the string of extinct volcanoes and counting the losses of middle age. Without looking back at her husband, she said, "You know how I feel about the subject of K'Rin."

"I do," Pl'Don answered. "But I need your advice. You know K'Rin and the Rin Clan much better than I do. In fact you were very close to K'Rin until his father fell into disgrace."

"You need not remind me of unpleasant memories." R'Oueu turned from the wall.

Pl'Don plucked a floribundant sprig of jasmine and offered it to R'Oueu. She accepted. Pl'Don purred, "I trust your counsel better than any other in Heptar."

"Thank you." She was not mollified. But she offered him a smile that guarded her privacy without rebuffing Pl'Don's inquiring gaze—a mixture of condescension and kindness. "What advice do you need from me?"

Pl'Don led her to a seat in some shade. "K'Rin has always tried to worm his way back onto the council with fear-mongering and intrigue. I believe he would start a war to improve his standing with the council. In fact, against direct orders to the contrary, K'Rin has instigated an act of war with the Cor Ordinate. Therefore, I think I can prove treason."

Even the disciplined R'Oueu felt color coming to her neck, an impulse that she quickly reversed. She had during her life at Heptar become expert at fighting her emotions. "Have you spoken with K'Rin?"

"No, but the facts speak for themselves. He launched a covert operation against Cor to provoke a conflict. The whole Alliance is at stake because of that megalomaniac. Even if I give him the benefit of a thousand doubts, we still need to try, convict, and punish him to avoid a galactic war that might cost millions of innocent lives. I may need to hand him over to the Cor Ordinate—however unprecedented—to face their justice."

"If you have no choice, why do you want my opinion?" She opened her book but she could not make herself read.

Pl'Don laid his hand over the page to recapture his wife's attention. "We do have choices in how we go about it. How will the Rin Clan react if I arrest their headman?"

R'Oueu's eyes grew vacant as she looked at her husband. She answered as if by rote. "They'll obey their oaths till they die." She turned her eyes away to hide the pain they might reveal to one as astute as her husband.

Her heart recalled an old painful oath. A rash young K'Rin swore that he'd never marry except R'Oueu. She likewise swore herself to K'Rin. He refused his family's match for him, incurring their wrath for many years. Then R'Oueu spurned K'Rin when his father and clan fell into disgrace.

R'Oueu closed her eyes. She broke her adolescent

oath, and according to her family's wish, she married the fast-ascending Pl'Don. With a sad but gracious smile, K'Rin forgave her their private betrothal: *We were just stupid children, I more than you.* Then he said something that hurt them both: *I was foolish to exact an oath that I could not enforce.* She remembered his cynical laugh. Even so, K'Rin remained true to his oath. He never married.

"What does that matter to me?" Pl'Don's question brought her back to the matters at hand.

She looked down on her husband and said, "If a Rin joins the Fleet and takes the oath to obey, you can be sure they will obey their Fleet officers. If they join the Rin household guard, the Tenebrea, you can be sure they'll carry out that oath to the death. Which means, husband, if you arrest K'Rin, the Tenebrea will come after him. If you kill K'Rin, they will come after you." She dropped the sprig of jasmine onto the white pebble walkway.

"I thought so. The rest of the clans, how will they react?"

"That depends on your case against K'Rin. I don't think you can build a strong enough case with circumstantial evidence to convict K'Rin of treason. The Rin Clan is known foremost as defenders of Jod. He has many friends in the Fleet and even in the assembly. No offense, my husband, but K'Rin's opposition to you does not necessarily amount to treason. If you overreach to punish K'Rin, you may do more harm to yourself."

"You are right, of course." Pl'Don pressed his fingertips together, forming a small cage with his thick hands. "He enjoys the protection of a good reputation. Therefore, we need to demolish his reputation in order to keep the peace."

"Caution, my husband."

Pl'Don pressed the palms of his hands together. "Am I not always cautious? Today I learned something very interesting from one of K'Rin's associates. K'Rin is trafficking in illegal youth drugs, Quazel Protein."

R'Oueu's eyes widened. She clutched her small book to her chest. Her voice remained steady. "Don't believe everything you hear. K'Rin fought in the drug wars. He knows Quazel is deadly. He knows that trafficking is a capital offense: life imprisonment on Jod, execution elsewhere. How can you prove such an allegation?"

Pl'Don grinned. "We need only take a blood sample and he convicts himself. K'Rin has taken Quazel."

R'Oueu blanched slightly. "That would be suicide."

"Quite the contrary, my dear. According to my source, K'Rin's scientists have discovered an enzyme that controls the negative effects of Quazel. I always thought he aged gracefully, but I attributed his vitality to his lack of vices." Pl'Don chuckled. "Now we know better."

R'Oueu held her breath as she said, "K'Rin could outlive us by a hundred years or more."

Pl'Don looked at his old hands and his aging wife. He leaned over and whispered in her ear. "Or we, too, could live another hundred years if we likewise learn how to make the enzyme. Imagine, R'Oueu, what we could do if we had a second lifetime."

Andrea spent the loneliest hundred hours of her life on the trip to Yuseat. She was alone with her thoughts: painful memories of her former life, restlessness with her present, and anxiety about the future. She remained withdrawn and distracted.

H'Roo occupied himself studying the voluminous

files on the strange moon. A couple of times he tried to
share interesting tidbits with Andrea, but Andrea
refused distractions. She remained so distant that
H'Roo, despite his junior rank, assumed command of
the flight. Andrea hardly noticed and didn't care. In the
tight living arrangement, Andrea periodically collided
with Eric. Occasionally she felt the sharp pangs of sex-
ual attraction—memories colliding with the present.
Eric did, after all, look like the man with whom she'd
shared her bed for five years. Coarse reality threatened
to pervert her cherished memories.

Andrea feared that she was forgetting Steve and
Glennie. She berated herself. Was she now such a hard-
bitten survivor that she could forget Steve? Certainly
their love was enduring. In some ways, comparing
Steve and Eric refreshed her fading memory and for
that she was grudgingly grateful. Yet she felt a wave of
guilt wash over her when so many details about Steve
resurfaced only upon inspection of this stranger, his
physical double, a clone who lived in his place. *Remembering is hard work. Remembering is pain.*

Eric's presence polluted her daydreams about hap-
pier days, and for that she was angry. Eric's presence
kept her mind focused on the Harbor Massacre, the
day her happiness was wrenched from her soul. Eric
was a constant imposition on her private anguish, and
her animosity toward him grew by the hour. She was
pleased that Eric had let his beard grow into a thick
black stubble, because she disapproved of Steve when
he let his beard loose at sea. She wanted reasons to dis-
like Eric. Disliking him became a project to separate
Eric from Steve. But it was like trying to separate the
reflection from the mirror. *Am I going crazy?* she wondered.

Andrea catalogued the little differences. Eric had Steve's posture but not Steve's easy gait. Eric walked with birdlike alertness and balanced, not like a sailor, but like a kick-boxer. The eyes were different. Although the flesh that anatomically defines the shape of the eyes was alike, the eyes had a different glint. Steve's eyes, she thought, were a deeper blue—perhaps reflecting water and sky. Eric did not raise his left eyebrow to shrug off controversy or close his eyes for moments of contemplation. Likewise Eric's lips were dry and cold compared to Steve's. She had a thousand times moistened Steve's lips with her own. The clone's lips lacked the small imperfection, a swelling caused by a scar from a childhood diving accident. She wondered, *How important are these minor physical differences?*

Little differences comprise the greater part of reality. Andrea lost herself for a moment with the memory. She knew Steve's imperfections—his scars, habits, and foibles—and she ached as she remembered how much she loved to look at him, worry about him, and contemplate him. Feel him. These little differences were major because they screamed the truth that Steve was dead, and all the little stories about him, all their shared experiences, were memories already fading with the passage of time.

On one of Andrea's shifts, during the others' sleep cycle, she bumped into Eric in the captain's galley. He filled the doorframe with outstretched arms. He whispered, "I know why you look at me all the time."

Andrea muttered, "No you don't." She motioned for Eric to get out of her way.

Eric dropped his arms to open the passage, but he grinned and said, "You've been looking at me like I was your husband. I'd say yours is a hungry look."

The stark truth stopped Andrea in her tracks. She glared back but said nothing.

Eric relaxed. "I wondered what I'd do if I were in your place. Let's say I got so attached to Tara that I couldn't function without her. It happens. Let's suppose something awful happened to Tara: wanna know what I'd do? I'd find me another TRA model—wouldn't be the same of course, but damn close. I'd expect Tara to do the same thing if I got canceled." Eric's grin faded to a serious invitation. "Think about it."

Andrea brushed by him and said, "Just stay away from me."

At the preprogrammed time, the *Benwoi*'s main engines came to life. The bridge filled with bright light, and sweet air replaced the blend of stale odors. After a series of system's checks, and some last-minute calculations from the navigation computer, the *Benwoi* slowed to kinetic speed, the forward screens showed the familiar black of space, and they cruised toward the Thule system.

Andrea took her seat next to H'Roo, who occupied the captain's chair. Tara sat at the system's console. Eric took a crew seat behind.

The *Benwoi* approached the Yuseat Sigma moon, flying over the major landmass covered by one black cloud. Tara announced, "I locked coordinates into the auto-land sequence."

H'Roo hailed the Yuseat Laboratory, then turned to Andrea saying, "They won't answer." He ordered Tara, "Engage auto-landing."

The *Benwoi* dipped forward and began a rapid descent. In the high atmosphere the sky was a crystal blue, contrasted by the slate-colored table of murky clouds below. They slipped into the clouds and lost visibility.

"Full sensor array. Infrared to screens." H'Roo reached over to execute his own command and found his hand colliding with Tara's. She simply withdrew her hand and watched to make sure H'Roo calibrated the sensors correctly to accommodate Yuseat's strong magnetic field. From her vantage, Andrea wondered if H'Roo would ever appreciate Tara's competence.

The forward screen showed a dull image of terrain in shades ranging from yellow to black. A couple of thermal vents glowed white. A large flat indigo surface conformed to the shape of the cold lake. The screen overlaid maps showing lines of elevation that helped interpret the moon's surface. The map showed an orange dot at the lab's coordinates.

The Yuseat Lab did not afford the luxury of laser guidance. In fact, the lab had thick shields to hide even the faintest electromagnetic pulse. The *Benwoi*'s infrared sensors compared terrain with its banks and guided them to the surface using the old method of triangulation from key terrain features. The computer deftly adjusted the map overlay to infrared image. The orange dot grew into a line drawing of the lab plus a square landing apron, until it filled the screen.

The *Benwoi* slowed and dipped below the heavy cloud cover into a sliver of clear air. H'Roo toggled the screen to visual and steered closer to the low black ceiling. The ground was likewise black, hard, and glistening wet, with odd patches of colors muted by the poor light. Andrea suddenly felt claustrophobic. She unbuckled herself and walked to a porthole, grabbing a metal eyelet to steady herself, as she watched the scene below.

They flew over a section of the lake that looked like a pool of crude oil. On a spit of black land, she saw white cones of light intersecting on the landing pad. Andrea saw a windowless bunker overgrown with mounds of fleshy fungi. The bunker and its immediate environs pulsated and glowed with a pale-green phosphorescent light.

They descended vertically. Andrea's field of vision through the porthole was momentarily restricted to gazing at the murky air about the laboratory and shards of reflected light. H'Roo read the altimeter, "Ten meters . . . five . . . three . . ." They felt a slight jolt, and H'Roo announced, "Weight on gear."

Andrea stood on her toes to look down through the porthole onto the illuminated landing pad. "What are those guys doing?" She saw a team of men in glistening, puffy plastic surface suits. Their suits glowed a pale green that waxed and waned as they expended effort or rested. The exertion was evident in the heavy breathing, their clear facemasks fogged about their nostrils as they exhaled. One man cut away slides of the thick pulsating slime mold with a ruby laser, while the other squeegeed the pulpy mass off the walkway.

H'Roo answered matter-of-factly. "They're clearing the walkway. Slime molds cover everything—very slippery stuff if you don't have the right shoes. The Yuseat Laboratory is remarkably low-tech in some ways."

"Why do their suits glow?" Andrea asked.

H'Roo quoted from his research. "They dope the suit material with phosphorescence. Some of the more toxic fungi glow to ward off the predatory slime molds." H'Roo pointed to the glowing mounds clinging to the lab and said, "Also, they cultivate phosphorescent molds around the lab to ward off predators."

Andrea remembered. "Slime cats." *Amusing. Molds on the prowl.* In a matter of minutes, a Jod corpsman entered the bridge. He wore a plastic suit that hung a bit limp about his shoulders. His detached headpiece hung over his back. His face glistened—not from sweat, but from the moisture of his own breath. The corpsman had high cheekbones, exaggerated jaw, and deep temples. He had quick eyes, and yellow teeth. "Welcome to Yuseat. I'm Sep Fal'Dar, senior technician at the lab."

Some of the Yuseat air followed the corpsman into the *Benwoi,* and with it a nauseating cocktail of odors. Andrea backpedaled as the corpsman approached. Tara held her hand over her mouth to suppress the gag reflex. Fal'Dar noticed their discomfort and dispassionately told them, "You get used to the smell."

"I doubt that." Tara winced.

"Your olfactory sense adjusts in a day or two." Fal'Dar showed no sympathy.

Andrea wondered if she really wanted to get used to the stink.

Fal'Dar pulled a small cylinder from a clear plastic pouch. "We're ready to take you inside as soon as you've all had an antihistamine injection." He turned to Andrea and noticed her uniform and rank. "I heard the rumor we had a Terran female in the Tenebrea. I didn't believe it."

"Mat Flores." Andrea introduced herself formally.

Fal'Dar seemed completely at ease with the pair of Tenebrea officers. They were just his latest pair of wards in this hostile environment. "Okay, Mat Flores, I must adjust the dosage for a human female—I guessed seventy to seventy-five kilos, but now that I look at you and . . ."

Andrea bristled and held up her hand. "Don't bother to guess—sixty-two kilos."

"I thought so." The corpsman twisted a dial on the hypo, then pressed it against Andrea's skin on the neck muscle below her ear. "I'm sorry we don't have enough suits to go around. We don't get many visitors, but the antihistamine ought to hold you for a couple minutes' exposure."

The Jod turned to Tara and measured her with a careful look. Tara snipped, "I'll take the same dose, thank you."

He injected Tara, then adjusted his hypo again, injecting Eric, then H'Roo.

H'Roo volunteered, "We have face shields."

"Please don't use them here. You'll be cleaning them for days. Most Yuseat fungi grow on plastics. Even if you kill 'em, the smell hangs on for a long time. We use plastics doped with anti-fungal chemicals. So, let's not foul your gear. I'm going to have to send in a crew to sterilize your ship as it is."

Tara, still sickened from the odor, echoed the sentiment. "I concur."

The corpsman finished inoculating the small crew of the *Benwoi*. Then he beckoned them to the door. "We'll walk quickly into the decontamination chamber. Try not to breathe deeply."

Andrea grunted, "No problem."

"The walkway is slippery as fish guts, so don't run. Once inside, we'll figure out how to bunk you. We don't have much living space. I was told to put the clone female in the same room with the clone male." Fal'Dar pointed to Tara and Eric. "You two are the clones, right?"

Eric and Tara nodded.

Fal'Dar pulled his headgear over his face, patting down the seals. Immediately the skin of the suit began to puff. His voice sounded hollow through the plastic faceplate. "When we get you inside, we'll need to decontaminate your clothes. Then, my staff will show you around the lab. Later, you'll meet Dr. Carai after he finishes his nap." He finished with his last instruction: "You four go straight to the lab entrance. I'll seal the *Benwoi*'s hatch. Don't run. The ground is slippery as old Putu cheese."

chapter 7

Andrea and H'Roo quickly traversed the gauntlet of fungi to the safety of the lab entrance, never looking back. Andrea found a faucet and sink and began splashing water in her burning eyes. H'Roo seemed less affected.

Tara slipped and sprawled into the slime mold. Eric hauled her to her feet and dragged her toward the lab, cursing her for slowing him down. Overwhelmed by the spores, their eyes flooded with copious tears and they groped their way toward the light. Tara doubled over to vomit. Eric continued to curse her as he held her up by her belt. Eric slipped and fell over Tara and he, too, began to retch.

Finally, Fal'Dar corralled the two sick clones into the lab entrance. He called out, "Ti'Maj! Bir-Tod! Disinfect these two. Zu'Pah, take H'Roo Parh to his quarters."

Andrea could barely see the drama swimming before her burning eyes. She blinked to occasionally image the surroundings: blurred shadows of persons, stainless steel, and white enamel. Splashing handfuls of water in her eyes, she asked, "Are they going to be all right?"

Fal'Dar replied, "The clones got too much exposure, but they will recover. Apparently, you humans need a bigger dose of antihistamine." He went to the medicine locker.

Eric and Tara were covered with gray slime. Two Jod technicians in suits unceremoniously stripped Tara and Eric of their clothes. Eric resisted when they pulled off his tunic, but to no avail. The Jod manhandled the naked clones into a hot shower. Eric and Tara shut their eyes tight against the stinging irritation of the spores. They were completely docile to the touch of gloved hands that sponged them with soapy water and disinfectant. Tara wheezed. Her bronchial passages had swollen shut. "Can't breathe!" she gasped. Tara began to struggle.

"Stay calm!" The Jod admonished her.

Andrea stepped forward, groping her way past the Jod to comfort Tara. Although blinded by her own tears, Andrea grabbed Tara firmly, pinning Tara's arms to her side. "I'm here. Don't be afraid."

Tara opened her raw, red eyes. She saw Andrea's flooded eyes squinting back, mucus streaming from her nose. She let her head slump into Andrea's chest. Andrea rested her chin on Tara's wet hair. Both unable to see, they comforted each other with touch. Fal'Dar stepped into the shower with a second autoinjector. He administered a blend of antihistamine, sedative, and bronchial dilator to the three humans. Tara slumped quickly. Andrea helped drag Tara into the room where the Jod wrapped her in towels and laid her on the floor. One of the curious Jod touched Tara's gullwing tattoo, and Andrea slapped his hand away. Andrea sat next to Tara with her back to the wall. Soon, she fell asleep. The Jod left Eric sitting comatose in the warm shower.

Andrea woke in a bed with her head on a pillow. She was dressed in a clean cotton outfit, with a drawstring tied loosely at her waist. She was barefoot. Her uniform was missing, she assumed taken for cleaning. Her hair was still damp. Her tiny billet was smaller than a broom closet: a cot, folding table, and portable data console. She had a slight headache and chapped lips, but she could see and she could breathe. She had a new and profound respect for the fungi moon, Yuseat Sigma.

Late in the day, Andrea answered a knock at her door. Fal'Dar stood with an autoinjector in his hand. He asked, "Are you better? Your eyes are still very red. I gave the clones another dose."

Andrea pulled her hair back. "I'm okay, thank you."

"Good. Then I can introduce you to the staff. Follow me."

Fal'Dar turned and left. Wearing the gauzy pajamas, Andrea followed him through a warren of narrow passages leading past other small living quarters, a small kitchen, and finally into an open work area, where three Jod technicians sat at benches like three owls.

Fal'Dar introduced them from right to left. "Zu'Pah." Zu'Pah was a thin Jod with painfully deep eyes. He bowed. His neck was a bundle of sinews. "Ti'Maj." The middle Jod had the barest hint of a double chin to soften his otherwise angular features: square jaw and straight nose. "Bir-Tod." The third Jod had a round face and small ears.

"Gentlemen," Andrea acknowledged. She wondered who among these three had bathed her, dressed her, and put her to bed. Nothing in their faces gave a clue.

Fal'Dar tersely ended the introductions and led Andrea to Dr. Carai's office. He waved Andrea in, then followed. The room was a disorganized mess. The wall was festooned with long sheets of paper, scribbled with diagrams and formulae. Pushpins held photographs of microorganisms magnified thousands of times—each appeared like some hideously malformed and tormented creature. A tray of half-eaten hardtack and cheese sat precariously on an end table. In the midst of the chaos was one clear table with an ultraviolet light shining down upon a cluster of tiny bromeliads, each sprouting a flowering stalk of iridescent rainbow colors.

"Dr. Carai?" Fal'Dar reached high and knocked lightly on the door lintel. "We have a visitor to meet you."

A plush but dilapidated chair turned languidly. In the chair, a slump-shouldered Artrix carefully laid down a tissue sample and removed the magnifying glasses from his broad face. His fur was still matted where the glasses had pressed his face.

"Come in. Always interested in meeting a new species." Carai's voice was high-pitched and scratchy. His words ended in an annoying whistle intended for emphasis among his species, but distracting everywhere else.

Andrea stepped forward. Fal'Dar excused himself to attend to his work.

"The human Tenebrea, Mat Flores. Interesting." Dr. Carai looked at Andrea intently, but she was not in the least self-conscious, as she likewise studied the old

Artrix. He had soft brown eyes, silky fur with a warm honey hue, tinged with gray. He had a narrow concave chest, the picture of an asthmatic, although such was not the case. His spine hunched—the consequence of a sedentary life on a large moon with gravity greater than his homeworld. Nevertheless, he carried himself with the confidence of one possessed of physical stamina. He had the smugness of a man who had little to do all day but was always late.

Dr. Carai said, "I have spent the last fifty years studying Earth, but I never got to go there. Look!" Dr. Carai pointed to a bookshelf filled with old, tattered books. "I collect Earth literature. Also, I have recordings. You can explain some of the metaphors to me."

"If I can."

Carai bobbed his head. Small dewlaps jiggled beneath the Artrix's chin. He said confidently, "I've seen plenty of Jod, but you're my first human. I approve of your hair, little that you have, but some is better than none." He uttered a breathy snort. Through a drooping mustache he curled his lip into a disapproving smile.

Dr. Carai wore no clothes, but his fur covered his nakedness completely except for his left leg. It was bare and spindly, all tendons and stringy muscle below the knee, mottled pink and brown.

"Are you staring at my leg?" Dr. Carai accused.

Andrea averted her eyes. "I, uh . . . yes," she admitted.

Carai held out his leg and turned his ankle, taunting Andrea with his old wound. "A slime cat got me."

Andrea bent down to take a closer look. "A fungus did that?"

"Slime mold, actually—a cousin to fungus. Slime mold is a microorganism that straddles the animal and vegetable kingdoms," the old Artrix answered acerbically.

Andrea responded with an incredulous look. "Straddle?"

"You don't know much about our slime cats, do you?" Carai's upper lip curled into his thick mustache.

"Just a fact or two from the files." Andrea looked for a place to sit, but the only other chair in the office was piled high with moldy specimens in small plastic jars.

"Fascinating creatures. On my first trip as a research scientist to Yuseat, I learned about slime cats the hard way. In this case, reading is a reasonable substitute for experience, but"—Carai held out his leg for inspection—"experience leaves an indelible lesson, right?"

Andrea asked, "Just what exactly are slime cats?"

Carai settled back in his easy chair. The springs creaked as he rocked. "Earth has a similar species of slime mold, what you call dictyostelium discoideum. You probably had them in your garden and didn't know."

Andrea reflected back to the little cottage where she and Steve had lived. *I kept a small garden of tomatoes and peppers. Glendon used to play . . .*

The Artrix's high-pitched voice dragged her back into the conversation. He said, "The Yuseat slime cat is similar, just one thousand times larger with much stronger digestive secretions." Carai measured a space about a meter long with his hands. "They're faster than their Earth cousins as well."

"Faster? How do they move?" Andrea rested against a table.

"The slime cat spends part of its life as millions of individual myxoamoebae living in a colony. The colony mass looks like a thin spill of black oil. Each member of the colony feeds on the bacteria usually found on decaying plant life. However, the cats aren't particular. When they feed, you see what appears to be pulsating. Gases created by the digesting process collect into bubbles, then dissipate. When their food is gone, the members swarm together into little streams, and those little streams congeal. Your Earth discoideum congeals into a structure that looks like your garden slug, a *grex* to use the proper language. On Earth your grex is just one to three centimeters long."

Dr. Carai measured the size with his forefinger and thumb. "Then the millions of myxoamoebae behave like a multicellular creature, undulating in a manner to locomote, and by that cooperative undulation, the grex slithers in search of more food. When it finds something to eat, the slime cat quickly disperses itself into the oil slick, spreading itself thinly over the food source. An Earth grex is harmless, but a Yuseat slime cat can digest any form of long string polymer—your suit for instance. Slime cats much prefer simple carbons—they just love hair and skin." He pointed to his scars.

Andrea bent over to look at the scars that looked as if someone had boiled away the skin. Carai continued his lecture on slime cats saying, "Near the end of the life cycle, the feeding cat metamorphoses again, forming a mass like a lazy bubble covered with hairlike stalks and spores. In the spore stage, the cats are benign. In their grex-mode, the cat is the dominant species on Yuseat. The only thing that limits them is food supply, which you, by coming to Yuseat, have increased."

Andrea shook her head. "It's an ill wind that blows no good."

"Indeed!" Carai gave a high-pitched laugh that

ended with a wheeze. "Fortunately, the cats are slow, but they can surround you. To a slime cat you are just one fat bacterium. Your body radiates considerable heat and you exhale delicious carbon dioxide. Without precautionary measures, you can attract a pack of slime cats in a manner of minutes. The cat spreads itself over you like a thick molasses. Then they digest you. You can't fight them: they're millions of single-celled creatures. I'd rather face an animal with claws and fangs."

"Has anybody at the lab—besides you—been injured by a slime cat?"

"No." Carai chewed the edge of his mustache.

"So your precautions work well."

Dr. Carai nodded. "We avoid the cats, and we try to make the cats avoid us.

Andrea observed, "I saw the phosphorescent work suits."

Carai raised an eyebrow and smiled through the thin mustache that hung over his upper lip. "Several fungi on Yuseat are rich with nitric oxide, toxic to the slime cat. These toxic fungi advertise by their phosphorescence. Other fungi mimic. Many of the copycats are not poisonous, delectable, in fact. We simply learn from nature and apply her defenses. The phosphorescent suits keep slime cats at bay. As an added precaution, we lace the air in the lab and in our suits with fatty acids to discourage all kinds of fungi. We adapt. After all, most of our work on Yuseat is out there."

Carai pointed a bony finger toward the lab's main door. "I hope you'll join us on one of our excursions into hell's basement where we harvest the Quazel enzyme." Again his laugh faded to a bothersome wheeze.

Andrea's eyes still itched. But her curiosity prodded her. "Sure. I'll go."

K'Rin looked up the black obsidian cliffs to the high fortress of Heptar. He wore civilian attire as ordered: a plain tunic and straight-legged pants. Compared to most Jod fashion, his family garb was somber: midnight blue with a thin silver border about the sleeves and neck with the Rin Triskelion embroidered on his chest. He turned to Kip who stood by the open door to the turbo-lift. K'Rin said, "My orders are to go in without staff or guard. I want you to stay onboard the shuttle and remain in communication with the *Tyker*."

"I wish I could go with you. I've always dreamed of seeing the inside." Kip's eyes were as wide as a child's.

K'Rin remembered his first visit into the Heptar Fortress with his father. He remembered gawking at the epicenter of Jod wealth and culture—all the things a young boy mustn't touch. He cleared his throat, and said, "After a week in that gilded cage you'd beg for a transfer to a ship." With that, K'Rin, gave his credentials to a uniformed guard, who without comment ushered K'Rin into the turbo-lift for the swift ride to the top of the butte.

At the top, K'Rin passed through another set of security scans before the guards released K'Rin into the fortress. He walked up the forty-four steps of rose marble into the inner palace of Heptar—the ancient seat of Jod power. The palace was, in fact, a maze of buildings interconnected with malls and gardens.

K'Rin had not been inside the Heptar Fortress since the year the council ostracized his father, not since they disenfranchised the Rin Clan. He could count the number of times he'd been inside the palace on one hand.

He had always thought Heptar was more mausoleum than palace.

As he passed familiar sites, K'Rin remembered his father. The old Rin's presence seemed palpable here, and K'Rin felt slightly unnerved, whereas he'd expected to be bolstered. His father, the old Rin, jealously separated the rhythms of his family life from the rhythms of the council, because as he admitted late in life, he despised his rapacious colleagues. He warned the young K'Rin: Inside the family, honor is spirit; inside the council, honor is perception. K'Rin always thought his father too cryptic—abstract. Now, he understood completely.

He walked into the grand mall that served as a covered courtyard. Built in the classical style centuries before the devastating Clan Wars, the walls tapered into soaring arches sixty feet overhead. At the peak of the intersecting arches, the heavy keystones protruded back into the empty space: brightly polished, milky, and translucent. These reverse spires were hollow bright lamps that filled the hall with soft light that reflected from the polished walls. With so many sources of overhead light, shadows blurred. By the large columns, guards stood in their stiff dusky uniforms, exuding anguished—and to K'Rin's mind exaggerated—ceremony. Other pedestrians walked in pairs or small groups through the mall: officials and family members. The multitude of conversations, like the shadows, blurred into a soft din.

The mall abruptly ended at a corridor closed by a floor-to-ceiling grill of brilliant platinum veneer upon tons of steel. It looked like an ornamental screen of filigree from a distance, but the sheer mass quickly convinced otherwise. The double doors, big enough to

accommodate fifty Jod standing abreast, were shut, and
it took a keen eye to find the sliver gap between door
and frame. K'Rin had been fascinated by these doors
when he was a boy visiting the council chambers for
the first time. The doors had no hinges; rather, they
operated by magnetism—levitated such that a child
might push them open. Likewise the giant doors locked
as the magnet pulled them into the doorframe. Mostly
a curiosity, the large doors rarely opened. Instead, by
the wall, a small gate with conventional hinge and
deadbolt opened. K'Rin approached the smaller
entrance.

A guard stepped forward to block his path. "This
area is restricted."

K'Rin handed the ornately uniformed guard his identification. The guard merely glanced at the document.
He was not in the least intimidated by an admiral who
bore the noble rank of Hal. Tall and aristocratic, with
impeccable manners, the guard demonstrated the odd
mix of command presence and subservience. K'Rin
thought, *An excellent doorman but a poor soldier.* The
guard asked, "What is your business?"

K'Rin answered, "I am answering a summons from
the council."

Without comment, the guard held a small retinal
scanner to K'Rin's face. "Focus on the blue dot, sir."

K'Rin obeyed, pressing his chin and forehead
against the device. The guard examined a small readout
on the back of the scanner. "Yes, sir, I see that you have
an appointment. I will take you to the west conference
room. Please, come in."

K'Rin stepped through the door into the inner sanc-
tum, and the guard followed, ducking his head to clear
the lintel. The young aristocrat motioned one of his

cohorts to mind the door while he led K'Rin deeper into the hall. Then he surprised K'Rin by saying, "I'm honored to meet you."

"Why? Are we kin?" K'Rin asked rhetorically. No Rin was allowed within Heptar's walls.

Unflustered, the guard replied, "No, sir. I'm aware of your reputation."

K'Rin look sideways at the young man, whose face betrayed no hint of emotion. "Reputation," K'Rin spoke as to an aide, "either exaggerates or understates." Looking up into the young aristocrat's eyes he added, "Always discount reputation—especially your own."

The young guard nodded at the offhanded rebuke. He stopped at a door, opening it for K'Rin, saying, "I'll leave you now."

K'Rin stepped into the room to find seven of the venerable council members seated. They fixed their eyes on K'Rin: silent accusatory looks. K'Rin observed various shades of tension about their necks fading rapidly as he entered the room. Lips were pursed. Clearly, they had instructions not to talk to K'Rin or talk in front of him before the official start of the meeting.

At the end of the crystal table, Pl'Don sat in complete serenity—a stark contrast to the other six. K'Rin remembered a warning his father gave him: *Pl'Don casually starts a brawl, stays out of it, then provides a premeditated remedy that leaves both factions beholden to him. He has his own peculiar genius.*

The long pause was uncomfortable for everyone in the room. The councilors looked as if they had seen a ghost. Indeed K'Rin looked just like his father, when the old Rin was in his prime. Just like his father, he wore dark clothes reminiscent of the uniform of the Rin household guard, the Tenebrea.

K'Rin, who aged slowly—unnaturally so—was almost alarmed to see the frail geriatrics surrounding the table. Many were protégés of his father, these soulless bastards who cast off the venerable Rin in favor of Pl'Don. They looked like bags of bones draped in gaudy silks, their gem-studded necklaces weighed them down, their rings, trapped between swollen knuckles, slipped loose upon their bony fingers. Better to look alive in black cotton than past dead in silk brocade.

Pl'Don broke the awkward silence. "Please sit down, Hal K'Rin."

"I'll stand, thank you." K'Rin's rebuff caused the other six heads to wag.

"Suit yourself." Pl'Don wasted no time getting to the subject of the meeting. "K'Rin, as an admiral, you serve at the pleasure of the council, and today we meet to determine your fitness to serve." He paused to see how his announcement played with K'Rin.

K'Rin stood impassively and listened. He often suspected that Pl'Don allowed his promotion to admiral to get him out of the protective arms of the Fleet.

Pl'Don spoke without consulting notes. "Admiral, two years ago, you sent a series of reports arguing that the Cor Ordinate presented an imminent threat to the Alliance in general and the Jod Empire in particular. Those dire predictions have thus far failed to materialize. Please remind us what you based those early warnings on—what verifiable information?"

K'Rin answered, "I interviewed refugees from the Cor system."

"Clones?"

"Mostly clones plus a few disaffected Cor civilians."

Pl'Don furled his brow and commented, "A rather

disreputable source on which to jeopardize galactic peace, don't you think?"

K'Rin looked at Pl'Don, ignoring the councilors present. "In addition, we monitored Cor shipping into the Chelle system. We watched the Chelle transfer military technology to the Cor. We have some corroborating reports from other Chelle sources."

"The Chelle?" A councilman interrupted. "I wouldn't trust them to give us the right time of day. How much did you have to spend for their fallacious information?"

K'Rin ignored the question. He spoke directly to Pl'Don. "We also noted a geometric rise in incidents involving Cor Ordinate Hunter teams. They made bold incursions into Alliance space to cancel renegade clones. I think they had a secondary mission of collecting intelligence against us. In any case, their activity indicates a certain boldness. They no longer think the balance of power inevitably belongs to Jod. Or the Alliance."

"You spoke with a Hunter?" Pl'Don probed.

"No. We have never taken a Hunter alive."

"You've never captured one of their ships for exploitation, either."

"Correct. The Ordinate have excellent countermeasures, including some technologies that we don't fully understand."

"So to put this in layman's terms, you have a hunch that the Cor Ordinate poses a threat." The spindly chorus of councilors nodded derisively.

"Sir, I'm not a layman, and I do not act on hunches."

"Nevertheless, your estimate is heavy with speculation. If true, where is this Cor threat now? Surely we ought to see more evidence if the threat is as great as you claim—or maybe you exaggerate. Many of us think you want the Cor threat to be true, because the Rin Clan and the Fleet might regain some of the prominence eroded by our policy of mutual reliance to maintain the peace."

"If it pleases the council, I have more evidence."

Pl'Don interrupted. "I'm sure you do. In fact, I know you do. Let me provide the big picture for my colleagues here; then perhaps you can fill in the details." Pl'Don looked left and right at his colleagues at the table. Then he pointed an accusing finger at K'Rin. "One of your allies in the Fleet allowed you to have operational control of a heavy cruiser, that just happened to intercept a pair of Cor Ordinate military vessels pursuing an Ordinate civilian craft—"

"An armed merchant." K'Rin corrected the record.

"Thank you. Our Jod cruiser destroyed one of the pursuing Ordinate vessels. The other fled. The civilian—pardon me—armed merchant is, I presume, in your custody."

"Yes. I have the *Benwoi.*"

Pl'Don looked around the table to gauge the effect of K'Rin's admission. "Since then, the Cor Ordinate contacted the council by means of the Chelle ambassador. They claim that an agent provocateur started a clone insurrection that involved a large terrorist attack in their capital city. They presume that because some of the responsible parties escaped to Jod, coincidentally rescued by a Jod cruiser, we are responsible for this outrage. Am I accurate thus far?"

K'Rin looked down the table. All eyes shifted from Pl'Don to him. "I ran a surveillance operation against the Cor. The survival of Jod is at stake."

"You disobeyed a direct order from this council." An old councilor grunted, "You ought to be garroted."

K'Rin paused to stare the councilor down, inviting him with a look to step down from the dais to carry out his threat. Across the long table, the silence was deafening, albeit fainthearted concurrence. K'Rin suddenly felt acutely mortal.

Pl'Don raised a hand. "None of that talk here. Let's ascertain the facts, if we can. Hal K'Rin, continue."

K'Rin stood with his hands clutched behind his back to prevent himself from gesticulating. "I recruited a Terran female into my household guard and trained her for a special mission. I intended to provide us plausible denial in the event of her capture. She infiltrated Cor by way of the port city of Clemnos. She had orders to bring back evidence proving or disproving reports of Cor capabilities. Multiple sources had informed me that Cor was about to bring on-line a new generation of clones: clones so physically and mentally acute yet spiritually dormant that they might become the perfect army. Manufactured as such, these clones would be as reliable and expendable as ammunition. I had to be sure. I wanted to present you proof of their capabilities and their intent. The Terran female found that proof."

K'Rin reached into his pocket and put a data cube on the table. "Watch this file at your leisure and you will see the clone army that we will eventually have to fight—indisputable evidence. During her mission, the Terran female discovered that the first crop of NewGen clones, as they're called, would hatch in months. Realizing that Jod's peril was imminent, she helped organized a small insurrection of the old-order clones to destroy that crop and buy us much-needed time. She also brought secondhand reports that Cor is at present manufacturing a fleet of military attack craft: J-Class, displacement less than thirty tons."

The nearest councilor passed the data cube down the table to Pl'Don. Pl'Don folded his hands on the table, thinking out loud. "J-Class? Long-range escorts, aren't they? Close support and defensive by nature. They can't threaten us."

K'Rin shook his head. "A swarm of forty J-Class attack craft, aggressively piloted and armed with torpedoes, can overwhelm a dreadnought."

An octogenarian at the table huffed at that suggestion. "Preposterous!"

K'Rin bluntly repulsed the councilor's bluster. "I have served on a dreadnought and I have flown as a tactical pilot. You haven't. You civilians are the only ones who think weapons are invincible. Determined pilots and soldiers—not weapons—make the difference."

Pl'Don asked, "Assuming what you say is true, how much time do you estimate we have before Cor can manufacture their armies?"

"I can't say for sure. The growth cycle for a NewGen clone is a bit less than five years. If the Terran female wrecked Cor's only NewGen crop, she bought five years. However, our reports suggest that the Ordinate have other clone factories. We don't know if they converted their other factories to the NewGen technology. Six months or five years: if we do not stop the Cor soon, they will manufacture armies faster than we can mobilize."

Pl'Don pressed his hands together. "Hal K'Rin, you and I have a problem. The majority of the council believes you fabricated your first reports of Cor activity in a crass attempt to manufacture a crisis and thereby reclaim the Rin seat on the council. I don't know what to believe, but what I know is this: Cor believes Jod committed an act of war. You! You, Hal K'Rin, committed an act of war! If your assessment of their capabilities is true, I believe we must prepare for the worst."

K'Rin sloughed the assault on his intentions. "Gentlemen, Jod must mobilize, regardless of whether you retain my services or not. The Fleet must prepare for a very different kind of war."

Pl'Don raised an accusing finger. "You are very sly, K'Rin. You alone know the true threat, if it exists. You have used subterfuge to force our hand. Now, I have two choices: I can exile you and deal with the Cor without your resources, or I can incorporate you into the council. As a member of the council with a military background, you would become the civilian responsible for the unilateral mobilization of Jod forces, and you alone would bear the responsibility for the worst policy disaster in a millennium—the likely dissolution of the Alliance. You may outdo your father yet."

K'Rin thought, *Kip called this one precisely. I must congratulate him.* He said, "I'll take that risk."

"How convenient for us," Pl'Don said sarcastically, then raised his hand to forestall the outrage percolating around the table. "We have another problem, Hal K'Rin. You've tied us together by this disaster. I'll tell you outright: I resent it, but tied together we are. At present, I don't trust you, and you don't trust me. So"— Pl'Don showed his hands palms outward, an ancient sign of goodwill—"we must give each other some assurances backed with deeds, concessions as it were."

K'Rin stood silent, waiting for the conditions. He was unprepared for Pl'Don's frankness. In an odd way, he admired his adversary's realistic appraisal of their relationship, even if Pl'Don failed to grasp the extent of the Cor threat.

Pl'Don said, "For my part, I've decided to restore the Rin seat and invite you into the council. I want you close where I can keep an eye on you, K'Rin. I have already arranged the ceremony to take place in forty days. I asked your old friend in the assembly, Hal B'Yuon, to sponsor the proclamation and make the arrangements. I understand you two have kept in contact these many years."

K'Rin had always thought that he and B'Yuon had successfully hid their correspondence. At some point, B'Yuon must have compromised himself. Yet B'Yuon flourished in the assembly. K'Rin wrestled with this juxtaposed good and bad news. He watched the other six members on the executive council. They accepted Pl'Don's decision without the slightest emotion. *This meeting has been rehearsed.*

Pl'Don continued, "You will oversee the mobilization of the Fleet. I will control you with my budget and with council resolutions. If there is a war with Cor, I want your solemn promise before these councilors here that when we achieve an armistice, you will retire from the council, from the Fleet, and you will abdicate as headman of your clan. I will not give up my seat as First Among Equals to a war hero who manufactured his own war."

K'Rin flared, then calming himself said, "I resent your implication. I'll retire from the council and Fleet, but I do not throw away my birthright. I am the headman of the Rin Clan as long as I live."

Pl'Don looked up and down the table at the stony faces and said, "I suppose that's reasonable." He turned back to K'Rin and said, "Furthermore, I have arranged to forestall this armed conflict by ceding to several Ordinate demands. You will make sure that we meet their demands. First, you will return their ship, the *Benwoi,* by way of the Chelle. Also, you will return the clone female that escaped on the *Benwoi.* Finally, you will extradite the Terran female to Cor where she will stand trial for terrorism. In addition, we are negotiating with the Chelle to arrange a cash settlement, reparations for the damage at Sarhn. You ought to be able to verify the Ordinate's claim for damage based on reports from your Terran female."

"I am still studying the Cor ship and interrogating the clone." K'Rin studied Pl'Don trying to detect any sign of displeasure. He had expected more animosity. "I need more time. We can learn much about Cor's command and control, their technology, their capabilities, and their weaknesses. We must take advantage of this opportunity."

Pl'Don's face remained inscrutable. K'Rin would have preferred malice and suspicion. Pl'Don ordered, "Be quick about it. I'll placate the Cor as best I can. But in the end, I need to give them what they ask to buy time. Time is what you value most, am I correct?"

K'Rin answered quickly, fearing Pl'Don might read the hesitation in his mind. "Time is the essence."

"Good. We understand each other. Everything and everyone else is expendable. By the way, who else outside your immediate staff knows about your misadventure on Cor?"

K'Rin answered, "The information that makes up the whole picture is compartmented. Many on my staff know their piece. I and a half dozen others know the complete situation."

"For now, let's keep it that way."

"I must inform the Fleet as soon as possible."

Pl'Don rose to his feet and slammed his open hand

on the table, jarring the old councilors into startled good posture. Raising his voice, Pl'Don said, "You will do no such thing! The Chelle and the Ordinate are watching us for signs of mobilization even now. I can buy time through diplomatic maneuvers, but I won't have your ham-fisted reactions undoing our careful work. You will not consult with anyone in the Fleet until we have installed you in the council and given you such authority. If you are going to become the civilian head of the armed forces, then you'd better learn to act like it."

Pl'Don sat down again to end the outburst that flustered the other councilors. Calming his voice from its high pitch, Pl'Don said, "War and diplomacy are two sides of the same coin. If we are going to mobilize, exhaust our treasury, and possibly ruin our carefully crafted diplomatic ties, then we will do so with some measure of deliberateness and utmost sobriety. Even your father understood that much."

K'Rin glowered at the backhanded comment about his father, saying, "My father understood more than you realize."

"Time will tell." Pl'Don looked down on K'Rin with a tight smile. "Remember, you serve at the pleasure of this council. Your authority emanates from us. Your usefulness to Jod is directly proportional to your ability—and your willingness—to carry out your lawful orders. As a cautionary word, let me remind you that any action contrary to our wishes at this point we'll consider tantamount to an attempted military coup."

"I understand." K'Rin knew that Pl'Don's cautionary word was as good as another's threat.

chapter 8

As K'Rin left the council chambers, he was greeted by an overfed, grinning, ebullient Jod. He wore rich robes with a gold sunburst covering his chest. His neck was festooned with heavy gold braid. From his left ear, a large ruby sparkled. K'Rin looked into the eyes set deep into a puffy face and a grin exaggerated by heavy jowls. Then K'Rin recognized his childhood friend, who was once the better athlete by virtue of height, speed, and agility.

"B'Yuon?"

"K'Rin!" B'Yuon stood back to look at his old friend, head to toe. "You haven't changed a bit in twenty years!"

"Nor you." K'Rin returned the compliment automatically if not awkwardly.

B'Yuon patted himself on the chest. "I've gotten fat and old. You are kind to turn a blind eye."

"And rich." K'Rin noticed that the broad sash draped over B'Youn's shoulder was in fact a fine mesh of platinum.

"I am overjoyed to see you again. We'll dine in my

quarters." B'Yuon embraced K'Rin. We have so much to talk about. Pl'Don has finally seen how much we need you on the council."

K'Rin withdrew. "He thinks I can be useful."

"Of course. What do we care what his motives are? We're back together again. Soon it will be old times. I knew you'd eventually come back. Moreover, dear friend, I get to manage the ceremony!" B'Yuon spread his thick arms. "We are going to have a show that Heptar will never forget! We will reinstate the Rin seat with all the pomp and ceremony the occasion deserves."

"I'd rather keep a low profile."

"Nonsense!" B'Yuon flourished. "They made a spectacle of your clan when they exiled your father. We will have a greater spectacle exonerating him. Your friends on the assembly have been kept down for a generation. We want to share this moment with you and your father's ghost." He lowered his voice to a dramatic whisper. "For twenty years I hid your father's chair in my home. We are having your family crest re-enameled—at my expense. I can't wait to see Pl'Don's jaw drop when he sees your father's chair on the dais."

K'Rin smiled carefully. "We mustn't antagonize Pl'Don. Not yet."

"I am overjoyed!" B'Yuon repeated himself in a forced whisper. He led K'Rin down the hall as he expounded on his plans for the ceremony. "Picture this: your household guard, the Tenebrea, leads you into the Assembly Hall. Do they still have those drab black uniforms?"

"Yes." K'Rin had to slow his pace to accommodate his corpulent friend.

"Hmmm. Well, sometimes less is more." B'Yuon unconsciously tugged at the gold braid around his neck. "Through the great gate, they march in formation into the Assembly Hall. Then, I have the honor of reading the proclamation reinstating the Rin seat."

Rapt in the drama of his own scene, B'Yuon painted a grand mural with his hands. "The Tenebrea presents you to the executive council to fill the Rin seat. Then you, representing the Clan Rin, take the oath. The entire assembly observes from the gallery above." B'Yuon painted a wide arch above his head with his fleshy hand.

"For this special day they proxy their votes to your Tenebrea, who have the unparalleled honor of voting you onto the executive council." B'Yuon patted himself on the chest. "That was my idea, and I consider it a good omen that nobody in the assembly refused."

"I am touched by the symbolism."

"Indeed. Your Tenebrea shall remember that day to their children and grandchildren. Very few Jod have ever seen the Assembly Hall, let alone cast a vote." B'Yuon ended, saying, "I cannot tell you how happy I am for you."

K'Rin stopped and faced his friend. "You must know that I agreed to resign when the Ordinate threat is finished."

"That means nothing!" B'Yuon shirked the idea of resignation. "After you save Jod from a disastrous war, I think we can find enough votes in the assembly to reject your resignation. In fact," and B'Yuon lowered his voice to a whisper, "I'm sure that in due course you can have your father's seat as First Among Equals. Everyone on Jod will know that you earned it."

*   *   *

H'Roo, Tara, and Eric continued to exploit the contents of technology and files of the Cor merchant ship *Benwoi*. To ease their daily commutes from the bunker to the ship, they fabricated a sterile tunnel of clear plastic. H'Roo had the unsavory job of putting on a work suit and spraying the *Benwoi* with fungicides. Fal'Dar and his three compatriots stayed busy working in the lab "milking bacteria," a process by which they extracted the Quazel enzyme from the nodules of crown gall collected from the Papuyoosa cedars. Dr. Carai divided his work between his disheveled office and the lab. He continued his life's work, a two-prong attack to solve the problem of manufacturing Quazel enzyme. Genetic engineering was the long-term solution, but at present, he worked on developing a synthetic enzyme.

Andrea excused herself from working on the *Benwoi*. She needed a break from Eric. H'Roo concurred. She was disinclined to help the Yuseat staff with their tedious lab work. So she spent her days in the minuscule Yuseat gym, and she availed herself of Dr. Carai's library where she listened to his collection of recordings—all opera.

Returning one of Dr. Carai's recordings, Andrea found him in the lab proper, peering into an electron microscope. Periodically, he stopped, wrote a note on a pad of paper, and rubbed his eyes. He noticed her in the background and asked, "What did you listen to, today?"

Andrea handed him the chip. "I can't speak Italian."

Dr. Carai squinted to look at the title. "My favorite: *L'albalba sepa'ra dalla luce l'ombra*, performed by the twenty-first-century maestro Antonio Salvatore Giuliano. I am very jealous of the human voice. We Artrix have an unerring sense of hearing, but we lack voices." Carai mocked his own high-pitched voice. "Nevertheless, my mother used to say that I have a nice voice."

"Your voice was music to her ears, I promise you." Andrea pursued Carai's interest to amuse her host. "I thought the Artrix had a reputation for music."

"For music, but not for song. We Artrix can make beautiful melodies with machines, but we cannot get much of a song from our voices. Consequently, we do not encumber our music with language. I always thought the two—music and words—were dipolar, but then I chanced upon Giuliano's songs, and I knew that words and music were meant for each other. Like male and female, song is organic."

Andrea sat on the stainless steel stool by the lab table. "What are you doing now?"

Dr. Carai set his notes aside, welcoming this interruption in his work. "What I always do. I'm trying to make a synthetic Quazel enzyme. You would think that with a molecular replicator we'd have no problem, but the replicator just gives us the blueprint. Nature is very stingy with her secrets. I suppose if I can figure out the secret of making a synthetic, I might be able to get off this rancid hell." Carai shifted his weight in his chair and asked, "How do you like our secluded little part of the universe?"

Andrea detected the bitter resignation underlying Carai's words. She looked at the old Artrix, his eyes framed by soft fur with a slightly lighter hue. The short fur hid the wrinkles and other imperfections of aging skin, giving the face a youthful appearance. But his dark eyes showed age and frustration. She said, "I'm looking forward to moving on. No offense."

"I say good for you. You get to leave in a few months. I'm stuck here." Carai looked around his tiny domain. "I'm stuck here, because Yuseat is the only place with just the right complex of stygian life that produces the Quazel enzyme in nature. If ever I make a synthetic."

"I thought you invented the Quazel enzyme." Andrea glanced at the paper notes strewn over the table. The handwriting was small and precise, the margins exact.

"No, some bacteria invented it. I just found it. The humbling aspect of being a biologist is that there's always some seemingly insignificant one-celled creature that can do things you can't." He reached down and scratched the old wounds on his leg.

"K'Rin and Feld Jo'Orom didn't tell us much about the enzyme." Andrea tapped her finger on the small bumps under her arm. "They give us enzyme implants to offset the other stuff."

"Stuff?" Carai sniffed. "Quazel-P is a replicating protein, a prion. It commandeers cells to create more of itself."

"Like a virus?"

"Worse in terms of pathology. A virus has genetic material that we can attack. Prions do not."

She asked, "Then how do they replicate?"

Carai raised an eyebrow and lowered his voice and measured his words to disgorge an uncomfortable secret. "We don't really know. I think that the healthy cell recognizes that the prion is a much tougher material. The cell unwittingly directs itself to copy the tougher material to rebuild itself—a Darwinian adaptation at the cellular level."

"Some adaptation," Andrea mused. "Quazel kills."

"Cells are"—Carai struggled for an analogy—"are shortsighted. They don't figure out the downside until it's too late. Look here." Carai directed Andrea to an electron microscope. "Take a look at this tissue. This piece comes from a Bentoplast, a very short-lived multi-cellular creature, near the bottom of the Yuseat food chain. I'm going to introduce the prion and you can see the entire Quazel cycle in a matter of a seconds."

Andrea pressed her small face to the eyepiece, putting her hands above her brow to seal out the light. "I'll introduce the Quazel now." Carai spoke in the background directing her attention over a field of cells shaped like a cluster of eyes with black pupils. However, she saw and understood without need of commentary. On the left side of the slide the Quazel invaded one cell. The solitary cell spasmed: the plasma edges turned from smooth irregular to fine oblique angles. The nucleus expanded slightly and turned a shade darker—in fact, denser. Almost immediately the adjacent cells were transfigured in similar fashion and the cells all locked together in rigid formation, more like living crystals than organisms, beautiful regularity. Cell division slowed to a stop. The small ocean of cells was becalmed. Andrea started to back away from the microscope when Carai admonished her, "It's not over yet. Now you'll see the effect of Quazel senescence."

Andrea settled back and watched. The left side of the slide began a second transformation. The cells lost their luster and turned opaque, as if some skim milk washed from left to right, not in the smooth collective transference of Quazel but in the individual passages of time. The nuclei changed from many-sided polygons into black shards. The cells began to shrink and crack like a sunbaked lakebed.

Andrea withdrew and sensed a tingling in her hands. "The Bentoplast is a little worse for the wear."

Dr. Carai switched off the microscope. "Prions are tough—a lot tougher than viruses. In fact, they are tougher than any of the body's normal tissues. We can't get rid of an infectious prion with heat or disinfectants, because we need to use such intense heat or toxicity that we kill the host before making a dent in the prion. I remember thinking that if we could arrest the Quazel cycle just before senescence—the aging and death of individual cells—we could make cells and therefore tissue practically indestructible, because in biological terms, the protein is practically indestructible. I'll bet you haven't been sick a day since your Quazel injection."

Andrea agreed. Her body's strength, endurance, and ability to heal continued to surprise her.

Carai turned off the electron microscope. "Normally, your body stamps out prions with its own enzymes. However, a few prions, like Quazel, don't react with your body's enzymes; therefore, we must supplement what the body can't produce."

He held up a gnarled sphere of wood fused onto a stick. "Here's the source of Quazel enzyme, crown gall from the Papuyoosa cedar. We're going out tomorrow to harvest more. Yuseat's climate is murder on robotics, so we use old-fashioned manual labor. We could use another strong back, and you might learn something." He handed Andrea the wooden knot.

She looked at the lifeless lump. "Okay. I'll earn my keep."

Fal'Dar rousted Andrea from her quarters early. "You coming to harvest crown gall with us?"

"I said I would." Andrea regretted promising Carai to help, but then she wanted to stay on his good side.

He was the person who manufactured the enzyme that kept her alive.

Through the door, Fal'Dar handed her a soft synthetic body stocking, chalk white and barely two ounces of cloth. "You wear this under the spore suit. Nothing else. Don't worry, it stretches. Hurry. Put it on and come down to the equipment room. The fog lifts in an hour, and we're anxious to get started." He closed the door and left.

Andrea handled the flimsy garment, and held it up to inspect what looked like a small child's pajamas complete with tiny feet. *Yeah, I'll bet it stretches . . .* The deep-cut V-neck stretched wide enough to step through. She carefully worked the flexible but durable fabric up her legs and over her hips. With some effort she poked her arms through the sleeves and then adjusted the front together forcing the V-neck closed. She paused to inspect herself in a small mirror. She was stark white from neck to toe. *I've seen thicker coats of paint.*

A bit self-conscious, Andrea walked to the equipment room. She found Dr. Carai and the work party of three Jod in various stages of putting on their plastic suits. Dr. Carai looked emaciated with his fur matted under the body stocking.

Andrea donned her baggy outer work suit. It was limber and easy to work in. The curved plastic mask tended to warp one's peripheral vision. The boots rose to the knee with tough shin guards. The soles of her boots were three-inch spikes from heel to toe, essential for gripping the slick surface outside, but awkward on the ceramic floor. "You get used to walking with more of your weight on your toes." Fal'Dar's voice was muffled by his faceplate. Puffs of vapor momentarily condensed below his mouth, evaporating almost as quickly.

On their backs each wore a large, but light filtering system good for twelve hours of work in the Yuseat atmosphere before the spores clogged the filters. Each carried a second set of clean filters packed in a cylinder attached to the backpack. Fal'Dar helped her assemble some plumbing associated with the suit. "When you breathe, air passes through thin panels on your back and shoulders. Filtered air enters your helmet through this hose." He helped Andrea locate the hose by touch. "Don't pinch the intake hose."

She felt the ribbed hose about an inch in diameter. "Got it."

"You exhale through the one-way valve below your chin." He pointed to the round button on her faceplate. "As you breathe, you maintain a slight overpressure of filtered air in your suit. So if you get a pinhole leak in your suit, you need not worry, the overpressure will keep the spores out." Then he taped her headgear to her shoulders. "Now you are breathing filtered air."

Next, Fal'Dar helped Andrea strap on a butt pack in which she would carry part of the harvest of crown gall. Others carried tools to dig and cut. After a final check, they stepped through a shower of a powerful formic acid, a fungicide to protect the suit. At Dr. Carai's order, they manhandled a hatch and stepped into the dismal damp. Ti'Maj handed Andrea an eight-foot-tall walking staff with a metal spike at the bottom and a broad serrated blade at the top.

They walked single file, carrying their equipment down the path shoveled down to a bare concrete walkway. The sides were three feet high, like drifts of black and brown mottled snow. The artificial lights from the building glistened from the wet slime fungus that piled up along the side of the walk.

Soon, the concrete ended and the work party stepped onto a narrow path marked with metal stakes. As they walked down the path, leaving the artificial lights behind, Andrea's eyes grew accustomed to the gloom. Away from the artificial lights, their work suits luminesced, and she felt part of a column of ghosts. She walked directly behind the lanky Dr. Carai. Pulsating ribs of slime mold lay across the path. Dr. Carai paused to jab his walking stick into a bulge in the mold. Gas escaped and the hissing mold collapsed on itself.

Red metal stakes led them to the edge of a black lake. Without a hint of moving air, the lake surface stretched like glass, disappearing into the fog. A tiny rivulet of treacle, runoff laden with ooze of dead fungi, added to the lake's stygian waters. At the water's edge, they found three glass canoes turned upside down, beached on a cushion of putrefied fungi. Fal'Dar and Zu'Pah righted one canoe and stowed their goods, took their seats, and used their walking staves to pole themselves from the slick bank into the shallow water. The pale green glow of their work suits reflected from the black water.

Ti'Maj prepared the other two canoes, launching Andrea and Dr. Carai who sat facing each other. Andrea noticed the gunwales were barely visible above the smooth water. She had no fear of water. She was an excellent swimmer. But she thought this particular water was a sinister liquor. With each stab of her staff to the soft lake bottom, she churned up a black cloud of sediment, and she marveled that anything below the surface could be as black as the turbid water itself.

Carai pointed to shadowy stalks that rose from the lake like damned souls. "Ahead you see the Papuyoosa orchard."

A thick grove of the stalwart trees rose above the water. Cypress knees rose from the water to fetch oxygen for the root system. The knees looked like melted wax, caked with the black sludge showing a slight rise and fall of the lake's water line.

"What are they doing ahead?" Andrea referred to Fal'Dar's canoe. They poled from tree to tree, reaching the lower branches and scoring them with the serrated ends of their staffs. Reaching into one of their packs, they pressed a pinch of black dirt into the fresh wounds they'd cut in the tree.

Carai answered, "They infect the Papuyoosa to create the crown gall." Carai pointed to other trees with burls swelling at forks in their branches. "Those knobs are the crown gall. Inside the gall live the bacteria that cause the swelling."

Andrea looked at the ugly burls growing on the branches. She had not realized that an entire subsystem lived in those lumps of wood. "So a bacterial infection causes the swelling?"

"Not exactly. These specific bacteria alter the genetic structure of the plant tissue that they infect, in this case, the Papuyoosa cedar. The swelling that we call crown gall is a neoplastic disease, like a cancer. In other words, the gall is a tumor. Hundreds of different species of woody plants get the disease—even on Earth. The disease results from infection of wounds by soil bacteria, Agrobacterium tumefaciens."

"So you give the trees a cancer." Apologetically she added, "I didn't take much biology."

"Sadly evident." Carai wagged his head.

Andrea marveled. "How did you make the connection among the Papuyoosa, the crown gall, the bacteria, and the enzyme?"

Carai smiled. "By simple observation. I'll show you. The Papuyoosa survives among Yuseat's fungi, because it is rich in Quazel Protein: tough as petrified wood. The fine needles suffer from Quazel poisoning, but those simply get brittle and exfoliate. The wood tissue has the bulk and rigidity to withstand the hardening. Because Yuseat has practically no wind, the brittle cedars don't need to bend. Essentially they grow until they become top-heavy and snap." Carai again pointed with his staff. "See that dead cypress?"

Carai's movement jostled the small boat, threatening to slosh some of the black water over the gunwales. Andrea shifted her weight to compensate. "Yes."

Carai said, "Note that Papuyoosa has a powerful resistance to the fungi while alive. Once dead, fungi practically dissolve the massive trees in a couple months. Some of these fungi that grow on the fallen cypress are edible, some taste good. But the point is: the Quazel prion requires a living host."

Andrea saw the giant leaning against some healthy specimens. Reddish fungi protruded from the wooden carcass. Gray puffballs seemed to march up the trunk. Bluish tendrils hung down to the water and white patches of mold covered the branches like fresh snow.

"When I noticed the crown gall on the Papuyoosa, I knew that something had broken down the Quazel defense. I analyzed the crown gall genetic material, which revealed the presence of certain unique plasmid-like DNA and other genetic products. The bacterial cells had introduced part of their genetic information into the plants. In turn, the tissue in the crown gall manufactured an enzyme that subverted the Quazel protein and allowed the tumor to grow. We collect the crown gall and distill the enzymes from it."

Andrea looked at Ti'Maj and Bir-Tod struggling in their canoe. "This is a stiff price to pay for a longer life."

Carai laughed sardonically, filling his facemask with vapor and the quiet with his shrill wheeze. "We're stuck now, aren't we?"

"I miss the sun." Andrea dragged a chair past a set of whining turbine pumps.

Tara followed with a second chair. "Are you sure this will work?"

"We're going to make a little tanning booth. If we get any paler, they'll think we're a couple of sickly Jod with hair. Already, you look like death warmed over, and I'm starting to feel like a case of the rickets just waiting to happen."

They ducked under a low ceiling of glass pipes and stationed their chairs under the banks of ultraviolet lights used to sterilize the water. They stripped to their underwear, sat down, and each put on a set of dark clumsy goggles designed for the larger Jod head. Andrea looked at Tara and thought the clone's improved diet and sedentary work were beginning to show in a pleasant roundness. Andrea lay back like a lizard on a rock. She asked, "How's your work coming on the *Benwoi?*"

"Good. H'Roo has the technical readout on the power plant and weapons. I have the data bank stripped down to elements. In fact"—Tara turned on her side and grinned—"I broke into their encryption system."

Andrea kept her face toward the light, deflating Tara with faint praise. "Good for you. Tell me, how is Eric doing?"

"He's bored." Tara kept her answer short.

"I'm bored, too. We have that much in common. I'm getting pretty tired of eating synthetics and mushrooms." Andrea felt the warmth of the light on her bare stomach.

Tara demurred. "I, ah . . . at first I didn't understand your reaction to seeing Eric."

Without looking, Andrea raised her arm and poked Tara's soft shoulder. "It's not your fault. Please don't start that again."

"I think I can give you some perspective."

Andrea took a deep breath. *I'm going to hear her spiel whether I want to or not.* She lay back with her goggles on and tried to blank her mind.

Tara sat up and removed her goggles, looking down on Andrea. "As a clone, I was used to seeing doubles, not only of myself, but of everyone I cared about. Every day a clone might see a dozen others that look identical to his or her mate. Until the Ordinate canceled all the ERC models, I'd see scores of clones identical to Eric every day. We clones can only know each other intimately. We cannot associate our feelings with outward appearances. On one hand, it must be wonderful to look across a room and see a face and know that that unique person is yours. In your case, it must have been just as devastating to see Eric."

Andrea lay motionless under the lights. "Are we finally through with your apologetics on physiognomy?"

Tara slumped back into her chair and adjusted the cumbersome goggles over her eyes. "I was just trying to help."

After a long uncomfortable pause, Andrea resuscitated the conversation. "I had an interesting talk with Dr. Carai yesterday. He's really quite a brilliant biolo-

gist. He asked me about you and Eric. I told him how
you clones were engineered to be sterile. I told him
about your crazy pipe dream of replacing the Ordinate
by creating a batch of fertile clones that would then
replicate in the normal way. Guess what he said."

Tara's interest peaked. She sat up again and swung
her legs around. Anxiously, she asked, "What?"

"First, Carai said you aren't technically clones:
you're really twins. Second, he said he could easily
reverse-engineer the sterility of the old-order clones."

Without a word, Tara grabbed her clothes and left,
dressing herself as she walked. Andrea banged her
head on a glass pipe as she rose to follow.

Andrea caught up with Tara in Dr. Carai's office. The
two were already in an animated conversation. Tara
acknowledged Andrea as she entered the room, then
continued without missing a beat. "But I saw the nurs-
eries in the Clone Welfare Institute." Tara's nostrils
flared as she talked excitedly. "I worked there. I saw
TRA models, identical to me."

Dr. Carai tried to calm Tara. "Yes. Yes. All that you
describe sounds mechanically sophisticated. I am
impressed by the neurological imprints and by the artificial wombs, but biologically speaking, what you
describe is child's play. It's not cloning! The Ordinate
procedure uses an egg—so far just like nature. Then
they splice out the undesirable DNA and splice in the
desirable DNA." Carai's face tightened into a fastidious
wince. "Don't even call the procedure cloning. What a
bunch of arrogant second-rate lab technicians!"

Andrea pushed aside an empty cup and a stack of
dog-eared photographs to lean against a cabinet. She
interjected, "Yesterday, you called it twinning."

"Precisely." The Artrix shrugged. He turned his attention back to Tara. "The Ordinate are just making twins—pretty much the way Nature does, except the Ordinate uses brute force."

Tara shook her head. Her cheeks were flushed from the brief stint in Andrea's makeshift tanning booth and from excitement. "I don't understand. What's the difference between being a clone and an identical twin?"

"The difference!" The old Artrix bared his yellow teeth. "Identical twins have parents. Strictly speaking, a properly manufactured clone does not. The only difference between you and a natural set of identical twins is that you don't know who your parents are. At some point in the process, your genetic code must have derived from the normal combination of sperm and egg, from a male and female: a biological mother and a father. When the Ordinate acquires a model they wish to duplicate, they splice the nuclei of a model's cell into adulterated eggs, and thereby grow fetuses from identical DNA. The effect is the same as if a fertilized egg in the womb split to become identical twins. Tara, your parents are some unknown human beings—most likely an Ordinate man and woman. You have hundreds or maybe thousands of identical twin sisters."

Tara sat down on a box of specimen slides.

Andrea watched Tara's face as the full impact of Carai's revelation took root in consciousness. The idea of mother and father, no matter how remote, apparently held some appeal for Tara. Andrea surmised that Tara had barely a clue of what she had missed. Perhaps the concept intrigued Tara because she suddenly had more than she had previously thought. Andrea put her hand on Tara's shoulder and said to Carai, "You told me you can reverse her sterility?"

"Not hers, but I can modify the next crop of old-order clones so that they can reproduce." Dr. Carai nodded confidently. "Tara is barren because the Ordinate harvested her eggs when she was still in what they call the larva stage. Human females, like Artrix females, are born with all the eggs they'll ever have. Tara has no eggs. From what you describe, I think Cor also genetically engineered both sexes to be deficient in key hormones. We can solve that problem several ways. In any case, I could take some of Tara's DNA and make a clone that is fully sexually functional."

Tara looked up. "Then I could perhaps become a grandmother."

Ever precise in his terminology, Carai replied, "Actually, you might become an aunt."

Tara looked at Andrea with melancholy eyes. "I'd like that. I could settle for being an aunt. Excuse me." She walked to Carai's door. "I must share this news with Eric immediately."

Andrea watched Tara disappear down the hall, then turned to Dr. Carai. "Fascinating. Imagine hundreds—even thousands of identical twins."

Dr. Carai brushed his mustache from his mouth. "Not a bad way to breed cattle, I suppose."

"You know"—Andrea took Tara's place on the box—"sometimes I think Eric could be the identical twin to my husband. The Cor killed my husband thinking he was Eric."

"I'm sure that's not possible no matter how much Eric and Steve favor each other."

"I'm sure you're right. But Eric and Steve share the same skin color, same voice, same eyes, same height. Both have the same nose, a slight rise on the bridge, the same arched brows and high cheekbones. Even the hairline and the cowlick are the same. Eric is a bit more muscular. He looks just like Steve did five years ago. It's been making me a little crazy, seeing him every day. Do you think everybody has a double?"

"Outward appearance is but a small part of a person's genetic code. I'm sure somewhere on Earth you can find someone who looks just like you." Dr. Carai paused to consider his answer. "It's all an approximation. Two persons can look very much alike and only be distantly related or not related at all."

Andrea's temper flared. "Let's say they are identical but not related. What are the odds?"

Dr. Carai scowled. "Steve and Eric, identical? Those odds are insignificant—practically zero. But I'll tell you my hypothesis. Your memory is playing tricks on you. Your imagination is wandering off the path of reason. Eric and Steve are not as similar as you believe. Just look at the facts. Eric is a clone manufactured on Cor. You and Steve were born and raised on Earth—light years apart."

Andrea had no ready rebuttal. "I suppose you're right."

"Simple science." Dr. Carai wheezed, "Do you want your late husband and Eric to be twins?"

"No. Absolutely not."

"Then accept the obvious, the simple answer. You are beginning to forget a painful memory and you may thank providence for fading memory. Don't use the circumstantial similarities between Eric and Steve to pick at old wounds."

Forget Steve? Andrea left Carai's office at first shaken in her convictions. Perhaps she was losing her mind. Carai had not so delicately suggested as much. Her father once told her that insanity is just living an unreal existence. How often had her mind cried out: this can't be real!

She thought willpower might rescue her, but now her will vacillated: Is it better to forget or to remember? Is forgetting reality self-willed insanity? Is remembering pain self-abuse? Andrea's head ached. She was trapped in her circumstance, and she sensed that the only door out was the truth. *And the path to the truth is pain.*

Her resolve stiffened. In the quiet of her room, she attacked Dr. Carai's argument. She recalled Steve, having been adopted by the Dewinters as an infant, never met his parents. He had no interest in finding his birth parents, who according to the Dewinters, lived anonymously in Southern Europe. Andrea was surprised how much she didn't know about her husband. She had such a healthy focus on Steve in the present that she did not even consider Steve's ambiguous past. Now she was impaled on the seemingly irrelevant past. She decided she would pay a visit to the taciturn Dewinters. Steve may not have cared who his biological parents were, but she did.

chapter 9

The Chelle emissary, Firbin, ignored the isolated flakes of snow that swirled around his feet. He admired the soaring spires of Sarhn; fortunate, because he was now a permanent "guest" of the Ordinate for the duration of their present crisis with the Jod. As a loyal civil servant of the Chelle Guild, he accepted this dangerous assignment. Brulk required Firbin's physical presence on Cor: the unspoken threat was that if Chelle played false, Firbin would pay the ultimate price. In the meantime, Firbin lived in luxury with the promise of a large bonus from the Ordinate treasury when the Cor prevailed against the Jod. Firbin finished his short walk from his sumptuous apartment to the Ministry Building. He crossed the formal garden with its charming antique elegance. Firbin paused for a critical glance at the row of ornamental cast-iron gas lamps with their dim blue and yellow flames. Inefficient. He dismissed the gas lamps with a shrug of his small shoulders and entered the large wooden doors into the building.

Admiral Brulk paid well for information; nevertheless, Firbin resented him. As a Chelle, he was keenly perceptive. He considered Brulk's demeanor ungracious—obviously Brulk had formed an opinion of him. Brulk had no right to form an opinion. What was particularly galling was that Firbin could not divine Brulk's opinion and must therefore assume the worst. But Brulk paid well, and the guild had assigned Firbin to placate the Ordinate and help them weaken the Jod. With today's information, he'd make a small fortune and upset the balance of power. A delicious moment for any Chelle.

Brulk met Firbin in the antechamber. "Do you have the technical readouts?"

Firbin held up a data cube between two spindly fingers. "These data are the fruit of seventy-five years' research and cataloguing Jod assets. We learned many painful lessons from our brief war against Jod aggression. Since we joined the Alliance, we have learned the entire Jod order of battle, and a few of our fleet officers have served on joint tours on Jod starships. I prepared an overview for you."

Brulk warmed. "Please come into my office—let's have a look." He followed the small Chelle into his room and directed him to a chair. Being too small for the furniture, Firbin sat uncomfortably at the edge, his beige smock hiked to his knees, his toes barely brushing the floor.

Brulk took the cube and held it before his steel blue eyes as if he could read the cube without a machine. Then he carefully placed the cube in his console. The wall screen illuminated with the Chelle logo, a Möbius loop, followed by a detailed line drawing of a Jod battle cruiser.

"Next screen," Firbin said, and the computer advanced to a photograph of a Jod dreadnought in orbit above a barren planet. The dreadnought looked like a sea creature—perhaps a ray, with thick wings frozen with the tips curled down and inward. The bow of the giant ship was a round protuberance. Thick multicolored rings on the nose served as the ship's insignia. "The Jod have seven dreadnoughts on active duty. They have another five old copies taken out of service and mothballed in deep space. A Jod dreadnought features the largest onboard power system of any vessel known, and consequently they have superb long-range gunnery. In a head-to-head match, you'd never get the chance to fire your weapons." Firbin looked sideways to see Brulk's reaction.

"I wasn't planning on a conventional engagement." Brulk scratched his chin as he looked at the scale placed next to the dreadnought. The Jod ship dwarfed the Cor J-Class attack ships. His small armada would be like a swarm of mosquitoes trying to drag down a bear—except that his attack ships carried two-hundred-pound quark missiles, each with the destructive capacity to flatten the entire city of Sarhn. "Just tell me their capabilities. What kind of shields do they have?"

"They have energy-repulse shields that extend four to twenty kilometers from the hull—a seamless three hundred sixty degrees. They can stop a relentless barrage of energy weapons. Lasers and torpedoes are useless when fired outside the shield. Likewise, torpedoes detonate at a safe distance."

"Unless they are fired at point blank range. We would have to get past their kinetic shields." Brulk raised one of his thick eyebrows as he queried Firbin with a look.

Firbin pointed to the wall screen with an elongated finger. "The Jod don't use kinetic shields. Instead, they use short-range cannon and small fighters to eliminate boarding threats. Not to mention that to get to a Jod dreadnought, you must have already run a gauntlet of destroyers, then cruisers. But mostly, the dreadnoughts rely on their long-range guns. Nobody has ever gotten within fifteen thousand kilometers of a dreadnought to even fire a salvo. In addition, despite their tremendous size, the Jod craft are more nimble than most smaller ships."

"I doubt that," Brulk replied incredulously. "Something that large must be difficult to maneuver. The inertia must be incredible."

Firbin tugged at his smock, trying to cover his bony gray knees. "In truth, the Jod ships are highly maneuverable—they have an exotic technology, a neural couch. The helmsman is neurally connected to the ship and the ship's computer. Decisions for course corrections and targeting adjustments are instantaneous. Their probability of navigational error when entering and exiting FTL speed is negligible. In open space, they have you beat in speed, maneuverability, range, and accuracy."

Brulk took a deep breath to control his growing impatience with Firbin. *I'm being lectured on naval strategy by a civilian, but I do need his information.*

Firbin pursed his colorless lips. "You can still settle this conflict using Chelle diplomacy. Our ambassador succeeded in pressing your demands, thus far. After all, you will get reparations."

Brulk tuned out Firbin's voice as he studied the photograph of the Jod ship. He observed: *Most of the ship's weapons are on the port and starboard. If only we could get them bunched together and standing still. . . .*

Firbin cleared his throat to distract Brulk. "I said, the Jod Council has accepted your terms."

"Really?" Brulk fully expected the Jod to accept the terms. He would have done the same, then use the lull to plan and execute a final assault.

"Our ambassador to the Jod reports that the Jod Council of Elders regrets any loss of life and agrees to a fair schedule of restitution. They agree to let us, the Chelle, survey the damage. They claim that Jod was not officially involved in any aggression directed toward Cor."

Brulk grunted, "Of course—an unofficial act of war?"

The brass clock on his desk chimed softly. Firbin paused for the interruption, then said, "Actually, the Jod Council is investigating the possibility that a rogue element of their armed forces may be responsible or at least culpable. Specifically, the council blames the incident on a rogue military commander, whom they intend to try for treason."

"Will they send the malefactor to Cor to face our justice?"

"I don't think the Jod political system allows that."

"How convenient. Nevertheless, keep insisting on extradition." Brulk glared for Firbin's benefit.

Firbin swallowed hard as he saw Brulk's ire rise. "So far, the Jod are still trying to locate the *Benwoi,* the Terran, and the clone. They promise to hand over those assets as soon as they can."

"Meanwhile they'd like us to wait around for their next assault. Is that right?"

"No. No." Firbin clapped his hands, a nervous habit. "The Jod agreed to stand down their fleet as a gesture of goodwill. I might add that the Chelle invoked our rights under the Alliance Charter, demanding that the Jod withdraw their patrols from our space. I can say with authority that they have withdrawn from Chelle."

Brulk simply looked down at Firbin, relaying his suspicions through silence. He knew that Firbin was speaking the Chelle's collective mind. Apparently, the Chelle were harboring second thoughts about Cor's ability to win the war. But the Chelle always had second thoughts. Their history was replete with precipitous beginnings (usually to settle an old score), then second thoughts, a pusillanimous execution of a modified plan, failure, then an attempt at compromise—all combined into a muddled, missed opportunity.

Firbin, in speech considered bold for his species, handed Brulk a mild rebuke. "You mustn't assume that the Jod Council is insincere. Their society is not as orderly as yours and ours. Within their own species, they tend to be divisive. As you well know, Admiral Brulk, I have no love for the Jod, but in this case, I believe their story."

Brulk listened to Firbin anyway, without comment. The instability of the Jod political order and their claim about a rogue element in their military did not appease him. *If a rogue element in the Jod military has enough resources to cripple Cor clone production and instigate a clone uprising, we dare not wait for them to organize.*

Firbin waited for a moment to add another point. "Lastly, the Jod invite the Ordinate to establish diplomatic relations. The Jod seek permission to send an emissary to visit you. Likewise, they invite you to visit Heptar on Jod." Firbin opened his large black eyes wide and said triumphantly, "To that end, the Chelle would be honored to broker an exchange of emissaries."

Brulk leaned back in his chair and pressed his folded hands against his thin lips to hide a creeping smile. "I'll relate your news to Madame Prefect. Meanwhile, I want you to transmit another request to the Jod. Everything they've told me through you is unsubstantiated. If we come to Heptar, I'll want to see their Fleet in port above Heptar. I will not have part of our government visiting Jod while Jod dreadnoughts might at the same time be paying a visit to Cor. Remind them that the Cor have no capital ships. Our largest vessels are smaller than their light cruisers. You understand our concerns."

Firbin slid off the chair and bowed slightly. "I think you are being most reasonable. When the Jod delegation comes to Sarhn, I suggest you reiterate that request in person. Meanwhile, I'll plant the idea where it can grow."

"You have been most helpful." Brulk handed Firbin a small envelope. "This receipt confirms a substantial transfer to your private account."

Firbin took the envelope and slid it up his sleeve. He bowed again and left.

Brulk performed the tactical calculus. I have seven hundred and ninety-one NewGens salvaged from the institute fire, five hundred of which are now programmed to pilot our four hundred and eighty J-Class attack craft. If I can catch the Jod Fleet in one spot, I can knock out their dreadnoughts and heavy cruisers. With the Jod Fleet out of commission, we can beat them in the race to mobilize. We must attack while they consider us weak. Brulk considered the irony: *The perception of weakness is my shield. Audacity is my spear.*

Suddenly, the lights flickered out in his office.

The attack was supposed to be a diversion to draw security away from the food stores, where the main party of Brigon's men waited for a signal to steal much-needed supplies.

Sixty flywheel batteries, each comprising tons of polished steel, turned at hypersonic speeds, frictionless, suspended by magnetism. Then the power failed. Magnetic cushions collapsed. The flywheels broke from their mounts, crashing through the long building, flattening everything in their path. Sparks splashed. "Look out!" Brigon yelled. An eight-foot disk of polished steel accelerated past him, instantly killing one of his fighters before crashing through a cinder block wall. There was no time to run, only to dodge crushing steel. Brigon had not anticipated the complete effect of sabotaging all the transformers at the solar power plant.

The flywheels ripped through the plant like a scythe. Clone laborers scattered, but many were caught by the deadly metal dervishes. The clones did not have time to shout warnings or even emit fear. Death was instant. Or if one were spared, spared instantly. Despite all the screeching of steel abrading concrete, and the crash of metal and block wall, human voices remained mute.

Brigon's pulse raced. He retrieved the weapon and the badly torn wilderness cloak from his dead comrade and fled the plant. At the rendezvous, he counted seven wide-eyed, panting men, and thanked providence that he'd lost only one dead.

"Quick! We must help the others haul grain." Brigon and his men left their dead comrade where he lay.

Dr. Carai sat across a gaming table. He was teaching a frustrated H'Roo Parh how to play an Earth game called chess. While H'Roo contemplated his next move, Carai muddled the game with incessant lecture. "At one time on Earth, certain potentates used to play this game using people instead of inanimate figurines . . ."

In the next room, the Yuseat Lab communications

suite lit up. The technician announced, "We're getting a hail. Encryption is good. Set the table. We're going to eat well tonight."

Carai grinned and gave the order. "Put up the navigational link and be sure to tell them to park next to *Benwoi,* not on it. Tell Fal'Dar to prepare the enzyme shipment." Carai turned to H'Roo and said, "Every one hundred twenty days, the supply ship comes. For a couple weeks we eat like kings: fresh fruit and vegetables. Plus the news."

"Your move." H'Roo tried to focus on the game. He was winning for the first time.

Carai effortlessly moved his knight, forking H'Roo's queen and a rook. "The temptation is to read all one hundred twenty days' news at once to get caught up, but what's the point? On Yuseat, the purpose of news is to kill time. So I carefully limit myself to one journal per day. By coincidence, I read my last journal yesterday."

"Please!" H'Roo protested. He looked across the table at the Artrix, who now sulked in silence, playing with his flaxen mustache. H'Roo spared Carai's queen.

Dr. Carai retaliated by pulling his queen diagonally across the board. "Checkmate."

H'Roo politely thanked Dr. Carai for the game and privately resolved never to play another game of chess with any creature possessing vocal cords. He retired to the solitude of the *Benwoi.*

Brigon led his men into the caves. The steward came out to meet the raiding party. "What did you bring me?" He ordered several idle men to unload the sleds.

Brigon grabbed the steward's arm and gave him the bad news. "I'm sorry, Hart. We found only four hundred pounds of grain." The steward's countenance fell.

He walked over to the sleds and pulled back the tarp. "What's this?" He pointed at the long bales of metal rods.

Brigon answered, "Nickel-titanium alloy-Nitinol-shape memory metal." He pulled off his gloves and stuffed them into his belt. He ran his hand through his sweaty, tawny hair. His cheeks were sunburned, his beard irregular, his lips chapped.

"We can't eat Nitinol." Hart threw the tarp over the rods. He stepped closer to Brigon and spoke in hushed tones. Referring to the cluster of clones loitering near the cave entrance, he said softly, "They're coming by the hundreds now: starving, sick. How do you expect me to feed them?"

Brigon lowered his gaze and whispered, "The precinct clones are being deliberately starved by the Ordinate, and they don't know it. When they do figure it out, they'll come by the thousands."

The impromptu bearers carried the bundles of Nitinol, following Brigon deep into the caves. As they walked, they felt the breath of warm air and with it the smell of sulfur. Brigon led them to a large, well-lighted subterranean room filled with uncomfortable heat. Inside, a group of fourteen wilderness clones, wearing meager loincloths and glistening with sweat, tended to the generators.

Brigon paused to inspect the generators that provided electricity to his growing underground city. Behind the workers, Brigon saw a line of pulleys along a greased shaft of steel. Over each pulley, a thick Nitinol cable turned the shaft that turned the generator. The cables disappeared deep into a gaping hole where a dim red glow indicated the source of great heat, perhaps two hundred feet below. The heat below caused the Nitinol cable to straighten itself, thereby pulling slack from above. The relatively cooler air above made the Nitinol more supple, creating slack. Therefore, by attempting to remember its former shape, the Nitinol turned perpetually. They had four such generators, each capable of three kilowatts per hour.

Above he saw a chimney cut through the rock to exhaust the noxious vapors. The chimney disappeared into blackness. Although the machinery made no noise, the room was filled with sound. At the base of the natural chimney, the clones had rigged wind chimes of clanging scrap metal, tinkling glass, and hollowed tubes of hardwood. The utilitarian clones had fashioned the wind chimes to assure them that the sulfurous vapors were indeed exhausting away.

A grizzled engineer, an old clone, approached Brigon. He too was naked from the waist up. "How much raw Nit did you get?"

"About two thousand pounds." Brigon stripped off his outer garment. His dirty hair was matted into small ringlets on his forehead.

"Good." The engineer scratched his stubby gray whiskers. "We're setting up generators for the clones in the south mountains, and we need more cable. I found a new way to extrude the bars and make thinner, stronger cable."

"Okay, you can help set up power in the the south mountain caves. We sure can't handle any more refugees here."

The small Yuseat Laboratory bustled at the arrival of the supply ship. Andrea recognized the crew. They wore the same baggy cut of clothes as before, cleaner perhaps, and now each festooned himself with gold necklaces. They wore gaudy gemstones tacked to their large ears. The sarcasm embedded in their faces was unmistakable. "You guys are from the *Kam-Gi*."

"Yes, we are," the senior of the three crew members answered. "The Old Man held us over after we ferried you and that other fellow"—he pointed to H'Roo Parh—"to Clemnos. Offered us steady work, free repairs, and he threatened to kill us if we declined." He laughed. His two comrades didn't.

Andrea agreed with the two somber crew members. "Hal K'Rin wasn't bluffing."

"Well, we've never made better money doing less work. All we have to do is fly where K'Rin tells us and keep our mouths shut. We pick up his medical supplies from you; then we rendezvous with his ship at some coordinates in deep space, well off the trade routes, and make the handoff. Best of all, he pays cash."

Andrea quipped, "A regular guy, I know."

"Have you heard? He's getting a big promotion. He asked us to lay low for a while. I don't think he wants us stirring up any trouble, if you know what I mean. Also, he told me to give you or your friend a message."

"I can take it." Andrea held out her hand.

The pilot dug through his numerous pockets. Turning to the stout Jod behind him, he said, "Did I hand you the— Oh, here it is." He fished a chip from a vest pocket and handed it to her.

Back in her quarters, Andrea put the message chip into her desk console. K'Rin's face appeared on a small screen. He spoke as if rushed but not excited. "Andrea. H'Roo Parh. The council has decided to reinstall the Rin seat. The ceremony takes place on the fifteenth day of the month of Corol—about forty days from now. The entire

Tenebrea will stand in the Assembly Hall with me. A handful must remain at their posts on the *Tyker*, at the academy, and on Vintell to maintain security.

"I must insist that you two stay far away from the Jod system and wait for orders. The Cor Ordinate have demanded that we surrender Eric and Tara. Also, they demand that we extradite Andrea to stand trial for terrorism. Hal Pl'Don wants me to give you up. You must not fall into the hands of Jod regulars. Work exclusively—I say again, exclusively—with Tenebrea personnel until I direct you otherwise. If war with the Cor Ordinate begins, extradition is, of course, moot.

"Meanwhile my freedom of movement is greatly restricted to the environs of Heptar. Kip will serve as my chief liaison to the Tenebrea. I shall be in charge of mobilizing Jod to meet the Cor Ordinate threat. Assure Eric and Tara that plans will undoubtedly include returning them to Cor to open a ground campaign. Andrea, I may not see you again for a long time.

"H'Roo, you are hereby assigned to pilot the *Benwoi*. I charge you to protect Andrea as well as your ship. The watchword is Patience. Farewell."

K'Rin's message, which should have been celebratory, was filled with understated dread. Andrea cared little about the threat of extradition.

To hell with patience. Andrea grit her teeth. K'Rin's message simply suggested more impediment to solving her problem: Steve's past. She thought, *I can't wait here for K'Rin to solidify his position on Jod.* She forwarded the message to H'Roo, adding a note: *I need a favor.*

House rules said that at a Yuseat feast no one may eat synthetics. The Jod may for a change prepare their dishes to excess—what Dr. Carai called rambunctious cuisine.

Yuseat staff and the crew of *Kam-Gi* prepared a huge spread of fine foods. They worked side by side in the kitchen, enthusiastically sampling their wares and complimenting each other's culinary exploits. The small kitchen became odoriferous with strong spices that made Andrea's eyes sting. She retreated, remembering her first painful encounter with flannerberries.

Dr. Carai, wearing a facemask with filters, joined the celebratory food preparation. Like humans, he could not tolerate Jod spices. He sautéed a pan of tentacled shellfish and prepared a mild cheese sauce spiked with fortified wine. He boiled a dark red grain into a pilaf that he tossed with bits of dried fruit and roasted pine nuts. He prepared enough for himself and the three humans.

Fal'Dar and Eric dragged tables into the largest room, the Quazel distillation lab. The Jod chefs arrived with their communal platter of spiced meats, tubers, and pastes—all smothered with a piquant sauce that reeked of flannerberries. The Jod sat at one end of the feast with their communal platter and personal bowls. Fal'Dar considered the ventilation in the room and sat Dr. Carai and the humans with separate plates at the other end of the table, up wind, as it were, from the steaming, spicy Jod food. Heavy crystal mugs sat at each place, and a large plastic bladder of Baldinale sat in the middle of the table with a spigot facing Fal'Dar.

House rules also required everyone to wear their best clothes. The Tenebrea wore their uniforms. Eric wore a loose-fitting shirt that gathered at the waist and wrists. Tara wore a gauzy off-the-shoulder smock revealing her gullwing tattoo. The old Artrix wore only his fine fur and a heavy garland of amber, a honey-colored mineral, fossilized sap, each bead an irregular lump polished to a luster subdued by two centuries of wear and restored somewhat by the Artrix's own body oils. The three *Kam-Gi* crew members each added a sash to their already garish clothes.

H'Roo sat next to Andrea. Together, they provided the demarcation of the Jod and non-Jod ends of the table. Andrea leaned aside and continued a thorny conversation in a low voice, "H'Roo, I'd prefer to go with your help, but I'll go with or without you."

H'Roo arched his brow. "Are you going to steal my ship?"

"I stole it from the last owners." Andrea didn't smile.

"You don't know enough to pilot cross-galaxy by yourself. Forget taking Tara. She won't go without Eric."

Andrea leaned toward H'Roo. "That's why I need you."

H'Roo shook his head emphatically. "Forget it. K'Rin would bust us to Pek and stick us in a listening post at the Chelle frontier for the rest of our long lives."

Andrea's voice was a blend of petition and threat. "I've got to talk with my husband's parents."

H'Roo looked down at his empty bowl, his face a mask of frustration. "No, you don't."

She poked H'Roo in the chest, her finger jabbing the bony chest plate. She measured her words, biting the syllables. Under her breath she said, "I am slowly going insane here. I am sitting across from a clone that looks exactly like my dead husband. I want to know why. The more I try to sort out the facts, the worse it gets. I want to believe in coincidence, but I don't. I don't even trust my memory anymore. To make matters worse, I can't recall details about my Steve's past. Hell, I don't recall ever seeing a baby picture of Steve."

"Oh, Andrea!" H'Roo raised his hands in frustrated supplication.

"Let it go." He looked away.

"I can't." Andrea nudged H'Roo again to grab his attention. "The Dewinters can answer some questions." She reflected. "Until now, I never paid them much mind. I thought they were just soured on old age and jealous of our happiness. But I think they are hiding something. I'm going back to find out what they know."

H'Roo pushed her hand away. "What is the point? Steve is gone. What if you can never know? Not every question in life has an answer. Now, you're making me crazy!" He looked away again, as if afraid of Andrea's face.

"Look at me when I talk to you." She pulled his chin around and fixed H'Roo with her own dark eyes. "The point is I want to know that something in my life is real. H'Roo, I am not being melodramatic. I can't stand it. I thought I could when I insisted that K'Rin send me to this hellhole. But the not knowing is killing me. You've got to help me."

H'Roo's chin fell to his broad chest. He muttered, "I'm under orders to protect you. I suppose that means protecting you from yourself."

"Any excuse will do." Andrea forced a bitter smile. "You can protect me and the ship by taking me to Earth. Besides, you've always wanted to visit Earth."

"We're not finished exploiting the *Benwoi*'s systems yet. Half her electronics are laid out on the deck. The lambda intake to the FTL drive is off-line. If you're going to hijack the *Benwoi*, you'd better wait for me to put her back together."

"I'll help." Andrea nodded. "I'm tired of the mushroom hunt, anyway."

"We might just get some real work out of you," H'Roo jibed. "You can help me reassemble the systems. We can get the *Benwoi* space-worthy faster; then you can commandeer a ship you know something about." He rolled his hazel eyes. "Listen to me: I'm aiding and abetting a mutiny aboard my own ship."

Andrea patted H'Roo on the chest as if to soothe the prods. "I really need to know. Thank you."

H'Roo folded his arms across his chest and looked over at the steaming platter laden with Jod delicacies. He said, "Now, I'm going to try to enjoy this meal despite you."

"To the Rin! To the Light! To the Tenebrea!" The Jod rapped their knuckles on the table and emptied their first tumbler of Baldinale.

Everyone ate great amounts of food and drank the strong ale. Tara and Eric had never tried Baldinale, and Andrea cautioned them both. Tara prudently heeded Andrea's advice and abstained. Eric didn't.

Eric was an unpleasant drunk: belligerent, loud. The crew of the *Kam-Gi* encouraged Eric's boorish behavior. Tara's face turned bright red with humiliation as Eric became unwitting sport for the rough contingent of the Jod party. Andrea gestured that she and H'Roo ought to manhandle Eric to his quarters and sober him up. Tara concurred, but Eric rudely jerked his arm away when Tara tried to coax him from the table. "Don't touch me! I prefer a woman who drinks." Eric raised his mug to salute Andrea. "I'll bet you can be a lot of fun if you want to."

Andrea cut her eyes to Tara, who seethed alone in

her disapproval of this sport. Her auburn hair exaggerated her fierce blush.

Dr. Carai instructed Tara to sit down. Then to Tara's horror, Carai ordered Fal'Dar to refill Eric's mug to the brim, whispering aside, "The Baldinale started it; the Baldinale will finish it." Meaning Eric.

Eric drank with abandon. For a moment he commanded the attention of the entire party. He obviously enjoyed the attention as he related an incoherent rambling of his first skirmish with the Ordinate security forces. Although his eyes drooped, his cheeks burned, and he grinned with self-satisfaction. "You guys come with me to Cor, and I'll show you a good fight."

He tried to stand but his legs failed him and he fell back into his chair. So he launched into a soliloquy sitting down. "I'm going to personally kill as many of those Ordinate bastards as I can lay hands on. You'll see. The ones I don't kill, we're going to make them our slaves. They'll do the dirty work for a change. They'll eat nothing but our scraps for a change. They're going to wish they were never born."

Eric drained his mug and waggled it at Fal'Dar, signaling that he wished it refilled. "When the Ordinate bastards get too old to work . . . oh, crap."

Eric never finished the sentence. He passed out. His mug crashed to the table, his hand stuck in the handle. He slumped forward, propped precariously in his chair and on the table, his face flat in a cold plate of seafood au gratin. The *Kam-Gi* crew erupted in boisterous laughter.

"Eric!" Tara left her chair to minister to her fallen mate. Rubbing salt into the wound, Andrea said with mock disgust, "Oh, leave the conquering hero where he lies. We'll clear him with the rest of the dirty dishes."

Tara turned her wrath at Andrea. "You have no right to speak to him like that! You're drunk, too."

"Well excuse me!" Andrea laughed. She put her finger to her lips. "Please don't tell Eric that I insulted him. What he doesn't know can't hurt him."

Again, the *Kam-Gi* crew howled with laughter. Tara was horrified, almost in tears. She cajoled the *Kam-Gi* crew to help her drag her comatose mate to their quarters. Accepting Carai's advice, Tara left to find a bucket.

The table became quiet. Andrea studied the bemused look on the Artrix's face. She accused him, "You enjoyed that, didn't you?"

Carai brushed his mustache aside. "I enjoy any novelty. I've been here on Yuseat longer than you've been alive. I don't get to see many foibles firsthand. I'm just an unfortunate expatriate like you."

H'Roo, beginning to feel the ale, interjected, "A fugitive, more like it."

"That was a long time ago. Anyone who could testify against me is dead by now." Carai glared, raising a lip, showing teeth stained yellow.

Andrea rested her elbows on the table, cradling her chin in her hands. "So how did you get stuck here?" she asked the Artrix.

Dr. Carai took another sip of Baldinale and settled back into his comfortable chair to tell his story. "I have a rare but debilitating genetic disorder: the Artrix name is Stynsix Langsuum—means slow madness. The disease causes the deterioration of the corpus callosum—a thicket of fibers that joins the hemispheres of the brain. Normally, cells that comprise the corpus callosum are sturdy, but with Stynsix, those cells are short-lived. The cell walls are weak and easily disrupted." Dr. Carai pointed to his head. "One quite literally spends a short existence where the left side of the brain quite literally doesn't know what the right side is doing." He laughed and wheezed.

"Don't you have gene therapy on Artrix?"

"We certainly do—unfortunately not for Stynsix disease. In the advanced stages of the disease, the post-adolescent Artrix affected by the disorder develops holes in the spinal cord and eventually pools of unusable brain. One brain function that remains is the sensation of pain, and Stynsix eventually creates the false signal that one is on fire."

H'Roo shuddered. "That's awful."

Dr. Carai sat back and rested his glass of Baldinale on his chest. "When I was a cub, the doctor discovered the aberrant gene in me, and he informed my parents of my condition, emphasizing in his own sympathetic way that whereas I would be a fairly normal cub, I'd eventually show symptoms as an adolescent. When I reached maturity, my parents would have a two-year ordeal of watching me die a miserable death."

"Your poor parents," Andrea murmured.

"My mother was especially distraught. However, my siblings took the news with heroic stoicism." Carai smirked at his own sarcasm. "Since I was good as dead, my every wish was a dying wish and therefore granted. To say that I was spoiled is an understatement. However, I had but one true desire—to study my own disease."

H'Roo commented through his stupor, "Admirable."

"My family thought my passion was the early onset of the disease itself. My research eventually brought me to Quazel Protein as the only sure way to strengthen the nerve cell walls. However, the consequences of using Quazel were well known even then. I studied

Quazel in nature. Quazel occurs naturally in some plants. The protein hardens pulpy tissue into rigid beams of wood. Iron hemp has Quazel, and in ancient times its light fibers were used to weave armor and shields. Until Quazel was outlawed, aquaculturalists injected the prion into low-order invertebrates. Farmers used it for certain livestock that they naturally intended to slaughter before the onset of Quazel poisoning—rather controversial, but nevertheless practical because the Quazel made the livestock extremely disease resistant. But as it happens with most scientific advances, abuses finally led to a total ban.

"Yet, I thought salvation from my certain demise lay with Quazel, so I secretly continued my research. I traveled to outlying botanical reserves to find natural occurrences of Quazel Protein. The greatest occurrence is here on Yuseat. I traveled here as the lone botanist with a surveying crew. We camped above the tree line in the mountain ice, well above spore-laden air. I donned an overpressure suit and made short forays to catalogue the many new species of fungi. I learned that on Yuseat like everywhere else, there is a food chain, and the high-order fungi don't wait for the less prolific forms to die."

Carai held out his naked leg. "I discovered slime cats, or they discovered me. I also discovered crown gall on the Papuyoosa cedar, and subsequently the enzyme to manage the effects of Quazel Protein."

The Artrix's old eyes lit up as he said, "Nature is wonderful to behold. She seems so unaware of her own presiding intelligence. I injected myself with the Quazel Protein, then worked up a protocol for administering the enzyme. That took some time to work out the proper release.

"I kept the specifics of my discovery secret for years. As I said, Quazel was illegal, and I knew that if they ever denied me free access to Yuseat, I'd no longer be able to harvest the crown gall from the Papuyoosa cedar, extract the enzyme—in other words, I'd pretty soon perish from Quazel poisoning.

"But my secret didn't last for long. My brother noticed, with dismay I might add, that I did not succumb to the symptoms typical of one with a degenerative disorder of the central nervous system. I'll explain the awkward custom of Artrix primogeniture to you some other time."

Dr. Carai took a long drink of Baldinale to refresh his dry mouth. "I told him that I had beaten the disorder. 'Impossible!' he claimed. 'You're lying!' he accused. He loudly and publicly accused me of purposefully trying to distress my parents—give them false hopes—with such outrageous stories. He defamed me to my kin. Because I would not give specifics about my cure, it appeared that I was indeed caught in a lie. In a short while, he had most of my kin despising me as a fraud and a liar. So I made the fateful mistake of defending myself by telling my family that I was working on developing a cure by experimenting with Quazel. I didn't tell them that I had already injected myself. Before I could even get into my explanation of how I had discovered the enzyme, my brother ran from the room and summoned the police. Trafficking Quazel is a capital crime, even today.

"If guilty, I would be condemned to garroting." Carai held his hands to his throat and squeezed. "Not a pretty sight. I fled before the police arrived. Then, I lived for many years as a fugitive in the Jod system. Basically, I worked as a biologist to raise money to finance brief excursions back to Yuseat to harvest a supply of the enzyme. I never could develop a synthetic—still can't." Carai shook his head.

"The Artrix government posted me as one of their most dangerous criminals—there's not a lot of crime on Artrix. I fell into the class of criminal known as Quazel traffickers. In fact I had the notoriety of being the only Quazel trafficker from Artrix.

"During the Quazel Drug Wars, a Jod special operations officer, K'Rin, found me working at a hydroponics farm on Corondor Six. A simple blood test showed I had the Quazel Protein. I was doomed, so I told K'Rin that I knew how to make Quazel enzyme. I told him that I'd make the enzyme for him if he would not deliver me to Artrix, where I'd certainly be executed. K'Rin faked my death. Apparently I was killed while trying to escape. The Artrix authorities closed the case, and now I am a nonperson."

Andrea turned and looked at H'Roo, then at Dr. Carai. Death is the perfect anonymity. No one hunts a dead man. Or a dead renegade clone. She looked at Eric's empty chair.

Carai drew his hands over his face like a curtain. "As a nonperson, I was theoretically liberated. Then, K'Rin put me in another kind of jail—this laboratory on this wretched planet. I run the lab, manufacture the enzyme for all the Tenebrea, and conduct research for a synthetic."

Andrea set her Baldinale down. "Faked your death, how?"

"I don't know." Carai shook his head. "But whatever he did sure convinced the authorities on Artrix." Carai placed the tips of his ten furred fingers together to catch a thought. "Ever since, I've always felt expendable. My first lab assistant, an eminent Jod scientist, crossed K'Rin, attempting to share our secret. K'Rin withheld the enzyme and the poor creature subsequently suffered Quazel poisoning. He died, a suicide in a mental institution. Sometimes I wonder why K'Rin keeps me alive."

H'Roo defended K'Rin. "He is just."

Carai emitted a high-pitched laugh that ended with a cynical wheeze. "Please spare me from the just!"

chapter 10

Andrea felt her legs cramp. She had sat cross-legged on the floor of the *Benwoi* computer closet beneath a glaring lamp, reading Tara's instructions and replacing hundreds of data cubes into numbered slots.

"Ugh." She stood and straightened her legs, then leaned over with her palms flat on the floor as she stretched her hamstrings. Looking through her legs she saw Eric grinning back at her.

"Don't you have any work to do?" She stood and faced him. He didn't seem very traumatized by his first encounter with Baldinale.

"Just admiring the view." He stretched his arm across the hatch to block her exit.

Andrea stiff-armed Eric, knocking him against the bulkhead as she walked past him toward the bridge. Eric chuckled, then followed her. "You're not so tough. I've seen the way you look at me."

"You dumb bastard," Andrea said without turning around. As she stepped onto the bridge, she felt an arm wrap around her waist. She spun around and found herself in Eric's strong arms.

He gave her a bear hug, lifting her from the floor, grinning. "We're going to have to learn how to work together."

Andrea arched her back, then smashed Eric with a head butt, knocking him unconscious. His arms fell slack and Andrea landed like a cat as Eric crashed onto the deck, bleeding from a gash above his left eye. Andrea looked up and saw Tara, who had witnessed the brief altercation. Andrea snarled, "When your friend wakes up, explain to him in simple words that if he ever touches me like that again, I'll kill him."

Tara sat down in the navigator's chair. She turned pale.

H'Roo found Andrea in her room. She had a cold pack on the back of her neck and a compress on her forehead. "You gave Eric a concussion. He bit a pretty nasty hole in his tongue."

"I saw a couple stars myself." She rolled her neck. "You know, that stupid clone was coming on to me?"

"Well, you should see the way you've been looking at him."

Andrea flashed H'Roo a look warning him away from that argument. H'Roo prudently retreated from opinion to fact. "Tara is in the dispensary nursing Eric and cussing him at the same time." H'Roo smiled in spite of himself. "Clones. Do you think she loves him?"

"She does," Andrea answered tersely.

"Then love is blind." H'Roo smirked.

Andrea shook her head, disagreeing silently. She removed her compress, then said, "If Tara doesn't domesticate Eric soon, I'll give him far worse than a concussion."

H'Roo rubbed his eyes. "I think we ought to get away for a couple weeks. Tara finished assembling the electronics. I can finish the lambda jet tomorrow. Tara and Carai can continue work on the wilderness cloaks while we're gone."

"I'm packed." Andrea looked up and smiled wanly through her headache. "What changed your mind?"

H'Roo rolled his eyes toward the ceiling. "At this rate, somebody is going to murder somebody else. Eric's injured. Tara's about ready to burst a blood vessel. Do you know why? You're dysfunctional. You are useless to the mission in your present state of mind. So I'm going to take you to Earth and settle this nonsense once and for all. The Eric-Steve similarity is a fluke, a coincidence. If you can't get past that simple albeit painful truth, then we can't work together."

H'Roo tossed Andrea a plastic bag, vacuum-sealed. Inside was a blood-soaked pad of gauze. "It's Eric's blood from his head wound. You can match his DNA with Steve's. I presume you Terrans keep records."

Andrea bristled at the criticism but nodded appreciatively. She took the small packet and put it in her breast pocket. "Thank you. I can use Dr. Carai's lab. Fifteen minutes with Carai's equipment and I'll have Eric's DNA on film."

"Be careful. Use the lab tonight after everyone is on sleep cycle. Nobody needs to know why we're leaving or where we're going. I would prefer that they think I'm taking you away for a little diversion and to preserve the peace on Yuseat."

Andrea felt the bump at her hairline. "That's certainly plausible."

"I'll arrange provisions. Report to the *Benwoi* at 0500 hours."

One hundred and seventy-four of the Tenebrea bivouacked outside the city of Heptar. Their multicolored tents haphazardly surrounded the crystal pool of an artesian spring. The spring had for millennia spewed red sand from the nether regions which according to local legend created a beach for damned souls furloughed from their eternal torment. The perfection of the water, sand, and sun was thought to accentuate the bitterness of the liquid sulfur, nettles, and pitch black of Jod hell—the afterlife of traitors and cowards. Such is myth.

The mood in the camp was a festival, a family reunion. The far-flung Tenebrea gathered in groups to recount their exploits and compare duties. The most frequent sound was the eruption of laughter and plaudits.

Jo'Orom stood in the shade of a gnarled oak surveying the camp. He cradled a bottle of water in the crook of his arm. He wore his field uniform, complete with utility belt, but the holster for his handlance was empty. Beside him at a folding table, Kip studied the protocol for the ceremony to reinstate Hal K'Rin to the council. Jo'Orom muttered, "I don't like the smell of it."

Not looking up, Kip replied, "You just hate the drill and ceremony."

"I'm not worried about our troops making a good show. They can walk in a straight line." Jo'Orom took a drink from his water bottle, rinsed his mouth, and spit. "No, this just doesn't feel right. I don't see the local troops. They should be hanging around eyeing the newcomers. I've never heard of soldiers that weren't curious. Nobody's watching. Very unlike soldiers. They've been told to stay away. I wish I knew why."

Kip answered, "Count your blessings. We don't need the distractions. You've got your dress rehearsal this afternoon."

Kip looked up. "I spoke with councillor B'Yuon. You'll be pleased to know that we can wear our ceremonial daggers. The Jod Marine Third Regiment will post guards to secure our armory and encampment so everyone can attend."

Jo'Orom felt his empty holster. K'Rin normally would never allow others to secure Tenebrea weapons. He muttered, "I'm going to miss K'Rin."

Kip set his screen aside. "You can have any billet you want in Heptar. You know that K'Rin wants you on his staff."

"No, thank you." Jo'Orom shook his head. "Looks like we might have a real war this time. At my age, the Cor Ordinate War is my last chance to get into a fight."

Hal K'Rin remained aboard the *Tyker*. He annotated a list of the Fleet admirals, noting the ones he considered imbued with the warrior spirit, capable of managing violence and those who simply excelled at managing men and matériel. He walked the decks of the *Tyker*, now empty except for a bare maintenance crew who volunteered to skip the pageantry below.

He made a final entry in his log, commending the crew; then he sat in his chair on the bridge. He chuckled at his own emotions: *I'll be damned if I'm not getting homesick.*

The *Tyker*, more than any single place, had been his home since he left his mother's house. He did not even know what his apartment looked like on Heptar. He'd never owned much furniture. His few utilitarian personal effects had been crated and shipped to his new quarters in the Heptar Palace weeks ago. Since he left his mother's house as a young man, K'Rin had not accumulated much of anything but experiences and loyalties.

He thought about the Tenebrea that comprised his crew and executed his will. They were more than his eyes and ears, and his strong arms. They were his intimates, his family. Compared to them, the Rin Clan was a mere formality—even a burden. He realized painfully that he had no family at Heptar: no wife, no children. He thought about R'Oueu and wondered if seeing her again after so many years would be awkward or perhaps worse. Social contact was unavoidable. Fortunately he'd be too busy to be lonely.

K'Rin would miss daily contact with the Tenebrea, and therein lay the greatest sacrifice. He had few, if any, friends at Heptar—political allies perhaps, but few friends, and many enemies. Even B'Yuon had become a stranger after so many years. He thought he might populate his Heptar staff with old comrades, but he refused to deplete the small cadre of officers and leave the Tenebrea without effective leadership. Nor did he think they would like the gilded cage of Heptar any better than he did.

"Sir, the shuttle is ready."

K'Rin turned and saw a uniformed Tenebrea holding a garment bag with K'Rin's uniforms. K'Rin's eyes instinctively glanced toward the crew member's nametag and rank. "Sep Gem-Bar. You were in Andrea's class. I remember you."

"Yes, sir." Gem-Bar shied from making small talk with the admiral, yet he managed to ask, "Is she here at Heptar?"

"No, she's safe." K'Rin caught himself. "I mean, she's on a critical mission; however, she is safe." He continued to wonder what would be the price of success on the council. Pl'Don would insist that he give up Andrea to the Cor Ordinate. *The hard practicality is*

*that Pl'Don is right: we can buy a couple months with
which to mobilize. I could give her up and disavow any
knowledge of her misadventure on Cor. Is it better that
one person be sacrificed than for the whole Jod race to
perish? Heretofore, my answer was so obviously, yes.
The ultimate practical consideration of survival alone
made the answer obvious! But Andrea? My personal
motives mustn't cloud my judgment. Not now. I have
always had to make the hard, practical decisions. One
would think these decisions might get easier.*

"Sir?" Gem-Bar tried to engage K'Rin. "We must
leave in five minutes or wait for the next orbit."

"Let's go." K'Rin followed Gem-Bar to the shuttle.
On the way to the surface, Gem-Bar said nothing.
Upon disembarking from the shuttle, K'Rin asked
Gem-Bar, "Do you consider yourself practical?"

Gem-Bar answered, "I try to be, sir."

K'Rin looked at the young Tenebrea and admonished, "Well, don't try too hard. It erodes one's charac-
ter."

The Tenebrea gathered in ranks in the mall outside
the Assembly Hall. The giant gate yawned open to welcome them to their destiny. They checked their gig lines
and the placement of their awards. They adjusted their
belts and daggers. Each stood on a piece of tape mark-
ing the interval. When they didn't fuss with their uniforms, they gawked at the majestic building, the high
walls, the intricate inlay of the polished floors, and the
larger-than-life statuary. Few of the Tenebrea ever suspected that such wealth existed.

At the appointed time, the commander of the
Heptar Regiment gave a hand signal. Jo'Orom, Kip,
and Bal'Don—commandant of the Tenebrea School—

marched to the fore, and turned about. Jo'Orom barked, "A—tten—shun!"

The slight din in the mall fell to utter silence. One synchronized padded thud echoed as the Tenebrea planted their left feet and softly slapped their hands to their sides. From inside the assembly, they heard a trumpet fanfare followed by solemn martial music punctuated with muffled drums.

From the rear, K'Rin marched. He reviewed his beloved Tenebrea as he walked through their ranks. At his side, dressed in heavy brocade of gold and silver, walked Councilor B'Yuon, who held in his fat fist the parchment with the proclamation restoring K'Rin to his father's seat. B'Yuon struggled to keep pace with K'Rin's longer stride.

As K'Rin approached the head of the formation, the doors to the Assembly Hall swung open slowly. As he crossed the threshold, the band finished a measure and stopped. K'Rin led the Tenebrea inside.

The Tenebrea marched into the empty Assembly Hall in two columns. Each column stopped at chalk marks on the polished marble floor, breaking smartly into ranks. The footfalls were barely audible, like padded cat feet. No music played; no cadence called. One hundred and seventy-four Tenebrea stood in two formations like heavy shadows on the bright rose and tan marble floors. Their uniforms, stripped of their deadly hardware, were unusually crisp. The officers wore platinum belts with ceremonial dagger sheathed. The enlisted wore the shorter utility knife strapped to their leg below the knee. These muscular soldiers were quiet as ghosts. All eyes faced the empty dais and the councilors' ornate chairs. On the far right, the Rin chair sparkled with its lacquered finish and enameled crest.

Hal K'Rin and Feld Jo'Orom stood several paces to the front. Jo'Orom wore the service stripes and decorations earned in his stint in the regular Fleet. Splotches of color stood out like poppies on his broad chest. K'Rin wore no decorations except thin gold braid on his sleeves, indicating his rank, and he wore a red sash over his dark uniform—the same sash his father wore at the council more than twenty years ago. Vindication.

Above, the assembly members sat with their wives at ten-foot intervals in the mezzanine gallery on the left. Their faces remained in the shadows although their robes, especially their sleeves, caught the light. K'Rin surveyed the faces, hoping to catch a glimpse of R'Oueu. He was not surprised that she was absent—certainly less awkward for both of them.

While they waited for the ceremony to begin, K'Rin thought of the months to come. He joined a council divided in opinion regarding the Ordinate. He was not fool enough to believe that his enemies would now embrace him and his assessment of the threat. He had little time to convince them to mobilize, although with Pl'Don's help the ultimate decision was secure.

Ironically, if the Ordinate caught them unaware, these same assembly members honoring him today would heap the blame on him and make him suffer history's opprobrium. Nevertheless, K'Rin had longed for this day. Although, now that he was moments away from being installed on the council, his inner peace was shaken. He had accepted the prospect of loneliness. For the first time since he left his mother's house to join the Fleet, he felt the corrosive fear of failure.

A panel in the wall opened, and a large Jod wearing a saffron-colored mantle stepped into the room to announce the council. "All rise!" The assembly rose.

Their stiff robes rustled. The council members entered from the left and proceeded the length of the dais. All wore mantles of subdued colors, embroidered with ancient runes from different Jodic dialects. K'Rin recognized his enemies and took some inner delight, noticing that they were pale, even nervous. He thought they squirmed. Each took a place at the table. The dour councilors turned and faced the Tenebrea. Obviously, the wizened old toadies were not happy by K'Rin's return. Resigned, yes. Obedient to Pl'Don's pronouncement, yes. Happy, no.

When the Rin House led the council, these tepid councilors had little influence. Under Pl'Don they had marginally more. Now their fears of the Ordinate outweighed their fear of losing what power they enjoyed. Now they must swallow the loathsome truth that they needed the Rin Clan more than the Rin Clan needed them. One chair remained empty. True to his word, B'Yuon had restored K'Rin's father's chair. On the high back, the Rin Triskelion sparkled in crimson enamel. K'Rin turned slightly to nod his appreciation to B'Yuon who, freed from military convention, embraced K'Rin, kissing him on the cheek. He then walked the remaining fifty paces to the dais and took his place behind the lectern.

Then Pl'Don entered and briskly walked to his place. He wore a dark green mantle with a blue and silver sash. He paused to make eye contact with K'Rin. "Please be seated."

Jo'Orom barked, "Tenebrea! At ease." His voice echoed though the hall. The Tenebrea silently but smartly shifted to a more comfortable position: a wider stance with their thick hands now placed as fists on their waists above their belts, elbows extended slightly.

The rest of the council slowly lowered their frail bodies into their cushioned seats, and young pages appeared from behind curtains to gently shove the clumsy chairs toward the table.

K'Rin tried to read Pl'Don's face and couldn't. Pl'Don seemed annoyed by the crowd, yet continued to speak through an unctuous smile. "Council members. It is good that you are all here today to witness an event that forever puts to rest the nagging contradiction that exists between the Clan Rin and the rest of the council." Pl'Don spoke in stentorian tones.

B'Yuon unrolled his parchment and looked to Pl'Don for his cue. The assembly members rose to their feet to hear the proclamation. Then Pl'Don raised his voice and pointed a finger at Hal K'Rin. "By the consent of the executive council and by my authority as the First Among Equals, I hereby order that you, Hal K'Rin, be arrested for high treason. We sentence you to be incarcerated on Klamdara for the rest of your natural life. Likewise the entire Tenebrea is outlawed and their freedom forfeit."

Instantly, the side doors of the chamber opened. In poured Jod infantry wearing body armor. They brandished proton lances. As quickly as the threat arrived, the Tenebrea closed ranks around K'Rin. The officers drew their daggers and the enlisted men their utility knives. A large Jod infantryman closed in first for the honor of arresting Hal K'Rin. He held his lance ready to fire in one hand, hand manacles in the other. He growled, "Out of my way!"

The hall filled with armed men and the sound of boots and the whine of lances powering up. K'Rin looked up at the dais to see Pl'Don's confident smirk, and K'Rin's neck flushed scarlet. *Pl'Don wants a blood-*

bath. He wants to provoke us to suicide. Discipline, not courage, is our only ally today.

Before K'Rin could utter an order, a young Tenebrea broke from the gray and black huddle. With a fluid motion, he ducked to the floor, avoiding a blast from the oncoming lance. Continuing the motion, the Tenebrea swept the feet of the infantryman and appeared to somersault over the large supine soldier. Instead, the Tenebrea sprang to his feet while the infantryman lay shivering on the floor, a short titanium handle protruding behind his ear. K'Rin shrugged away his entourage and plowed his way back to the front of the formation.

The bold young Tenebrea turned to face a volley of lances knocking him down, buckling his knees, killing him. A second Tenebrea leaped from the huddle to help his fallen comrade and was instantly cut down by lance fire. He fell over his dead comrade and his lifeless arms involuntarily embraced his friend. Both lay at the feet of Jo'Orom and K'Rin—the dead Tenebreas' eyes frozen on some distant thought, grinning at some poignant irony, chests smoldering from the lethal volley. Disrupted tissue and blood oozed past the charred flesh.

K'Rin raised his hand and ordered loudly, "Stop! Tenebrea, stand fast." His voice pierced the growing din. K'Rin looked briefly at the dais where B'Yuon stood quivering in terror.

A plaintive voice challenged. "Let us at least die fighting!"

"Silence!" K'Rin bellowed to staunch the same esprit he'd trained into his fighters. Then to offer them some hope, however false, he muttered somberly, "Not here. Not now. Pass the word." The Tenebrea obeyed and stopped resistance. K'Rin detected a shadow cross Pl'Don's face, and he knew he was right. Pl'Don wanted him dead. He wanted the excuse to kill K'Rin and the Tenebrea without the political backlash associated with massacre. He even arranged to have the entire assembly present to witness the Jod regulars defending themselves from a bunch of armed fanatics. But K'Rin denied Pl'Don his excuse.

The Jod infantry took the Tenebrea's daggers and knives, slapped manacles on their wrists. In two minutes the Tenebrea was reduced to a sullen mass, their necks inflamed with anger.

K'Rin spoke. "Pl'Don, let my men go. You have me."

Pl'Don laughed cruelly. "Oh, no. I can't have two hundred trained assassins wandering about the Jod system wrestling with their conflicted loyalties. I'd never get another good night's sleep. Even you Bal'Don." He pointed to the Tenebrea School commandant standing next to K'Rin. "Although you are kinsman, you'll remain with your comrades. Besides, nepotism is unseemly in my position."

Bal'Don shouted back, "You dishonor our clan!" A guard struck Bal'Don with a closed fist to silence him.

Pl'Don offered a bemused smile. "You see, it's best that we keep K'Rin's little brood of assassins intact."

Suddenly, a small commotion broke out in the ranks behind K'Rin. K'Rin turned to see a manacled Tamor-Kyl shoving his way from the center of the formation past K'Rin toward the dais. Tamor's eyes were wild, but his neck showed no signs of fear. The infantry did not intercede, but let Tamor pass, although a hundred weapons were aimed at him, ready to cut him down in one violent moment.

As Tamor passed, K'Rin said firmly, "Tamor! I order you to stand down. Don't throw your life away like this. I forbid it!"

Tamor stopped and looked at K'Rin with utter contempt. "Weak old man . . ." He turned his back to K'Rin and walked toward the dais. K'Rin braced himself to see the unarmed and shackled Tamor cut down in cold blood.

Pl'Don raised a hand to give a signal to the Jod officers, allowing the manacled Tamor to approach the dais. Then he said, "Set Tamor-Kyl loose. He has earned our clemency and our gratitude."

K'Rin walked in the lead down the cobblestone street. The jingle of chains and the long column of black uniforms attracted a crowd of civilians. They watched in awe as the Tenebrea, shackled together in leg irons, shuffled single file. Two Jod regulars in full battle gear flanked each prisoner. Each guard had his handlance pointed at a prisoner's head, with his finger on the firing button.

K'Rin sensed fear everywhere, and he was humbled by the Tenebrea's stern rejection of their fears and their faith in him. How misplaced! His heart sank knowing he was so directly responsible for their plight. Did they still believe that K'Rin would finesse this disaster? He had presumed too much: that the council did need him, or at least would never risk strife with the Rin Clan. To be so wrong! K'Rin struggled to conceal his doubts from his soldiers.

The Tenebrea marched through the old bronze gates of the Heptar barracks down a worn cobblestone avenue toward the landing pad below. Diplomats, support staff, off-duty soldiers, and shop owners lined the way gawking, pointing in critical but hushed tones. Even in manacles, the Tenebrea walked with their heads up, alert— their eyes soaking in details, such as the faces of their detractors. Many of those who came to gawk nervously averted their eyes lest their gloating invite the Tenebrea's retribution. As they approached the bulky troop transport, a familiar figure stepped forward to halt the column: Tamor-Kyl. He wore the uniform of a Jod Fleet Commodore. He dismissed K'Rin's guards and stood toe to toe with his former superior. Tamor spoke quietly so that other Jod ears might not discern their conversation. "I've been promoted." Tamor pointed to the stripes on his sleeve. "Now, instead of a dead-end desk assignment, I'm going to work in the field with a command. By the way, the council has graciously given me command of your former vessel. I have taken the *Tyker.*"

K'Rin looked around. "What did you do with the crew?"

"I killed them. Pity, actually. They resisted the boarding party. It was really quite senseless—Gem-Bar especially. I liked him. However, I was very disappointed when I didn't find your pet, Andrea, aboard."

"You would be dead if you had." K'Rin made his point as if stating a simple theorem.

"Then perhaps you'll tell me where she is." Tamor leaned forward and grinned.

K'Rin forced a smile of his own. "I'm counting on her to find you. All things considered, I think I'll sleep better than you will."

Abruptly, Tamor changed the tack of his informal interrogation. "You must tell me how to procure the Quazel enzyme."

"Why? Are you due for your dosage?" K'Rin's sense of irony buttressed his flagging spirits.

Tamor plied him with reason. "In a few months, you and your men will start to show the effects of Quazel poisoning. If you tell me how to procure the enzyme, I promise you everybody will continue to get enzyme implants."

"Your promise is worthless." K'Rin's eyes blazed with contempt.

Tamor's neck turned a burnt orange. "If you don't tell me, you are responsible for their agonizing deaths."

K'Rin replied, "I am already responsible for their deaths. By withholding the enzyme I can be responsible for your death, too. You failed to think your operation through to completion. Now, you can't extract yourself. Can it be that we both outsmarted ourselves? Now you're as dead as I am. My death will be bad enough. Yours will be horrible; you are a coward, after all."

Tamor slapped K'Rin across the face with full force. K'Rin did not flinch. Tamor raised his hand again, when a Heptar guard intervened. "Sir! To strike a clan headsman, a Hal no less, is a serious crime!"

Tamor quickly looked around to see if any council member might have witnessed this sacrilege. K'Rin licked a trickle of blood from his lip and said mockingly, "Commodore Tamor-Kyl, enjoy your promotion and command of the *Tyker:* you only have six months to live."

"Nevertheless," Tamor returned the taunt, "while you rot in Klamdara Prison, I'll find the Quazel. I'll find your pet, Andrea, too. The Rin Family name and your rank won't save you. I'll watch all of you die, then I'll rebuild the Tenebrea under my leadership."

chapter 11

The *Benwoi* slowed to kinetic speed. The forward screen flickered to life with a graphic display overlaying the Terran system and providing their relative position. Andrea explained the rudiments of Terran security regarding space traffic. "We're an armed merchant, therefore, not eligible for a civilian spaceport. We need to land at a secure facility, and we need an alias for ground control." Andrea looked over the charts. "The Baltimore Spaceport Facility can handle armed merchants. So, who are we?"

H'Roo queried the Jod Fleet registry. The Jod merchant marine consisted of almost five thousand starships. H'Roo's family, the Parh Clan, owned the registrations for more than three hundred of them; several were armed merchants commissioned before the days of the Alliance. As they began deceleration toward Earth, H'Roo typed a few keys and announced, "Now we are the armed merchant *Lan'Pfin,* one of the Parhs' old ships. Your Terran control won't know the difference."

Looking at the forward screen, and a magnification of Earth, H'Roo added, "So much blue water."

Andrea felt a twinge of homesickness. "Maybe we can mix a little pleasure with business." She wanted to be lost in a crowd again. Noticing the tilt of the Earth with the North Pole in daylight, she said, "It must be summer in Baltimore."

Andrea saw the distinct outlines of the Earth continents, more or less shrouded in white swirling clouds. They made their approach over the East Coast of North America where she pointed to the mouth of the Chesapeake Bay, a small body of water pinched by a long finger of land. Slightly to the west was a gray corridor: a thick mesh of roads, rail, houses, and tall office buildings, where Washington blended into Baltimore, and Baltimore stretched to Wilmington and beyond.

She remembered that during summer weekends, the city of Baltimore closed the streets to vehicles, and people poured in to fill the vacuum. Beer tents popped up like lilies in the sun. People crammed the alleys; vendors lit outdoor grills. The aroma of sausages, waffles, fried fish, and potatoes stirred through the harbor. Street musicians played all sorts of instruments: pipes, guitars, mandolins, and every kind of percussion— empty oilcans, bells, and big drums. All kinds of food and music from all over the world. In the evening, the Baltimore Consort gave concerts of Renaissance music. Baltimore was never so alive as when they stopped to celebrate. On such a day, the Ordinate Hunters murdered her family. Andrea banished the memory.

"Are you okay?" H'Roo asked.

"I'll be fine." She sat down.

The sun was just above the horizon as they landed at the Baltimore Spaceport Facility on the flats northeast of the city. H'Roo set the fraudulently named *Lan'Pfin* on one of the hundreds of square concrete aprons. He invoked his father's name and the family's considerable line of credit to secure a hangar and fuel for their ship. "My father will be none too pleased when he gets this bill for services."

Port security boarded to safety-lock the ship's main weapons. In addition, they sealed the *Benwoi*'s small arms in a locker. Andrea and H'Roo were in no position to argue.

Using H'Roo's line of credit, they procured a debit card and some cash. H'Roo inspected the curious green notes, before handing them to Andrea. Then, they rented personal ground transport, a small two-seater vehicle that burned hydrogen. She fastened her seat belt and cautioned H'Roo to do the same.

"Why? Are we going tactical?" H'Roo asked as he pulled the straps over his head.

Andrea raised an eyebrow, then accelerated out of the parking lot. They drove over the winding congested roads south, toward the small city of Annapolis. "We just missed the azaleas." Andrea pointed to the bushes in the road median, a tired bumper of flowers. The whites and pinks were burned and drooping.

Andrea drove unerringly to the center of Annapolis and parked in front of the Maryland Bureau of Vital Statistics. From her breast pocket she pulled the piece of film that contained Eric's DNA data. She held it before the sun. The film was an elaborate set of bar codes of varying widths, lengths, and primary colors. H'Roo asked, "Are you sure you want to go through with this?"

"I'm sure." She led H'Roo up the limestone steps into the utilitarian building. A clerk, a small torpid man who seemed fused into a Plexiglas window, directed Andrea to a keyboard to make her request, a copy of Steve Dewinter's DNA record.

From his side of the glass, the clerk read the request with one eye fixed on Andrea. Most DNA match requests came with a court order to resolve some unsavory affair. Wives who sought their husband's DNA almost always had divorce on their minds—or homicide. But the records showed that Steve Dewinter was already deceased, and the cause of death was homicide. That an alien Jod accompanied the woman simply raised suspicions. The clerk sighed, "I need proof of identification. Please rest your chin on the eye scanner."

Andrea did as she was told.

The clerk's voice remained monotone. "Okay, Mrs. Dewinter. Do you want film or digital?"

"Film."

"That takes a minute to print. I'll authorize your request. Ten dollars, please."

Andrea slipped a note through the slot at the bottom of the thick Plexiglas.

"You should have gotten your husband's DNA scan when you copied your records—could've saved you the ten dollars."

"I didn't request my records." Andrea thought for a second that she misunderstood the clerk.

"Sure you did." The clerk asserted blandly. He pivoted his screen around to show the data entry. Pointing with his finger, "Four days ago, Office of Military Affairs, Brussels, European Federation. Says here, you requested a copy of your records; reason, originals lost in fire. You downloaded all your records: birth certificate, school transcripts, military records, marriage certificate, tax account records—everything."

"You are sure about that?" She asked rhetorically. She believed her eyes, but found the news disturbing. *Who would be looking for me?*

The clerk shrugged his round shoulders. "Not my job to be sure."

Andrea accepted a small white envelope with a film record of Steve's DNA, signing a chit to complete the transaction. She preceded H'Roo into the hall and found a bench in the arboretum that filled the foyer. She fumbled with the small envelope. "Here, you look. My hands are shaking." She shoved the envelope toward H'Roo, then handed him the film of Eric's scan. "Tell me what you see." Andrea looked down at the floor and set her face like flint.

"With pleasure." H'Roo took the two pieces of film. "Now we can put an end to this ridiculous"—he put one piece of film on top of the other; then held them up to the sun pouring through a skylight—"this ridiculous . . ." H'Roo's voice faltered. He carefully slid the top film a fraction of a millimeter. His confidence crumbled. He looked sideways at Andrea.

"What?" Andrea demanded.

"Oh, I'm so sorry." H'Roo handed the film to Andrea. "Steve's and Eric's DNA are an exact match. Exact."

Andrea grabbed the film and held it up to the light, repeating H'Roo's motions. She became pale as she herself became certain of the match. "I was afraid—I mean, I knew they were too similar. Oh . . ." Andrea groaned. *Steve, how could you?*

She turned to H'Roo and uttered her worst suspicion, "Steve was a clone, wasn't he?"

"The DNA is a match. I cannot think of any other explanation. I'm really sorry." He reached over to take her hand.

Andrea looked away from H'Roo as she felt herself begin to choke. The certitude took her breath away. She looked at the glass ceiling of the arboretum. *I didn't know . . . Steve was a clone—a copy, just another drudge like the hundreds of drudges I saw on Cor. Manufactured! Oh, dear God. And Glendon? What was she?* A tear ran down her cheek and she quickly wiped it away on her sleeve. *I won't cry—I won't! Steve was singular in so many ways—in ways that matter. His spirit was no copy—his happiness was not manufactured. Most of all, I know for certain that he loved me as he could love no other woman—not because I am unique, but because he was unique, because together we were unique. One thing I must find out—did Steve know he was a clone? I can stand anything, even his death, but not such a monstrous lie that would cheapen our love and break our vows before we took them.* In her mind she saw Steve in the last moments of his life, huddled over their daughter, shielding the child from the hail of Ordinate bullets. *Nothing about Steve was cheap.*

She turned to H'Roo. "I don't think Steve was aware that he was a clone."

"What difference does that make?" H'Roo said, mystified.

"None to you. Everything to me. We're going to Nabbs Creek and visit the Dewinters."

They drove down a narrow asphalt road that meandered around lazy water. A drawbridge stopped them and they waited for a racing sloop to motor in from the bay. The sun began to cast long shadows. Andrea pointed up the creek. "The Dewinters live in a small cottage in the middle of ten acres past that bend in the creek."

She turned off the pavement onto a lane marked

with a green sign: Shore Loop. Beneath the sign were two rusted mailboxes with house numbers painted. The loop was a washboard of ruts. Gravel made of old pulverized clamshells crackled under the car wheels. In the distance, a large dog barked aggressively.

Andrea followed the loop clockwise to the water's edge. She parked in the mottled shade of a willow tree next to a weather-beaten pier occupied by only a ratty chicken-wire crab pot and several neat coils of line, a green garden hose, and a faded plastic owl nailed to a pylon.

"We'll walk the rest of the way." Andrea killed the motor. "The Dewinters live up the hill in the middle of those tall oaks."

"They must be wealthy." H'Roo got out of the car and surveyed the area.

Andrea laughed, "Not really. The channel favors the other side. The real wealth is over there."

H'Roo walked onto the decrepit dock. Andrea joined him. The opposite side of Nabbs Creek was crowded with pleasure craft—mostly large sailboats. They lined the far shore, nestled together along wooden piers. Larger craft, fifty feet and longer, sat off-shore on the glassy water tethered by lines to round red and white mooring buoys.

The day's activities at the far shore marina were coming to an end. Day sailors coiled their sheets and washed the salt from the teak decks. On the land surrounding the marina, scores of boats sat cradled on wooden platforms. Scruffy men scraped and sanded barnacles from boat bottoms.

Andrea explained wistfully, "We used to sail up Nabbs Creek and tie up at the marina. Steve used to dinghy over here to see his folks. I stayed over there at the marina with Glendon. I rarely came over here to the Dewinters' house." She gazed at the black water. "I never felt comfortable over here."

A female mallard corralled a clutch of her ducklings in the shade of a pier. A gray heron stood in the shallows as still as a weather vane. H'Roo had never seen such waterfowl. A faint breeze tossed a field of ripples across the black water. Halyards slapped the old aluminum masts, filling the air with metallic clanks. H'Roo commented, "Sounds like the Gyre Temple Bells."

She turned around and said, "Follow me." They walked uphill through a short field of tall grass toward a stand of chestnut oaks. Overgrown boxwoods, ten feet tall, formed a barrier. Andrea confidently took H'Roo around the far side to a cracked and potholed driveway. A fat tabby cat meandered defiantly into the front yard to inspect the interlopers, yet stayed prudently two short steps from the thick boxwoods and safety. A dilapidated sedan sat forlornly in the driveway.

Noting the car, she said, "They're home." She pushed open a wooden gate, long in need of some white paint. A fresh crop of weeds choked the flagstone walk. Dandelions dotted the lawn with their cheerful yellow flowers and white fuzz balls. Except for the cat, the small brick cottage looked abandoned. Andrea walked onto the stoop and knocked.

Nobody came. She noticed a furtive shadow cross a room at the back of the house. She knocked again and called out. "Jason! Leslie! I know you're home. Answer the door! It's me, your daughter-in-law, Andrea."

Andrea raised her fist to pound on the door, when an old man shuffled through the living room to the door. His voice complained, "You should not have come back." After a click of a dead bolt, the door cracked opened to reveal a glimpse of a scowling face: Mr. Dewinter. "What do you want?"

Andrea braced the door open with her body. "My friend and I want to come in and ask you a few questions." Andrea nodded toward H'Roo. When Mr. Dewinter saw the Jod behind her, he backed away from the door. His eyes betrayed both fear and recognition. "Who sent you?" he asked.

Andrea didn't wait for a further invitation; she pressed open the door and walked into the living room. Andrea demanded, "Go get Leslie," and the old man backed way.

Under her breath, she told H'Roo, "When he saw you, he acted like he'd seen a ghost." H'Roo didn't reply; rather, he stood back, a reluctant invader of the Dewinters' privacy.

Andrea looked about the living room. In any other old home, the sideboard would be littered with silver frames bearing photographs of family. The Dewinters had no such mementos. In fact, the house was devoid of memory: no memory of Steve, no memory of places traveled, no artifacts for sentimental value—nothing. Looking at the walls and dusty surfaces, at the old-fashioned Venetian blinds pulled down, one might conclude that nobody lived here. Indeed, she thought, the old occupants of this house were hiding—not living—here.

Andrea stepped through the plain living room into the small alcove of a dining room. Mr. Dewinter's pipe lay next to a porcelain ashtray. Behind her she heard a weak voice, "Andrea?" She turned to see a pair of tired slate gray eyes peering from a pale wrinkled face. Mrs. Dewinter tapped a chair with her plastic cane and said, "Do sit down and ask your questions. Would you like something cold to drink?" The old woman looked at H'Roo closely as if she recognized him. Andrea wondered, *Why are they afraid of H'Roo?*

Andrea answered with more civility, "No thank you."

The Dewinters sat together on a threadbare sofa, nervous as if anticipating a rough interrogation. Andrea said, "First, let me introduce you to my comrade, H'Roo Parh from Jod. H'Roo, meet my in-laws: Jason and Leslie Dewinter."

Mr. Dewinter asserted impatiently, "Please ask your questions, then leave."

Andrea continued, "Before I ask my questions, let me tell you where I've been. Mostly, I spent some time on Jod, then I spent several months on a planet called Cor."

Leslie turned to her husband. Her face sagged.

"That's impossible!" Jason Dewinter exclaimed.

Andrea watched the Dewinters closely. "How so?" Andrea asked.

Jason fumbled for an answer. "I . . . I don't know. I just thought that Cor was a closed system."

Andrea pretended to accept his explanation. "During my travels, I stumbled upon the most amazing fact, that—well I must admit—shocked the hell out of me." Andrea's face darkened, her lips drew tight such that H'Roo and Jason Dewinter saw immediately that she was a tumult inside. Her calm discourse almost seemed irrational. "I met an ERC clone that looks just like Steve—identical, in fact. Could be his twin! In fact, the ERC's DNA matches Steve's." She pulled the two pieces of film from her breast pocket.

The old woman pulled her hand away from her husband as she cried, "Oh, no! Jason, she knows."

"Be quiet, Leslie."

Andrea pounded her fist on the table with such

vehemence that the china cups in the adjacent cabinet clattered. "You came from Cor, didn't you? You didn't adopt Steve: you manufactured him."

Leslie Dewinter cried, "But I did adopt Steve!"

"Then why don't you just tell me the whole truth?" Andrea's voice softened in sympathy for the old mother who now appeared heartbroken.

Leslie Dewinter covered her face with her hands and emitted a pitiful groan.

"All right, all right!" Jason Dewinter answered as he tried to console his wife. The old man looked at his frail wife with strained affection. "Leslie and I are not from Earth. We're Ordinate. Leslie worked in the Clone Welfare Institute as a genetic engineer for the New Products Division. I was an economist."

"Go on," Andrea ordered.

The old man began to relax. "We had a good life. I was happy, but Leslie was not happy, and she did not have the courage to tell me why. She wanted children and I never did."

He looked contritely at his aged wife. "Leslie began work on a new model clone—the new constable model. They took DNA from some Ordinate donor and produced the usual six clones."

"Preclones." Leslie Dewinter softly corrected her husband.

"That's right. Preclones are not yet altered for sterility. So they hatched the preclones at an early stage, equivalent of four years old, and then each of the geneticists, Leslie being one, worked with a candidate. They subjected them to batteries of physical and neurological tests. At the conclusion of the tests, they selected two candidates for alteration and replication. The rejected preclones, including Leslie's, were to be canceled."

Andrea interrupted with a question. "Did Steve know that he was a clone?"

Mrs. Dewinter looked knowingly at Andrea. Her old eyes still mourned the loss of her adopted son. "We never told him. It was safer for everyone that he not know. He never suspected he was anything but my adopted child. He had no memories of Cor. Steve never hid anything from you."

"Thank you." Andrea felt her heart pounding against her ribs. She had just heard the first comforting words since Steve and Glendon's murder.

Andrea looked at the ceiling to avoid eye contact. Her mind sorted the data and so far every piece fit. Steve and Eric were not a coincidence. She was not exaggerating their physical similarities. She was not going crazy. Now she had a handle on the truth. That Steve died in Eric's place was tragic, but not senseless, not bad luck. Everything has cause and effect. But she knew Steve's story was incomplete. Andrea took a deep breath and turned toward Jason Dewinter. "Tell me everything."

Jason Dewinter shook his head. "The rest of this story is pure insanity. I still don't understand what we were thinking. Leslie did not deliver her preclone back to the lab nursery for cancellation that night. When I came home, I found her shaking with fear. She took me into our bedroom and there wrapped in a blanket was a small boy with dark shaggy hair. The child was frightened of its new surroundings. I knew instantly what had happened, and I knew the consequences. Harboring a clone is treason, a capital crime for which the sentence is automatic. There, sitting on my bed was my wife's death warrant. First, I developed a plan to sneak the child back into the laboratory and try to gloss the short absence, but Leslie refused. I thought of killing the preclone myself and concocting a story to save Leslie, but I knew she'd hate me for it."

"I suppose it was selfish of me," Mrs. Dewinter admitted.

Mr. Dewinter did not contradict his wife. Turning back to Andrea he continued, "Anyway, the damage was done. I knew that within hours, the institute authorities would know that the preclone was missing. They'd immediately implicate Leslie. The Ordinate hangs traitors."

Mr. Dewinter stammered as he tried to collect his emotions, "I, ah . . . I couldn't let that happen. I wouldn't want to live without you." He reached over and grabbed his wife's hand.

"Then what happened?" Andrea prodded Mr. Dewinter back to his story line.

"I smuggled Leslie and the boy offworld with a substantial bribe and a lie: she was my mistress, the child was illegitimate, we were escaping a disgrace. We sought asylum in the Jod system where we were handed over to their offworld security force." Dewinter looked at H'Roo. "The case officer brought us to Earth where we started a new life and raised Steve. Every day of our lives we've lived in fear that the Ordinate would find us. From time to time, Jod security informs us whenever they suspect Hunter team activity in the Terran system. But all we can do is hide."

Andrea interrupted, pointedly, "Who is your point of contact in Jod security?"

"Some new fellow named Mat Gro'Zhen."

H'Roo mentioned to Andrea, "He's Tenebrea. I've heard of him."

Jason Dewinter returned to his train of thought. "For instance, two days ago we got a message." From his pants pocket, Jason pulled a crumpled note in his own hand-writing. He read out loud. "Suspected Hunter team, Benelux area. At least they're four thousand miles away."

Andrea thought, Benelux . . . Belgium? Someone in Brussels was looking for me . . . they have my records! Cor Hunters? Andrea felt the hair stand on her neck. She decided not to alarm the Dewinters with her spec-ulations until she had the information she came for. She asked, "Before Mat Gro'Zhen, who handled you?"

Jason Dewinter looked at Andrea as if he were sur-prised at her question. "Why, Hal K'Rin, himself. He took a special interest in us."

Andrea was stunned, and yet the pieces came together in a perfect fit. No wonder K'Rin felt remorse for Steve! He detours on his mission to Earth. He sees Eric and immediately realizes the Hunter team is chas-ing Eric but might find Steve. He races back to Earth, of course, straight to Baltimore to protect Steve. But he's too late. He feels responsible for Steve's widow. *He does not want me to know that I was married to a clone, so he hides the truth. I must apologize for all the mistrust I heaped on K'Rin.*

She looked around the modest house, Steve's child-hood home. She looked at the unhappy old woman who sat on the old sofa, her life spun around by her decision to save a young boy. She looked at the tired old man whose life was drawn into the maelstrom of his wife's decision. She had always thought ill of them; now she admired Leslie's compassion and Jason's fidelity. No wonder Steve was such a good man. I owe the Dewinters an apology, too. She was about to tell them what she felt when she heard a dog barking loudly, frantically. Through the window she saw head-lights beyond a stand of trees: the beams bouncing because of the ruts in the road. The headlights illuminated the house, then abruptly switched off. She asked rhetorically, "Are you expecting anybody else tonight?"

"No," Jason Dewinter replied in a worried tone.

"Your neighbor?" Andrea asked with increased urgency.

Leslie answered, "He doesn't have a car. He borrows ours, and . . ."

Andrea cut her off. "H'Roo, come with me. Jason, do you have a place you can hide?"

"The cellar crawl space." He stood up alarmed.

"Take Leslie. Stay out of sight. Go now." Andrea was already on her feet heading for the kitchen with H'Roo. "May be nothing. We're going to check on that panel truck pulling into your driveway."

On her way through the kitchen, Andrea jerked open the utensil drawers. The Dewinter home was a poor armory. As she rummaged through the drawers she briefed H'Roo. "I think it's a Hunter team. They got my records in Brussels. They'd have this address. Take this." She gave H'Roo an eight-inch French knife. She found a skinning knife and an ice pick. She turned off the lights; the two of them slipped out the back door. They ran crouched along a chain-link fence, enmeshed with floriferous honeysuckle.

The faint sound of gravel crunching beneath tires grew louder. Peering through the leaves of the honeysuckle, she saw a van with headlights off slowly rolling to a stop behind the Dewinters' old car. The van's sliding door opened. A large man with a military haircut jumped out with a pistol and a palm radio. He began to patrol the grounds, establishing perimeter security.

A second silhouette emerged from the van and went up the front walk toward the front door. Andrea heard a knock, then she heard the door open; it was left unlocked. A third man exited the driver's side. He peered into the Dewinters' old car, then followed his colleague into the house. Andrea whispered to H'Roo, "Only three. I'll get the perimeter guard. You stay close to the house. Don't do anything until I get back." She didn't wait for a reply but slipped away.

She crouched at the edge of the boxwood and looked down the gravel road. Her target walked toward the water. He stopped suddenly and brought a communications disk to his mouth. "Wait for my signal. There's a car parked at the dock!" He pulled a short pistol from the pocket of his light jacket.

Andrea followed, weighing each footfall to maintain silence. The man walked to the car and peered inside the windows. He looked at the decals in the windshield, then looked around the area. He put his hand on the hood of the car. He raised the comm-disk. "Nobody's here. It's a rental. The engine is still warm."

A voice replied, barely audible to Andrea, "I'm coming out to help. We'd better sweep the area."

"Understood." He put the comm-disk back into his pocket and walked cautiously onto the dock, to get a better look up and down the shoreline. He nudged the old crab pot with his toe.

Andrea darted to the car. She ducked and hid, peering around the side. The Ordinate stood with his back to her as he studied the large sloops moored offshore. She pulled the boning knife from her waistband and began to creep behind him. She watched his shoulders carefully, knowing that she must dart to his blind side when he turned around. Her first concern must be his right hand that held the pistol.

She managed three steps onto the pier when a loose

board creaked under her weight. He spun around clockwise and she bounded forward and kicked. She struck the pistol, knocking it from the Ordinate's hand and into the black water. The Ordinate countered with a punch to her ribs that knocked her down to the wood. She rolled, crashing into the chicken-wire crab pot. She scrambled to her feet and raised her knife and slashed the Ordinate's leg as he kicked at her head.

He grunted, pausing only to look at the bleeding gash below the knee. The cut was to the shinbone, painful but ineffectual. Andrea crouched, holding the knife backhanded to slash rather than stab. She leaped at her unarmed enemy.

He stepped into her attack and grabbed her wrist. He suffered further deep cuts to his fingers, but turned her hand violently against her wrist and ligaments. He was strong, taller by five inches, and outweighed her by eighty pounds. Andrea lost her grip on the knife, dropping it to the wood. She kicked it into the water as the Ordinate reached down to claim the weapon. At the same time, she smashed him in the jaw with her knee, breaking his hold.

He rushed her, endured a punch to the face, then wrestled Andrea to the wood. He grabbed her neck with his large hand. He knew exactly where to press the carotid arteries. Andrea's arms were pinned beneath his bulk, but she managed to reach the ice pick in her waistband, turning the point toward the Ordinate and slowly driving it into the man's abdomen. "Arrh!" He slammed her head against the pier as he pushed himself off her.

He pulled the ice pick from his gut and took it in his good hand. "I'm going to put this right through your eye." He lunged at her. He was now winded—slower.

Andrea rolled just as the ice pick grazed her scalp.

The force of the blow buried the pick deep into the dry boards. She scrambled to her feet as the Ordinate tugged at the ice pick.

She grabbed the coil of rope by the crab pot and quickly threw a clove hitch around the Ordinate's neck and pulled with all her might. He reared up, grabbed at the line about his neck, then flailed his arms trying to turn himself to face his attacker. She jerked back as hard as she could and with a sweeping kick knocked the Ordinate's feet out from under him. He crashed to the pier. With his waning strength he reached back and purchased a grip on Andrea's hand, but she felt the grip fade and finally go limp. She looked down at the dead man. In the moonlight, his hands were white. His face was purple, his lips dark, his swollen black tongue clenched between ivory teeth.

"Tom!" A hoarse voice called from behind. She saw the second man walk down the driveway toward her car and the pier. He saw her. He raised his gun, and Andrea threw herself into the shallow water. When she stood, the silt bottom sucked at her feet. She huddled under the dock, figuring that an attempt to make deeper water would only expose her to deadly fire.

She heard the footfall on the pier and soon saw the shadow of a figure pass over the slots between the planking. Directly above, she heard the second Ordinate report in a harsh whisper, "Tom's dead! We're compromised."

The comm-disk hissed and a voice replied, "Recover the body. Get back here! I'll call for backup."

The shadow struggled to lift the weight of the dead man, pausing to untie the gangly cord from the swollen neck. Then he lumbered from the pier up the gravel road toward the house. Andrea crawled out of the muck and water by a stand of cattails. She ran through brambles up the hill to beat them. Her bruised rib ached. She reached the house too late. She saw the smaller Ordinate shrug the dead body from his shoulders to the ground next to the van. He opened the side panel door, then seemed to lose his footing, staggering back. He stumbled and fired a round wildly into the van. He fell backward, dead before he hit the ground. The wooden handle of a kitchen knife protruded from his chest.

H'Roo jumped from the van, reached down, and retrieved the pistol, leaving the knife. Then he limped into the shadows.

Andrea ran to the side of the house and peered through the window. The third Ordinate saw her silhouette in the window and fired his pistol repeatedly, punching holes through the glass. As he fired, he yelled into his communicator, "Bring backup!"

A small shard cut Andrea's face below the left eye as she ducked to the side. As she lay on the ground contemplating her next move, she heard another pair of shots, followed by a third; then H'Roo's voice, "Andrea!"

She stood and peered in the window again. H'Roo stood over the body of the Ordinate, who had three black holes in his back. A pool of blood spread slowly on the wood floor beside the dead Ordinate. A similar large dark stain spread on H'Roo's shirt. Andrea waved through the window, then ran to the front door. "H'Roo, you're hit."

"I would know." H'Roo sat in a chair at the maple table. He tore off his shirt and inspected the holes where the bullet entered his waist above the hipbone then exited. Andrea handed him a thin pillow to staunch the bleeding.

At that moment, Jason peered around the door at the carnage in his living room. Andrea tersely announced, "We've got to get out of here. He," and she pointed to the dead Ordinate, "called their ship." Andrea helped H'Roo back to his feet. Jason returned to the cellar to get his wife.

As they left by the front door, H'Roo complained, "Andrea, you are nothing but trouble. You'll be the death of me yet."

"That little hole won't kill you." Andrea hustled H'Roo down the hill toward their car. "You hear that?" The whine of the turbines alerted her, then the lights. "The ship." Andrea instinctively shoved H'Roo down behind a large oak tree.

The Cor ship raced overhead, then hovered above the Dewinter house. It paused for a moment, bathing the house in a bright bluish light. Then at point blank range, the ship fired a weapon. The small house became a spasm of blast, heat, and wood fragments. The ship instantly turned skyward, accelerating out of sight. Small fires burned in the grass and trees. Smoldering debris rained down.

Andrea asked H'Roo, "Are you all right?" The thick oak had shielded them from the blast.

He grimaced, "Yeah."

Andrea peered around the tree and the vacant lot. She walked back up the hill. The Hunter team had thoroughly eradicated the evidence of their abortive visit. The weapon had blasted a shallow crater where the house, car, and van once stood. The clean bowl-shaped crater indicated a quark grenade.

chapter 12

The steel ramp lowered slowly. The blinding white Klamdara sunlight and dry heat poured in. K'Rin blinked away the pain as he looked out from the shadows of the prison transport.

"Move!" A guard prodded with a stun stick.

K'Rin slowly walked to the top of the ramp that stretched to the dusty surface. He heard the clank of metal chains and garbled threats behind him. The Tenebrea's defiance was changing to a low-grade fever of sullen resistance. On their tedious journey on the slow prison transport, they had lived in cramped space, breathed stale air, and eaten prison rations of boiled maize and water.

K'Rin squinted through the bright sunlight to look at their new world, most likely their grave. On the ochre field, two phalanxes of Jod regulars stood at rigid attention, their weapons drawn. They wore dark face shades to save their eyes from the harsh light, and brown cloth tied over nose and mouth to protect them from the fine dust that rose with the merest breath of moving air. Behind the brigade of soldiers stood the

Klamdara fortress walls: forty feet of concrete. Streaks of rust ran down the walls like dried blood. The fortress stood at the face of a gigantic cat cut into the face of red cliffs. Million of years ago, ocean tides smashed inland, blunting their advance on these cliffs, cutting away miles of rock, leaving an overhang that he'd only read about, yet never imagined being so immense. The overhang provided shade from the blistering sun, and also provided some deep cisterns for the rare water. Finally, the overhang—five hundred feet of red sandstone—shielded the fortress from aerial bombardment.

Klamdara had an eerie quiet. A thousand meters to the right lay a giant pit, around which lay giant hulks of mining equipment, prostrate, torn apart for scrap. Once mighty machines ripped iron ore from the Klamdara bedrock, now they dissolved into dry puddles of rust.

A new solar farm occupied the rocky soil to the east. Fifteen-foot towers stood like stalks brandishing rectangular jet-black panels, more like deathweed flower petals: each solar collector bent like heliotropes toward the rising Klamdara sun. New construction. Judging by the number of stalks, K'Rin guessed they had sufficient power to arm long-range laser cannon. In any case, these preparations were substantial, yet recent—months of intensive effort in secret. K'Rin rebuked himself with the thought, *Too busy looking for traps outside, I fell into one here in the Jod system. Pl'Don has prepared for months. I underestimated him, and I overestimated my own knowledge of his activities.*

One of the jailers prodded K'Rin between his shoulder blades, and K'Rin moved down the metal ramp. He knew that a second prod would also include an electric shock to punish and motivate.

K'Rin's military mind suppressed his immediate discouragement. He studied the Klamdara fortress. The walls leaned outward, about a seven-degree pitch, creating a reverse slope to frustrate would-be invaders. At the base of the wall, the ancient engineers dug a trench and filled it with iron spikes as tall as a man, blunted with age but no less deadly. The wall surface was smooth: no towers. Instead, the wall had periodic protuberances, like chins, providing defenders fields of fire along the walls. Escape over the walls appeared most unlikely.

He walked past the two phalanxes of Jod regulars toward the iron gates: solid black iron, and thick as a man. A spindly bridge of graphite composite crossed the trench over the threatening spikes. K'Rin stopped to inspect the gate. Here, he figured, was the only way out. The gate fit into stone rails, heavily greased. They had raised the gate just enough so the men need not stoop to pass beneath. Inside, K'Rin looked overhead. The screw gear that raised the massive gate appeared refurbished. Hydraulics turned the screw: no amount of flesh and bone could budge the weight in that gate. Once inside the gate groaned as it closed.

Within the walls, the fortress opened to a large plaza of rough-hewn, irregular stone. Between the plaza and wall lay ten acres of furrowed soil baked by the sun. Deeper in the fortress, within the shade of the overhang, stood rows of makeshift barracks, built hastily from cheap plastics and aluminum rods. K'Rin thought, *They don't expect us to survive here long.* Behind the makeshift barracks stood two boxy structures, the old prison cells, built of yellow brick on a cement slab.

A guard stepped in front of K'Rin and with his weapon signaled K'Rin to halt. Behind, K'Rin heard the shuffle of feet and clatter of chains fade to quiet. He contemplated his men's morale as they faced their bleak future. They had nothing but their bare hands, their training and discipline, and each other. *We will learn the measure of ourselves.*

Slowly the Tenebrea filled in ranks behind him. Feld Jo'Orom stood at K'Rin's right, Kip on his left. Both appeared unperturbed, and K'Rin was momentarily relieved that some unit cohesion remained—but for how long? While one set of guards held their weapons ready, another group removed the chains. Having removed the Tenebrea's chains, the guards turned and faced a glass booth halfway up the wall.

A small door slid open and down the steps walked the commandant. He carried a long gnarled stick, a formidable club that he used as a walking staff.

Without fanfare, he stood in front of K'Rin and said, "I am Pel D'Cru, commandant of the Klamdara fortress. My orders are to ensure that none of you get out of this fortress alive. The penalty for any infraction of camp rules is summary execution. It would be my distinct pleasure to kill each one of you." His eyes were not so much cruel as vacant.

D'Cru looked past K'Rin to the Tenebrea arrayed in uneven lines. "Given your reputation, I fully expect you to attempt to escape. In fact, I removed your chains as an invitation to try. I want to test some new ideas I have for physical security in this rather aboriginal setting. Therefore, I fully expect that my soldiers and I will at some point have the opportunity to see each one of you die. The sooner the better, actually. All of us want to leave this forsaken rock."

D'Cru walked toward the wall and raised his voice for all the prisoners. "The rules are simple. Do what we tell you when we tell you. Don't step on the plowed dirt. When you step onto the plowed dirt, you leave footprints." He pointed at his own footprints in the plowed dirt. "My soldiers have orders to shoot to kill any prisoner who steps onto the dirt. Their response time is a matter of seconds."

He proceeded toward the wall. "You may think that the inside wall has a rough surface—even a few places for handholds perhaps. I know you Tenebrea consider yourselves expert climbers. Some of you might think you can climb this wall, but climbing the wall is really quite impossible." D'Cru pointed to one of the Tenebrea who gazed past D'Cru with practiced indifference. "You, there."

A guard reached forward with his prod to move the Tenebrea forward from formation. D'Cru continued, "Come here. Don't worry. What's your name, soldier?"

The young Tenebrea looked back at Jo'Orom who assented with a nod. The young Tenebrea replied crisply, "My name is Har'Got."

"Relax. I won't let my men shoot you when you step onto the dirt."

Again, the Tenebrea glanced back at Jo'Orom and K'Rin, then grudgingly stepped forward ahead of the prod. He stiffened as he stepped onto the dirt, but no weapons fired. "Come here, come here," D'Cru coaxed. "I just want you take a close look at the wall, so you can tell your comrades how futile it is to attempt to scale the wall."

D'Cru motioned with his stick. "Go ahead. See if you can find a handhold." Har'Got just looked back at D'Cru, glancing toward K'Rin for confirmation. K'Rin tried to communicate a message with his eyes: Be careful.

With a paternal lilt to his voice, D'Cru coaxed, "Go on." Har'Got inched cautiously forward, looking back at

D'Cru who leaned on his stick and watched with a casual smile. Har'Got reached forward with his hand trying to sense any wire, any pressure, or any tingle that might trigger an alarm. He looked down the wall from side to side. The back wall was pocked with age and showed many edges left from scaffolding and buildings that had once lined the inside wall. The ancient wall was thick at the base, providing a helpful five-degree incline to the top. He turned around. D'Cru hadn't moved, hadn't changed his expression in the least.

Har'Got reached up to purchase a grip in a crevice. Upon touching the wall, everyone recoiled at two violent bursts of green light from the upper corners of the wall. The bolts of light converged instantly to the pressure point on the wall, colliding with a white crash. He turned from the wall holding up a smoldering stump where his hand had been.

"Now isn't that an excellent deterrent?" D'Cru exclaimed, mocking the Tenebrea's wound.

The young warrior's eyes blazed from anger more than pain. He bolted toward D'Cru with his good hand outstretched, intent on killing.

D'Cru met the attack with his staff raised, crashing a blow across Har'Got's face, knocking him unconscious. Har'Got lay facedown in the dirt, bleeding from a scalp wound.

Jo'Orom stepped forward, but K'Rin grabbed a fistful of Jo'Orom's tunic, whispering, "Do nothing. Not now." Kip stood wide-eyed, watching as K'Rin restrained the senior noncom.

"The touch-activated wall cannon is my personal idea." D'Cru came forward to bait Jo'Orom and K'Rin.

K'Rin's neck flared a murderous crimson, which brought a smile to D'Cru's face.

D'Cru stood nose to nose with K'Rin and taunted loudly, "If you so much as twitch I'll kill the little bastard where he lies. If any of you assault a guard, the penalty is immediate summary execution." Spittle flew as he yelled his final threat. "I'd just as soon kill you all now, so why not give me an excuse!"

K'Rin stood like flint. He did not even wipe the offensive spit from his face. But Jo'Orom and Kip and the Tenebrea near the front saw K'Rin's eyes, and they had never seen pure rage contained before. The Tenebrea knew it was for their welfare alone that K'Rin bowed his head.

The next morning, K'Rin awoke with a thin film of dew on his black uniform. He rose with a stiff back from sleeping on the concrete floor in one of the old cells with his blanket rolled as a pillow for his head. The Klamdara dawn cast a deep fleshy pink light throughout the cell. He let the others in his cell sleep as he stepped outside.

He heard his name whispered, "K'Rin!"

He turned to see a big Jod, obviously a civilian; his face concealed deep within a heavy cowl. A thin linen cloth protected the Jod's nose and mouth. The soft fat hands were folded across a large stomach and they were decked with valuable rings. K'Rin answered, "B'Yuon?"

The figure raised a finger to his lips and motioned to the guards who accompanied him. B'Yuon was barely in control of his emotions. K'Rin looked at his old friend with contempt, and asked, "Why are you here?"

B'Yuon choked back a sob, "I am betrayed with you—to my everlasting shame. If Pl'Don would eliminate you, then my time is short. So I sneaked out of

Heptar. I am a fugitive. I came straight here, before the council discovers my absence. At present, D'Cru thinks I'm here on assembly business."

K'Rin watched the Jod guards as he listened to B'Yuon. He said quietly, "Restrain yourself, B'Yuon. Act like a councilor. The guards are becoming suspicious."

B'Yuon straightened his posture. "I can't help myself. I wear this stifling cowl to hide my shameful blush. I came here to clear my name with you. I saw your face in the Assembly Hall. I felt like a coward for standing there and watching them take you away. I am a coward."

K'Rin stroked his chin and looked into the shadow of the cowl to see B'Yuon's glistening eyes. His friend was weeping. K'Rin changed positions, standing beside B'Yuon with his back to the guards. Ahead was the yawning chasm of the natural cave. K'Rin whispered, "There was nothing you could do then, but you can do something for me now."

"I can't go back to Jod!" B'Yuon's eyes showed cold fear. B'Yuon's genuine fear gave K'Rin the confidence to trust the soft, old councilor. K'Rin answered, "I don't want you to go back to Jod. I want you to fly to the Artrix system, to Yuseat Sigma in the Thule system."

"I've never heard of it."

"Few have. However, it's on the standard charts. I want you to broadcast a message to the surface. Tell them exactly what happened and that we're doomed. Tell them to stay away from the Jod system. In particular, tell Mat Flores—first name Andrea—that the council wants to extradite her and the clones to Cor. My guess is that they'll send the traitor Tamor-Kyl to find her. They must stay out of Jod space. Promise me you'll deliver this message."

The heavy cowl nodded.

"Good. In warning them, you redeem yourself." K'Rin directed B'Yuon to sit on a block of stone that lay on the ground. K'Rin rested on his haunches. "Any other news?"

"Yes. Pl'Don ordered the Fleet to stand down to demonstrate our peaceful intentions toward the Cor Ordinate. He recalled the capital ships to Heptar, and he intends to purge the fleet of any officers from the Rin Clan. He's afraid the Fleet might have sympathies for you. He is correct in that assessment. Also, Pl'Don sent his cousin Xi-Don and a Jod delegation to Cor to negotiate a peace to be brokered by the Chelle."

K'Rin drew the Rin Triskelion in the red dust. He commented, "Bad news. Pl'Don has exposed the Fleet in a meaningless gesture. He may incite the war he so desperately wants to avoid." K'Rin stood and brushed the dust from his pants. He added with a tone of indifference, "I probably won't live to see the end of Jod. You, my poor friend, probably will."

B'Yuon reached out but resisted touching K'Rin. "You must have hope. The Fleet is strong. The Rin Clan remains intact. Time changes all things."

K'Rin smiled ruefully. "We don't have time, my friend. All of us are infected with Quazel Protein. We'll be dead, some of us in three months, others nine; me, I figure I've got five months."

"Is it true?" B'Yuon asked. "Did you run Quazel?"

K'Rin shook his head. "How we got infected is now irrelevant."

K'Rin walked to his friend, clasped his hand, and looked on his soft round face. "I'll die easier if I know that you've delivered my message to Yuseat Sigma."

"I'll live easier knowing I fulfilled your last wish."

B'Yuon pulled back his cowl. He turned and slowly walked away. The pair of armed guards followed him toward the gate.

Andrea used a clumsy brass key to let herself into the dark room, carefully locking the door behind her. She set a small red box on an end table and crossed the room. "Did you get any sleep?" she asked.

"A little." H'Roo lay on his side in a reclining chair with a towel wrapped around his waist.

"You'll sleep like a baby pretty soon." Andrea walked to the window and opened the thick drapes. Their little bed and breakfast overlooked Town Creek. She gazed through the anonymous fog that stilled the water and shrouded the yachts. Across the way was the ancient Byeberry House. The Cutts and Case Boatyard still boasted the finest reproductions of monohull yachts, adorned with rare woods, lacquered to shine like copper and gold. Andrea had brought H'Roo to Oxford to hide. She knew Oxford and the self-isolated people who lived there. In fact, she thought she recognized some of the faces she'd known when she and Steve frequented the harbor.

The morning fog began to lift. Dappled light penetrated to carve patches of white on the gray water. A pair of oyster boats slowly meandered toward the bay. Men in yellow slickers gathered their tackle, straightened lines, and tested the long tongs used to pull the smug mollusks from their beds.

Andrea returned to the business at hand. In the light, H'Roo looked paler than usual. She retrieved her red box and emptied its contents on the bed. "Laudanum." She held up a small brown bottle before H'Roo's eyes. "You'll like this stuff." She measured a generous dose of the amber liquid into a short glass. "Drink this. In a couple of minutes, you'll feel no pain."

H'Roo tried to sit up straight, but the pain and the effort defeated him. He slumped back. Andrea admonished him, "Lie still. Quazel doesn't make us bulletproof; nor is it a guarantee against sepsis."

H'Roo's chest heaved as he took a deep breath. Then he panted from fever. He calmed himself, then drank the saccharine-bitter liquid and grimaced. "Nasty stuff . . . burns the throat."

"But you'll love the afterglow." Andrea peeked under the bloody towel. The entrance and exit wounds were crusting; the swollen flesh was pink and warm to the touch. She said, "I've got to drain the wound before you fester. You just look at the boats." She dragged his chair to the window to offer H'Roo a distraction and to get better light.

He mumbled, "Nice boats." The drug began to dull his speech.

Andrea rummaged through the first aid supplies she had pilfered from a couple of large pleasure boats anchored at a nearby marina. She felt guilty violating a man's ship, but she knew that a bluewater sailor would have a fairly complete medical kit aboard. She fashioned two thick gauze bandages with tape. Then she opened a sharp penknife and doused it with rubbing alcohol. She wanted to make light of the procedure and the fact that she had no experience, having only read manuals. "How do you like Earth so far?"

H'Roo continued to focus on the boats and the mewing seagulls outside his window. "Jus' like I pictured it."

She poked him with the point of the blade. "Feel that?"

"Na' really. Wha' is laudanum?"

"Opium and alcohol—nothing better." Andrea slipped the short blade into the entrance wound, breaking the crust. The pressure of the swelling immediately expelled a short gush of pink fluids, followed by a trickle of fresh blood. She dabbed with a warm wet towel. Opaque fluids drained from the hole. She likewise reopened and cleaned the exit wound. "Almost done." She poured some tincture of iodine over the oozing holes, then bound him with the gauze bandages. "You'll be able to travel in a few days." She expected H'Roo's Quazel would accelerate the healing.

H'Roo didn't answer. Andrea looked up concerned, but found him sleeping gently in the arms of the narcotic.

Tamor-Kyl continued to wear the black and gray uniform of the Tenebrea. As far as he was concerned, he was the Tenebrea now. With the Quazel enzyme, he could be more: he could own Pl'Don by offering him another century of life. Tamor could quite literally rule the man who ruled Jod. On the other hand, without the enzyme Tamor would be dead within six to nine months.

He had searched the Tenebrea Academy medical station and found nothing. The records showed that the annual shipment of the Quazel enzyme was due within the month. From where?

Tamor searched the *Tyker*'s libraries and K'Rin's logs for clues. Nothing! He took a company of Jod infantry to Vintell and sacked the safehouse looking for information that might lead him to the Quazel laboratory. Still nothing. Of the four Tenebrea stationed there, three died in the melee, and one survived grievous wounds. An excruciating interrogation proved only that the survivor knew nothing or was prepared to die to protect the secret. Tamor brought the dying soldier to Klamdara and deposited him at Jo'Orom's feet.

Jo'Orom looked down at the suffering Tenebrea. He recognized the face despite the beating, even if he did not recall the name. The black uniform was torn and stained with blood. The young Jod breathed with difficulty. He coughed thick caramel-colored phlegm. Two lance burns on the chest told the fatal tale. His right lung was disrupted and without a surgeon, the young soldier would soon drown on his own lymph. His eyes were glazed, lacking focus, but the dying Jod seemed at peace, almost pitying the older noncom. Both knew that there were worse ways to die.

Jo'Orom dropped to one knee to put his face closer to the dying soldier. He turned to Tamor and said bitterly, "You must take him to the dispensary. At least make him comfortable."

Tamor signaled the guards who jerked Jo'Orom to his feet. "I'm taking you to the dispensary."

As they led Jo'Orom away, he said to one of the other prisoners, "Get him water. Clean him up, and keep him company."

The dispensary was a cold room with white ceramic tile walls and glass cabinets stocked with medicines and surgical tools. The guards ripped off Jo'Orom's shirt and bound his wrists to the arms of a heavy steel chair. Jo'Orom sat like a sphinx.

Tamor approached him with a scalpel. "I very much wanted to cut up Hal K'Rin—perhaps he'd find my technique more suited for special operations instead of staff duty. What do you think?" Jo'Orom glared contempt.

"Unfortunately, the council thinks we would set a bad example by shedding the blood of the noble born. A bit oversqueamish, don't you think?" Tamor brightened as if he'd just grasped a new gem of knowledge. He waved the scalpel at Jo'Orom and said, "But you, Jo'Orom, you're just a common Jod, like me. Nobody will miss you." Tamor walked behind the chair, bent down, and whispered in Jo'Orom's ear. "I don't want to hurt anybody. I just want a piece of information. No one seems to know where I can find the shipment of enzyme or where I can find the Quazel laboratory. You know, don't you?"

Jo'Orom said nothing.

Tamor held the scalpel under Jo'Orom's eye and said, "I promised K'Rin that I'd supply all you prisoners with the enzyme, but K'Rin, that old paranoid, prefers that you and all your companions die from Quazel poisoning rather than share that bit of information with me. However, I know that you care more for your troops than he does. Those brave young Tenebrea out there are like . . ." Tamor shrugged his shoulders and smiled with mocking affection. "Like your own sons. So why not tell me?"

Jo'Orom said nothing.

"You know I'll find out anyway. I'll interrogate every last prisoner. I have so many resources: truth drugs, pain, empathy, and fear. The trick is to select the right tool for the right candidate." Tamor walked behind Jo'Orom and bent down to speak softly in Jo'Orom's ear. "My guess is that you can resist the drugs, the pain, and the fear. But can you watch all your young Tenebrea die so senselessly?"

Jo'Orom sat ramrod straight and stared at the blank white wall. He strained at the cord that bound his wrists to the arms of the chair.

Tamor grabbed Jo'Orom's left arm above the elbow, exposing a set of beads buried beneath the skin. With the scalpel he sliced them away. Jo'Orom emitted a low groan as the scalpel sliced his flesh. Bright blood ran down his arm, dripping from the elbow.

Tamor came around and in his bloody hand he held six gray pellets, the Quazel enzyme. "Perhaps the onset of Quazel poisoning will help your memory. As you get sick, just remember that you've condemned all the others to the same fate. You can save them. Even if you decide to be the martyr, the others will see how horribly you die as your tissues crystallize. They'll save themselves."

Jo'Orom looked at the small wound in his arm and knew it was mortal. "How they live and die is their business. How I live and die is mine."

Tamor-Kyl leaned over, grinning in Jo'Orom's face. "Suit yourself."

The Jod guards led the bleeding Jo'Orom back to K'Rin, then randomly grabbed another Tenebrea for interrogation. The young soldier set his jaw; he and Jo'Orom shared a brief but bonding look.

Jo'Orom watched until they had turned the corner. He asked the group, "How is the soldier from Vintell?"

K'Rin answered with one word. "Dead."

Jo'Orom nodded. He spoke softly for K'Rin's ears only. "If we get out of here, we're going to need the enzyme. You know Tamor will eventually get to the lab. Only you and I know where to find the *Kam-Gi* shipment, but a dozen or more know about the lab, and Tamor will break someone. Do you think the *Kam-Gi* will wait at the rendezvous?"

K'Rin looked around suspiciously. "I think they'll

wait. Fear and greed are powerful motivators and I have the *Kam-Gi* by both handles."

Late that evening, Tamor broke a young Tenebrea completely using the drugs. The poor wretch, a former Yuseat lab technician, never knew that he betrayed the secret, but K'Rin knew and he announced the loss to his inner circle.

"How do you know?" Kip asked.

"Obvious—" K'Rin shook his head at Kip's obtuseness. "The interrogations suddenly stopped, and Tamor-Kyl left." K'Rin also knew that Andrea was now in danger.

chapter 13

When Andrea and H'Roo returned to the Yuseat Lab, they found the inhabitants arming themselves. Fal'Dar and his men had shed their white lab coats and donned their black field uniforms with utility belts and weapons. Eric's face was grim as death. He too was dressed to fight. Tara wore a shoulder holster with a handlance. They had been waiting anxiously for the return of the *Benwoi*. Dr. Carai immediately briefed them on the news as relayed a week earlier by B'Yuon: Tamor-Kyl's betrayal and the Tenebrea's bitter incarceration on Klamdara; the council's overtures to Cor. Carai addressed Andrea directly. "K'Rin wants you to stay away from the Jod system. Tamor-Kyl has the *Tyker* and he's hunting you to take you back to Cor. Apparently, the council feels that your neck in a noose might pacify the Cor Ordinate."

Andrea pulled her raven hair back into a ponytail. "It appears that the rest of you intend to disobey K'Rin's orders. Right?"

Fal'Dar glared back. "We've got to try. If we don't get them out, they'll die from Quazel poisoning."

Ti'Maj and the other Tenebrea raised their voices to consent.

H'Roo withdrew pensively. He said, "The Klamdara fortress was infamous when it garrisoned the penal colony after the Clan Wars. Recalcitrant clansmen spent their last days on Klamdara mining iron. No one ever escaped, even with outside help. I read all about it when I was a boy."

"Are you suggesting that we do nothing?" Fal'Dar accused.

"No. We'll do something; what, I don't know." H'Roo pulled up a stainless steel stool and sat down. He took a deep breath. "Besides the fortifications, they will have at least a regiment: eight hundred marines with heavy weapons. They might have two regiments. We won't know until we get there. Plus, Klamdara can get reinforcements in less than forty-eight hours. Even if you manage to fight your way in, you'll have an even greater challenge fighting your way out. If you do get K'Rin and the Tenebrea off Klamdara, most likely, you'll be in open space in a small merchant ship pursued by dreadnoughts."

Fal'Dar stepped up ready to throttle H'Roo. "I've got a brother on Klamdara! We all have kin in the Tenebrea."

Andrea stepped in between the two Jod. She turned to Fal'Dar and bluntly stated, "Don't forget, we have only six Tenebrea here. No offense, but have any of you lab rats been on a field mission lately? Or ever?"

Silence. "I thought so." She looked around the room. "Eric has some experience."

"More than you," Eric challenged. Eric folded his arms across his chest. His left eye was still faintly purple.

Andrea ignored him. "Tara's been on a raid. Dr.

Carai is a civilian. The nine of us against eight hundred marines. Those are bad odds."

Fal'Dar stood eye to eye with Andrea and said, "If you two are—"

Andrea pushed him away, "Don't say anything you'll regret, soldier. Listen and learn something." She turned to H'Roo and asked, "So how would we crack Klamdara?"

H'Roo gazed at Fal'Dar sympathetically. Nevertheless, he said, "The Jod garrison will see us coming from a half million kilometers. We must assume they have long-range surface-to-space cannon."

Andrea immediately answered H'Roo's objection. "We can approach Klamdara from the reverse side, then stay below the horizon."

H'Roo asked incredulously, "You mean march the last thirty miles? We'll have Jod marines crawling all over us."

"We can sharpshoot the details later. Assume we get to the Klamdara fortress."

H'Roo swallowed. "Assuming we get to the fortress, the first order of business is to cut their communications to the outside. If they can't make the call, they can't get the reinforcements. For the same reason, we need to seize their launch facility. At the same time, we need to breach the walls, secure their armory, and liberate K'Rin and the Tenebrea. We need at least five hundred soldiers and heavy fire support for a mission this big." He looked at Fal'Dar and added sarcastically, "The nine of us might as well walk up to the fortress gate and knock. Then, you can explain to them that you came to retrieve your brother."

Tara interrupted. "Walk up to the gate and knock? That's a better idea than you think." She rummaged through her pack, untying a strip of cloth, unfurling one of the wilderness cloaks. "I brought these from the *Benwoi* to show to you guys. I guess now's as good a time as any." She threw the cloak around her own shoulders, then activated a small brass button. As her body slowly energized the cloak, she began to disappear from the neck down.

Dr. Carai reached over and touched the putatively invisible fabric, causing the image to warp at the end of his long finger. "Remarkable!"

Andrea agreed. "Two of us can get close enough to perform one piece of the mission, but only one piece, which is not good enough. We need more cloaks and more men. I know where we can get help."

Tara punctuated Andrea's thought, saying, "Brigon."

Andrea surveyed the faces of her fellow Tenebrea. Their doubt was palpable.

"Brigon, the clone?" H'Roo shook his head in disbelief. "We're going to risk our necks going to Cor to do what? Recruit some clone labor to help us assault a fortress garrisoned with a regiment of the best marine infantry in the Jod system—are you out of your mind?"

"Brigon fought by our side when we burned the Clone Welfare Institute. His fighters are well trained and well armed. Brigon would be extremely valuable on a mission to Klamdara. Unless you have a better idea, hear me out." Andrea explained her plan. She explained how they might travel to Cor. Using the codes that Tara had broken, they would slip by their security and land in the wilderness beyond the city of Sarhn. Brigon and thirty of his best fighters would travel with them to Klamdara. They would use the wilderness cloaks to surprise the Klamdara garrison: take out the comms, secure the arsenal, and rearm the Tenebrea prisoners. "I think two hundred Tenebrea—

even sick from Quazel poisoning—can outfight a Jod regiment."

H'Roo turned to Eric. "What do you know about this clone?"

Eric shrugged his shoulders and damned Brigon with faint praise. "I never met him. He lives in the wilderness well beyond the security interests of Sarhn." Pointing at Tara's head that seemed to float in midair, Eric added, "Apparently, he's clever with technology. But I don't think I'd rely on him. He's basically a thief interested only in himself."

Tara unwrapped herself and switched off the cloak, laying it on the lab table. She turned a cold disapproving eye toward Eric, chagrined as she contradicted her mate. "Brigon promised that he'd take charge of the Resistance when I left."

Eric sniped, "I'll believe that when I see it. Brigon can't lead the Resistance. I'm sure he's hiding in his cave somewhere—his promise to you long forgotten. Even if you found him, I doubt that he'd come on a suicide mission to Klamdara."

Andrea interrupted. "He'll come. Don't worry about Brigon."

Andrea was surprised at how quickly she defended Brigon. Yes, Brigon. How she had berated him when he first refused to help her! Tara had refused to leave Cor unless Brigon promised to lead the remnant of her Underground organization. Brigon accepted only when Andrea promised to return to him by the summer, with or without Jod help. At the time, her promise was little more than expedient. She sensed his affection, albeit misplaced.

Andrea felt a twinge of guilt for her callous indifference to Brigon. She recalled that no sooner had she left

Cor with Tara than the expedience of her promise to return degraded into ambivalence. At first, the image of Brigon cooling his heels amused her; then a perverse sense of duty crept into her subconscious. Finally, the oddest sensation of remorse wheedled its way into her mind. The thought of Brigon's disappointment stirred feelings she had long buried. She pictured him waiting in the wilderness—waiting until the autumn, then dismissing her with a curse. Now she wanted to see his face again and assure him that the promise was true. The only awkwardness she felt was that instead of bringing help, she was asking again. Yet, she knew he'd oblige her. Andrea had not realized it before, but she cared what Brigon thought of her.

Dr. Carai asked, "Do you plan to tell Brigon how bad the odds are on Klamdara?"

"Yes." She answered quietly as if speaking to herself, "He's never known anything but bad odds." Andrea was sure of Brigon's answer when she was sure of little else. He would say yes. No qualifications. No conditions. Just a simple yes. Moreover, knowing the certainty of his consent unsettled her. The certainty of his will, not the actual help, obligated her. Andrea held her hand over the pit of her stomach. She felt a bit of her self-control slipping away. She thought, *We had a contract: you manage Tara's Resistance; I bring help. How easy it is to break a contract. Now it appears we have a one-sided covenant—you have made yourself vulnerable to me. Now you want me to make myself vulnerable to you. I think not. Not yet.*

The group huddled to plan the particulars of their rescue mission. Fal'Dar wanted to leave immediately, but Dr. Carai insisted, "We need seven days. We must pack all the Quazel enzyme, food supplies, and the medical gear.

Fal'Dar, you need to harvest as much Papuyoosa crown gall as you can. I'll need to create at least a year's supply of the enzyme or our efforts are at best a temporary reprieve. We gain little if we save the Tenebrea for only six months, just to run out of the enzyme again. Who knows when we can return to Yuseat? Later, I'll need to dismantle the lab." Carai tugged at his beard. "Seven days, if we work around the clock."

Tamor-Kyl stood at the helm of the *Tyker* as they approached Yuseat. He looked at the forward screen and smugly remembered how easy it was to extract the whereabouts of the lab—northern hemisphere of Yuseat Sigma. *Soon I'll own the secret of the enzyme. Then, I alone can dispense the miracle of longevity. Pl'Don will give anything to double his life.*

The navigator spoke. "Sir, we are entering Yuseat Sigma's gravity well."

Tamor ordered, "Scan the landmasses in a standard pattern." He turned to the marine combat team leader and ordered, "Is your team ready?"

"We're ready to board the shuttle to the surface."

"Good, as soon as we have a fix, we descend. I'm going with you."

"That is your prerogative, sir. We expect a fight." He folded his arms and watched the forward screen.

Tamor's face soured. He said, "Remember. The lab must be taken intact. The scientific data in that lab are crucial—do you hear me? I want all weapons on semi-automatic, powered low to avoid combustion. There's an old Artrix scientist down there. We must take him alive. If anyone kills that Artrix, I will personally cut that marine's heart out!"

The team leader chafed at the threats from a

younger, seemingly less experienced officer, mysteriously promoted by special order of the council to be his superior in rank. But he and his men hadn't been in a real fight for a long time, and he wasn't going to let some prig with council connections spoil the mood. They had, after all, volunteered for this mission. "Yes, sir. We'll spare the Artrix."

"We may run into a Terran female down there. The council wants her taken alive if possible."

"Is there anybody at the lab we're allowed to kill?" the team leader asked derisively.

Fal'Dar rushed into the lab where two Jod technicians and Dr. Carai worked doggedly, extracting Quazel enzyme. Breathlessly, Fal'Dar announced, "We've been scanned! The ship is trying to establish a laser link to our computer."

A tired Dr. Carai rose from his stool. "Recall the surface party! What do we know about the intruder?"

"They are in orbit. They are scanning the surface at the low and high end of the spectrum. Their electronic signature indicates a Jod command frigate or cruiser— my guess: the *Tyker*." Fal'Dar directed his next order to Ti'Maj. "Go white. Power down everything! Take down the navigational suite, communications, everything. Shut down the generators. The ship must finish another orbit before descent. We have about eighty minutes."

A half hour later, the surface party returned. Andrea was wet with perspiration as she peeled off her suit. Her black hair stuck to her forehead. H'Roo's face was flushed from exertion. He tossed his sack of crown gall on the floor and grabbed a bottle of water. Eric's and

Tara's faces showed the strain of working without sleep, but their eyes sparked with energy and will. Dr. Carai met them at the decontamination room. "We've less than an hour!" He nervously tugged his beard with his thin fingers as he talked. "Tamor-Kyl must have learned our location. He's after a supply of Quazel, I'd wager. Quick! Bir-Tod, you and Eric pack all the Quazel into satchels. Clean the surface suits and stow them aboard the *Benwoi*. Bring as many filters as we can carry; destroy the rest."

He pulled Andrea and H'Roo-Parh aside. "Can we get out of here in the *Benwoi?*"

Andrea shook her head. "Not with the *Tyker* above us."

"So, what do we do?" Carai's voice rose with his anxiety.

Andrea sat down on a bench. She stopped peeling off her suit. The skintight undergarment stuck to her skin. "If we walk out, they'll capture the *Benwoi* and we'll be marooned here. We've got to move the *Benwoi.*"

Carai asked, "Won't they just find us with their onboard sensors?"

"Not necessarily," H'Roo countered. "We can move a short distance while the *Tyker*'s orbit has her over the horizon. We need to hide from the *Tyker*'s sensors. We need something to attenuate heat, mass, and emissions. We need to get under dirt, water. . . ."

"Or fungi." Dr. Carai raised his index finger. "We'll land in a bog. The *Benwoi* will sink to her belly. We'll spray nutrients over the hull. In a few hours, not a square centimeter of metal will show. In a day, we'll be under four inches of fungus. The Jod could walk over us and never know. They would have to be extremely lucky to find us."

Andrea smirked. "Tamor-Kyl is not a lucky person. He won't find us." She wiped her headpiece out with a dry rag. "I guess we'll be going back out in a minute."

Carai's mood brightened. The glad prospect of leaving Yuseat outweighed the immediate danger. That this execrable life form, fungi, was to be both his shield and his sword improved his spirits even more. He laughed with a wheeze. "So, let him try. A standard Jod surface suit is useless on Yuseat. If Tamor strays from his shuttle, Yuseat will kill him—literally eat him alive."

"You'd better get your suit on," Andrea prodded Carai.

He seemed not to hear Andrea; rather, he gazed around his confined world, thinking of the new set of problems. "We can't leave the lab intact. Tamor might camp in the lab and try to see what he can learn." The old Artrix pursed his lips as he thought out loud. "He's desperate for the enzyme. Plus we need him to vacate Yuseat as soon as possible. Therefore, we need to make the lab as inhospitable as Yuseat itself."

Andrea suggested, "We might set an explosion and kill a few of them."

Carai laughed wickedly as he looked around the pristine lab. "Yours is a crude solution, Mat Flores. We just need to leave the door open."

The lab became a flurry of activity as the crew hustled the last satchels of Quazel and sacks of crown gall aboard the *Benwoi*. Everyone hauled as much as they could carry through the sanitary plastic tube that led to the *Benwoi*. Each dumped his or her load in the *Benwoi*'s bay: food, water, surface gear, filters, satchels of enzyme, and fifty-pound sacks of crown gall. Tara rummaged through the pile making an inventory. Most importantly, she ensured that they had the two wilderness cloaks.

The air rapidly grew stale as the air circulation ceased. Frantically the entire crew hauled supplies. They worked in dim lights powered by batteries. Dr. Carai stuffed his pockets with data cubes. "How much time?" he yelled in his high-pitched voice.

Fal'Dar manned the array of passive sensors. He reported. "By extrapolation, I calculate that the *Tyker* is still twenty-four minutes away. When she clears the horizon she'll be able to detect movement, mass—even our batteries. Figure that they'll be here in ten minutes or less."

"Weapons check!" Fal'Dar bellowed. Everyone answered. All weapons accounted for. Fal'Dar gave Dr. Carai the word, "We're ready to leave."

"Everybody get aboard the *Benwoi*." He handed Fal'Dar a facemask. "Open inner and outer doors," Dr. Carai ordered.

Fal'Dar obeyed and a heavy vapor of moist air and spores wafted into the laboratory.

Then Dr. Carai spoke to the computer, "Execute program to degas library."

The computer replied almost instantly, "All data cubes dark."

Then Dr. Carai opened a wall panel filled with small mechanical switches and he murmured, "Good night." He flipped entire rows of switches with the side of his hand and as he did, whole systems blinked off. The ubiquitous hum of pumps and fans fell silent, lights extinguished. The crystal displays faded, and the room turned into a pitch black.

Fal'Dar switched on a handheld lightbar. Carai walked to his workbench and lifted a large brown bottle and dashed it to the floor. The yellow liquid began to evaporate into a heavier-than-air gas that spread over the floor toward the open laboratory door. Carai grinned through the plastic facemask. "Sort of a catnip for slime cats."

Fal'Dar said, "It'll take us months to clean up this mess when we get back."

"If we ever come back—" Dr. Carai looked at the young Jod incredulously and followed him to the *Benwoi*.

The shuttle from the *Tyker* hovered above the lab. Piercing xenon lights settled on the concrete apron banked with glistening fungi. The shuttle landed and dropped the ramp, disgorging thirty Jod marines with weapons held ready. The first two slipped on the slick surface and fell into the slime. Within moments their eyes flushed with copious tears and mucus streamed from their noses. A swarm of midges descended like a thick black cloud, adding to their misery. Blinded by their own tears, they coughed and sneezed as they staggered back into the ship.

The leader of the combat team clawed at his eyes, saying, "Didn't see anyone near the compound. No resistance." A corpsman handed him a wet towel for his eyes.

Tamor-Kyl ordered, "Put on surface suits. I want a thorough search of the facility."

Fresh troops left the shuttle in standard surface suits. Lights from their helmets slashed the mist and dissipated. With weapons raised, they encircled the lab. Several slipped and fell in the muck, cursing. Quickly they learned to slow their movements, and measure every step to gauge their grip on the slippery surface before shifting weight. Most stood gaping at the gloom, their arms slack, their weapons pointed at the ground.

Tamor-Kyl followed. His heart sank when he saw the lab door open and no light. Nobody was home. He called for more illumination, then entered the lab. The floor was covered with a thick white blanket of downy fungus that clung like hoarfrost. Underfoot, the white feathery fibers crushed, leaving a black stain footprint. Already, a thicker auburn fungus fed upon the dying hoarfrost. Some of the tissues had the aspect of stone, yet underfoot they smooshed like overripe fruit. The walls were black with mildew and brown drops fell from the ceiling: residue from a pulsating slime mold that streaked the surface. Tamor looked around the lab at the aggressive molds destroying everything as thoroughly as fire. Panic began to grab him.

He walked into Carai's office. He thought he saw small black shadows slither out of the light, but he paid no heed: he went to the computer and flipped the red switch. Nothing happened. "Get some power in here!" He barked.

Two marines ran in with a long yellow cable from the shuttle. They plugged the universal coupling into the computer's power source. Again, Tamor flipped the red switch. The screen glowed but offered nothing but a terse message: ZERO FILES.

Tamor howled. He struck the screen with his gloved fist, bending the surface. The operating system was gone. The chair was a rot of slime. The papers had become host to thousands of spindly mushrooms. "Search every room, every drawer!"

"What are we looking for?"

"Small gray pellets about this big." Tamor held up his thumb and forefinger. The marines scattered to search the rest of the building.

Tamor looked around. The destruction was deliberate. He looked at his sleeve and noticed that the aggressive molds had already begun to discolor his suit. He could disinfect the place, but what good would that do? He had no idea how to make the enzyme, and all the information was gone. The lab equipment was quite ordinary and gave no clues to the process.

He turned to leave and saw the black shadows again. This time they did not eschew the light but edged toward him in a slow undulation like giant garden slugs. They surrounded him. "Damn molds!" Tamor needed something to strike. He raised his boot and stepped on the largest sluglike creature, grinding it into the floor with his toe. In the next few minutes, Tamor-Kyl learned all about slime cats.

He looked down. The slime cat was gone. Instead, he began to see a black slick spreading over his foot up to his ankle and higher. Like a thin molasses it spread upward, defying gravity. Then the black slick began to pulsate as if it were on a slow boil. While he watched the metamorphosis, a second sluglike creature collided with his other foot and spread itself into an oily slick. Tamor reached down and tried to wipe the black from his shins. The black matter stuck to his gloves. His suit at the lower legs was pocked where the colony of creatures had digested the plastic. The pulsating slicks continued to spread slowly. Tamor realized he might be in trouble and started to walk toward the lab exit. He had to walk through a gauntlet of slime cats that quickly adhered to his feet and slithered over each other to adhere to his suit.

He looked down the hall and saw another marine with a large pulsating black stain on his back. Hollering for help, the marine flailed away with his arms, trying to reach a growing pain between his shoulder blades. His buddy swiped the black with his hand, revealing a large hole in the suit and blistered skin. All around Tamor heard shrill cries of pain. He saw many staggering back to the shuttle, tearing off their protective suits and adding to their misery a lung full of spores.

Tamor began running toward the shuttle. He began to itch all over his legs, his right hand, and his neck. He saw some of the black ooze spreading over his face-plate. From the inside, he saw the plastic pit and bubble. The itch turned into a searing burn, and while he was still meters away from the shuttle, he began ripping his gear off. Immediately the spores attacked his lungs and sinuses. His eyes burned, tearing profusely.

The black had spread up his neck, over his ear. He blocked its progress toward his eyes, allowing the hungry slime cat to eat the skin and flesh from his fingers instead. He fought the urge to scream as he stumbled up the ramp into the shuttle. "Raise the ramp! Seal the doors!" Tamor yelled.

"Belay that order!" the combat team leader yelled. "I still have troops out there!"

"They're as good as dead!" Tamor growled in pain. "Corpsman!"

The officer bulled his way past Tamor to retrieve the wounded, some of whom lay in agony on the ground. Others were indeed dead, covered in a pulsating shroud of black.

The medical corpsman had three injured marines lying on the floor, sedated. His own hands were raw flesh where the slime cats had eaten through his surgical gloves. He sprayed liquid nitrogen on the slime, rendering the black slicks dormant and brittle. He directed others to peel the black away, carefully disposing the creatures in a steel can, in which he added ethylene oxide, constantly reminding them, "Keep the lid on the can. The vapors can kill you."

The corpsman quickly turned his attention to Tamor. The slime had oozed beyond the dam Tamor had built with his hand—threatening Tamor's right eye.

"Hurry!" Tamor screeched. The corpsman put a thick bandage over the eye to protect it from the icy nitrogen. He sprayed. The nitrogen left a white coating. He pulled the sheet away and with it dead and digested skin. Half of Tamor's face was raw meat. The right ear had dissolved like hot wax. Even the corpsman felt a surge in his gut, and he had to fight his gag reflex.

Tamor inspected his hand, which looked as if the skin had been a glove removed. The numbing effect of the supercold nitrogen wore off, and the searing pain returned. A scream welled up in his throat, but the corpsman mercifully injected a powerful painkiller that put Tamor unconscious.

The combat team leader dragged the last of the living up the ramp. "Pilot! Get us the hell out of here!"

Just five kilometers from the lab, the *Benwoi* stood knee-deep in a slime bog. She listed ten degrees port due to the uneven bottom. The outer hull was crusted with several inches of wet molds—nothing that a hypersonic lap through Yuseat's atmosphere couldn't burn away.

Tara watched the solitary console. The rest lounged about the ship counting the hours. She announced, "The *Tyker* just left orbit in a big hurry on a bearing for the Jod system."

H'Roo stood up. "Alert the rest of the crew. We wait till the *Tyker* makes the jump to FTL speed. Our next stop is Cor."

chapter 14

Admiral Brulk directed Lt. Botchi to lead the Jod delegation on a tour of Sarhn's military facilities. He made his excuses to the Jod emissary, retired Admiral Xi-Don, truthfully saying that he was overwhelmed by his schedule.

Indeed, Brulk was stretched. He was busy planning the preemptive decapitation strike against the Jod. He had to manage ground operations against two clone precincts, where starvation had finally moved a sizable portion of their older population to revolt. His plan was to isolate them, contain them, use them as long as possible, then let the winter kill them: all of them, even the passive spectators. He lamented the loss of so much labor, but he knew that a clone, having simply witnessed an insurrection, was potentially dangerous.

The Minister of the Economy, Grundig, grumbled but did nothing to impede Brulk's schedule. Madame Prefect watched with stony silence, and bid the rest of her cabinet to do likewise. She did, however, question the protocol of having young Botchi guide Xi-Don around the city.

Brulk answered with a sly smile, "A bit of one-upmanship, Madame Prefect. I want my officers to see a Jod admiral plus entourage led around Sarhn by an Ordinate lieutenant."

Lt. Botchi first took his wards to the supply officer to fit them in cold-weather gear. Each Jod wore a heavy white parka against the biting cold. Unfortunately, the Ordinate did not have boots to fit wide Jod feet. Xi-Don looked pale as death in the parka. The seven rings beneath his eyes looked ghoulish, but the old Jod's eyes were lit with new purpose. Lt. Botchi noted that several times, Xi-Don remarked how glad he was to be out of retirement, doing something useful.

Botchi hid his amusement as the docile Jod delegation cringed at the cold but remained mute to avoid offending their Ordinate hosts. The hairless Jod, used to temperate and tropical climates, shuddered with each blast of winter wind that whipped through the streets. The sky was a crisp pale blue, scrubbed clean by the most recent blizzard. Evergreens wore heavy coats of snow. Drifts piled up randomly and sparkled in the sunlight. Preoccupied with their miserable feet, the Jod failed to see the bedazzling sight of Sarhn in winter.

Botchi spoke to the senior Jod, Admiral Xi-Don. "I apologize for the uncommonly cold weather. Cor's orbit is significantly elliptical, and we are at the aphelion. Also, the Cor star is variable with fairly pronounced swings and a short cycle of barely twenty-five years. Consequently we are at present experiencing a hard winter. However, this too shall pass."

Botchi's explanation did nothing to relieve the Jod's discomfort, but Xi-Don graciously conceded, "You need not apologize for Nature."

"Actually, we hope the temperature will fall another thirty degrees to dry the air and stop the kkona storms. Meanwhile the snow has one good effect." Botchi looked around to read the shivering Jod's faces and see that they rejected his statement out of hand. "The deep snow in the mountains has all but shut down the operations of the wilderness clones, and the cold helps us contain the precinct clones and subdue their periodic flare-ups. So we in the Ordinate suffer this cold gladly. It's an ill wind, eh?"

Xi-Don replied, "When you and your ambassadors come to Jod, we shall be in our late spring. Do plan to stay an extra couple weeks. I'll personally escort you to Plaginial Springs and put you in my family's summer palace."

"I look forward to it." Botchi kept a straight face. His orders were to be scrupulously polite but not friendly.

Across the street, a parade of clone laborers, thinly attired in orange coveralls, shoveled the thick snow from the streets, carting it to the city walls, and dumping it over the side. Botchi saw that the Jod averted their eyes. He couldn't tell whether the Jod were sympathetic or disinterested in the clones. Botchi goaded Xi-Don. "You disapprove of us using clone labor, don't you?"

"I didn't come here to judge the Ordinate."

Lt. Botchi smiled. His eyes reflected the cold blue sky. "You can be frank with me. As I understand history, the Alliance proscription against cloning started with the Jod."

Looking over Botchi's shoulder, Xi-Don saw one of the clones sit down on the curb, clutching her knees to her chest. The young female's bare legs were white. She closed her eyes as if to numb the reality of the life-sapping cold. The other clones stolidly worked around her. Xi-Don said, "Policies change."

"As does technology, Admiral." Botchi directed the delegation to look at a platoon of NewGens standing in formation receiving orders. The NewGens wore simple body armor and a thin white poncho. Much of their exposed flesh, faces, and hands bore the burn scars from the fire that destroyed the Clone Welfare Institute. They seemed impervious to the cold.

Botchi had orders never to miss an opportunity to remind the Jod of their culpability. "One of the tragedies of your operation against Cor is that you inadvertently slowed our progress toward ending the kind of cloning that your species so strenuously condemns. Take a close look at the New Generation Clones."

The delegation saw the NewGen clones. A voice from the back muttered, "They're hideous."

Botchi overheard and said, "Normally, the NewGens are quite pleasant to look at. Most of this crop was burned when your agent and a band of old-order clones sabotaged the institute. We rescued fewer than eight hundred copies from the fire." Glossing the truth, Botchi added, "We had not sufficiently prepared ourselves to withstand such an attack. Until you provoked them, the old-order clones and the Ordinate had always lived peaceably with the understanding that the clones would not exist, except for the Ordinate. You contributed to undermining that peace. However, we are much better prepared now."

Xi-Don bristled at the lieutenant's impudence. Nevertheless, he merely replied, "In time you'll come to understand that the Jod government had nothing to do with this catastrophe. We have arrested and punished the guilty party. The Terran female is still a fugitive. We hope to capture her and the *Benwoi* before your delegation visits Heptar. Our leader, Hal Pl'Don will gladly hand them to you then, and you may execute justice according to your custom."

"We hang terrorists and spies." Lt. Botchi returned the Jod admiral's disapproving glare. He recalled Admiral Brulk's appraisal of the Jod. The Jod are rotten and therefore easy to crush. Without blinking an eye, the Jod will sacrifice the Earth alien and one of their own chiefs to purchase an arrangement with us. Such a society quickly dissolves into every man for himself. Such a society is easier to defeat. As Botchi considered the measure of the Jod admiral against his own Admiral Brulk, he felt assured of the Ordinate's ultimate success.

Xi-Don changed the subject back to the NewGen clones. "I see you are using clones for military purposes. Some fear that you may raise clone armies."

Again lying to his enemy, Botchi replied, "We would not arm the NewGens except for self-defense. You instigated an insurrection. We need to augment our tiny defensive force of Ordinate security police. Lately, we have considered the possibility of needing to raise a clone army to withstand Jod aggression. Ironically, whether we use NewGen clones for military purposes has more to do with your policies than ours."

Admiral X-Don's neck flushed with exasperation. Through his teeth he said, "If Cor can show some forbearance, I'm sure we can find a simple means to monitor each other's military capabilities. You need not overreact in fear of our fleet, and we need not overreact from fear of your NewGen technology."

They continued with their walk toward the Sarhn barracks.

266   *Roxann Dawson and Daniel Graham*

Botchi's tone turned more amiable. "We had hoped that the invention of the NewGen technology would remove the Alliance's objections to including us in the Family of Species. You refer to the Alliance that way, don't you?"

Xi-Don nodded crisply, huddling against a blast of biting wind.

Botchi continued to take malicious pleasure in the Jods' misery. So he paused a mere fifty paces from the barracks' entrance to finish his long, even slightly philosophical point. "In a real sense, we feel responsible for the flaws in the old-order model. Despite our best efforts, their life is sometimes conflicted. They have some vestiges of what you might call free will. Often their free will becomes disordered. Witness the present insurrection against us, their creators. So we built the NewGen model and have pretty much eliminated free will. Life is so much less complicated without free will, so much more peaceful for the NewGens that are genetically engineered without will or aspiration. They have no more sense of self than a well-trained dog. I assume that your objection to cloning is that the old-order clone serves against his or her will."

Xi-Don answered, "I believe the sentience of the old-order model was the basis of the Alliance's objection." The Jod stepped gingerly around a sheet of ice toward the barracks.

Botchi walked ahead, halting their progression again. "You can assure your leaders that the NewGen model is a departure from the cloning technology that you currently reject on ethical scruples. The NewGens are more accurately described as a new species. Using genetic engineering, we developed a model that is hermaphroditic and propagates by parthenogenesis. When each NewGen hatches, we remove the already fertilized eggs—about three hundred or so—and immediately begin growing as many replacements as needed. We cryogenically save the extras. The NewGens grow with very little intervention on our part except to incubate the eggs and nurture them. While they are larvae, we program them for menial tasks. The NewGen clone is more like a benign Terran bee. Do you have bees on Jod?"

Xi-Don grumbled, "We have a similar species, but ours do not have stingers."

Botchi smiled with a note of reproof. "Ours do." Botchi suddenly feigned surprise. "Gentlemen! Are you that cold? Please, let's get you indoors before you get ill."

As they hustled through the snow toward the barracks they saw two squadrons of light attack hovercraft fly overhead in tight formation. The hovercraft disappeared beyond the forest that stood as a buffer between Sarhn and the clone precincts.

Chaos consumed Precinct 18. Thousands of old-order clones huddled at the base of the new perimeter wall; they crouched low in the triangular ditch, up to their knees in fresh snow. Rebels had taken the precinct by force and these loyal clones fled to the protection of the Security Troops at the wall.

Many held their hands over their faces as if not seeing and not hearing the fighting provided protection. Their arms were mere sticks, their clothes but shreds of cloth. Hunger had eaten them to the bone. A few wrapped themselves in thin blankets. Most wore kerchiefs or homemade caps. They wrapped their hands in bandages, not having any gloves or mittens. Their faces were pale blue from the cold.

Directly above them in the perimeter towers,

Ordinate Security Troops stood behind thick bullet-proof glass. They returned bursts of machine gun fire to suppress the rebels who hid behind barricades in the streets.

Light rail cars that carried the clones to and from Sarhn lay on their sides with the thick undercarriages facing the machine guns. The rebels plugged the gaps between the cars with an assortment of tables, chairs, and mattresses—even their dead. Behind the barricades they kept fire barrels blazing.

The rebel clones also looked thin, but not desperately so. Their faces were masks of rage without a spark of hope: they intended to die that day and take as many of their tormenters with them as possible. But they intended to die with a full stomach. They passed sacks of bread, crocks of butter, and blocks of cheese around. Jugs of milk and cider likewise passed from hand to hand. The rebels rose periodically to fire their weapons, an assortment of crude rifles and slings. They taunted the loyalist clones at the wall by tossing half-eaten chunks of bread and empty jugs into the open. They ducked behind the overturned rail cars whenever they saw the white flashes from the Ordinate tower machine guns—some too late.

Ten hovercrafts landed on a grassy field within the Clone Precinct 18. A mix of Security Troops and NewGen clones, all wearing heavy body armor and helmets ran from the ships and spread out on the field in prone positions waiting for the order to fire.

The captain of the operation stepped from his ship speaking into his headset, gesticulating. A squad of troops rose in unison and ran to the left to flank the clones at the barricade. One of the emaciated clones hiding in the ditch, ran toward the captain and volunteered, "I am the WRT 2001 who called you!"

The captain pulled the breathless clone behind his ship for cover, then pressed a button on the side of his helmet to open the faceplate: "What happened here?"

The WRT pointed with his thin finger toward the cluster of dormitories. "We found out where they have been hoarding food in tunnels beneath the precinct. They have a cache with thousands of sacks of grain. We tried to apprehend them, but they had weapons, too! You must protect us!"

The captain acknowledged saying, "Go back to your ditch and hide." The WRT nodded eagerly and scampered back.

The firefight that ensued was violent but brief. The clone rifles lacked the punch to penetrate the Ordinate body armor. The security troops and NewGens methodically killed all those who stayed at the barricade, dispatching the wounded, and refusing to take prisoners. They hunted those who fled into the interior of the precinct. Everywhere, the snow was stained red. The Ordinate left the dead clones where they lay frozen. They dumped snow in the fire barrels to extinguish the only heat.

Having pacified the precinct, the captain found the WRT 2001 who obediently showed the Ordinate the food cache. Then following the captain's orders, the WRT assembled forty of the still-obedient clones, who spent the remainder of the day loading the sacks of grain onto the Ordinate hovercraft while the armed Security Troops and NewGens watched. The clones were so weak from hunger that they could barely lift and carry the forty-pound sacks of grain.

At the end of the day, the exhausted and bewildered

precinct clones stood and watched the hovercraft depart. The sun was down, the temperature plunged even further, and fresh snow fell to bury the dead.

Klamdara's morning sun warmed the back of K'Rin's neck as he walked into the yellow brick cell carrying two bowls of porridge. He stomped some of the red dust from his boots. Jo'Orom sat up in his cot, then doubled over in pain. K'Rin watched as the ailing Jod planted his feet on the ground and stood. Jo'Orom gritted his teeth to prepare himself to endure the next movement: he stood erect, forcing his knees to lock, slowly straightening his spine and raising his chin. K'Rin saw the agony written on Jo'Orom's face. K'Rin held out the bowl and said, "Take some food, Feld Jo'Orom."

Jo'Orom whispered hoarsely, "I can't. Thank you." He gently patted his abdomen. Jo'Orom shuffled slowly, turning to face his commanding officer. He whispered, "Lying in bed is bad for morale."

"Yes, Feld Jo'Orom." K'Rin forced himself to look upon his sick friend. He set both bowls on the floor and took Jo'Orom's arm. Jo'Orom frowned feebly, "You should assign a junior enlisted to be my nurse. You have more important matters to attend, sir." He shuffled across the cement floor.

K'Rin affected a stern voice. "I only tend to you in my leisure time."

"Fair enough." Jo'Orom changed the subject. "Have the Tenebrea performed their morning exercise?"

"Yes." K'Rin looked into Jo'Orom's dimming eyes. The rings beneath the old Jod's eyes were losing their color, blending into a sickly muddy brown.

"Good. We must be ready to fight. We must study

the guards' patterns." Jo'Orom labored to breathe. "We must keep discipline. Let D'Cru's guards think we have given up the struggle. They will make mistakes. Yesterday, I saw a guard with his weapon slung over his shoulder. Bored soldiers make mistakes."

"I know." K'Rin felt the thin arm in his grasp. K'Rin had not spent this amount of time with his own father at the end. He couldn't remember why he postponed his leave to visit his father's sickbed. *I suppose I thought he wouldn't die, or that I was indispensable . . .*

"We are still watching and planning." K'Rin assured Jo'Orom. Indeed, the captive Tenebrea studied the minutest details of prison routine. They memorized the change of the guards. They memorized which guards were slack and which guards remained alert, which were right-handed, which favored their left hand. They noticed that the guards on the wall stopped wearing the heavy body armor in favor of loose cloth uniforms. The Tenebrea studied the reverse slope of red rock that hung overhead, calculating the number of pitons and the length of rope needed to climb out—pointless because they had neither pitons nor rope.

They collected anything metal and hid their finds, painstakingly manufacturing crude spikes from bits of pipe or metal bars. They used innocuous hand signals to alert each other to approaching guards. They practiced encroaching on the guards' tactical space, making them comfortable standing within four meters of a Tenebrea; three meters; then two. The unarmed Tenebrea would need to get close to the guards to surprise them.

K'Rin's staff watched supply ships come and go. They knew that ships unloaded their wares with their engines hot—ready to bolt at the slightest sign of danger. The Fleet still treated the Tenebrea with all tactical caution, even if D'Cru's infantry did not.

Whereas Jo'Orom believed in earnest that the Tenebrea would somehow subdue their jailers, capture a supply ship, and escape, K'Rin thought the plan was at best a wholesome fantasy. K'Rin oscillated between hopeful scenarios and reality. He imagined Andrea Flores and H'Roo Parh disobeying his orders and effecting a rescue, however impractical, and it amused him to contemplate her unorthodoxy. The thought of a rescue was so ludicrous that K'Rin would not give the thought the legitimacy of the spoken word. Upon sober reflection, K'Rin was satisfied to think that Andrea was safely disengaged, hiding on Earth perhaps. *Is hope incompatible with reality? Is false hope better than no hope?* K'Rin turned to the dying Jo'Orom and wondered.

K'Rin decided Jo'Orom's hope was contagious; his simple plan might work. When each Tenebrea had a crude weapon, they would make an attempt to seize Klamdara and hopefully to capture a ship.

K'Rin blamed himself for the Tenebrea's loss of freedom. All his practical machinations had come to naught and now the troops survived on Jo'Orom's hope. K'Rin would sooner take away their ration of real water than deprive them of this intangible hope. So K'Rin embraced Jo'Orom's plan completely. He exacted one promise from his men. The privilege of killing D'Cru was his alone.

K'Rin helped Jo'Orom walk to the door of their cell. Jo'Orom shook K'Rin's arm away, then walked into the bright sunlight under his own power, stiff and halting, but erect. His steps became more deliberate as he approached the flimsy huts arrayed in the Klamdara yard. An enlisted Tenebrea ran forward to receive an order.

Jo'Orom said in a raspy voice, "Today I'll inspect hygiene."

Before he took his leave, K'Rin said in a low voice, "D'Cru and his bastards won't give us a pain management collar or even narcotics to ease your pain."

Jo'Orom closed his eyes. "Then I will have to endure death like the ancients." He forced a feeble smile. "I'm beginning to admire them greatly."

Another blizzard engulfed Sarhn. Admiral Brulk stood at his window and looked at the thick white flakes flying horizontal in the stiff wind. White—everything was white. Sheet lightning flashed, illuminating Brulk's face, highlighting the gray stubble in his short hair. Despite the harsh white flashes, Brulk did not blink. The thick glass muffled the booming thunder to a low moan. Without turning away from the storm, Brulk asked, "Gentlemen, what do you think of Cor?"

Xi-Don sat in a comfortable chair, yet he appeared uncomfortable. He answered carefully, "Your world appears harsh to a Jod's eyes."

"Harsh indeed." Brulk turned. He folded his arms across his chest as he said, "The Chelle brought our ancestors here from Earth. I suspect they wanted to see if humans were rugged enough and resourceful enough to withstand Cor's variable climate. We survived. We grew. We don't care if the Alliance disapproves of our methods."

Xi-Don interjected, "I am sympathetic with your point of view. The Jod government simply wants assurances that the Ordinate will keep the peace."

Brulk scowled. He fought the invective rising in his

throat. He thought the Jod more arrogant than the Chelle. "We did not violate the peace."

He walked toward the Jod emissary and stood over him and lied masterfully. "You may think this ironic, but I am the chief advocate of peace within the Cor government."

Xi-Don nodded solemnly. "Military men are usually the most loath to start a war. We are the ones who suffer after all."

Brulk looked and sounded conciliatory. Despising his Jod counterpart as he did, Brulk wanted to smother him with bogus goodwill. "We can avert this war that will surely cripple the Jod but will mostly likely extinguish the Ordinate. I have studied the odds, but I have yet to convince my civilian counterparts. I need your help."

"What do you want me to do?" Xi-Don asked.

Brulk sat down in a wingback chair next to Xi-Don. He leaned toward Xi-Don to share a delicate confidence. "The Cor civil government wants the Jod Fleet to stand down as a show of goodwill. I, however, want you to amass a show of force."

Xi-Don's eyes widened. "Go on."

Brulk let his countenance turn grave. "My government has no idea of the power of your dreadnoughts. I want the Madame Prefect to see with her own eyes the size of your Fleet. You need to assemble all your capital ships above Heptar when we arrive with our delegation to initiate diplomatic relations—all seven dreadnoughts and as many heavy cruisers as you can muster. I will personally put the Prefect on the bridge of my ship as we troop the line. She will see that your assets dwarf ours. I can promise you that the shock of seeing your Fleet will make her want to accept your offer of reparation."

Xi-Don nodded soberly. "With due regard to your accomplishments here on Cor, your assessment is correct: the Jod Fleet is indomitable. I think the best use of our Fleet is precisely to deter futile military campaigns. I can guarantee that your Prefect will see the Jod Fleet."

"Good man. Do you have the authority to offer that guarantee?"

Xi-Don demurred. "The head of the Jod government is my cousin. Also, we have our own reasons for assembling the Fleet. I told you about the possible rogue element in our Fleet, an admiral from an influential family. As we speak, we are recalling and decommissioning all officers who might have ties to the guilty party. You see, Admiral Brulk, we are quite serious about keeping the peace."

Brulk feigned speechlessness, then uttered, "I hope Madame Prefect can someday appreciate the goodwill expressed here today. In the meantime, I still think it wise to impress her with your assembled Fleet."

Xi-Don smiled—a paternal smile. "Perhaps she will realize that the Jod Fleet serves the entire Alliance. In a manner of speaking, if Cor joins the Alliance, the Jod Fleet will then serve your interests as well."

"I am eternally grateful. For the first time since the destruction of the Clone Welfare Institute, I feel Cor's future is secure."

Xi-Don stood and bowed. "Will I see the Madame Prefect and your cabinet before we leave?"

"No." Admiral Brulk shook his head. "The Prefect would only repeat her accusations and demands. I want to send you home with my heartfelt plea for cooperation. When we arrive at Heptar, you can deliver the Terran female and her Jod chief to Madame Prefect to satisfy her dignity. Meanwhile, assemble your Fleet as a show of force to give her a dose of humility. For my part, we shall continue to retire the old-order clone technology by natural attrition, removing the Alliance objections to Cor's participation in your union."

Xi-Don approved. "Most encouraging. I believe I can speak for my cousin, Hal Pl'Don: you shall have your demonstration. Your Prefect will see our military might as well as our restraint. Restraint is the key to these negotiations, patience and restraint."

"Good. Then let's not waste time. The storms will only get worse in the coming weeks. I suggest you begin your journey as soon as possible. As agreed I'll send an advance party or employ the Chelle to ensure that you have made your preparations and to choreograph our entrance. Let me assure you, the Prefect is impressed by pomp."

"Our hospitality will impress you even more than the size of our Fleet."

"We will do our best to reciprocate." Admiral Brulk returned Xi-Don's genteel bow.

As the Jod left his office, Brulk felt secure in his plans. Chaos, then order. He sensed that the grand plans must be distilled into minimal language. He considered himself a self-trained philosopher, whom fortune molded into a military leader, that rarest of creations: a visionary who can act.

His great mission was to interrupt the Ordinate's natural entropy with a momentary spasm of chaos from which the survivors would improve the social order for the next millennium. Years of preparation now converged, a life's work intersecting with the future. His destiny and Cor's were singular.

The insufferable itch would not go away. Tamor grabbed the arms of the surgical couch and dug his fingers into the cushions. Delicate hands peeled the thin strips of linen away. As the wraps of cloth fell away, the light intensity grew from deep gray to opaque beige, finally to stark glare of white. Tamor's eyes blinked as he tried to acclimate to the light. He saw the surgeon's hands withdraw. He saw the concern in the surgeon's eyes. An assistant flushed pale orange about the neck—disgust or fear.

Tamor sat up and growled. "A mi'or! Han' me a mi'or!" His misshapen mouth garbled the order.

Nervously, a female wheeled a tripod with a mirror to the surgical couch. Tamor snatched it from her and pulled it to his face. The surgery had exacerbated the damage done by the slime cats. His nose was half-eaten. The cartilage graft failed completely, leaving nostrils that looked skull-like. Over the right side of his face and down his neck, his pale smooth Jod skin was a rippled purple sore, congealed into a scar. His right ear was a nub of twisted cartilage outlining a small black hole. The scarring about his right eyelid caused a drooping aspect associated with stupidity.

The surgeon had successfully sewn shut the hole in his cheek where the fungus had eaten through. The wound still showed a deep divot. He held up his hand, which also looked like it was on fire. The fingernails were gone, replaced with scabs, his thumb reduced by one joint. Tamor ripped the mirror from the tripod and smashed it on the arm of the surgical couch, lacerating his hand.

The surgeon backed away as he explained. "Tamor-Kyl. All the grafting failed. The laser reconstruction techniques failed—nothing worked. Your skin, all the way through your subcutis, has begun to show early stages of Quazel poisoning. The cells that make up

your cartilage and skin are no longer supple enough to
respond to treatment. If we could manage the effects of
the Quazel, I believe we could try the operation again."

Tamor tossed the bandages away and shoved his
way past the surgical staff, toward the door.

chapter 15

Eric slapped the console and muttered an expletive. He spun around in his chair and looked at H'Roo, who paced the floor. "They want to know why we're using the old code."

Andrea looked up from her tactical display of Cor and looked at H'Roo for an answer. He suggested, "Tell them we had an onboard fire that ruined the epsilon series data cubes. Tell them we need immediate clearance to land."

Andrea shrugged, and Tara keyed the response. They held their breath.

Two minutes later, Eric read his console. "We are cleared into the Cor system. But they are sending assistance in case we need help with the fire damage. Now what?"

H'Roo answered quickly. "Simply acknowledge and close the channel." Turning to Tara he added, "Now, we've got to put this ship down directly—no orbits." He switched on shipwide comms and announced, "We're going down tactical."

Andrea ordered, "Tara, find us something flat to land

on, about five hundred kilometers in the mountains north of Sarhn. Coordinates 45 degrees 8 minutes, by 52 degrees 22 minutes. Search area, a thousand square kilometers. Preferably, find us some terrain that can give us some defilade."

Tara, who sat in the navigator's chair, brought up the *Benwoi*'s forward screen and magnified the image of Cor a thousand times. The computer smoothed the grainy image. They saw thick waves of dense clouds rolling off the ocean, smothering the land. The clouds disappeared into the shadows of nightfall. Lightning flashes lit the clouds like paper lanterns. Tara shook her head. "We'll have to land with instruments only."

H'Roo fumed. "No land-based navigation. No landing apron. A major storm. At night." H'Roo turned sideways to read the data: estimated surface wind speeds gusting to eighty kilometers per hour. High altitude winds were five times that. He turned to Andrea. "This ship becomes aerodynamic during descent. It uses wings to stall, and then braking rockets to land vertically. That wind can flip us on our back."

Andrea stared back at him coldly. "And?"

"We don't know if the *Benwoi* is built to take this kind of weather. If we wreck the ship, we're stranded on Cor. I recommend we abort."

Dr. Carai stepped forward to listen to H'Roo, but Andrea motioned the Artrix to stand back.

Andrea left her seat and walked to H'Roo. She put her face close to his. She wanted him to feel her hot breath as well as hear her words. She talked softly so that none might hear but H'Roo.

"Never," she whispered, "take counsel of your fears. The time for plans is behind us. Now we execute."

H'Roo set his jaw. He suddenly looked years older. He replied, "I am not afraid."

"Well, ship's captain, I believe you. But they don't." She motioned with her head to the other Tenebrea standing together watching this contretemps between the two officers. Andrea finished saying, "I suggest you take us down."

H'Roo didn't nod or give any other sign that he agreed with Andrea. He turned to Tara. "Put flight controls to manual on my mark." He took the pilot's seat. "Pass control."

Tara looked sideways at H'Roo, who glanced back with a wan grin. She ordered the computer, "Put up the virtual overlay." Tara superimposed key cartographic features over the virtual image. Sarhn and the clone precincts stood out as red line drawings in the thick of the storms—the mountains were drawn in green. The storm clouds reached deep inland, all the way to the badlands, two thousand kilometers east of the mountain range. They had no choice but to take their chances in the tempest below. Tara's face fell with disappointment as she announced, "Entering outer atmosphere."

H'Roo placed his hands over the pilot controls and rehearsed. The ship jarred left and right with the slightest pressure on the steering ball. Pointing to the gray virtual image on the forward screen, he selected a broad checkered valley with a thin black river—presumed frozen—that snaked randomly. He gave a series of short commands. "Tara, pick landing coordinates toward the leeward side of a steep wall of rock."

"Done," Tara replied without taking her eyes from her console.

"Eric, move over and take weapons control. We may

have forest beneath us when we land. I want you to use
the laser cannon to mow the trees down. You'll have
maybe five seconds to burn us a pad."

"Understood." Eric changed seats. He set a pattern
with the two forward cannon to shave the ground.

"Everybody strap yourselves in. We're going in hot."
H'Roo pulled over his shoulder straps and buckled
himself into his seat. The others quickly followed his
example. He began to bank the *Benwoi* toward the
north on a long arch.

Cor's gravity accelerated their descent. Giant cumu-
lous clouds reached up to grab them. Even Andrea felt
her knees buckle as they plunged toward the roiling
mass of electrostatically charged clouds. The *Benwoi's*
wings protruded gracefully to slow the ship's fall. Hull
temperature rose despite forward shields. They plummeted without incident until they hit the high altitude
winds that reached four hundred kilometers per hour.
The ship shuddered, then began to wobble slightly
from side to side. H'Roo gently adjusted the nose of
the ship, afraid that a harmonic undulation might set
in. He held the crosshair steady on the forward screen,
which continued to provide a virtual image of their
rapid descent.

When the *Benwoi* hit the storm clouds, the ship
jerked wildly, nearly ripping the crew from their seats.
The jolt slammed H'Roo forward into his shoulder
straps, knocking the wind out of him, then slamming
him back into his seat, momentarily ripping his hand
from the steering ball.

The *Benwoi* fell into a spin. They spun so fast that
the onboard computer could not process the virtual
image. The screen churned into milk white. The back-
drop of the image was nothing but snow in all direc-

tions—black clouds, white snow, and blue lightning. The altimeter became a blur of decreasing numbers. H'Roo knew better than to attempt to right the floundering ship himself. He felt the blood draining from his head into his limbs. His vision narrowed and he fought to stay conscious. He yelled a vocal command to the computer. "Autopilot!"

The computer made corrections in pitch and yaw faster than any flesh and blood could. The spin became a series of violent jerks that quickly subsided to broad swings port and starboard. The wild swings diminished to an uncomfortable bounce through the atmosphere. The autopilot pulled the nose of the craft up, using the wings and braking rockets to slow the plunge.

The front screen stabilized. Tara, strapped in her seat and pale as a ghost, groped her console. She found the *Benwoi*'s position. "We're way off course."

H'Roo refocused his eyes. The virtual image showed them flying toward the ground. The autopilot was sending a request for landing instructions to the coordinates in the valley. H'Roo reassumed manual control. "Hard to port." He executed his own orders.

The *Benwoi* banked. H'Roo used the long turn to slow the ship to subsonic speed. He cleared the forward peak of the mountain range and turned up the valley. For a moment, they saw a break in the clouds, but the scene below was nothing but unintelligible white. On the leeward side of the mountain, they found themselves below the clouds and in shadow. Dark as a moonless night. The snow blew horizontal, creating a billowing floor of white that the landing lights failed to penetrate. The snow merely reflected the light back to the sensors: they were snow-blind. The virtual image remained H'Roo's best guide. The screen depicted their impromptu landing site with a pale red light.

The *Benwoi* shuddered as H'Roo poured on power to break their fall. As they slipped below five hundred feet, the virtual image left the screen, having no better resolution to offer. Landing lights offered a feeble intermittent glimpse of the ground below—also maddeningly white. The computer replaced the virtual images with radar-enhanced optics that filtered the worst effects of the heavy snowfall. The landing site was not as level as they had hoped. The ground was thick with tall conifers, bent under the burden of snow and ice. H'Roo's neck discolored, a mix of frustration and fear.

H'Roo fired the braking rockets again for final approach. Eric set loose his laser cannon in a rectangular crossing pattern to blast the trees near their roots. Shards of woods and clouds of snow erupted from the laser blasts, obscuring forward vision completely.

The high winds pushed the *Benwoi* to the left of Eric's expedient clearing. H'Roo compensated with the steering ball, but only by intuition. Snow-blind and bucking gale-force winds in an unfamiliar ship, H'Roo announced, "I'm putting her down now." The *Benwoi* settled with a jolt onto the heavy debris of fallen trees. They heard the metal groan as the weight of the ship rested lopsided with the port landing gear ensnared among the thick logs. The port wing was bent and unable to retract. "Cut the engines." H'Roo drooped in his seat to catch his breath.

Andrea felt lightheaded. Rough trip. She looked around the ship. What a mess. Everything not tied down had been tossed during the spin. Round objects, plastic cups mostly, rolled to the port side of the *Benwoi*, which listed at a precarious angle. Messes can be cleaned. The old Artrix lay limp, unconscious in his straps, breathing easily. Blacked out in the spin. Tara staggered back to the crew quarters to relieve a bout of nausea. Fal'Dar and his comrades just seemed glad to be alive. They unfastened their harnesses and massaged the bruises on their shoulders.

Andrea smelled ozone from electric arcing, caused by strained circuits. "Power down the mains. Auxiliary for environmental suite only." Turning to the crew she added, "We're not going anywhere until sunup."

The ship's lights dimmed and the hum from the engine room faded into silence. Andrea presumed the ship had suffered structural damage. The forward screen flickered with static, indicating some damage to sensors on the outer hull.

H'Roo shook his head in self-rebuke. He said, "A better pilot could have put her down without damage."

"We didn't have a better pilot." Andrea slowly unbuckled herself. "If we can't fix this one, we'll steal another." She looked into H'Roo's eyes and saw something different. A new ring. She reached out with a slender finger and gently stroked the skin beneath H'Roo's eye—the thin claret ring beginning to show beneath the amber and indigo.

"What?" H'Roo asked, withdrawing from her touch.

"You're a three-ringer now."

The Sarhn Barracks operations center was particularly quiet as everybody hunkered down, waiting for the storm to pass. "Sir!" A young technician barked an alert and pointed to his screen.

The abrupt call startled Lt. Botchi. He sloshed some tepid tea on his uniform. Slowly, he composed himself and turned to discipline the technician at the console.

But before he could lecture the young man on ops-center composure, the raw recruit blurted out, "It's the *Benwoi!*"

"What!" Botchi set his glass on the counter and leaned over to inspect the console. In the dark operations center, the console's pale green light reflected in the technician's wide eyes.

"Perimeter control reported a distressed ship, the freighter *Roth*, using an old code. They matched the hull signature with their call sign. No match. It wasn't the Roth. However, the hull signature does match the *Benwoi.*"

"Where is she?" Botchi dabbed his shirt with a napkin.

"Disappeared in the storm clouds. Satellite tracking lost her west of Sarhn, heading southeast. She was spinning out of control in a free fall—presumed crashed in the mountains."

"Radar?"

"Nothing, sir. The storm limits effective range to ten kilometers."

"Get a best estimate on the crash site from the last trajectory. Task the imagery satellites to focus around the crash site. If she augered in, she probably broke her engine seals. She'll leave a hot spot for days. As soon as we can put up aerial reconnaissance I want that ship found."

"Yes, sir." The technician turned around. "The extrapolation of trajectory puts her down in the south range."

"Did the *Benwoi* send any communications?"

The technician turned and stroked a few keys, then waited. "No record of a transmission except the hail to Perimeter Control. Sir, the chance that the *Benwoi* survived is practically nil."

"We must be certain." Botchi drummed his fingers on the table.

"They may have detected our fleet assembling at Lynx. Our whole strategy is built on surprise. If we're compromised, we're defeated before we begin. I want confirmation that the *Benwoi* is down. I want the crew captured or killed."

"Damage?" Andrea sat in her chair, turned to face uphill.

Fal'Dar reported, "No damage to the main engines. Computers are on-line. We have a break in the floor filament for the artificial gravity grid in the galley. A ventilation fan burned a bearing. Also, we found a couple of busted hoses that we've already repaired. I'd say we're lucky."

"Can we straighten the ship?"

"We can't raise or lower the landing gear. The legs are either bent or jammed. We'll need to go outside to see."

Andrea looked at the chronometer. "We have daylight now. How's the weather outside?"

Tara trod carefully to avoid slipping on the tilted floor. She consulted her array and answered, "According to the sensors, hull temperature is minus two degrees Celsius, wind is zero, luminous flux is also near zero."

"What?" Andrea responded with a quizzical look. "You mean it's still dark outside?"

Tara shook her head. "My guess is that we're under three or four feet of snow."

H'Roo entered the bridge wearing layers of clothing over his uniform. "We can't lower the ramp. I'm going up to the top maintenance hatch."

Andrea followed H'Roo. She wormed her way through the narrow bulkhead that constricted further into a narrow passage of cables and pipes. She squeezed by Fal'Dar and Zu'Pah who worked in the maintenance bay, then climbed the short metal stairs leading to the hatch. With some difficulty, she manually unlocked the hatch and slid it open.

The stark white sheet of crusted snow reflected the warm yellow hues of the *Benwoi*'s artificial light. Andrea reached overhead to touch ice shaped in the shallow dome left by the *Benwoi*'s smooth hull—snow melted on the hot skin of the *Benwoi*, refrozen into a convex sheet of translucent ice. The glassy crust supported several feet of loose snow.

Andrea tapped the icy crust with her finger. "I never did like the cold." She put on a pair of leather gloves, then smashed the ice crust with the heel of her hand. A torrent of white powder fell over her. She smiled at herself and wiped the snow from her wet face, shaking the loose snow from her hair and digging bits of melting snow from her collar.

Looking up the white chimney and blinking at the bright light above, she said, "About three—maybe four—feet of fresh snow." The sky was a crystal, eternal blue, scrubbed clean by the storm. Sunlight sparkled from the snow crystals. A light breeze blew wisps of snow into the ship.

Andrea stepped up the slippery ladder, finally bracing her foot against the hull. She stood to her full height and poked her head up for a look around.

Thick trees surrounded the *Benwoi*, many tossed by the cannon blasts, broken and leaning against others. The crisp air smelled of pinesap. Steep volcanic mountains rose beyond the trees, stretching forever toward the sky.

She turned around to get a look into the valley and saw the cold steel barrel of a carbine pointed at her face. Startled, she lost her balance. Reflex thrust Andrea's arms out to break the fall, but she found nothing but loose snow. A thick mitten stuck out and grabbed a handful of her clothing in the middle of her chest. Andrea instinctively purchased a grip on the rifleman's wrist. She hung on that powerful arm for a moment, as she shuffled her feet back onto the ladder. She steadied herself.

The rifleman was swathed in a white mantle: ragtag, not uniform. Thick wraps of dirty linen covered his neck, chin, and ears. A thick frost-encrusted mustache covered his lips. His eyes hid behind dark round goggles. A thick cloak draped over his shoulder. He sat on his haunches above her, propped with plastic snowshoes. A wilderness clone.

His unshaven cheeks were red from the cold and sun. The mustache turned up as the man's facial muscles tightened. He pointed the rifle barrel aside. He cradled the weapon in his left hand covered by a mitten made of fur. His right hand was naked; the trigger finger rested loosely on the lethal lever. Andrea slowly raised her hands to show that she was unarmed and said, "We are friends of Brigon."

"I know." The rifleman pushed his goggles onto his forehead and pulled the linen wraps from his chin. His steamy breath disappeared in the crisp air. "I didn't mean to scare you like that."

Andrea recognized the dark gray-blue eyes and the playful smirk behind the unkempt beard caked with ice and frost. He smiled broadly. "You came back early." Brigon pulled off his left mitten and reached down and put his bare hand against her cheek. His hand was warm and moist against her cold skin.

H'Roo called up from the maintenance bay. "You all right? What's going on?"

Andrea ducked her head back into the ship. "H'Roo! Tell Tara, Brigon's here."

She turned back to face Brigon. "How did you find us?"

"You made a lot of noise coming down. A sentry"— Brigon pointed to the steep mountain wall on the other side of the valley—"saw some laser blasts last night and reported a downed ship. We came to scavenge the wreckage. I didn't expect to see an intact ship. I certainly didn't expect to see you."

Brigon reached down and grabbed Andrea's wrist. "Let me get a better look at you." He pulled her out of the ship with her cooperation. But she sank in cold snow up to her chest. The snow found every crevice in her clothing, nipping at her ankles, slipping down her waistband. She ignored the trickles of prickly cold against her skin. Andrea enjoyed the warm comfort of looking into familiar eyes in this most unfamiliar world. After a moment, she said, "I can hardly move."

Above her, Brigon squatted on his haunches and laughed at her predicament. "Do you know how to use snowshoes?"

"No."

"Today would be a good day to learn. How soon can you leave the ship?"

"Thirty minutes." She turned slowly toward the hatch. Plowing through the snow to the *Benwoi*'s hatch she said, "We need to offload some gear, and I need to change into some heavier clothes."

Brigon lent her a hand to extract herself from her pocket of snow. He said, "Tell your people to bring all the food and medicine that you have." As Andrea lowered herself into the ship, Brigon asked, "How many people are in your crew?"

"Three humans—Tara, Eric, and me—five Jod, and one Artrix. Nine altogether."

Brigon turned and shouted a command, "Hey, Stubbs! Go down to the sled and bring up the small showshoes and short skis. Nine sets." Turning back to Andrea he asked, "What in hell is an Artrix?"

Andrea looked back and smiled. "Dr. Carai can explain himself better than I can."

The *Benwoi* crew members and wilderness clones paired off for the march back to their base. The wilderness clones carried the heavy packs stuffed with provisions. They took turns dragging the sled stacked high with provisions from the *Benwoi,* and still they challenged the unburdened *Benwoi* crew to keep pace.

Brigon's people backtracked, taking advantage of the trail they had already cut through the snow. In many places, however, drifts had partially covered or completely filled the shallow troughs. With snowshoes, they shooshed through the powder. Every ten minutes the lead pair stopped and waited for the column to pass. In that way, everybody pulled duty plowing the drifts and packing virgin snow—everybody but Dr. Carai who suffered the most from the rapid pace.

They traveled in haste. Andrea calculated that they traversed eight kilometers in the first hour on the downhill run. Their path weaved through thick stands of pine that leaned away, almost perpendicular to the slope. Heliotropes: the straight pines obeyed the sun more than gravity. The snow-covered pines allowed only meager shafts of sun through, further skewing any vertical reference to the sky. The combined downward slope and heliotrope trees played tricks on the mind.

Although Andrea felt the gravity lengthening her downhill strides, her eyes fooled her inner ear's sense of equilibrium into thinking that she plowed uphill. Andrea fell, sprawled in the white powder. Brigon hoisted her back to her feet, brushed the snow off her body, and said, "Takes some getting used to."

The ground gradually leveled, and the thick pines gave way to spindly hornbeam trees and meadow. Brown tufts of stiff grass poked through the snow, like cattails, but the clusters of bearded seeds looked more like oats. Several wilderness clones detoured and quickly stripped the grain from the stalks, considerable effort for a mouthful of grain. Andrea asked Brigon discreetly, "Your men— must they forage?"

Brigon didn't answer. Nor did he comment on the breach of discipline: his men leaving the column. Andrea noted, *Their faces are too thin.*

Brigon kept the same pace on the flats. Andrea felt the burn in her thighs. Her lungs rebelled, refusing to fill themselves to capacity with the icy air, and she felt her limbs threatening to cramp. Sweat dripped down her forehead. Her collar, wet about her hot neck, became stiff, chafing her skin exposed to the freezing air. How ironic to suffer a heat injury in this wicked cold. Andrea loosened the straps on her outer garments, partly to release the heat, partly to unconstrict her lungs. As she looked at the uphill slopes ahead she asked Brigon, "Are we in a hurry?"

Brigon peeled back the wrist coverlet on his mitten and looked at his chronometer. "A pair of Ordinate satellites will be overhead in about fifty-three minutes with IR and motion detection."

Andrea looked back to see Dr. Carai struggling. "Some of my people are having a rough go." She talked in short bursts between breaths. "Can't we hide under your wilderness cloaks?"

"The Ordinate has a string of birds that stay overhead for about two and a half hours. That's a long time to sit still in a snowdrift. Your Jod friends will freeze for sure. You and me, we might be able to find a way to keep warm under my cloak." Brigon turned and grinned, almost losing his balance, scuffing up a spray of powdery snow.

"Keep your eyes on the road," Andrea huffed.

"Also, if we rest now, the sun goes down, the temp falls another twenty degrees, and the wind picks up. You don't want to travel at night if you don't have to." Pointing ahead, Brigon said, "We want to reach some small caves at the cliffs if possible. With some hustle, we can get under shelter out of the snow, where we can rest and take a meal."

"Understood." Andrea hadn't enough wind to converse and snowplow at the same time. She distracted herself from her body's complaints by looking at the terrain and sky. Cirrus clouds had begun to blow overhead. A billowing fog hung in the shadows of the mountains further up the valley. Black crows with white chevrons on their wings picked at the few tufts of grass that poked through the snow.

As they arrived at a wall of ragged black rock and ice, Brigon called loudly to the column, "Four minutes!"

He pointed to a small opening where a trickle of water flowed onto an ever-growing table of ice. He told Andrea, "This is the cave I told you about."

A thick curtain of ice blocked most of the entrance. The wilderness clones deftly axed one of the narrow entrances to provide a passage. "Hurry!" Brigon waved his arms to herd the exhausted party into the cave. He looked at his chronometer. "Three minutes." Everyone quickly shuffled inside.

Andrea collapsed on the cold damp floor softened by dry straw. She caught her breath and looked around. A soft bluish light filtered through the opaque wall of ice. The hollow space was shaped like the hull of a long canoe turned on its side. One end of the cave housed a primitive galley: a small rusted stove, a copper basin, and a low table with legs carefully cut to compensate for the uneven floor.

The wilderness clones sat in a semicircle using their packs as back rests. They stacked their carbines together, loosened their utility belts, and unbuttoned their parkas. Steam and the odor of wet wool rose from their chests. Then they broke out dry rations: rolled oats, cheese, and dried meat.

Eric and Tara sat with them. They unpacked compact kits of vacuum-sealed nutrient bars. Everyone shared food with unaffected hospitality. Andrea watched, amused at the routine as old as human experience.

Dr. Carai and the Yuseat Jod huddled together. Andrea could hear Carai's high-pitched grumbles echoing from the cave walls. One of the Jod snapped backed, "At least you've got fur!"

H'Roo joined Andrea. He squatted on his haunches. Still out of breath, he said, "I thought that crazy clone, Brigon, was going to run us to death. If I didn't know better, I'd say Jo'Orom sent him to plague us."

Andrea closed her eyes and nodded. Sitting with her legs flat on the stone floor, she bent at the waist stretching her hamstrings before the cold made them tight.

As if to confirm H'Roo's suspicion, Brigon walked into the middle of the cave and barked a few laconic commands. "Change socks. Where's Stubbs?"

A voice from the semicircle responded. "Ho!"

"Make some tea. Everybody drinks at least one quart. One more thing, the latrine is at that—that—end!" He pointed down to a dark narrow end of the cave, farthest from the galley. He unshouldered his pack and carbine, then walked to the latrine unfastening his harness as he went.

An anonymous voice spoke loud enough for the assembly. "Lead by example!" Brigon turned and grinned. He had recognized the voice, "That's right, Bedal! When I found you, you didn't even know how to piss on a wall." The clones guffawed and heaped their own ridicule onto the outspoken clone.

Obeying his simple orders, Stubbs, with a pair of his comrades, gathered large chunks of ice and dumped them noisily into the copper basin. He then reached into his pocket and retrieved a steel ball the size of an egg. He pulled a safety pin out, pressed two buttons, and tossed the ball onto the ice. The ball glowed white hot as it melted through the ice and disappeared. Within five minutes, the basin was a roiling boil of water issuing a chimney of steam that dissipated in the cold cave air.

Brigon came back. He walked over to Andrea, dropped his pack, and sat down between her and H'Roo. He didn't waste time and used his brusque command voice. "Obviously, you didn't bring the Jod Fleet." He motioned with his thumb at the handful of Jod clustered together. "What's the story?"

Andrea answered, "Remember the Jod admiral I spoke of? Hal K'Rin."

"I remember. He's the one who'll bring the Jod Fleet to defeat the Ordinate—so you said." Brigon's eyes narrowed, braced for bad news.

"He went to the Jod Council to insist that the Jod mobilize to fight the Cor. We don't know the details. The ruling faction fears his influence with the Fleet. They brought him and his guard, the Tenebrea, to Heptar under the pretense of reinstating his seat on the ruling council. But it was a treacherous ruse. They imprisoned K'Rin with his personal guard and sent them to the penal colony of Klamdara. He was taking your side."

Brigon waved off any tangential responsibility. "Don't even try to suggest that I owe your K'Rin anything. He doesn't know me. He doesn't know what my side is. He's finished. That's all I need to know." Disappointment displaced the hope in Brigon's dark eyes and he suddenly looked ten years older. "Eventually, so are we."

Andrea realized she had hurt her own case. She tried another tack. "If we leave him in Klamdara Prison, he and his men will die. They have a sickness; Dr. Carai has the cure."

"So?"

"If K'Rin dies, you have no chance for Jod assistance."

"What chance have we now?"

"If we save him, he may yet rally his clan. At the very least, you'll have the Tenebrea at your disposal. Maybe we can still defeat the Cor."

Brigon issued a side glance to the silent H'Roo. "Like this guy?" Then he turned his gaze onto Andrea. His voice mocked. "You say maybe we can defeat the entire Cor Ordinate? Maybe? How stupid do you think I am? Even if your K'Rin lives, he's got no power. He can't do you any good. He can't do me any good."

H'Roo interjected, "Not so. Hal K'Rin has many resources outside the Jod government. You would have a powerful Jod indebted to you."

Brigon silenced H'Roo with a look, adding, "Powerful men rarely honor their debts. I may live in a cave, but I'm not that naive. Face facts, Andrea. Your man in prison is finished."

Andrea blurted out, "He's not my man; I don't have a man. I am part of his household guard. I need you and about thirty of your men armed and wearing your cloaks to get K'Rin and his guard out of Klamdara. I have a responsibility to try to save him."

"I don't." Brigon's wet beard glistened. His tawny hair matted down, formed a ramshackle part that ran down the middle of his scalp to his forehead. Andrea looked at Brigon and listened to him. She knew that he and K'Rin truly had little or nothing in common.

Brigon leaned back. "You haven't giving me a single reason why I should help you solve K'Rin's personal problems."

Andrea had expected that the argument might come down to a personal request. She said softly, "I have to try to save K'Rin." She lowered her eyes. "I need your help. I would be indebted to you."

Brigon paused. He scratched his chin through his beard. "You, indebted to me? That's interesting. How do you intend to repay the debt?" Again, he glanced at H'Roo, trying to communicate that H'Roo ought to excuse himself. H'Roo clearly caught the signal and refused the unspoken request.

Andrea folded her arms across her chest and said, "If

you come to Klamdara and fight with me, whatever the outcome, I'll return with you to Cor and fight by your side."

"Is that all? I have plenty of companions who can fight."

Andrea's voice turned as cold as the cave. "What more do you intend to ask?"

Brigon put up his hands to surrender. "Whatever you think is fair." He looked around to ensure that none of his men were within earshot. He whispered, "I'll come with you, Andrea. Not for K'Rin's sake, but for mine. Cor has become a killing ground. I'd just as soon die with you on Klamdara than die without you here."

Andrea lowered her eyes. *He comes because I asked him to.* She had anticipated Brigon's reaction exactly. She was at the same time pleased with her acuity and somewhat ashamed of her methods.

chapter 16

Tamor-Kyl sat in the shadows of Pl'Don's office and waited. He wore a smoke-colored face shield. The Quazel had made his eyes hypersensitive to light. The scars on the left side of his face drew pitiful gawking. The surgeons managed to repair the muscle tissue on his cheek and lips, enough to restore his speech, but cosmetically, they accomplished little.

Waiting had become insufferable, for with each passing moment the Quazel Proteins stiffened his limbs. The early symptoms of Quazel hardening served as a harbinger of the agony to come if Tamor failed to find the Tenebrea's cache of enzyme. He had waited that morning for a doctor to give him something to abate the symptoms. Now he waited as Pl'Don's first appointment of the day. He was alone with his thoughts.

Tamor raised his hand to his throat and felt the pain management collar about his neck. Usually, the PMC indicated that the wearer was terminal. Through tiny tubes entering the base of the skull, the collar dosed him with a combination of electrical and chemical neu-

ral blockers, automatically calibrated to perfectly neu-
tralize the sensation of pain. The doctor had assured
Tamor: The medicines do not inhibit motor response.
You can still work. Then, Tamor asked cynically, Why
doesn't everyone wear PMCs all the time? The doctor
replied with cold realism: Because the sensation of
pain is helpful to most organisms. Healthy organisms
react positively to pain. Tamor thought seriously about
murdering the doctor.

Instead, he seethed alone in his personal hell and
bitterly asked: So what happens when the pain
becomes unbearable? The doctor assured Tamor that
the collar was invincible against pain. Invincible?
Tamor forced a stark confession from the doctor: The
pain management collar and your body's pain fight for
control of your consciousness. But the pain never wins.
Always staying ahead of the pain, the collar finally
strips you of consciousness, at which point you die.

The naked truth. You die. Tamor touched the collar
with loathing and affection. He looked at the doctor
with more hate than gratitude. The astute doctor had
read his eyes. The doctor demurred: The collar doesn't
kill you. I certainly am not responsible for killing you.
Your body is killing itself.

Pl'Don swept into his office and was startled to see
Tamor waiting for him. As Tamor stepped into the
light, Pl'Don recovered and said, "I heard that you had
an accident."

"An accident?" Tamor echoed the acerbic words. His
anger swelled. "Four dead; six injured." Tamor lifted his
faceplate to let Pl'Don see the twisted flesh that was
his face. He pointed to the pain management collar
around his neck. "Because of the Quazel hardening, the
surgeons can't repair these scars."

Pl'Don withdrew behind his desk, bumping his simple stool aside. He remained standing, straightening his saffron robe. "Then you failed to acquire the enzyme. Therefore, I may presume that you also failed to return with the *Benwoi*, the other property of the Ordinate, and you failed to capture the Terran female."

The pain management collar did not numb the sting to Tamor's pride. "I did not fail. Our mission was sabotaged. Somehow the Tenebrea at the Yuseat Lab received warning. They escaped with the supply of enzyme. They ruined the laboratory and erased all the files." Tamor's voice was edged with accusation. "You have a security leak."

Pl'Don pressed his hands on his desk and surmised, "Nevertheless, I think we can objectively say that you did not succeed. As for the security leak—yes—one of the assembly members, one Hal B'Yuon disappeared from Heptar shortly after we incarcerated K'Rin. We have reason to believe he visited K'Rin at Klamdara using false papers."

"You believe! Don't you know?"

Pl'Don unconsciously raised his hand to touch the emerald pendant that hung from his filigree gold necklace, his badge of rank. Pl'Don answered impatiently, "Our offworld intelligence assets are greatly diminished at the moment with K'Rin and the Tenebrea on Klamdara. Tamor-Kyl, you are my offworld intelligence arm at present. I would like you to rebuild the Tenebrea's capabilities as soon as practical."

Tamor slammed his fist on the desk and bellowed, "I'll be dead in three months without the enzyme!"

Pl'Don dismissed Tamor's outburst coolly. "Then, I suggest you make finding the *Benwoi* a priority. If you find the *Benwoi*, you'll find the enzyme. My guess is that you'll also find the clones, and the Terran female. You are wasting valuable time here."

"You must let me interrogate K'Rin in my own fashion."

Pl'Don shook his head and wagged his finger, "No, no, no. I don't care what you do to the others, but I am not going to set a precedent of torturing the noble born, especially a headman of the Clan Rin. I would thereby compromise my own position. Do not raise the subject again."

Tamor roared, "Damn you Pl'Don! I gave you K'Rin! You owe me!" The commotion attracted the council guard. Immediately, Pl'Don's chamber doors flew open and in rushed a dozen large Jod with handlances drawn. They surrounded Tamor and watched Pl'Don for a signal. Pl'Don responded with dignity, "Our friend Tamor-Kyl is not feeling himself today." Turning to Tamor he said, "Compose yourself. I give you full access to Fleet resources to complete your mission. However, you may not lay a finger on Hal K'Rin. I will not have a blood feud on my hands because of you. D'Cru has those orders as well, so don't be tempted to disobey me. However, what you do to Jo'Orom and the others is your business."

Tamor spewed contempt. "You faithless ingrate!"

Pl'Don glanced at the captain of the guard, raising his pale hand to signal restraint. Then he cautioned Tamor, "Don't insult me again. I may hand you over as a traitor."

"Really? What would you do? Have me executed?"

"No." Pl'Don smiled. "I would take away your pain management collar and then order my surgeons to keep you alive."

*   *   *

As they trudged through a narrow canyon, Brigon saluted a pair of marksmen hidden in the ice-covered rocks above. So high and steep were the black canyon walls that the path remained in shadows. The rock-strewn floor meandered as a lazy S following a small frozen stream.

Brigon led his column past a series of regular mounds, large trapezoidal humps softened by the fresh snow and drifts on the windward side: the only man-made structure she'd seen on their trek through the valley floor. A fifth mound was unfinished, shorter, and stair-stepped.

Andrea asked, "What are the mounds?"

Brigon answered without looking at the mounds. "The dead."

The coldness of his answer startled Andrea into silence. She remeasured the mounds with her eyes and calculated that they held several thousand corpses stacked one upon the other.

Brigon trudged ahead and explained. "Precinct clones. They stumble around the wilderness: starved, diseased. We find them already half-dead. They waste a couple rations of grain, then they die. I can't spare the manpower or take the risk of hauling their bodies into the desert." Brigon looked around the frozen valley. "With the onset of winter, we can't dig through the frozen ground to bury them, so there they lie. If we make it through the winter, we'll figure out what to do: bury the bodies or leave before the rot drives us away."

They walked toward a wall of black volcanic stone. The base was a mix of ice and scree—bits of stone chipped loose by heave and vegetation. Brigon led them to a hole in the wall, a lava tube opening encrusted with lime deposits from the coral and crustaceans that lived there millennia ago when land lay under sea water.

Andrea felt the warm breath of the cave as she entered.

"Thermals?"

Brigon turned and answered, "Yes. We have all the energy we need. These mountains are riddled with caves like this one. They fill up with refugees from the precincts. We have no fewer than five thousand clones hiding in the caves throughout the mountains."

Andrea was impressed. "That's a lot of manpower."

"They are untrained, useless to me and to themselves. They don't even know how to survive. They barely know how to hide in the caves. They eat and defecate. Hunger and disease are the greatest enemies now." He looked back at Tara who busily conversed with the other wilderness clones. "I would be happy to give them all back to Tara Gullwing."

Inside the lava tube, the party walked into a dimly lit antechamber. Three separate tunnels fed into the larger space. Brigon commanded his men, "Billet the Jod and Dr. Carai at your dormitory. I want them escorted wherever they go."

Dr. Carai emitted a high-pitched wheeze of disapproval to which Brigon replied, "None of us has seen an Artrix before. My people are just as likely to shoot you, eat you, and make shoes out of your hide."

Although offended, Dr. Carai turned to his newfound companions for assurances. Stubbs pressed his dirty face next to Carai's, and licked his lips in grotesque exaggeration. When Carai backed away, Stubbs chuckled and mewed, "We would eat you."

Brigon continued. "Tara, Eric: you two can wander around. You'll find a fair number of your old Precinct

15 Underground intact in the second dormitory. I recommend that you bunk with them." Brigon motioned to the tunnel on the right.

Then, he pointed to a pair of men bearing large rucksacks. "Bring the medical supplies and follow me. You, too, Andrea."

Andrea observed Brigon's technique with grudging admiration. *He brings a foreign group inside his base and he separates them by rank or class into small, comfortable, but ineffectual groups. Clever tactic. How easy it would be to infiltrate a population of clones. This show of hospitality is not for our benefit but for security. Perhaps he doesn't trust us. Or perhaps he is just following the instinct that has kept him alive so far.*

The assembly broke up. Muttering echoed from the damp walls as the groups shuffled off. Brigon directed Andrea to the worn gravel path in the middle of the cave floor. He pointed to the pockmarked walls. "The sharp walls snag clothing."

The tunnel toward the dispensary was lit with pale electric lights spaced along the walls without evidence of wires. The air smelled of sulfur and urine. Brigon pulled a loose end of his linen neck wrapping over his nose and mouth.

An occasional trickle of cold water slipped down a patch of green slime that survived on the artificial light. The tube bisected once, then it again became wide. Brigon led her unerringly. The clones bearing the medical supplies followed fifty paces behind.

Suddenly, the halls were crowded with emaciated people, clustered in groups of four and five, murmuring conversations. Andrea noticed that the clones tended to arrange themselves by model. *How strange.* She recognized a foursome of TRA models, genetically identical, yet now unique in their deprivation. They were Tara's identical twins. One was sickly thin with sunken cheeks. Another had chapped and swollen lips. One TRA sat cross-legged and erect, indifferent to her poor state. The next sat on her haunches, slump-shouldered with resignation. Oddly, their shared wretchedness created greater solidarity than their shared DNA. Each clone wore several layers of clothes. The drab jackets and layered pants hid their starvation and exaggerated their thin hands and gaunt faces. Thinking back to the mounds of naked corpses outside, Andrea knew that clothing was probably the one thing of which they had ample supply.

She stood beside Brigon and looked at the huddled crowd of misery. Brigon loosened the wrap from his face and surmised cooly, "Half of these clones will be dead before the thaw. If we could just get into the fresh air and gather food." He shook his head. "I can't organize this many people. They are docile enough, but we don't have any leaders. All these clones were bred to take orders—not give them."

Andrea said, "At Klamdara, you have two hundred trained warriors, specialized in small unit tactics—just waiting for you. If you save the Tenebrea, you'll have two hundred warriors who owe you their lives. They can organize and train thousands of your clones. Hal K'Rin, Bol'Don, and Jo'Orom can turn your people into warriors that can beat anything the Cor can biologically engineer. They trained me." Andrea still wished Brigon would commit to the Klamdara mission for reasons that did not involve her personally. In part, she did not trust herself to endure as Brigon's motivation.

"You think they'll show that much gratitude?" Brigon shook his head.

"I guarantee it. K'Rin's mission and yours are the same except for motive."

"I have a mission?" Brigon raised an eyebrow.

Andrea answered with monotone frankness. "You'd be more effective if you'd admit it."

Brigon scratched his cheek through his beard. "With a few thousand fighters like you and me, we might not need the Jod Fleet." The bearers with the medicine brushed by them.

Andrea paused when she recognized a woman with thinning gray hair—a medical technician. "She's from the fifteenth precinct—one of Tara's people."

"Oh, that's Doc. She joined us immediately after you and Tara left Cor. I don't know how she stands it."

The woman worked at a rough-hewn wood table. At present, she ministered to a middle-aged man whose inner thighs were covered with hideous pus-filled lesions. The old woman applied chips of glistening fat to the lesions on the refugee's thighs.

"What's she doing?"

Brigon answered. "In the summer months the pungee fly stings and lays tiny eggs on the skin. Now, the maggots hatch and feed on the host's outer layer of adipose tissue. The itch is unbearable. I've seen where a wolf had chewed its own guts out trying to stop the itch. Without treatment, gangrene results and the host usually dies. The pungee larvae then pupate and in the spring, they break through the scabs of dead meat. If you stay in the wilderness long enough, Andrea, you'll have an experience with pungee flies." He held up his wrist and showed Andrea a ring of pockmarks.

Andrea swallowed and looked with newfound interest on the fatty poultice applied to the wounds. Brigon described what she saw. "The treatment looks odd, but it's very simple. The maggots prefer fatty tissue. They crawl from the skin into the bacon. Then, we throw the infected bacon into a fire."

She looked around at the thin people. Many had dark bruises on their arms and legs. Andrea pointed and commented, "They look like they've been beaten."

Brigon didn't seem to consider the matter a slur against his men. "You've never seen scurvy before, have you? What these clones need is some fruit and some sunlight, both in short supply down here."

They left the dispensary and walked uphill through the belly of the mountain until they came to another cavern built by a bubble of volcanic gas. A whiff of fresh air circulated in the room. A pair of female clones perched on wooden stools listened to jerryrigged headphones. Brigon announced with a modest shrug, "Welcome to my operations center. I want you to see— actually hear—something."

Brigon motioned to one of the technicians to leave her station. Brigon handed the earphones to Andrea and sat in front of a simple monochrome cathode ray tube. A piece of clear plastic covered the screen; the plastic was annotated with cryptic combinations of letters and one discernable word: Lynx. He said, "We rigged a passive collector to gather electromagnetic emissions. Normally we use it to track when Sarhn launches sorties to the precincts or to the wilderness area." Brigon smiled. "The Ordinate think we're too primitive to track them with technology: their snobbery works to our advantage."

Andrea pressed the earphones to her head. "I hear traffic now. Are the Ordinate attacking a precinct?"

"No. We're not listening to Sarhn now." He pointed

to the screen. "We're looking into space in the direction of the Lynx Colony. You hear lots of traffic, don't you?"

"Yes." Andrea cocked her head. "It's just noise to me."

"All ship-to-ship and surface-to-ship data transfers. You also hear navigational radar for close maneuvers, communications, and weapons ranging. We count four to five hundred ships assembled up there. They're getting ready to go someplace soon—twenty days from now, maybe thirty days."

The Ordinate did build a fleet of J-Class attack ships. They'll man them with NewGens for a suicide mission to decapitate the Jod government and cripple the Fleet. Under her breath, Andrea said, "They're going to attack Jod."

"That's my guess. The aggressor makes the rules. Admiral Brulk insists on making the rules."

"How do you know so much about the Ordinate high command?"

"I've studied Brulk all my life." A dark shadow fell over Brigon's eyes. "He probably doesn't know whether I exist." Brigon reached down to the old patchwork console. He gingerly tapped a few keys with his index fingers. After keying in a command, he hit a circular yellow button with a blue halo surrounding it. The color decals were practically rubbed down to the beige plastic.

Something about that yellow and blue key jogged Andrea's memory, a bit of flotsam in her mind: nothing specific. She pointed and asked, "What does that yellow key do?"

"The execute key. When the system demands double confirmation, you must hit the execute key. Now pay attention."

The execute key: yellow within a blue circle. Andrea stared at the old keyboard.

The chatter in her earphones abruptly changed from the Ordinate fleet comms and faded to silence. Andrea asked, "What are you doing now?"

Brigon turned a crude dial. "I'm going to share a little good news with you." He finished redirecting the sensors and Andrea's earphones picked up a loud ping. "You're now listening to surface radar that the Ordinate set up yesterday, about fifty miles south of here."

He reached over and gently removed the earphones. Andrea felt his large hand cup her head. He said, "Now look over here." He pointed to the second console where the technician carefully noted large rectangular areas on a crude glass-covered map. "The Cor have four satellites they use to map the surface of the planet. They can squeeze the focal area and use the same satellites for surveillance. They don't bother to encrypt their telemetry."

"Why not?"

"The Ordinate never considered the possibility that we might understand their surveillance or piece together the technology to frustrate their efforts. Sit down." Brigon grinned like a boy showing off a new gadget. He reached over her shoulder, brushing her neck with his forearm. "We intercept the Sarhn ground control station signals to their satellites, so we know when they shift their assets from surface mapping to reconnaissance. We know when they're looking for us and we hide while each satellite passes overhead."

Andrea observed, "So that's why you were timing your ground march so carefully."

"Exactly. We can disguise our numbers. We can mislead them about our intentions. We can misdirect their operations. Plus, we can anticipate their next ground operation. If they start heavy reconnaissance over the precincts, we know a punitive operation will follow in a matter of days."

Andrea added, "You could warn the precincts."

He shook his head. "No, Andrea. I don't share my secrets that easily. I still don't trust precinct clones. These tricks keep us alive out here."

Andrea didn't argue. In a roundabout way, Brigon was telling her that he trusted her with his life's secrets—his life, no less. She accepted the compliment.

Brigon tapped the screen. "Look. Fifty miles south, right where we heard the ping of their surface radar."

Andrea looked at the map and the crisscrossed rectangles. The technician had drawn a pair of red fans showing the sweep of the surface radar. Several green arches showed the flight paths of Ordinate hovercraft. Recognition lit up her eyes and Brigon responded, "Yes!"

Andrea said, "They're looking for the *Benwoi* in the wrong place!"

"Right now they are practically burning a hole in the southern range of the mountains, in the broader valleys—looking for the *Benwoi*. Fifty miles away!" Brigon squatted down to be in direct eye contact with Andrea.

He said, "We're going to help them deceive themselves. I've told my people down south to spread some metal junk out in the area. We might even find something a bit radioactive. Make it look like a crash site. Also, I want to harass any Ordinate who sets foot in the south mountain valley. We'll set some traps, take down their radar—generally make them think we're interested in salvaging a wreck in that area. Meanwhile, we can quietly make the *Benwoi* space-worthy." He exuded, "I love it when the Ordinate makes a mistake."

Andrea teased, "But do you rely on their mistakes?"

His grin crumpled at the jibe. "My whole life is one of their mistakes."

Tara dismissed her escort after a few awkward objections. Eric continued with the more formal tour.

She wandered alone through the tunnels, anonymously. Tara recognized a handful of old colleagues from her precinct organization. She spoke with them briefly and marveled at their detachment. She had a small pang as she realized that her people had completely transferred their loyalties to Brigon in a few short months.

Brigon had kept his word and offered her people sanctuary. Many rejected Brigon's offer and stayed in the precincts. Tara asked about those who stayed behind and her questions were answered with shrugged shoulders or a laconic euphemism. So-and-so didn't make it. Soon, Tara stopped asking, because too often she learned that the object of her affection died in the precinct or at present lay in the frozen mounds outside the cave entrance. She learned that Gerad's naked body lay frozen in one of those stacks.

"Tara Gullwing! Is it really you?"

Tara turned and saw a grinning face. The smile was lopsided from a thick red scar with suture tracks that raked vertically down the left side of his face from above the hairline, over the forehead, splitting the eyebrow, marring the cheek, bisecting the upper lip, and terminating at the chin. The eyes sparkled. "Remember me? I'm Airco." He lisped slightly because of the heavy scarring on his lips.

"Airco!" Tara grabbed him by the shoulders. "I'm glad to see you alive." She touched her own chin and asked, "A wound?"

"Knife wound. Got this cut fighting next to Coop. Probably would have been killed, except Coop ordered us back. Then I got a back full of shrapnel." Airco pulled up his jersey to expose a random splash of scarlet marks. "Brigon's men carried me to the mountains and patched me up. I feel great now."

Tara recalled. "The explosives you made for the raid on the institute: they worked like a charm."

"I know." Airco beamed as he tucked his jersey loosely into his britches. "I saw the fires as they carried me away. I still make a few explosives, but I want you to see my favorite new toy." Airco pulled an oily cloth from a table to reveal eight long rifles. The gray barrels were twice as long as the carbines that most of Brigon's men carried, making Airco's model less practical for the bush.

Airco handed one of the rifles to Tara. It weighed about twelve pounds—lighter than she imagined—with most of the weight in the stock. Tara found the bore size large, to the point of being awkward. She could jam her forefinger to the knuckle inside.

"What are you planning to shoot with this cannon?"

"Cor Ordinate, NewGens . . ." Airco shrugged and looked embarrassed for giving such an obvious answer.

The wood stock was bulky, although shaped with a cheek rest. Above the trigger guard, a bulky hinge fastened to a lever half as long as the barrel. The front post and rear sights were made of brass. A fine wormscrew raised and lowered a peephole to carefully etched notches. She ran her fingers over the rear of the weapon looking for a hammer or firing pin, or even the mechanism to chamber a round. She looked back at Airco. "I don't get it. How does it work?"

"It uses compressed air." Airco held up a shiny steel bullet without the brass jacket. "No gunpowder." The bullet had a round point at one end, tapered to flat bottom at the other. "You just drop the bullet into the barrel like so." He took the heavy rifle and set the butt on the floor, bracing the stock against his left foot. He dropped the steel slug down the barrel, nodding as he heard the metal clink. "Then you pump up the air pressure." He took the long lever and started working it up and down. Each downstroke was more difficult than the last. Airco strained on the last couple pumps. "If you . . . ugh . . . want to get a range . . . ugh . . . of a kilometer . . . there . . ." Airco straightened himself and finished his thought, "You need about fifteen strokes.

"Watch this." Airco rested the heavy barrel on a wooden yoke and pointed it to the back of his shop. "That mannequin has two sets of body armor. Behind the mannequin is a splash plate that will drop the round into sand."

Tara started to put her hands to her ears. Airco chuckled.

"Don't need to do that." With his forefinger, he released the safety, then carefully pulled the hair trigger. The weapon made a sudden spitting sound, followed instantly by a thud-whack as the bullet slammed through the mannequin and spent itself against the splash plate. "Doesn't have the kick of gunpowder."

Airco turned around. "I'm not the best shot here, but I can hit a target the size of that mannequin a kilometer away. This is the perfect sniper rifle for working these mountains. No sound. No flash. No smoke. The enemy can't extrapolate range. They just feel the seventy caliber round slam through their body armor, rip a whole through their torso, and punch its way out the back." He handed the air rifle back to Tara.

She raised it to her eyes to look down the iron sights. "Most impressive."

"I prefer fighting at long range." Airco pointed to the scar across his chin. "Don't you?"

"I'm sure I do." Tara handed the rifle back to Airco.

Andrea woke from a nap and sat up on a mat of reeds. As she pulled on her boots her mind suddenly made the connection with the yellow and blue execute key on the console. Random thoughts often collide in the subconscious. She had seen a yellow disk with blue halo before.

She closed her eyes and rested her forehead on her knees. That awful day. Steve showed me the acrylic tattoo that a street vendor—the clown with the purple hair—foisted on him: a yellow disk with blue corona. So that's it. One of the Ordinate Hunters marked him as a target for the others. An execute key, no less. Steve paid the clown two slips for that fatal mark.

Andrea forced herself to open her eyes. She was weary of replaying the scene at Baltimore Harbor.

From a clean room on top of an observation tower, Admiral Brulk supervised the last-minute preparations of his fleet on the planet Lynx. Twenty thousand miles above the planet's surface the Ordinate fleet of J-Class attack craft maintained orbit like a thin ring of debris. Less than eight light seconds away, Cor reflected a grayish shimmer.

The Ordinate used the Lynx Colony for heavy manufacturing. This sister planet of Cor occupied an outer orbit from the Cor-system star. Lynx's atmosphere was stingy with oxygen and rather too generous with ammonia. The planet's minerals were superabundant, especially rare heavy metals such as mercury and platinum. Due to long-term exposure to the elements on Lynx, clone labor typically depreciated faster, lasting half as long as clones on Cor. Unfortunate, but the increased investment in clone labor was greatly offset by isolating dangerous work to Lynx, far away from the civilian population on Cor.

Brulk wore a self-satisfied smile, having accomplished the impossible. No race had ever built a fleet of war ships so fast. The night sky above twinkled with a cluster of white specks: four hundred and eighty J-Class ships. All had finished their shakedown flights and each waited its turn to return to the surface to receive its payload of quark torpedoes. He felt so alive in these final days that he had little need to eat or sleep. Brulk felt wonderfully alive.

Brulk looked over the dark landscape. He owed much to the frowsy Lynx Colony, and Lynx owed everything to him. He alone saw the great potential in ugly, inhospitable Lynx. The Ordinate government gave him full authority here. Madame Prefect even referred to Lynx as Brulk's Kitchen. Consequently, Brulk could take shortcuts on Lynx. Here, using clone labor, he built the J-Class ship drives without the cumbersome radiation suits and heavy shielding that would have been required elsewhere. That efficiency alone cut the critical path of shipbuilding in half. On Lynx, he operated four small and widely dispersed munitions factories. Again he compressed time by carefully accepting certain risks when assembling the elements for his ships' quark torpedoes. An eighty-foot-deep crater marked the spot where a fifth munitions factory experienced an accident that gouged out ten thousand cubic yards of rock. The explosion killed three hundred clone technicians and two Ordinate supervisors and blinded a thousand or more clone laborers, who in turn had to be canceled. One by one, each J-Class ship landed by a lonely hangar twenty miles outside the Lynx munition factory. Brulk watched the activity in the hangar by means of remote cameras. On the hangar catwalk, a NewGen pilot stood by and watched passively as old-order clones provisioned the ship. Pilot NewGens wore lime-green flight suits. Each carried a heavy helmet with a set of loose wires dangling from the back.

Brulk looked down in the work bay, where a lone Ordinate civilian wearing a hermetic suit supervised. Two large clones carefully ushered in the cart that held the ten quark torpedoes, each powerful enough to chew a fatal hole in a Jod dreadnought. The forward laser cannon was oversized, designed to repel any small ships put forth as a screen to protect the Jod capital ships. Armed with the heavy torpedoes and an oversized cannon, the J-Class ships needed to cut weight elsewhere. They fueled the ship with enough for a one-way trip. They stocked the provisions, including the environmental suite for the twenty-day voyage to the Jod system, but nothing for the trip back. Brulk knew—indeed he expected that the NewGen pilots knew—that the J-Class ship firing at close range would engulf itself in its own quark blast.

Brulk's plan was brutal in its simplicity. Brulk had four hundred and eighty J-Class ships, each with a spread of ten torpedoes. They would swarm through the Jod capital ships' energy shields, overwhelm their close defenses, and fire their torpedoes at point blank range. The entire strike would take less than two minutes. The balance of power in the galaxy turned on two minutes. With the Jod Fleet annihilated, Cor's six light cruisers and eight troop ships would flatten Heptar and decapitate the Jod government so conveniently confined to such a small piece of real estate. Brulk calculated that he'd lose fifty to seventy-five percent of his craft to Jod defensive fire, but the remnant would gut the Jod Fleet. No Cor J-Class assault ship would survive the attack. They weren't supposed to.

Brulk knew that the Jod command would never anticipate tactics that involved self-immolation. The Chelle had shown him the Jod principles of space warfare. The Jod Fleet's prime directive read: The Fleet's first mission is to secure the Fleet. Translated, the Jod could not conceive of an attack that presupposed the annihilation of one's own fleet, like a chess player whose strategy hinges on the conviction that skilled opponents never swap queens.

Convictions are dangerous. Brulk sneered at the Jod's sentimentality regarding their huge machines, as if a ship were like the family seat, steeped in glory and tradition, as if a ship had a soul and required a certain dose of revisionist history to buff its image. Laughable. To him, ships and pilots were as much a kind of munitions as torpedoes.

A voice from behind interrupted his musings. "Admiral. You have a secure communication coming from Sarhn. Lt. Botchi."

"I'll take the call at my desk—audio only." Brulk sat down at his faux granite desk and powered up his comm suite in secure mode.

"Brulk here." He waited eight seconds for the round trip of signals.

The encrypted voice sounded slightly hollow but Brulk recognized the voice as Botchi's. "Lt. Botchi here. Update on the possible sighting of the *Benwoi*. We found widely scattered debris in the area where we think the *Benwoi* crashed. Also we've seen some signs that the wilderness clones have been scavenging the wreckage: tracks in the snows, sleds—just a handful of clones. I want to send in a patrol to confirm."

"Don't get distracted from your main mission. You've got enough problems containing a billion precinct clones while our forces are on the other side of the galaxy."

Eight long seconds passed. Brulk detected a note of complaint in Botchi's answer. "Yes, sir. I know. We have small units spread around all our cities. We are neutralizing the old-order clones on schedule." Botchi added sardonically, "I'm not worried about the old-order clones. They cooperate beyond my expectations. The cold is decimating them. Unfortunately, we're having more trouble from our own civilians. We had to disperse a handful of malcontents in front of the Ministry Building."

"All the more reason to keep your troops at Sarhn where you need them. Personally, I'm satisfied that the *Benwoi* is down. If the Jod learn about our plans, they'll disperse their Fleet. If they disperse their Fleet, the Chelle will warn us."

Botchi answered, "I don't trust the Chelle. I just want to make damn sure about the *Benwoi*. I'd like to get hold of the *Benwoi*'s recorders to make sure they didn't transmit anything that might give our plans away. I can't be sure from aerial reconnaissance. The wreckage is strewn over several square miles. We're not even sure we're looking at twisted pieces of the ship's hull or what. We're not going to get a definitive answer until we walk into that area and get our hands on the wreckage. Time is running out."

"How so?"

"We've had two meters of snow since the wreck, so most of the evidence is buried. We've got another series of storms blowing in for the next forty-eight hours. Pretty soon, we won't be able to find anything without shoveling the entire valley."

Brulk gave the matter a moment of silent thought. "Okay. I can't fault you for wanting to be sure. But don't spend too much time on the ground. Be careful," Brulk warned. "We can't absorb many ground losses until we get the NewGens fully on line. I want you to go with them. No mistakes. The wilderness clones almost shot down one of our hovercraft with small arms fire two months ago. I really don't want to contemplate what they might do if they captured an operational hovercraft."

Botchi's voice replied confidently. "We'll land at a safe distance, leave a heavy guard, and walk in."

"Remember, Lieutenant. Don't get distracted from your schedule." Admiral Brulk cut the communication. Why would the *Benwoi* return? Another mission to destabilize the clones, perhaps? *It doesn't matter: the Benwoi is rubble; the Jod explanation of this outrage will soon be irrelevant.*

chapter 17

A clone dressed in a shabby overcoat led Andrea up a narrow tunnel. He muttered in a monotonous heartbeat cadence. "We're late, you know. He'll blame me, you know. It's not my fault, you know. You weren't where he said you were."

Andrea stopped listening to the clone's soliloquy. As they walked up the corridor, motion detectors turned on lights ahead of them. Behind them, lights timed out. She had the sensation of walking on a treadmill set to a small incline, oddly similar to space travel where you carry your light with you, and all else is black, fore and aft.

The clone's drumbeat of commentary stopped when they arrived at a thick curtain, a threadbare pattern of gold flame on green blocking the passageway, the only likeness of a door that she'd seen at Brigon's base. The clone muttered, "Brigon's quarters," then he turned abruptly and retraced his steps, seeming to pull the light with him.

Andrea stepped through the curtain. A collection of familiar faces looked up from various discussions.

H'Roo and the four Jod from Yuseat, Eric and Tara, Brigon, and a dozen wilderness clones sat on cushions in a tight circle. Dr. Carai was absent.

Andrea looked around. She was surprised by the subterranean room. It was bright with some evidence of housekeeping. The rough volcanic walls had been plastered with white stucco. The naturally arched ceiling was fancifully painted with a rosy dawn beginning at the east wall, rising to bright pale yellow above and fading to a blood red sunset in the west. At one end was a wooden bed, roughly hewn without a headboard, but with a mattress and a down cover. A sturdy writing desk butted against the wall with two small chairs, each facing the other.

On the wall was a modest circle of wood painted with the face of a woman, stylized—oval face, round eyes, thin determined lips. Andrea knew by instinct that this woman was responsible for this bit of domesticity in the heart of the mountain.

"We're all here now." Brigon's voice caught her attention. "Andrea, come sit by me."

With his elbow, he quietly nudged a female clone who sat on a cushion next to him. The female, obviously a couple years older than Brigon, stood but did not vacate her space. She crossed her arms over her chest, and gave Andrea a look to kill.

Andrea made a quick study of the woman: willful, strong, and clumsy in proportion—broad shoulders and thick waist, not at all graceful. She had bright chestnut eyes and short black braids that looked limp next to her square—and at present, set—jaw.

Andrea replied, "No thank you. I'll sit with the Tenebrea." She wedged herself between H'Roo and Fal'Dar.

Brigon slapped the female clone on the rump, "Well, Chana, you scared off another one!" He grinned at Andrea as the woman reclaimed her seat. Then he said, "My people want to go to Klamdara to save your friend." He added with predictable sarcasm, "You know how it is: a chance to broaden one's experience, see new places, meet different people. They've never ridden on a spaceship before. Right, Chana?"

The female didn't answer, tried to look disapproving, but her eyes betrayed a certain satisfied mirth. An anonymous voice answered in her stead, "We've never ridden on a hovercraft."

"So," Brigon ignored the interruption, "what do we know about Klamdara?"

H'Roo answered, "The word *Klamdara* means iron anvil. It is the fourth planet from the Jod sun. It's rock and sand, mostly, a smallish planet, slightly smaller than Cor. The atmosphere is breathable but very dry. No snow."

"That's a plus," a voice behind him jibed.

H'Roo was annoyed by the interruption. "Most of the planet is not habitable because of the dearth of water. However, the surface is rich in iron and other heavy minerals. The government used convict labor from the Clan Wars to mine Klamdara. When the convict population died out, so did the mining. Klamdara shrank from a large penal colony to simply a prison for a few damned souls—traitors to the Jod government. The terrain around the prison is much like your mountains, except they are sandstone and lack vegetation."

"Otherwise identical . . ." The voice in the back chafed him again.

This time Brigon intervened. "Enough!"

H'Roo felt vindicated. "Along the valleys, however, you find deep fissures that swallow up any surface water that might otherwise improve the planet surface."

Then Brigon peppered H'Roo with questions about the Klamdara fortress: troop strength, armament, long-range guns, and terrain. At the conclusion he thought out loud. "So, we'll need to land out of range of their cannon."

"Exactly." Both H'Roo and Andrea said the word at the same time. H'Roo continued, "We've got to surprise them for more reasons than you think. They'll quickly ascertain where we land the *Benwoi.* We must abandon the ship and use wilderness cloaks to hide us as we travel overland to the Klamdara fortress. We can't defend the *Benwoi,* so we can't count on using her again. When we get to the fortress, we must cut their laser link to the fleet. They won't bother the fleet with a contact report about a merchant ship entering their space, but when we get inside the fortress walls, I assure you they'll call for reserves. The closest dreadnought will respond and we'll have at least a brigade—maybe two—of marines dumped on us. You can't imagine the firepower of a dreadnought or the fury of two thousand Jod marines."

The room turned quiet.

H'Roo laid out a sketch of Klamdara Prison. "I drew this from memory."

Brigon mocked, "You were there? Do you have a criminal past?"

"Gyre's bells, no!" H'Roo's neck tinged pale yellow. Several clones murmured, pointing to his neck.

Andrea nudged H'Roo and whispered, "Tough room."

H'Roo composed himself and said, "I read about Klamdara when I was a boy."

Chana challenged, "So you don't really know where anything is."

Brigon raised his hand to stifle the rising skepticism and end the baiting. He took the sketch in his hand and studied it. The picture had two parts: a frontal view and a top-down scale drawing showing the interior buildings. "That's a lot of cement." He turned to Chana. "I doubt that they have rearranged much." Then he asked, "Where is the laser link?"

H'Roo reached over and pointed to his sketch. "Chana is correct, I don't know exactly, but look here. The fortress sits under a giant overhang of sandstone, three hundred to four hundred feet high. The laser link requires line-of-sight to Jod or to one of the space relays. If the link were inside the fortress under the ledge, they'd lose more than half their coverage. To have constant communication, they've got to put the laser link outside the wall about one hundred meters. For the same reason, they've got to place their long-range cannon outside the walls."

Andrea nudged H'Roo. "That's great news. You didn't tell me that."

"I just figured it out last night when I sketched the fortress." H'Roo finished by saying, "After we take out their comms, the rest of the operation is an ordinary raid. First, we isolate the garrison troops as best we can by cutting their communications and seizing their small launch facility—also outside the walls."

Andrea added, "We'd better take the long-range cannon, too."

H'Roo nodded. "Second, we get inside the fortress and arm the Tenebrea, and defeat the garrison. The trick is that we must perform these first two main tasks simultaneously. Third, we wait for the next supply ship to come. We highjack the ship and all get off Klamdara. We can complete this mission with forty soldiers wearing wilderness cloaks."

The female clone Chana demanded, "What if the next ship is a dreadnought and not a supply ship?"

H'Roo looked at Andrea for an answer. Andrea simply turned to Chana and said, "A dreadnought is out of my league. Honey, if a dreadnought comes, I'm going to let you handle it."

Brigon burst out laughing, and the other wilderness clones nervously joined in. Even Chana managed a toothy grin. Brigon recovered first and said, "Chana, I want you to coordinate with H'Roo to plan a manifest for forty: the *Benwoi* crew plus thirty of our best fighters."

Chana suggested, "We'll need to travel light. Short barreled small arms. When we get inside the walls, we're going to be point blank and hand to hand."

"Don't forget to bring Airco's long rifles." Brigon addressed the entire group. "The ship ought to be ready in three more days. Be ready to travel." Then he dismissed the gathering. As the room began to empty, Brigon grabbed Andrea by the wrist to hold her back. "Don't go yet."

"Business?" She neither encouraged nor resisted his grasp.

Brigon let go. "Not really. I thought we might talk."

Before Andrea could respond, Eric and Tara stepped forward. Eric spoke for both, saying, "May I make a suggestion?"

Brigon turned impatiently to Eric. "What do you want?" Andrea used the interruption to back away. She stood back to see how Brigon handled Eric. Tara likewise watched the exchange intensely.

Eric said, "Tara and I have met a number of our old comrades from when we started the Precinct Underground."

"Good for you," Brigon replied with sarcasm. He looked around to make eye contact with Andrea.

Eric's face hardened at the resistance in Brigon's terse reply. "When you go to Klamdara, you leave behind thousands of clones without any kind of leadership. Tara and I at one time organized many clones to resist the Ordinate."

"What are you suggesting?"

"I suggest you leave the two of us behind to hold your organization together while you are away."

"I won't be gone that long." Brigon edged forward to get closer to Eric. Brigon was slightly taller than Eric, but in most respects they were physically well matched. But Brigon's thick tawny hair and full unkempt beard warned of an unrestrained temper.

Eric did not flinch. In clipped speech he said, "You might not come back at all. Leave us here to run things."

Brigon ushered Eric toward the door, brushing past Andrea. Tara followed, tight-jawed. He said, "You're coming with me to Klamdara. Want to know why?"

Eric scowled as Brigon answered his own question. "Because I don't know you, and I don't trust you. I'll see you follow a few orders before I let you give them." Brigon glanced back at Andrea and then at Tara, whose countenance was most disapproving. He defended himself to the two women, speaking as if Eric were not standing there. "I don't just give away my authority." He asked Andrea, "Would you?"

Kip raised the back of his hand to catch a trickle of blood dripping from his nostril that cut a dark trail through the Klamdara dust caked on his hand. The early onset of Quazel poisoning. Two dozen of his men had already experienced early symptoms such as nosebleeds.

In the background he saw K'Rin sitting next to Jo'Orom's cot. Jo'Orom's body was stiff, animated by only shallow painful breathing. He was blind. Already the cartilage in his joints was ossified and he lay with his arms across his chest like a corpse prepared for a funeral pyre.

"Sir, may I have a word with you in private?" Kip asked.

K'Rin rose stiffly. He handed the wet towel to another attendant who continued to moisten Jo'Orom's chapped and bleeding lips.

He straightened his dirty uniform and walked the few paces to Kip.

"Yes?"

Kip spoke aloud as if Jo'Orom was no longer alive to hear. "The Quazel will snuff us out one by one. Sir, you should let us die fighting—not like him." He pointed at Jo'Orom.

K'Rin answered. "We are making plans . . . patience."

"Patience is killing us! Please be practical. Face reality."

K'Rin pushed Kip out of the sickroom into the dusty courtyard and the bright Klamdara sunlight. "I'm killing you? Killing my people? Are you saying I am indifferent to the suffering here?" K'Rin winced at a small pain behind his eyes. Insulted by his aide and in utter frustration, K'Rin shoved Kip again. "What reality am I missing here? What practicality do you see that I don't? What's your plan?" With one last shove he braced Kip against the brick wall.

Kip's neck flared briefly, but the subordinate took the physical abuse with his arms at his side, fists clenched. "We want your permission to rush the gate."

"Denied."

"Your troops insist. We have a right to die fighting."

K'Rin's blood rose but fell quickly as he looked at the young aide, whose lip trembled in this confrontation with his mentor. K'Rin raised his hand and placed it gently on Kip's chest. "You must be in a lot of pain."

Kip did not reply. So K'Rin admitted for them both: "Me, too."

Kip remained braced against the wall with K'Rin's broad hand holding him in place. "Many of our people are in worse shape than you and me. I can't stand to watch them all die like sick animals."

"So your plan is to get everyone killed. Right? As fast and painlessly as possible. Right?"

Kip looked at the ground. "Better than wasting away slowly in a sickbed."

"Like Jo'Orom?"

"Yes."

"I understand." K'Rin turned and looked back at Jo'Orom. "The watching is as bad as the dying. Do you know Jo'Orom trained me to fly, to fight?"

"Yes, sir."

"In some ways I wanted his approval more than my own father's." K'Rin looked again over his shoulder at the anguished wizened body lying on the cot with disciplined stillness. "Jo'Orom knows he is as good as dead. So do I. Even a massive dose of the enzyme can't restore him now. But his heart is so strong that he won't die. His heart is too tough, maybe even cruel. With every beat, it pumps pain through his veins. As a kindness, I offered to dispatch the old Feld—I told him that I could take him in his sleep, end his excruciating pain, and return him to his ancestors."

Kip nodded agreement.

K'Rin squinted and shook his head sadly. "He condemned me with a look I'll never forget. He summoned his strength and uttered one word. Coward. He called me a coward."

"Sir, the old Feld is delusional. I'm sure he never meant . . ."

"He knew exactly what he meant." K'Rin contradicted Kip sharply. "The old Feld read my heart. He knew that I wished him gone to ease my burden, not his."

Kip shook his head. "No—"

K'Rin saw the doubt in Kip's eyes so he added, "It takes courage to endure the sufferings of others—sometimes more than it takes to endure our own suffering. I am not by nature a coward. I fall prey to malformed judgment like any Jod, but I learn from my mistakes and move on. You do the same, Kip."

"I'm sorry, sir, but your mistake is in waiting. Jo'Orom trained us to fight, so let us fight. Let us show the old Feld that we are not cowards. We can assault the guards' barracks and at least take some of the bastards with us." Kip bitterly added, "Let them share in our reality."

"Pain for pain? I thought the same way when I was your age." K'Rin's countenance turned hard. The frustration of captivity wore on him as much as the Quazel poisoning. His own rage bubbled up, clouding his judgment. Self-doubt followed the rage. "But let's put aside sentimental arguments for a minute and talk about your plan like a pair of professional soldiers. Your plan certainly doesn't require any tactical finesse."

Kip forced a weak smile. "My plan is simple enough." He lowered his eyes to the ground.

"Kip, look at me." K'Rin stood with his back to the morning sun. His long shadow fell on Kip's face. The young Jod's eyes were red from lack of sleep.

K'Rin argued, "Your plan is flawed. Your plan is just an expedient to sidestep reality. Look at the facts. We're in prison. Quazel has ironically made time our mortal enemy. Nevertheless, we are one hundred seventy warriors, albeit crudely armed. Our opposition is a regiment of well-armed infantry." K'Rin managed a smile. "It would appear that our situation is hopeless."

"My point exactly. But at least we can give them a good fight."

"To what end? Be honest, Kip. You don't want to win. You want some Jod infantryman to kill you and spare you the hard death that's staring you in the face now. If you come up with a plan that will actually get us off Klamdara, I'll be the first to listen. What you propose is just a murder-suicide."

Kip looked away. His neck tinged amber.

"Our situation is not hopeless." K'Rin pulled out a scrap of paper with charcoal etchings, schedules of movement. "You know that I'm working on a plan to get out of here."

"Yes, I know. But your plan hinges on luck."

"Circumstance, not luck. We've got to wait for the next supply ship to land—between twenty and thirty days from now. When they stand down the ship to offload supplies, we'll have thirty minutes to overwhelm the guard, cut communications, and seize the supply ship. I figure our casualties will exceed fifty percent. The remnant will rendezvous with the *Kam-Gi* to get the enzyme."

"So, what do we do for the next twenty to thirty days?"

"We continue to make weapons. We plan our three-prong assault. We wait. There is no tactical advantage in attacking before the supply ship arrives."

Kip looked away from K'Rin. "I don't want to die waiting."

K'Rin squared his shoulders and pointed past the huts to the foreboding Klamdara wall. "Anybody who wants to die quickly need only throw himself against that wall. The touch-activated laser cannon will do the rest. However, we're going to need every Tenebrea willing and able to fight if we are to have any chance of success. Kip, I don't want to fight beside anyone whose immediate goal is an expedient death. If that's what you want, just toss yourself against the wall and let the laser cannon put you down."

"It is a hard thing you are asking us to do—watch death creep up on us." He wiped another trickle of blood that ran down from his nostril over his lip.

K'Rin put his hand on Kip's shoulder. "Always take the harder road to confound the enemy. At present, it is harder to live than to die—harder to wait than to rush out in a blaze to a quick end. But mark my words, as we seem weaker, the guards relax. They get sloppy, easier to disarm and defeat. Let them think we are resigned to our fate. But don't be. Take consolation in knowing that if we die waiting, then we die doing our best."

K'Rin withdrew his hand from Kip's chest. "Somehow, we'll survive this torment, and when we do, the Tenebrea will be a band of brothers like no other."

Brigon looked at his chronometer. He looked over his shoulder to see the last men in the column sweep their trail in the snow. He surveyed the crash site. The wind had pushed the snow into drifts. The buried *Benwoi* looked like any number of snow-covered boulders. The fallen trees looked more like the victims of avalanche than laser cannon. One of the thicker trees provided support for a tunnel bored through the snow beneath the belly of the ship.

The only sounds were the complaints of hungry carrion crows and metal hammers. Brigon smelled moisture in the air. The temperature seemed to rise slightly, despite the lengthening shadows. Mottled skies indicated that another storm was building in the west.

The *Benwoi* remained buried under the fresh snow except for a small bald spot where the wind peeled away the white shroud to reveal the burnished hull. Brigon barked: "Ten minutes! Everybody inside! Cover your tracks."

Two lookouts hopped from ledge to ledge, holding their carbines high. Other laborers carefully backed toward the tunnel, using pine branches to brush their tracks. Brigon preceded them into the burrow beneath the *Benwoi.* He found Andrea and H'Roo Parh commiserating about the mangled port landing gear. "So?" Brigon asked, "How soon can we make a vertical jump to take off?"

Andrea pointed at the clone holding the light. "Ask him." One of Brigon's men, crammed in between logs like a contortionist, shone an oil lantern at the jagged crack in the metal where a thirty-inch thick log jammed the hinge. Sap oozed from gashes in the bark and filled the air with an antiseptic smell. He shimmied back. Sap stuck to his hair. Answering Brigon's earlier question, he said, "Six days."

"Six days!" Brigon cuffed the man on the shoulder

and called him by name. "Stubbs, I don't see six days' work here. What are you talking about?"

Stubbs set his jaw and silently backed away. Brigon pursued him. "Explain yourself."

Stubbs pointed with his lantern to the tight spaces under the *Benwoi*. "We can untangle the forward and starboard landing gear by cutting away the timber. But as you can see, Brigon"—Stubbs's words were measured—"the logs are thick and we can barely slip a blade between the hull and the wood. Plus we need to leave some of the wood in place as props—unless you want fifty tons to fall on you? I figure ten men, two days to clear the timber."

"That's two days. Go on."

"The lower half of the port landing gear is twisted—twisted enough that it won't retract into the hull." Stubbs used a straightedge to demonstrate where the leg was bent outside the landing gear well by four impossible inches.

"And?" Brigon looked under the fallen timber to view the damaged landing gear.

"I doubt we can put enough heat on the alloy to put the leg straight. Even if we could, I wouldn't want to soften the metal with the weight of the ship overhead. I can't think of a way to relieve the pressure without erecting a gin pole outside for everyone to see."

Brigon quietly asked, "Then how do you fix it?"

"I can think of only one option. First we prop her up with a trestle. Then we amputate the landing leg at the first joint—drill out the universal pin and uncouple the lower half. The problem is the drill. The *Benwoi*'s machine shop has a laser drill, but do you want to turn on the engines to power it?"

"We can't afford telltale emissions." Brigon saw the dilemma.

Stubbs agreed. "Then we'll have to use hand drills, and that will take two days working shifts—if everything goes right. She can land on a stump. She'll always have a gimp. Takeoff will be a bit trickier, but she'll fly without any trouble."

Brigon counted on his fingers. "Okay, that's four days. Why are telling me you need six days?"

"The extra two days are for me." Stubbs held his ground. "In case my estimate is wrong." Stubbs looked at Andrea plaintively.

Brigon grinned and put his arm around Stubbs. "I love engineers—I really do." Patting him on the back Brigon said, "Four days."

Andrea took Brigon aside and asked him privately, "We can't afford a mistake. Do you really want to rush your man?"

Brigon looked into her brown eyes. The dim lantern reflected small flames in her black pupils. He said, "We might have only four days."

"Why?"

"Ordinate operations have all but ceased in the precincts. I believe they are mobilizing to do a reconnaissance in force beginning at the southern range. I want to be gone before they stumble onto us. Don't worry about Stubbs: he has a strong sense of physics. He won't take any shortcuts—even for me. Meanwhile, we go back to the mountain to monitor the Ordinate. If they do bring a force into the valley, I want to prepare a suitable greeting."

Looking at his chronometer, he said, "Grab your gear. We leave in twenty minutes. I suggest we keep H'Roo here. He seems to know the ship better than you do. No offense."

Andrea answered through tight lips, "None taken."

chapter 18

While H'Roo and Stubbs worked feverishly at the *Benwoi*, Andrea wandered through the caves watching Brigon's cadre prepare for the Klamdara raid. The vast majority of the mountain denizens ignored the frantic preparations. The raid seemed like a sideshow compared to the burgeoning clone population's struggle to simply survive the winter.

That night, Andrea couldn't sleep. She had no physical aches or pains to keep her awake. Usually she could spot the source of her sleeplessness by cataloguing her anxieties. But tonight she didn't feel the specter of her past tugging at her sleeve. Despite her plans, the future remained amorphous. Andrea was fatalistic about the rescue mission to Klamdara. She was past caring about physical harm or death.

The present? Something about the present disturbed her. She remembered the sensation but struggled to attach a name to the feeling. Fear? No. Then the answer tumbled clumsily into her mind: Loneliness.

Andrea willfully rejected the thought. She rolled up her mat, and dressed. Fal'Dar and his Jod comrades lay scattered asleep, breathing heavily. Dr. Carai slept sitting with his back to a wall, his chin resting against his chest. A data tablet lay in his lap, likewise dormant.

Andrea meandered through the empty caves to the simple watch center. The few dim screens jerryrigged to provide warning of air and ground activity snoozed in front of the equally passive technicians. The technicians wore their earphones. They appeared to doze with their eyes open, but they were awake. They listened mostly to atmospheric static, but also to the signals emanating from the Cor Ordinate's assets.

The technicians periodically paused to key in notes. Andrea asked a middle-aged woman, "Do you have any more indicators that the Ordinate plan to send troops into the southern valley?" The woman looked at her notes. "Same stuff. They've assembled eight hovercrafts and two gunships. They're going to send a reinforced battalion somewhere."

"When?"

"Not yet. When they calibrate their navigational equipment, we can expect their operation to begin within two days."

"Thank you." Andrea paced the room, then asked, "Where's Brigon?" The woman pulled one of the ear pieces aside. "He's outside." The woman's tired profile reflected the pale green light from the screen. She gave Andrea directions, pointing her to a natural airshaft. She concluded with an offer, "Take my parka."

Andrea accepted. She walked up a precarious set of stairs beaten out of the rock. The shaft was lighted with a string of motion-detecting lights. So as she picked her way forward, she only saw ten feet ahead or behind, everything else black. She felt the rush of warmer air venting skyward.

Andrea stepped into the still night air: dry and crisp. Her breath became a plume of vapor. Isolated ice crystals drifted down from snow-laden pine boughs. The trees appeared to lean into the rock as if they suffered vertigo. The snow crunched beneath her boots.

Andrea found Brigon sitting on a rock, staring out above white mountains into the night sky. "Mind if I sit with you?"

"Please do." Brigon brushed the fresh snow from a flat rock with his heavy mitten.

Andrea sat down and said, "I couldn't sleep."

The air was still. The canopy of stars seemed to shiver from the cold. A quarter moon cast a white pall over the snow-covered mountains. Below, the luster of moonlight reflected from ground fog that filled the valleys like milk.

Brigon broke the silence with a note of self-commiseration. "I come here to get away from all the racket in the caves. I haven't had much peace and quiet these past months. I never imagined that I would find myself in charge of a rabble of precinct clones."

Andrea watched her steamy breath dissolve into the night air. "I am still surprised you accepted the burden. Have you risen above your bias against the old-order clones?"

He looked over the valley. "I guess so."

"What made you change your mind about them?"

Without comment, Brigon pointed at a meteor racing across the sky. He said, "I used to look at the mountains and the sky and I often thought that I was insignificant compared to the wonders out there."

Andrea nudged him. "I don't consider your admission particularly modest."

Brigon returned her glance and answered with a

grin, "Neither do I." He took a deep breath. "I knew for certain that the clones—so many of them simple, linear—were inferior to me, therefore, hardly worth a mention in the greater scheme of nature. One evening, sitting just about where we're sitting right now, I watched one of the new joiners gazing out into space. I knew her name, Simka. I knew because she was talking to herself, stupid prattle: 'Simka, look at the stars.' I thought she might be a little addle-minded. Slow-witted clones don't survive long in the wilderness."

"You felt sorry for her?"

"Not really. I felt rather superior. I spied on her—curious to see what she might do. The point is: this Simka was what I'd call a below-average clone. Anyway—" Brigon snugged himself in his parka and continued. "The sun had set. A thin layer of clouds blazed red and purple. A few of the brightest stars pricked the twilight. I wondered if Simka could appreciate the splendor of nature the way I did. I doubted she could grasp the sheer magnitude of the land and sky, the universe outstretched before us. I knew she couldn't."

Andrea jibed, "You're being awfully poetic."

Brigon sternly replied, "Don't mock me. Do you want an answer to your question?"

"I'm sorry. Yes."

"Then the clone pointed to the sky, to one of the brighter planets, and she began talking to herself. She said, 'Simka, there's Sofo!' At first, I thought, So what? A clone can look up at the sky and comprehend the planet Sofo. Then I thought, Yes, but Sofo cannot look down and say there's Simka."

Brigon exhaled a frosty breath and concluded, "A simple clone like Simka trumps nature by her basic comprehension." Brigon faced Andrea. His eyes caught a glint from the moon. "So now I have a better opinion of the old-order clones and myself."

Andrea chafed him. "Now you will be impossible."

Brigon then pressed the same question onto Andrea. "You also seem to have gotten over your bias toward the clones. I've seen the difference. What made you change?"

Andrea blew her warm breath through her cold hands, shoved them into the pockets of her parka, then answered, "My explanation is a lot shorter than yours. Less philosophical, anyway."

Annoyed by the oblique criticism, Brigon said, "Tell me anyway. I'm interested."

"Did you know I was married?"

"Yes. I asked around." Brigon looked up at the stars. "Tara?"

Brigon quickly added, "She was very circumspect. All I know is that you were married and your family were killed by the Ordinate, which explains a lot." He grimaced. "That was awkward—I apologize."

"Not necessary." She looked away from Brigon, turning her face toward the moon. "I loved Steve and Glendon more than my own life."

Brigon muttered, "I can't say that I ever loved anything that much."

Andrea turned her head to look at Brigon. His breath left a thick frost on his mustache. His cheeks were pinched red by the cold and his eyes glistened.

She said, "A month ago I learned that my husband, Steve, was a clone." Andrea turned to measure the comprehension in Brigon's eyes. She explained, "Steve never told me. But then, he never knew the truth about himself."

Briefly Andrea told how an institute scientist smuggled her laboratory specimen, a child—Steve—off Cor rather than cancel him. She explained, "Steve was source material for a new model of clone—" She swallowed hard. Her mouth suddenly felt dry as dust as she finished, "Made from the same genetic material that later made Eric."

Brigon sat in stunned silence for a minute until Andrea mercifully finished, "I can't despise these clones when I loved Steve as much as I did."

Brigon shook his head tentatively. "You were married to a clone like Eric?"

"Steve was not like Eric." Andrea bristled.

Brigon pulled at his beard. "Well, I'm sure you loved him."

They sat quietly together looking out at the frozen landscape. The only sound was the soft bumps of Andrea's boots as she rhythmically kicked her heels against the large stone they sat on. Brigon asked, "Are you cold? Do you want to go in?"

"Not yet."

"Actually, I did love one clone," Brigon volunteered.

"Lucky girl—" Andrea smirked.

Brigon elbowed Andrea and said, "My mother."

"Oh." Andrea tried to remember her mother, thin and pale, propped up in bed by giant pillows. Andrea remembered standing at the bed, her chin barely clearing the mattress and the cold steel rail. Her mother would pat her head with her bony fingers, whispering, "I'll get better."

Brigon interrupted Andrea's thoughts. "Did you know that my mother was a clone?"

Andrea nodded. "I think everybody knows that about you."

"That's all they need to know. I'd tell you the whole story."

"Why?"

"Because"—Brigon swiped away the frost on his mustache—"I was hoping that at some point you'd need to know."

Andrea's stomach tightened, almost a recollection of morning sickness, as she realized that she actually wanted to know his story—all of it, and why? Andrea refused to answer her own question. Instead, she sat still and listened.

"My mother was a domestic clone, named Plova. Did you see the picture of her in my quarters?"

"I saw it." Andrea looked at Brigon. "You must take after your father—except the eyes."

"I loved to look into her eyes." Brigon's face changed quickly from sad to curious as if he didn't know how his own story would end. "She was assigned to work for one of the important families in Sarhn. The son, a student with aspirations to join the Ordinate's defense force, became overly fond of his house servant. He routinely took her into his bed. A great shock to the young man: this sterile clone became pregnant. The young man did one decent thing—he forewarned my mother that if she were discovered with child, the Clone Welfare Institute would cancel her outright. My mother fled into the wilderness, where she had me.

"She hid us in these caves. The slight sulfur odor kept the dangerous creatures away when we slept. We learned how to avoid them as we foraged for food. She periodically went into the precincts and returned with a renegade clone. At first, I thought she was just soft-hearted, taking in strays of her own kind, but eventually I learned her meaning.

"The first duty of every renegade brought to the wilderness was to teach me everything he or she knew. Odd, but the entire technological knowledge of the Ordinate has been compartmented and stored piecemeal among the hundreds of varieties of clones. Think of it! One clone engineered to repair communications equipment has drilled into her consciousness the theorems of electricity. She in turn teaches me microelectronics. Another is a metallurgist who worked twenty years making materials for their ships, another a chemical engineer of sorts consigned to a small solvents manufacturing process. He teaches me his neural imprint augmented by his twenty years of practice. I always was a quick learner. I remember everything I hear.

"When I was sixteen years old, I could pass as a newly hatched clone. My mother took me to the precincts to see for myself what she'd told me about clone life. We moved about the precincts unmolested. One day, an older female clone of my mother's time recognized her mark."

Andrea asked, "What did her mark look like?"

"She had an intricate tattoo, a stylized flame on the nape of her neck. The other clone informed the authorities." Brigon interrupted his narrative to comment, "I had no reason to despise the precinct clones until that day."

"What happened?" Andrea knew too well the ruthlessness of Ordinate Hunters in pursuit of a runaway clone.

Brigon recited the events without emotion, or Andrea thought, with suppressed emotion. He said, "I remember the day as if it were yesterday. We were at the power plant. I was engrossed, watching a pair of clones repair the ceramic magneto-bearings on a generator. Suddenly, a pair of Hunters marched into the room led by the female clone. The informant basked in her good deed and newfound importance as she triumphantly pointed out my mother. I heard a few loud accusatory words, the word *renegade*. Then I saw my mother's face crumple as she gave me the hand signal to flee. It all happened fast.

"With her other hand she drew her weapon from a slender leather sheath. She carried a small spike—not lethal by itself, but she laced the point with curare. She plunged it into the closest Hunter. The clone informant screamed, alarmed at the violence—" Brigon's voice finally allowed anger. "The stupid cow." Brigon nervously wiped his mustache again. "The curare gripped the Hunter as he plucked the small spike from his side. His hand froze about the silver handle. His grimace became a grin as he stiffened and fell, eyes open, imploring help. The second Hunter reacted swiftly, putting his pistol to my mother's forehead. He said something to her that I did not hear. She looked obliquely in my direction, urgently signaled me to flee as the bastard pulled the trigger. The informant shrieked again and ran away."

"And you fled . . ."

"Oh, no." Brigon's eyes narrowed. "I grabbed a hammer that one of the clone workmen dropped to the floor. I ran up quietly behind the Hunter, now preoccupied, calling for medical aid and backup—his partner had a pulse. The curare stops the breathing but not the heart. I drove the hammer into the Hunter's skull to the handle."

Brigon held up an old heavy pistol, the dark finish rubbed and corroded away. "I took the Hunter's pistol. It is my favorite weapon for killing the Ordinate."

Andrea pulled her hand from her pocket and reached over to touch Brigon, but she hesitated. "You couldn't bury your mother."

"Never gave the matter any thought. I had no concept of disposing of the dead." He looked at her wryly. "I suppose I still don't."

"What did you do then?"

"I spent the next fifteen years surviving. I used clones—the capable ones—who sought sanctuary in the wilderness. I was just as happy to use them to hurt the precinct clones as well as the Ordinate. I had this fantasy where I blow up the entire planet and kill everything: the clones, the Ordinate, and me."

"What happened to your fantasy?"

"I got tired of hating everything. I even got tired of hating my own father."

"You know who he is?"

"Yes I do. This piece of data you must never tell anyone. My father is Admiral Adan Brulk. He is the head of all security matters for Cor."

Andrea pulled off her hood, believing that she had heard incorrectly. "What did you say?"

Brigon just nodded solemnly. "Before he became a full admiral, I use to hear his voice every now and then when we collected radio signals. For years, I used to think that he kept the security patrols out of the wilderness for my sake—so my mother also thought. She believed that Brulk was protecting us from afar, and I believed her. The reason I didn't want to go with you into Sarhn last year to attack the institute is that I didn't want to run into him. I thought it best that we stay in our separate worlds."

"You didn't know if you could kill him." Andrea recognized in Brigon a bitterness that she thought she alone knew.

He muttered, "I think I could kill him now."

"Then, why did you come back and help us at Sarhn?"

Brigon raised his hands in surrender. "Not my idea. My men would have gone in with or without me. I followed. Once inside, I led."

"I'm glad you came."

"So am I." Then Brigon pointed to the night sky. "The fleet assembling off the Lynx colony is Brulk's. He is responsible for the NewGen technology. He is responsible for the plan to starve the old-order clones to death. In addition, he is responsible for the plan to annihilate the Jod Fleet."

Andrea thought Brigon's eyes looked suddenly old and bewildered. She cautioned, "Brigon, eventually, he must kill you, too."

"I'm sure he rues the day he let my mother get away." Brigon laughed bitterly. "I suppose he'd call that a classic mistake of youthful inexperience. Now please don't take this the wrong way, Andrea, but by my calculations, your husband Steve was the lucky one. He got off this damnable planet. He got to Earth. He fell in love with you, and I'm sure those years were worth my whole lifetime. Mercifully, he never knew his past."

Andrea turned away and muttered, "Don't feel sorry for yourself."

Looking at Andrea, he said, "I'm sure Earth must be a wonderful place with wonderful people."

Andrea winced at this bit of flattery. She replied, "You don't know anything about Earth. The Ordinate originally came from Earth."

Brigon groped for some rationale. "Well, I'm sure the change of climate . . . the Chelle, the—hell, I don't know, Andrea. You came from Earth. I don't know what happened to the Ordinate after they got here."

Andrea's cheeks flushed. "Brigon, the planet does not make the people; the people make the planet."

"Okay. Okay," Brigon admitted. He looked out into the night sky. "I was just trying to say something nice about your home—just trying to be sociable." His warm breath seemed to hold his words in the cold dry air. "I'd be content just about anywhere if I could be with you: here, on Earth—"

Andrea reared back and laughed at him. "You, me, and Chana. I don't think she'll go along with that arrangement."

Brigon was flustered. "Chana? She's just one of my lieutenants. You think we. . . . No, no, no. I don't sleep with my lieutenants. She just likes the access."

"I bet—"

"I know she acts a bit possessive, but believe me, Andrea, Chana's not in the picture."

"Then you don't know much about women."

Brigon started to answer, but he was stumped. "I suppose I don't." He took off his mittens and reached over to touch Andrea's cheek. "You're cold as ice."

She pulled back. "I feel warm enough."

"I'm not going to hurt you," Brigon protested. "Now what's wrong?"

Andrea shook her head. "I don't know. I'm not . . ."

"Not what?" Brigon prodded.

Andrea looked away. A wisp of cloud veiled the moon, and the white light on Andrea's face dimmed. She repeated, "I don't know."

"Tell me. Am I wasting my time with you?" Brigon grabbed Andrea's arm to turn her face toward him. His hands were large for a man his size, and his grip was firm. "I don't have time to waste."

Andrea tugged her arm free and looked away at the cold stars.

Brigon's voice hardened. "I figure you're good for at least one straight answer. Are you just using me to solve your problem on Klamdara?" His voice had the edge of bitter resignation.

Andrea pursed her lips. She looked in Brigon's eyes and saw disappointment mingled with hope. She tried to concoct an answer to dodge the question, but she knew Brigon was no fool. He demanded a plain answer—yes or no. To parse words would harden him. She would not barter affection for help; she despised women who did so. Yet she desperately needed Brigon's help to complete her mission; and heretofore, scruples had not been an impediment. Andrea took a deep breath and exhaled; with the last bit of her breath she said, "Yes, Brigon. If you put the matter in those terms, yes, I am using you."

Brigon recoiled and muttered, "You've got a cold heart." His eyes caught the glint of the quarter moon.

"Brigon." Andrea pulled back on his parka. "I need you. I can't do what I have to do without your help. Is needing someone wrong?"

Brigon spoke through tight lips. "What if I need you?" Brigon didn't give Andrea a chance to answer. He stood up and blustered, "I can't believe I'm talking like this!" He laughed at himself. "I'm going to get myself killed on some rock at the other end of the galaxy to prove myself to you! To you! Why? Because you need my services? That's a laugh! Six months ago, I didn't give a damn what anybody thought. Now look at me. I'm trying to convince you that . . . oh, never mind. I'm no more rational than a newly hatched, pre-programmed clone. I ought to——"

Andrea slid from the rock to her feet. She grabbed Brigon's collar. "I care what you think about me."

Her words quashed Brigon's derision. He, in turn, grabbed her arms above the elbow and held her at arm's length. "I don't understand. You are willing to use me, but you care what I think? Now that must be uncomfortable. So tell me, after Klamdara, if we live through the wars, when you're not outnumbered and outgunned, do you think you'll still need me?"

Andrea could hardly breathe. *Is it the cold? Brigon's grip? Is needing someone a weakness?*

"Don't be coy." Brigon mocked her. "Don't worry about your answer. I'll still go with you to Klamdara. I don't have any other plans. So answer me. Are you going to need me when I'm no longer useful?"

She looked into Brigon's dark, angry eyes. Her answer was barely audible. "God forgive me, I believe I will."

chapter 19

Brigon spoke quietly with his steward. Hart was himself skin and bones; therefore, Brigon trusted him to be honest distributing the food. Food provisions were dangerously low. The influx of clones and the bitter winter had chased away most of the game, so meat was nonexistent. The granary shrank daily. In the best of seasons, Brigon could not steal enough. Clearly the Ordinate planned to use starvation as a weapon to eradicate the old-order clones. He knew the precinct granaries lay empty as well. His most closely guarded secret was that he allocated food disproportionally. His fighters received fifteen hundred calories per day, the refugees half that. "Hart, how long will the grain hold?" Brigon asked under his breath.

The steward replied in even lower tones, "At the present rate—assuming we take in no more runaways—sixty days. We can't cut back the rations much further. They are getting desperate. I heard one of the new arrivals observe that we have tons of frozen meat just outside the base."

"The mounds?" Brigon blanched.

"Yes, sir."

Brigon closed his eyes. "Somehow, I'll return with food. In the meantime, organize scavengers. Gather pine nuts, strip bark from the trees, trap and eat anything that moves."

"Brigon!" A runner entered the crowded subterranean mess hall. The clones parted, guarding their wooden bowls and meager daily ration. The din in the room subsided.

"Over here!" Brigon raised his hand.

The runner shoved his way through the crowd till he was next to Brigon. Out of breath, he spoke in hushed tones. "The Ordinate are making final preparations to sweep the valley in force."

Brigon demanded proof.

The runner recited the evidence. "All the pieces fit: the stand down of precinct operations, increased reconnaissance, maintenance, wireless traffic; plus they've tested a microwave comm link to coordinates at the southern end of the valley."

Brigon grabbed the runner's arm and started walking to the exit. "How many?"

"We estimate six transports and two gun ships— that's six hundred ground troops."

"When?" They turned up the tunnel toward the small operations center.

"Thirty-six hours."

They stopped at an intersection. Brigon commanded, "Assemble my staff and the *Benwoi* crew in the ops center immediately. Forewarn them that we leave with all combatants in ninety minutes."

Within ten minutes the ops center swelled with bodies, yet the room was quiet except for the rustle of clothes and the dull clunk of gear. Each wilderness clone carried a carbine and heavy blade for close fighting. Brigon stood on a block of stone. Looking down on his lieutenants, he quickly described the threat. No one seemed perturbed by the lopsided odds. Brigon said, "If the Ordinate discover that we manufactured a fake crash site for the *Benwoi*, we'll never get off Cor. We've got to ambush them as they disembark."

Then Brigon gave a series of crisp orders. "Send two runners to the southern caves and tell them to outfit as many fighters as they can muster. Chana, we'll take sixty men with carbines, grenades, and blades. Bring the high-velocity ammunition. Also, bring the twenty-five-millimeter gun."

"At last!" The heavy gunner raised his fist in the air.

Brigon translated the exuberance for the assembly. "The Ordinate doesn't know we have the big gun—about time they find out." He looked over the heads of his people, then barked, "Airco!"

"Here!" Airco stood on tiptoes and answered from the back of the room.

"Bring all eight snipers."

"With pleasure. I made three antipersonnel mines—fifty pounds of plastique and flachettes. Can I bring them?" Airco grinned.

"Why not?" Brigon approved. "Let's kick them out of our valley so fast that they forget why they came." Then Brigon said, "The crew of the *Benwoi* will stay here at base."

Andrea stepped forward and countermanded him flatly. "Any Tenebrea not working on the *Benwoi* will fight beside the wilderness clones."

Brigon turned and found Andrea standing with four Jod. They wore their black uniforms beneath heavy overcoats. Andrea's hair was pulled back tightly. Each Tenebrea carried a handlance and knife on his belt; each stood erect. Brigon could see that they were spoiling for a fight.

Brigon frowned. "I don't want the Ordinate to know our numbers. I don't want to risk them knowing that Jod are involved."

Andrea's face was taut, her high cheekbones more pronounced, her eyes pitiless. "Frankly, I want to see the looks on their faces when they see the Tenebrea. You must let us fight by your side. If not, you insult us. We will not have your people think that we shirk our duty."

The wilderness clones murmured approval.

Then Eric spoke. "Tara and I can raise another twenty men from the civilians in the caves—men and women that we trained years ago. I doubt they've forgotten how to kill Ordinate Security Troops. We need weapons."

Brigon looked at Tara, who affirmed her intentions. "We want to help. It's our fight, perhaps more than yours."

Brigon stepped down from the stone and stood face-to-face with Eric. "I'm not so sure you really want to become one of my lieutenants. I'm afraid you'll be a liability to us. Can you take orders without question?" He spoke loud enough so that the others might hear him disparage Eric.

Eric answered, "Obedience is part of my programming."

"Obedience to whom?"

Eric didn't answer, but merely repeated his offer. "I can increase your strength by twenty-five rifles."

Brigon saw that his fighters welcomed the additional firepower. The wilderness clones had never faced such a large force before. But he doubted that he could maintain control of his people, let alone the clones from the southern caves, Andrea's small unit, and now Eric's militia. Brigon thought, *I can't manage three or four separate battles! On the other hand, I can't dismiss capable riflemen—not in a fight this big.*

Brigon put on his war face. "Very well. We shall surprise them on all counts: our big gun and our numbers. We march within the hour. We travel tonight and the next day. If we're lucky, we'll get a half day's rest before the fight."

Then, Brigon stepped back onto his stone. "Chana, see that Eric and his men have weapons, and issue them the full meal ration. Send a runner to the *Benwoi.* Inform them of our situation." Brigon added sarcastically, "Extend my profound apologies that I cannot postpone this fight so that they might participate in our popular war."

Brigon frowned at Andrea and Eric. "Tell Stubbs and H'Roo Parh that we need the *Benwoi* ready to launch. We must get off Cor as soon as possible."

Brigon's augmented war party numbered ninety-nine. Their long column slipped into the cold night and snaked through the snow-filled woods. The wind was mercifully still. Low clouds blackened the night skies, wiping away the moon and stars. The minimal light lost itself within the trees, and the column had to travel more by instinct than by sight. Tiny ice crystals fell throughout the night, numbing faces, feet, and hands.

Andrea marched near the rear of the column with her Tenebrea. Behind her, Airco and his men walked with their long air rifles, and behind them a foursome pulled a sled with the 25mm automatic rifle and crate of belted ammunition for the big gun, and Airco's mines.

Silence was the rule. Each half hour, muffled voices passed back the order: "Send up the count!" Then the voices from the rear counted softly: one, two three . . . until the count reached Brigon: ninety-nine. No break in contact.

During one particularly miserable hour, the command rippled down the column, "Cloak!" Brigon anticipated a pass by one of the Ordinate's radar satellites. He doubted that the other Cor passive sensors could penetrate the thick clouds. However, he did not want to risk discovery by overhead radar, with so many moving targets in a column.

Those who lacked cloaks huddled with those who did. Andrea huddled with a pair of Airco's men. They squatted on their haunches in the snow, trying not to entangle their snowshoes. The clones suggested they arrange themselves back-to-back, and Andrea, as a guest in their makeshift shelter, complied. They used their backpacks for seats and nestled together. They forced themselves to drink slush liquids and eat sweet bars of dried fruit. They became stiff from inactivity in the freezing cold.

Except for similar forced respites under cloaks, Brigon's party trudged doggedly through the night and next day over familiar but unmarked trails. The fifty-mile march to the southern caves ended shortly after nightfall on the second day. The ninety-nine shared their fatigue and their aches with silent commiseration, as if honor demanded silence, as if their brotherhood depended on it. When they arrived at the southern caves, they had just enough time for a hot meal, a cat-

nap, a change of socks, and a weapons check. Brigon
had to forgo creature comforts to spend the time giving
last-minute instructions to his lieutenants.

The sun lit the snow-covered west mountains across
the valley. With perfect weather, the Ordinate would
arrive soon. Brigon surveyed the valley with his binoculars. He chewed a piece of black root, a stimulant. He
paused to spit some of the black treacle, staining the
snow at his feet.

Airco's snipers sat in the high ground at the
entrance of the valley where they could put the landing
craft in a deadly crossfire. Brigon placed the 25mm
gun in a crevice near Airco's position. He guessed that
the gunships would try to ferret out the snipers. He
wanted his big gun to shoot at the gunships from
above. The bellies of the gunships were heavily
armored.

Brigon knew Ordinate doctrine. They either retreat
into their ships at the first sign of conflict, or they
assault to suppress the ambush. He hoped for the first
and bet on the latter. He set the bulk of his forces along
the east mountain slope where the mountain sagged
into the form of a slight crescent. He put the south
mountain clones in the middle of this crescent. He
expected them to buckle under the strain of the
Ordinate assault. More importantly, he expected the
Ordinate to pursue. Eric's small group anchored the
left flank. Brigon's main force sat ready on the right to
sweep the Ordinate flank.

He shifted the stick of black root to the other cheek
and explained his plan to Andrea. "First, the snipers
sow confusion into the landing. Nothing causes panic
like an unseen, silent killer. Airco promises that in the

first three minutes his men can nail fifty Ordinate. Next, south mountain troops open fire, finally giving the Ordinate an object to attack.

Andrea looked down the long slope. "If the Ordinate troops run all the way up here, they'll be half-dead from exhaustion."

"NewGens don't get tired." He looked toward the center of his line. "When the NewGens reach them, the south mountain clones will falter."

"You sure of that?"

"I'm counting on it." Brigon spit another black spot on the snow. "They've never been in a fight before. When the center buckles, Eric's men on the left fire long-range. At that point the Ordinate force is decisively engaged. They can't retreat without accepting heavy losses. Moreover, the enemy will have their backs to me. We will have them in a crossfire. If we can kill half their force today, the Ordinate won't come back to the valley for months."

Andrea asked, "Where do you want the Tenebrea?"

He lowered his binoculars and said, "I want all five of you Tenebrea in reserve—behind me."

"Unacceptable."

Brigon leaned over and spit. "I don't have time to argue with you now. If you get yourself killed, I don't have much incentive to go to Klamdara, do I?" He looked back at Andrea. His face was calm as if slightly bothered by her interference in his otherwise routine approach to killing the Ordinate. "That's just a fact. Do with it what you wish."

Andrea pulled out her handlance. As she checked the settings, she said, "We won't stay in reserve. Where do you want us?"

Brigon grumbled, "If you won't stay in reserve, I'm

sure you can find lovely fighting all along the front."
He waved his arm in a broad arc.

Andrea turned her back and led the five Tenebrea
away.

Brigon goaded her. "Not even going to wish me
luck?" Then he raised his binoculars to look at the horizon and saw six craft flying in convoy. As yet he did
not hear the whine of the turbines.

Lt. Botchi rode on the lead hovercraft. Landing in
the flats, straddling a frozen stream in the middle of the
valley, the craft kicked up a cloud of snow, creating a
thick white curtain. Meanwhile, the two gunships flew
back and forth menacingly over the landing site.

Botchi left the craft with the first platoon. He carried
only his mapboard and a comm-disk. The men shuffled
down the ramp, slipped into their snowshoes, and
fanned out. The particles of snow blown skyward by
the propwash fell like a million diamonds, sparkling in
the morning sunlight, revealing a blue mantle of sky
and the raw beauty of the mountains.

Thud! Botchi turned left toward the sound. He saw
a soldier stop and look down.

"Keep moving!" Botchi ordered. Botchi was annoyed
that the soldier seemed indifferent to his orders.
"Soldier!"

The young man, seemingly preoccupied, touched a
black hole in his white suit, raised his hand to his face,
and manipulated his fingers smearing red liquid
between his thumb and forefinger. Then he fell to his
knees in the snow.

Two dull thuds and two more men crumpled and
groaned as they died. Botchi heard a whistle and a
sharp ping as a bullet missed him and struck the hover-

craft behind. He looked around. Already he had five hundred men in the valley. Most of them wandered off to do their jobs, unaware of the sniper fire.

Botchi was confused. He did not hear rifle reports. The whine of the hovercraft turbines was not loud enough to mask rifle reports. The vengeful silence coming from the mountain was beguiling. Botchi frantically looked around. Soldiers seemed to trip and fall, many crumpling without comment, others hurling epithets. Botchi heard a soldier cry, "I'm hit!" Another soldier replied, "I didn't hear anything."

Botchi dove into the deep snow, looked up, and yelled, "Where's that rifle fire coming from?"

Nobody answered. His platoon, now alert to the danger, crouched down with their weapons raised— some nervously firing blind. They surveyed the mountains in the general direction from which the bullets came, but they saw nothing: no smoke, no flash. They heard nothing but the deadly whistle of bullets and the fatal impact of metal against flesh and bone. Botchi wondered, *Should I withdraw? No. I can't let a handful of clones run a reinforced battalion from the field.*

Botchi pressed his communications disk to broadcast. "Sniper! Take cover!" Botchi crawled through the snow toward the underbelly of the hovercraft. "Gunships, suppress that fire! In the mountains due east. I'll send estimated position." Botchi raised his mapboard and drew a circle over the suspect area. The lead pilot responded over the comm-disk, "We copy."

Both gunships peeled around in a tight banking turn and rushed toward the face of the mountain. Botchi heard an agitated gunner announce, "I see 'em in the rocks! Five or ten of 'em." Botchi tapped another channel on his comm-disk. "Put half the NewGens aboard troop carrier four. Deploy them on the ridge behind the snipers. Flush them out." Again he sent coordinates by means of his mapboard. "We'll catch them front and rear."

Airco leaned against a large pumice boulder coughed up by an ancient volcano. He breathed deeply to quell his own pulse, put his cheek against the stock, and shifted slightly to place a tiny black silhouette above the steel post in his front sight. He squeezed the trigger, heard the spitting sound, and felt the pusillanimous kick. He looked up to see the silhouette stagger and clump into the snow. "Three for me!" He pulled his weapon back and began pumping the lever to recharge the gun.

"Look!" the sniper to the left bellowed.

Airco saw the gunships. One patrolled a section of the mountain farther north. The second turned and began a run toward them. "They see us!"

By the time the words left his lips, incoming bullets splashed the rocks around them. Airco ducked behind the boulder and felt it jar from the impact of the bullets. He looked to his left and saw a fellow sniper lying facedown in the snow in a spreading crimson stain. The gunship passed overhead, banking hard to the left, preparing for another run. Airco scurried over and found a second sniper with his cold white hand over a large-caliber wound through his chest. He called, "Darin!"

The wounded clone removed his hand. His erratic breathing made a sickening slurp as his lung drew air through the bleeding wound. He looked up at Airco and shook his head apologetically. He coughed a pink spray, instinctively raising his hand to cover his mouth.

"I'm feeling—" Darin struggled for a tortured breath, then exhaled. "So tired." His blood-soaked hand fell to his wet lap. The whine of the turbines announced another pass by the gunship.

Airco burrowed behind the rocks. Behind him, rocket fire blasted the slopes. A storm of pulverized rock rained down on him. The gunship went into a hover and gently slipped overhead to inspect the carnage. From the corner of his eye, Airco saw a gunner in a glass bubble looking back, prepared to sweep the area with his four-barrel Gatling gun. Airco turned his head and closed his eyes tightly, tensing every muscle in his body as he anticipated the pain of bullets tearing through him. *Just get it over with.*

Suddenly, he heard the loud burrup of automatic fire. He rolled over in time to see a second burst of the 25mm cannon rip through the gunship, tearing the starboard turbine and fuel cells to pieces. The gunship tried to retreat, putting all power to the port engine but to no avail. Airco sloughed the debris and stood to watch the gunship burst into flames and plunge into the valley floor below. The Ordinate pilot and gunner fled the wreckage as the fire began to cook the ammunition.

Brigon watched the developing battle from his perch. He saw a troop carrier reload with NewGens and depart. He ordered, "Keep an eye on that carrier. Tell me where it lands."

Meanwhile, he focused on the swarm of Ordinate troops that ran toward the slope and hid within the sparse cover of boulders lying at the base of the mountain. The remaining gunship patrolled the center with suppressing fire, but it held back, out of the 25mm gun's effective range.

The south mountain clones fired sporadically at the oncoming Ordinate troops. Brigon watched intently. "They're wasting ammunition!" he criticized. "They're not taking careful aim—too afraid of being hit."

He turned a few degrees to see Eric's men lying prone among the rocks, poised to unleash a volley from their weapons into the Ordinate's flank. Eric had traded expansive fields of fire for overhead protection. Brigon noted that Eric's positions offered little to the gunship overhead. Well done. Good trade.

Eric's hand rose and fell—a signal. Brigon saw Tara's auburn hair glint as she appeared from the shadow of a rock. She yelled something; then Brigon saw several muzzle flashes, and a dozen Ordinate fell.

The Ordinate troops turned to face the effective fire from their right flank. They hesitated, then hunkered down, bunching together. The gunship reeled around to assess the threat, still wary of antiair. After a moment of panicked indecision, the Ordinate ground troops hunkered down in a semicircle facing the south mountain clones and Eric's smaller but more effective ambush. Brigon grinned. "Now we've got them."

He saw almost a hundred exposed backs. He yelled to his men scattered among the rocks. "Now don't everybody shoot the same guy. Pick your target, left to right. Check your gun sights. Range is five hundred meters. Lay a round right between their shoulder blades. Make your first shot count." Brigon set his binoculars down and raised his carbine. "Fire at will!"

The volley decimated the Ordinate troops. The stunned Ordinate reeled around to return fire. Botchi stood alone in the middle. He tried to organize his men to attack, but the Ordinate ignored his commands. Their focus had shifted to staying alive.

Brigon whooped, "Pour it on!"

"Brigon!" One of the wilderness clones pointed far to the left outside Brigon's immediate interest. "The troop carrier landed above our positions, at the seam between the center and Eric's flank."

Brigon turned his binoculars and saw the carrier disgorge fifty troops. NewGens! The enemy split their force: half to envelop the south mountain clones, and half to beat Eric from his position. The terrain was brutal, a stair step of saw-toothed vertical drops. Brigon had walked those ridges before and knew that the NewGens needed twelve to fifteen minutes to travel the short distance. But the rugged terrain also hid them. Neither Airco nor he could touch them with direct fire.

"Damn!" Brigon's mind raced for a best course of action. "Our people won't see them till it's too late!" He cursed himself. "I should have laid landline."

His plan of pinning the Ordinate down and sniping them to death was history. Through his binoculars, he looked at Eric's people. They did not see the NewGens bearing down on their positions. Neither did the south mountain clones. Caught unaware, they'd be slaughtered. Before him was an opportunity to cripple the Ordinate Security Force by eradicating an entire battalion with little cost to his core unit. But at what cost to the others? He decided quickly. "Prepare to attack. We rush them and hope that the south mountain boys and Eric's people see us and follow suit." Brigon cinched his cloak to his belt and refixed his snowshoes. His men knew the danger of leaving the safety of their rocks for the open field, especially with a gunship prowling the area, but they obeyed.

Brigon turned to survey his men's last-minute preparations. "Where's Andrea?"

The rear echelon was vacant. Andrea was gone. Brigon pulled his binoculars up and scanned the ridgeline between his position and the south mountain clones. He saw her. She and four Jod ran along the rim. He noted grimly: She's gone to warn the others. She must have left as soon as she saw the transport land. More than anything he wanted to be with her now. Impossible. She's on her own.

"Sir, your orders?"

Brigon put his binoculars in his pouch as he stepped in front of his men. "Keep a wide spread of twenty-five meters between each man. Don't bunch yourselves for that gunship up there." He pointed at the dark ship now hovering above Eric's position trying to find a target. "Three of you, bring the flachette mines."

Another voice hollered down, "Don't forget to pull the caps and disconnect the klackers."

Brigon turned to see the blood-splattered Airco limping toward their position. "My second team is still in the rocks, but they're almost out of bullets."

Speed is security. Andrea ran with her four Tenebrea along the ridge. She kept a wary eye for the gunship that pounded the center and Eric's positions. But the heavy carnage was in the bottom of the bowl where Ordinate faced rifle fire from three sides. She also watched the ridge above, for she expected to see the NewGens appear at any moment.

They arrived at the outskirts of the center position. The gunship's handiwork was everywhere, bleeding and groaning. As she looked for the leader, she could not help but marvel at the different reactions of the wounded. Some simply sat and bled, patiently waiting for their lives to ebb as their blood soaked into the snow, almost content that the pain would soon subside forever. Others fought to stop the bleeding, some grimly comical in their futility. Others ignored their plight and continued to fire their weapons, not from any wrath, but almost from lack of having anything else to do. She had no idea how she'd act with a mortal wound; she hadn't given the matter any thought.

Ti'Maj tapped Andrea on the shoulder and pointed toward the valley. She saw Brigon's men advance along a wide front, moving with discipline, pausing to kneel and fire, rising to jog the next fifty meters. The lone gunship spun around to concentrate on Brigon's men while they were in the open. Her heart sank momentarily, but she forced Brigon's peril from her mind.

Andrea found the leader of the south mountain clones. He was shot through the shoulder in almost the same spot Andrea had received her wound. He was woozy from loss of blood, but still resolved to fight. She told him, "Twenty or more NewGens landed on the ridge above you. They're coming this way."

The man looked bewildered. He reached up and grabbed Andrea's hand. "Help us."

"We can't." She looked around for signs of NewGens. She jerked her hand free and said, "Stay here and fight the NewGens or join in the melee down the mountain." She gestured toward the thick pocket of Ordinate below. Then, she left him.

"Where are you going?" the south mountain leader protested.

She didn't stop, but called over her shoulder, "To Eric's position."

*　　　*　　　*

With the gunship brandishing weapons overhead, Brigon's men ran as fast as they could into the arms of the Ordinate ground troops. They fired their weapons as they ran, forcing the Ordinate to keep their heads down. Brigon noticed how his men turned their faces slightly aside, as if they were protecting their eyes in a sandstorm. Ten of his men fell from the bullets raining down from above and the front. The gunship paused in a hover a mere fifty feet from the ground to finish the men who fell wounded. Brigon and his men ran into the relative safety of the rocks strewn in the bowl. They crashed into the Ordinate, firing point blank and slashing. They had just thrown themselves into hand fighting with an enemy who, despite their losses, still outnumbered them four to one. Brigon knew he needed to mass his men but the gunship above made that option infeasible.

"Bring the flachette mines!" He hollered. Three men dragged the mines forward. Brigon took one of the mines and laid it facing skyward. He plugged in the blasting cap and connected the ignition wires to the klacker.

"Go! Go!" He waved the other men deeper into the fighting, and he took refuge behind a rock. Looking up at the gunship he muttered, "Come on, you sonovabitch!"

The gunship hovered above trying to find any clone not grappling with an Ordinate soldier. The quad barrels twitched but didn't fire, because any burst would kill as many Ordinate. Brigon raised his carbine and fired a round that hit the observation bubble of the gunner. Less than three hundred feet away, Brigon saw the gunner's face react: momentary surprise, then satisfaction—at last, a target in the open.

Brigon squatted behind the boulder as the gunship eased overhead, showering bursts around the rock. Bits of rock flew around, tearing Brigon's face and arms. Brigon pressed himself against the ragged rock trying to stay out of the direct line of fire, while coaxing the ship closer . . . closer . . . closer!

He pressed the klacker and dove for cover. The flachette mine exploded, sending an updraft of four-inch spikes that ripped the stubby wings off the gunship, shredded the vertical turbofan, and perforated the aft fuel tank. The gunship burst into flame, exploding as it fell. A wave of fire blew past Brigon. Smoldering debris rained down.

Eric recognized the target in his sights as one of Brigon's men. He screamed at the top of his lungs, "Cease fire!" He crawled out of his hole to survey the bedlam below.

When he saw the second gunship fall in flames, Eric called his fighters from their holes. The south mountain clones began to pour down the mountain to join the fray. "Tara! Report!"

Tara poked her head above a rock generously pocked. "Three dead, two wounded."

Then he heard a burst of automatic rifle fire from behind. He turned to yell cease fire again, when he saw uniformed soldiers bearing down from above. Instead, he yelled, "Get down!"

More rifle fire and the ricochets punctuated his command. "We've been flanked!" Eric yelled for anyone who could listen. Eric rose to see a platoon of large men, all identical in face and build, pour into his position. NewGen clones. All around he heard the struggle:

pistol and rifle reports, the grunts and groans of hand-to-hand fighting.

He had wondered how he would fare against the genetically superior model. He drew his handgun and knife and strode out for some close work. He found his first NewGen straddling a clone, driving a knife into the frantic man's chest. Eric fired point blank into the NewGen's back, too late to save his comrade. The NewGen turned to face Eric, struggling to its feet. The NewGen suffered a massive exit wound above the stomach. What kind of creature is this? Eric fired two more rounds into the NewGen's chest, finally knocking it down.

Less than fifty feet away, Tara fought ferociously. Wedged between two rocks, she spent her ammunition killing two NewGens. Then she heard the fateful *click* of the firing pin against an empty chamber. Tara left her crevice to join the desperate fighting in the rocks above. She brandished her hand weapon, a hatchet adorned with a thick three-inch spike.

Andrea arrived at the ridge. She waved the other Tenebrea forward. "We're late!" She admonished them, "Stay in pairs." Without a word, the Tenebrea shed their snowshoes and ran down the slope into the back door of the fight. Their handlances whined and stung.

Andrea surprised her first prey. She shot once. The stunned NewGen merely grunted and returned fire. Andrea dove aside to evade the shot. She fired again on a roll and hit the NewGen in the thigh with a bone-crushing bolt. The NewGen staggered, but refused to fall. A third shot hit the NewGen in the gut, a blast that surely must have ruptured the creature's small intestines. Yet the NewGen struggled to continue the fight.

A fourth blast to the face pulverized the eyes, and the blinded NewGen collapsed, groping for the weapon he had dropped.

A second NewGen attacked her. The sight of an identical foe almost unnerved her. *What? I didn't kill him! What if they can't be killed?* But she saw her opponent dead in the snow and she recovered her wits. *Control your fear!*

The five Tenebrea fought for mere yards. The chaos was magnificent. What the NewGens lacked in creativity, they had in brute tenacity. One by one, the Tenebrea's handlances failed. They pulled their utility knives and continued to fight defensively. They used the rocky terrain and suckered the NewGens into close quarters where two Jod could use their bulky strength to manhandle a NewGen: one Jod holding the genetically enhanced NewGen warrior, the second cutting the NewGen's throat.

Andrea knew that they had outclassed the NewGens in skill, but she feared fatigue. She looked at her comrades, whose white skin and white parkas now looked aflame in red.

Tara found herself face-to-face with another NewGen. Like her, he was out of bullets, but unlike her, he did not have a hand weapon. Tara raised her hatchet, holding the spike between her and her assailant. Pitiless cold eyes! The NewGen circled around her staying just out of reach of the hatchet. She invited him forward by lowering her stance.

As the NewGen moved toward her, Tara leaned forward and extended her arm as she swung the sharp hatchet, opening a neat slice through the NewGen's body armor across the ribs. The NewGen glanced at the bleeding wound with indifference, learning from his mistake. Unflinching, he studied Tara. He held his hands slightly forward to parry the next swipe of the hatchet. Tara knew she was in trouble. "Eric!"

The NewGen stepped closer, and she swung again. But the NewGen caught her hatchet by the handle, wrenching it from her hand. Tara tried to dart left, but the agile NewGen blocked her path. She expected the NewGen to smile at this triumph, but no. The expression didn't change. She cried desperately, "Eric!" Her cries seemed to annoy the NewGen. He slashed from left to right, and Tara jumped backward escaping the blade. He slashed again from top to bottom and Tara dodged sideways, but not far enough. The blade slashed her face from the hairline, missing her eye, but opening her cheek to the bone. The wound stunned her. She thought Eric must be dead, and although her instinct continued to fight for life, her heart accepted death. She staggered back and raised her arms to fend off the next blow.

The NewGen stepped forward and swung the hatchet, slicing her right arm off at the elbow. The blow spun Tara around and she fell to the ground. The NewGen changed his grip on the hatchet, preparing to drive the spike into her head. More overcome with nausea than pain, Tara held up her bleeding stump to ward off the mortal blow.

Then Eric's face appeared behind the NewGen. Tara had heard that a good death often recalled a pleasant image to compensate for the pain—as when a clone is retired or canceled. Eric. Her lips moved but she made no sound. The last thing she saw was Eric's strong arms grab the NewGen and wrestle him to the ground. Thus, Eric spared her the final, although probably unnecessary blow. As pleasant a sight as any to die with, she thought.

Eric and the NewGen rolled down the steep face of the mountain tangled in each other's grip. They slid down the frozen steep slope, bouncing against rocks. The NewGen's chest wound left a broad claret streak in the snow. They grappled furiously, holding onto each other, while keeping a grip onto the hatchet. Eric felt his grip on the hatchet waning. He knew he must lose a contest of raw strength.

Frantic, rolling, Eric sank his teeth into the base of the NewGen's neck. His mouth gushed salty, wet, and warm. The NewGen shoved Eric free and they spun untangled to a stop, leaving Eric slightly uphill. Eric looked around and saw that the NewGen had dropped the hatchet. The NewGen rose to his knees and put his hand to his throat. Eric had not severed the jugular vein.

Eric spit a piece of flesh from his mouth and scrambled to his feet, ignoring the deep bruises and cuts incurred during the fall. He wiped away the snow that clung to the sweat on his face. He panted, trying to summon more strength.

The NewGen squared off just below him. Eric took a deep breath, then attacked with his fists, smashing his fist into the NewGen's chest wound as hard as he could. He beat the NewGen backward down the slope. Again, he slammed his right fist into the wet wound. His knuckles felt a rib, scored by Tara's hatchet blow. Another punch and the rib snapped; Eric cut the palm of his hand against the jagged bone. He stood above the NewGen and roared that he would rip the bastard's heart out if he had to. The NewGen countered with a smashing fist to Eric's head, opening a cut above the eye.

Dizzy from the blow, Eric back-crawled up the slope, out of the NewGen's reach. He needed a couple seconds to clear his head. As he backed up the slope, he felt a sharp prick to his leg: the hatchet! Eric palmed the weapon, concealing it.

Below, the NewGen pulled a large rock from the snow and began trudging up the slope. *He'll crush my head like a melon.* Eric crouched and watched the NewGen carefully step toward him. Eric waited, calculating the distance and his advantage of height. The NewGen raised the heavy rock to smash Eric, when Eric lunged at him, swinging Tara's hatchet with all his might. He buried the metal head inside the NewGen's chest just above the wound Tara had made. The rock struck Eric with a glancing blow to the back, and they tumbled again in the snow for twenty feet.

The NewGen was stunned. He grabbed the base of the hatchet with one hand and Eric's harness with the other—still a powerful grip. The NewGen's eyes burned, relentless.

"Die, you sonovabitch. Die!" Eric yelled in the creature's face. Eric tugged at the hatchet, but it was ensnared behind the NewGen's ribs. He pulled with all his might, but his efforts only lifted the NewGen's bulk off the snow. Stuck! Eric abandoned the hatchet and wriggled free. "Ah, keep it!" Eric growled, and he turned to crawl up the slope.

Exhausted, Eric crawled up past the trail of frozen blood. The din of fighting above had slacked. He saw a pair of his men wielding machetes, furiously beating a NewGen prostrate on the ground. To his left, he saw the south mountain clones rush into the valley, adding to the mayhem. Everywhere, men lay dead and dying. Already, famished crows gathered at the outskirts of the battle to pick at the corpses. The Ordinate dead in their black uniforms looked like the husks of ants. Smoke from the burning gunships drifted back to Sarhn.

Eric felt a feeble hand grab his ankle. He turned and saw the NewGen, half-dead, coughing, grimacing, teeth bright red from fresh blood. He tried to pull Eric back. Eric felt his blood chill when he saw the NewGen grab the hatchet handle and slowly turn it clockwise, pulling the weapon from his chest as if it were simply stuck in its sheath. The NewGen slowly raised the hatchet to strike.

Eric felt a rush of rage. He shifted his weight, slid down, and kicked the NewGen in the forehead: once, opening a wound above the eye, ripping a flap of scalp; a second time, flattening the NewGen's nose. With a third kick, he broke the NewGen's grasp. The hatchet fell harmlessly to the ground. The battered, disfigured lump of flesh slid backward.

Lt. Botchi stood in the middle of his panicked men. Their perimeter shrank with each minute. He saw nothing but disaster. He had arrived with six hundred soldiers. More than half were dead. Most of the others were wounded. Who could have imagined that the wilderness clones had such numbers, weapons, and ability? He looked at the carnage and thought: *It is vain to stay here and die. In six months, the next crop of NewGens will hatch, and shortly thereafter, I'll return to eradicate these wilderness clones.*

"Fall back to the transports!" Botchi yelled to those around him and into his comm-disk.

The Ordinate troops began a disciplined retrograde. Brigon's clones prepared to pursue the Ordinate into the open, but Brigon restrained them. Instead, they stood safely behind the rocks, and those who still had a few bullets left, carefully dropped some of the retreating Ordinate.

Brigon quickly retrieved his binoculars and scanned the rocks where Eric's people had struggled against the NewGens. Where's Andrea? He held his breath as he counted the dead: clones and NewGens. He saw movement. Zooming in he saw Eric crawling up the slope, but he didn't see Andrea. He issued orders to the men nearby. "Gather all weapons—all gear. Meet at the south mountain caves." Brigon started up the mountain to find Andrea.

Eric crawled back up the hill, kicking footholds in the ice and snow. The fighting had stopped. Either his people had prevailed, or he was delivering himself to the remnant of NewGens and certain death. Numbed by fatigue and cold, he accepted either outcome. Finally, he pulled himself over the lip of rock where he found Tara. Her eyes were closed. Frozen tears sealed the eyelashes. Her lips were purple. Tara's severed right arm and hand had turned ghostly white in the snow. Her face was swollen with a wide gash raking her hairline to chin. She's canceled. His programming, his training, his experience told him to leave, but he found himself transfixed, gazing down on Tara's mangled face as one might look up at the stars. Eric started to leave, but he hesitated. He dropped to one knee. He touched Tara's cheek, but his frozen, insensate hands told him nothing. He bent his head down, cocking his ear to her mouth. He felt and heard the shallow breath. She's alive! The thought at first exhilarated, then depressed him.

Eric examined her. Her worst wound—the amputation—barely oozed blood and lymph through a frozen cap of flesh. The freezing cold had slowed her loss of blood and preserved her fragile hold on life. But the same cold nipped her flesh with frostbite. She would be lucky to keep the fingers on her left hand. Her ears felt stiff. What if she lost her toes or her feet? He knew of clones canceled for merely losing a thumb or a toe. The misery of gangrene . . . A voice from his faded neural imprint reminded him: *It is a mercy to cancel useless clones.*

He backed away. She lay unconscious, maimed, no longer able to do the kind of work she was made for. Her face, so pleasant to look at each morning, was now disfigured. Let her die unconscious. As he stood, Eric heard a voice ask, "Is she alive?" He turned and found Andrea, four Jod, and three wilderness clones. He answered, "Yes."

Andrea condemned their lethargy. "Damn you. Don't just stand there. Try to save her!"

Eric stood with his arms slack at his sides. "Save her for what?"

Andrea pushed one of the clones aside and stripped the other of his cloak. Her narrow, flashing eyes and curled lip warned the others to cooperate. And they did. They rolled each end of the cloak around a pair of carbines to make a litter. Then Eric and another carefully lifted Tara onto the makeshift stretcher. Andrea covered her with a second cloak.

Andrea used a piece of nylon cord to tie off Tara's seeping wound above the elbow. "Get her back to the caves." Her order sounded more like a threat. The

stretcher bearers shuffled ahead. Eric stopped. "We for-
got her arm!" He looked back. The blue and white
hand lay palm skyward, like a half-closed claw forced
to let go. Already the arm looked too small to have
been part of Tara.

"Forget it," the second litter bearer sniped. "We don't
have that kind of medicine. She probably won't live
through the night anyway."

chapter 20

The Klamdara heat sapped the Tenebrea's spirits. The still air let the stink of captivity linger. "Old friend, try to drink." K'Rin carefully poured a trickle of water into Jo'Orom's mouth.

In the adjacent cell, Bol'Don and a dozen Tenebrea, Jo'Orom's cadre at Tenebrea School, stood languidly and silently watched. Jo'Orom swallowed and winced. The simple contraction of the muscles needed to swallow sent shooting pain through Jo'Orom's neck, scoring the esophagus, burning the pain deep inside his chest. Jo'Orom felt every beat of his own heart like broken bone grating against broken bone. He exhaled, his only reaction to the grinding pain. Minor reflexes produced shooting pain, like blinking the eyelid to moisten his blind eyes. His gut was distended slightly due to internal bleeding. He breathed shallowly, another trade-off between his will to live and the excruciating pain.

Jo'Orom braced himself, then whispered, "Thank you."

"Don't speak." K'Rin witnessed the heavy price of

Jo'Orom's simple courtesy. He touched the old Jod's flesh and it felt like dried leather. K'Rin's neck began to show a building fury—a fury smoldering beneath frustration and impotence. Many will pay for this outrage against you, Jo'Orom.

K'Rin took a sponge to wipe the sallow skin, mottled with ruddy blotches. The rings under Jo'Orom's eyes turned dark indigo, announcing the onset of death. Jo'Orom summoned his last strength. He whispered, "Listen."

"Yes." K'Rin bent low to put his ear by Jo'Orom's cracked and scaly lips. He knew these were last words.

Barely audible, the hoarse voice uttered, "Don't despair."

"We won't."

Jo'Orom's hand raised, searching. K'Rin gingerly entwined his fingers in the old Jod's. K'Rin felt the shiver of pain in the thin, weak grasp. Jo'Orom whispered, "Despair is an act of will."

"I'll remember." K'Rin felt the grasp failing. "Rest, my friend."

Jo'Orom took a deep tortured breath. "Hope . . ." Jo'Orom's hand lost the last shred of animation. K'Rin suddenly felt that he held a stick. Jo'Orom arched his back and exhaled his last, his mouth gaping for a last gulp of air that he never took.

K'Rin took a small white silk handkerchief from his shirt pocket. He began to unfold it to place it over Jo'Orom's face to fulfill custom.

"Remove the cloth!" a voice at the doorway growled, Tamor-Kyl's voice.

K'Rin turned to see Tamor-Kyl and Commandant D'Cru. Tamor wore a dark face shield and the black and gray uniform of the Tenebrea. He raised a gloved fist, a calculated insult to K'Rin. Beside Tamor, D'Cru stood quietly and smirked. Behind D'Cru stood four heavily armed guards.

K'Rin left the small cloth over Jo'Orom's eyes. He stood and placed himself between the dead Jod and Tamor. His grief percolated into raw anger.

Tamor-Kyl saw K'Rin's neck darken, so he tried to bait him. "We shall display the ossified remains of Jo'Orom in the center yard for the rest of you to contemplate."

K'Rin scowled. "All of us will join Jo'Orom sooner or later—even you." K'Rin glared at Tamor. "The difference is Jo'Orom was not afraid, and you are."

Tamor stepped forward, but D'Cru restrained him, grabbing the junior officer's arm. Tamor looked disdainfully at D'Cru's hand, but he prudently relaxed. He said, "Let me bring you up-to-date. Soon, I am going to be promoted to your old job: Chief of Offworld Intelligence."

K'Rin said sarcastically, "Congratulations."

"I thought you'd like to know that your work continues."

"Now the blind will lead the blind."

"Don't be bitter about my success. You've got much more to be bitter about." Tamor's dark face shield hid his mangled face. "The Fleet is assembled above Heptar. Under council orders, the Fleet has relieved all officers with ties by blood or marriage to the Rin Clan. They sit at desk jobs in front of screens. They curse your name, Hal K'Rin, because your treachery has tainted their good names as well."

"You are the traitor," K'Rin accused. Voices from the cell behind K'Rin murmured, and K'Rin raised his hand to silence his men and spare them retribution.

K'Rin knew that his birth and rank protected him from physical abuse, but no law protected his men.

"Well, that's a matter of opinion, K'Rin. As long as you're rotting here in Klamdara, dying from Quazel poisoning, and I'm helping the council secure peace with the Cor Ordinate. As you may understand, only victors write history."

"Then the Cor Ordinate will write yours."

Tamor turned to D'Cru and commented. "That sounded like wishful thinking, didn't it, Pel D'Cru?"

K'Rin addressed both his tormentors as he would speak to marginally competent subordinates. "Are either of you going to make a point?"

D'Cru mocked K'Rin in return. "My point is simple. You aren't as highly regarded as you once were, K'Rin. In fact, I've received some thinly veiled threats against your life."

D'Cru tossed a packet of papers at K'Rin's feet. He raised his voice for all to hear. "I've received hundreds of communications from the families of your men. They despise you, K'Rin, for bringing their sons and brothers to ruin. I told them how you infected them with the Quazel Protein. I also told them that you knew where we might find the antidote to keep their sons alive, but that you refuse for selfish reasons to tell us where to find this life-saving enzyme."

K'Rin balled his hands into fists, and stood silently. The Tenebrea watched from the adjacent cell. They looked longingly at the paper transcripts.

D'Cru walked past K'Rin to take a closer look at Jo'Orom's wizened body. He addressed himself to the Tenebrea.

"Unfortunately, all of you are going to die needlessly like Jo'Orom. Meanwhile, your relatives are working feverishly to gain pardons for you, but what good are pardons if you're dead? You can read their letters if you like. In all of the letters, parents beg their sons to repudiate Hal K'Rin, and beg mercy from the council."

Tamor-Kyl chimed in, "Next month, a Cor delegation will visit Jod to pay their respects. We shall have an armistice to prevent the war K'Rin tried to instigate. I have even heard talk of amnesty. With the immediate danger of war out of the way, the council will begin hearing your cases—a slow process, but a fair one. Unfortunately, I doubt any of you will survive to benefit from a pardon."

Tamor turned to K'Rin. "You are doomed, Hal K'Rin, but you can release your men from their oaths and tell us how to procure the Quazel enzyme."

K'Rin stood as silent as death.

"Or," D'Cru addressed the other Tenebrea, "perhaps you poor wretches can beat the information out of him. We regulars, unfortunately, must operate within the constraints of Fleet policy. You don't. I see no reason why you should die in torment for the vanity of a disgraced leader. I leave you with that thought."

K'Rin faced his cadre of officers. He struggled to control his temper; the very thought that someone would try to incite his men against him inflamed his blood. Perhaps Kip was right: it is better to die fighting. The Tenebrea's expressionless faces hid their physical pain and masked their thoughts. Am I sacrificing them needlessly? His eyes met Kip's, and Kip looked away. K'Rin thought, *He's heartsick, and I don't blame him.*

Tamor and D'Cru turned abruptly to leave. K'Rin stepped after them and grabbed D'Cru by the arm to stop him—not forcefully as to invite intervention from the guards, but gently. D'Cru turned with a magnanimous smile. "Do you have something to tell me? It's not too late to save your people."

"Yes."

"Speak up, K'Rin. I can barely hear you." D'Cru encouraged K'Rin with false sympathy. Tamor anxiously stepped closer to hear. Softly, K'Rin spoke, and the softness of his voice pulled Tamor and D'Cru closer. K'Rin addressed Tamor. "I presume you've already been to the Yuseat moon. Because you persist, I may conclude that B'Yuon warned the lab, and that they fled with the Quazel enzyme. I can also conclude that they denied you the ability to make your own enzyme. I am very grateful to them." As a dig, K'Rin added, "Andrea Flores has a lifetime supply of the enzyme, and you don't."

Tamor shuddered. "Where did you send them?"

"I ordered them to leave the Jod system and never return. I did not specify where they ought to hide."

Tamor yelled, "You lie!"

"Perhaps." K'Rin kept his voice low. "I have nothing more to tell you, but I thank you for coming to cheer me up. Knowing that Andrea will outlive you is a consolation."

D'Cru restrained Tamor, whispering, "Let's leave for now." D'Cru leaned into K'Rin's face and growled, "I saw the look on your men's faces. I've heard talk. I predict that they will shortly beat you to death. They despise you, now."

K'Rin's face turned to flint. Again he spoke quietly. "I predict that somehow, someday soon, D'Cru, you will die at the end of my knife."

Andrea carried a small methane lantern to find her way through the corridors of the south mountain caves. She found Eric lingering by the entrance to the dispensary. "Have you seen Tara yet?" she asked.

Eric shook his head. "No. She's still in with Doc."

Andrea had washed her face and hands, but her dirty hair hung loosely behind her ears. Her clothes still showed the stains of sweat and smatterings of blood. "Brigon decided to take you to Klamdara. We lost half our strength in the valley, so we need every experienced fighter."

Eric showed no emotion, but said, "He ought to leave me here."

"You don't have a choice, Eric. If you're going to say good-bye to Tara, now is the time. We're going to eat a hot meal, then start our march up the valley before nightfall."

Eric looked at his feet. "Tara is ruined. Her face, her right arm . . . she lost two toes from her left foot. Frostbite."

"Will she live?"

"Oh, sure," he replied bitterly. "Yeah, she'll live. She's not dead yet. But Tara's got cancel written all over her. I mean . . . face facts, Andrea, she's useless now."

"Then why are you hanging around the dispensary?"

"I don't know," Eric answered belligerently.

A male attendant brushed by into the dispensary carrying a bowl of water and a tray of bandages. Andrea heard a few feverish groans from the shadows. The wounded endured their pain without the comfort of narcotics. Most drifted in and out of sleep. In this ward, most would survive their wounds.

Tara had the unenviable prognosis of surviving, yet she'd be maimed. She would not work a console as before. Most likely, a limp would slow her down. The scar that ran down her face like a rip in a portrait had become her new mark, supplanting the delicate and enticing gullwings. Everyone would now recognize her uniqueness by her deformities.

Eric looked in the shadows and said, "She's on the cot at the back of the chamber."

"How do you know?"

Eric bristled. "I asked. Tell her that I . . . that I wish her well." He turned and walked away.

"She'd rather see you than me. Why don't you tell her yourself?"

Eric kneaded his hands nervously. "She'd want to talk. I don't know what to say."

"What did you two talk about before?" Andrea asked with a genuine curiosity that penetrated her detachment.

"We made plans. We talked about doing things together. Tara liked to do things for other people. She liked to do things for me. I suppose it was the part of her neural implant that never faded. But now, she can't do anything. She'll go insane before long. I can tell you that she's lying in there wishing she were dead."

"You can't know that," Andrea argued.

Eric shot back, "I'd go insane if I were useless. You wouldn't understand. A clone cannot be still. All we have is our work." Again, Eric started to walk away.

Andrea looked down the dim corridor. Eric walked slowly, dejected and confused. She called after him, "So I guess you'll just go find another TRA model. Is that what you clones do?"

He stopped. Without showing his face, Eric gave a surly response. "That's not fair." He did not move, but stood slump-shouldered in the dark corridor. He complained, "Not fair."

Andrea watched and wondered if Eric would sum-

mon the courage to face her. "I don't despise you anymore, Eric. I pity you." Andrea spoke with clinical
detachment. Her voice carried through the corridor.
"You poor, stupid clone."

Eric turned. He appeared worried instead of angry.
He stood below a small light that created shadows
where his eyes ought to be. "You have no right. . . ."

"My husband, Steve, was made of the same genetic
material as you. You two are, biologically speaking,
twin brothers. But you knew that, didn't you?"

Eric didn't answer, but his eyes showed that he
understood completely. He retreated slightly into the
shadow. She continued. "Yet, you two are as different as
night and day. Actually, I think you're a rather poor
copy of Steve. Let me tell you what Steve would do if I
were lying broken in there. He wouldn't be paralyzed
by the fact that I was no longer useful to him. He'd be
animated with concern, figuring out he might be more
useful to me. I'm not trying to get a rise out of you,
Eric. I'm just stating a fact: you are more pathetic than
Tara is. As far as I'm concerned, you are worse than
useless if you can't help her."

Eric stepped into the light again. Andrea thought he
looked small. "What should I do?" he asked quietly.

"Talk to her. Encourage her to get well. Lie to her if
you must. Promise to come back and take care of her."
Andrea stepped out of his way to let him pass into the
dispensary.

"Aren't you coming in?" Eric asked plaintively.

"I'd be in the way." Andrea looked into the shadowy
ward to the spot where she thought Tara's cot must be.
She touched Eric's arm and said, "Tell her that I promised to bring you back from Klamdara in one piece."

"You shouldn't make promises you can't keep." Eric

backed away from Andrea's hand and walked into the ward. He shrank into the murky light, dropping to one knee beside Tara's cot.

Andrea watched from the shadows. She saw Tara's good arm rise to greet Eric. For a brief moment, Andrea thought she might want to trade places with Tara Gullwing.

Continued in Book III of The Tenebrea Trilogy:

Tenebrea Rising

Authors' Note

We would like to take this opportunity to present two worthy organizations that help children in need: Camp Heartland and Half the Sky Foundation.

Camp Heartland is the world's largest camping and outreach program for kids affected by HIV and AIDS. Half the Sky Foundation was created by adoptive parents of orphaned Chinese children to enrich the lives of and enhance the outcome for babies and young children in China who wait to be adopted.

To learn more about these organizations you can visit *www.roxanndawson.net* or go directly to the sites *www.campheartland.org* and *www.halfthesky.org.*

Thank you.